THE HOUSE OF ULLOA

The Countess Emilia Pardo Bazán was born in 1851 into a wealthy and educated family in the Galician town of La Coruña. She read avidly from an early age, acquiring an unusually broad education for a woman of her time in Spain. When she was sixteen, she married José Quiroga Pérez Pinal, a Carlist law student, from whom she later discreetly separated. Her interest in the novel began when she became familiar with the works of contemporary writers, such as Pedro de Alarcón and Benito Pérez Galdós (with whom she had an affair), and her first novel was *Pascual López: The Autobiography of a Medical Student*, published in 1879. She went on to become the leading exponent of Spanish Naturalism and a key figure in modern Spanish literature, with *The House of Ulloa* (1886) generally considered as her masterpiece. Altogether she produced nineteen novels, twenty-one novellas, over five hundred short stories, and several works of literary criticism, numerous essays and travelogues. She occupied a chair in literature at Madrid University from 1916 until her death in 1921.

Paul O'Prey is a writer and translator, whose publications include *A Reader's Guide to Graham Greene* and two volumes of Robert Graves's selected letters: *In Broken Images* and *Between Moon and Moon*; he is the editor of Graves's *Selected Poems* for Penguin and of Joseph Conrad's *Heart of Darkness* for Penguin Classics.

Lucia Graves was born in Devon in 1943. She read Spanish at St Anne's, Oxford, and has had a long career as a literary translator. Among her translations are Robert Graves's *The Greek Myths, Wife to Mr Milton, The Golden Fleece* and *Collected Short Stories*, the *Journals* of Anaïs Nin (into Spanish), and Columbus's *Barcelona Letter of 1493* (into English). She has lived in Barcelona for the last twenty years.

D1354144

EMILIA PARDO BAZÁN

THE
HOUSE OF ULLOA

TRANSLATED WITH AN INTRODUCTION BY
PAUL O'PREY AND LUCIA GRAVES

PENGUIN BOOKS

PENGUIN BOOKS

Published by the Penguin Group
27 Wrights Lane, London w8 5TZ, England
Viking Penguin, a division of Penguin Books USA Inc.
375 Hudson Street, New York, New York 10014, USA
Penguin Books Australia Ltd, Ringwood, Victoria, Australia
Penguin Books Canada Ltd, 2801 John Street, Markham, Ontario, Canada L3R 1B4
Penguin Books (NZ) Ltd, 182–190 Wairau Road, Auckland 10, New Zealand

Penguin Books Ltd, Registered Offices: Harmondsworth, Middlesex, England

This translation first published 1990
1 3 5 7 9 10 8 6 4 2

Filmset in Baskerville [Linotron 202] by CentraCet, Cambridge

Made and printed in Great Britain by
Cox & Wyman Ltd, Reading

For Pilar

Contents

Introduction

The House of Ulloa, first published in 1886, is not only one of the most outstanding of all nineteenth-century Spanish novels, but also is one of the first to herald a new age in both the society and literature of that country. The story is of social, political and psychological upheaval, and of men helpless in their attempts to interfere in the natural order of things and escape their destiny. It traces the moral and material decline of the old aristocratic and ecclesiastical order at the time of the Glorious Revolution (1868), while exposing the self-interest motivating many of its opponents. The novel's hero is a priest, Father Julián, a genuinely spiritual figure but one who is hopelessly ineffectual in his attempts to halt the inexorable decay of the House of Ulloa, and who is himself crushed by its fall – which is not only a human, but also a moral tragedy.

The novel's author, the Countess Emilia Pardo Bazán, is a key figure in modern Spanish literature. She was born in the Galician town of La Coruña on 16 September 1851, into a wealthy and educated family who encouraged her precocious intellectual ability and thirst for knowledge. At the age of sixteen she married José Quiroga Pérez Pinal, a Carlist law student, from whom she later discreetly separated as her literary activities became increasingly celebrated (or, as some saw it, notorious). Her father, José Pardo Bazán y Mosquera, was elected Deputy to the Cortes as a member of the Progressive Party after the September Revolution of 1868, at which point the whole family moved to Madrid. In 1873, in the midst of further political crisis, he judged it prudent for him and his family to leave the country, and so began a brief but enriching period of travel for Pardo Bazán.*

Once again in Madrid, she had three children in quick succession and resumed a set programme of intense study. She was a highly motivated and disciplined autodidact, who read extensively in the fields of theology, metaphysics and philosophy. She also kept abreast with politics and developments in the natural sciences, largely through her reading of foreign journals.

At first Pardo Bazán had little interest in the novel, though this changed after she became acquainted with the works of contemporary writers such as Pedro de Alarcón, Juan Valera and Benito Pérez Galdós, the greatest of Spanish nineteenth-century novelists, with whom she later had an affair. Her own first novel was *Pascual López, autobiografía de un estudiante de medicina* (*Pascual López: The Autobiography of a Medical Student*) published in 1879. Inspired by the Naturalism of contemporary French writers (in particular the Goncourt brothers and Émile Zola), she set out to portray the world in her fiction as accurately and truthfully as possible. This can be seen in *The House of Ulloa*, for example, in her endeavour to capture every detail of the wild Galician landscape, including its abrupt and dramatic changes of light and mood; in her pursuit of the psychological, physiological, genetic and social factors behind character and motive (something which we now, over a hundred years later, take for granted in a novel); in her brave exposure of moral decadence in the world of politics and the nobility; in her frank portrayal of violence and poverty; in her attempts at dialectal verisimilitude in the dialogue of her socially inferior characters. There is also a strong element of documentary writing within this Naturalistic

* Previous commentators have stated that the Pardo Bazán family left Spain after the installation of Amadeus of Savoy as king, in 1871; this, however, is at odds with what Pardo Bazán herself writes here in the 'Notes Towards an Autobiography' (see page 11), and would not seem to make sense from a political point of view. Pardo Bazán is quite clear that it was after Amadeus's abdication, in February 1873, when the ailing Progressive party to which her father belonged finally collapsed, and the new Republic was declared, that her father judged the situation unsafe and took his family abroad.

framework: to obtain the necessary background detail for her third novel, *La Tribuna* (*The Tribune*), Pardo Bazán went repeatedly to a cigarette factory in La Coruña – an extraordinary thing for an aristocratic woman of the time to have done, and one which gives her social observations considerable authority.

Pardo Bazán was a formidable figure in Spanish literary and intellectual circles, being both an energetic and dynamic woman as well as an extremely gifted and highly prolific writer, producing nineteen novels, twenty-one novellas, over five hundred short stories, several works of literary criticism, numerous essays and travelogues, and even two cookery books. Her work was always surrounded by controversy, particularly following her seminal study of Naturalism, *La Cuestión Palpitante* (*The Burning Question*) – a controversy aggravated, of course, by the fact that she was not only a woman, but an active feminist. She felt strongly about the plight of women in Spain and edited a series of books, the Women's Library, aimed specifically at educating women. Feminine experience in both her fiction and non-fiction is invariably portrayed as quintessentially unjust. She herself, thanks to her position, talent and fame, as well as to her strength of character and her unorthodox marital arrangements, was free from many of the usual constraints, so that, for example, she held a prestigious chair in literature at Madrid University from 1916 until her death in 1921. But there were limits to this freedom, as she discovered when she was refused membership of the all-male Royal Academy, the final accolade for a Spanish intellectual.

When *The House of Ulloa* was first published in 1886, it included an autobiographical essay as prologue. The essay, entitled *Apuntes autobiográficos* ('Notes towards an Autobiography'), avoided, for obvious reasons, any reference to her marital separation, or any other aspect of her frequently scandalous private life, such as her affair with Pérez Galdós. It is more a literary self-portrait, tracing her intellectual development and showing the influence of her extensive reading not only on her work but on her life. It reveals too the sources of her patriotism, her feminism, the paradox of her dogged conservatism and her passion for reform, her unwavering Christianity, and her dedication to the pursuit of truth in philosophy and literature which underlies all her writings. This essay, from which the following excerpts are taken, is over ninety pages long in its original form, and has never been republished.

NOTES TOWARDS AN AUTOBIOGRAPHY

My first literary recollection is of certain verses written on the occasion of a great historical event: the end of the African war. What these verses were like one can easily imagine, bearing in mind that I had only just reached that age when the Catholic Church assumes small children to have acquired the power of reason. However, I still preserve a clear memory of that time and of the patriotic enthusiasm that prompted my first burst into song, whereas I tend to forget other more recent events quite easily.

* * *

When the war was over and the peace agreement signed, it became known that part of the victorious army would disembark at La Coruña. I was very excited at this prospect, and would have given anything to grow little wings on my shoulders like a swallow and fly out to sea to welcome the ships bringing the troops home.

I will never forget that sunny day and the army's triumphant entry: a splendid sun danced on bayonets and naked swords, and made the colours of the Spanish flag – riddled with bullet-holes – seem gayer, more lively and brash; it made the laurel leaves on the garlands shine like varnish, and poured like a torrent of glory on the hardened, olive-brown faces of the merry young men, and on their dusty, patched and torn uniforms of which they boasted with martial pride. I was on a balcony in the calle Real, with my forehead pressed against the rail. I envied the grown-up señoritas as they waved their embroidered handkerchiefs and threw down handfuls of rose-petals, as well as bouquets and garlands tied with long silk ribbons. They seemed so in command of the situation, while *I* had to stand on tiptoe and try to squeeze between the thick bars of the balcony in order to get a better view of the parade, and could throw the victors nothing better than a look of heartfelt admiration. There can be no experience comparable to witnessing the return of the home troops, with winged Victory trapped between the folds of their flag!

* * *

I was aware that the conclusion of the war and the triumphal return of the army to La Coruña signified something great and worthy of celebration. I also realized that it was something unconnected with the Government, which I had often heard criticized at home. It symbolized instead something of a higher nature, something so exalted and majestic that everyone revered it: the Nation. And since nobody paid any attention to me, and I had no one on whom to relieve my tremendous enthusiasm, I took shelter in my room and scribbled my first verses – five-line stanzas, I seem to remember. Oh, and how I dreamt of proudly seeing them printed in the newspapers, which in those days were always full of poems with frilly frames around them!

It was a long time before any further poetic spark came out of me. What I feel I must say is that the sublime thrill of love for the homeland precedes any conscious awareness of the idea that produces it, and can be felt just as strongly by a child as by an adult. In my particular case this sentiment is one that has not been modified by any books I might have read, nor by any of the hazards of life, nor by certain sophisms that go around disguised as the latest word in philosophical scepticism, but which are in fact nothing but atrophy of the soul and an ill-fated sign of decadence in a nation. I find myself in this particular – and I say this with pride – equal to any woman of the people.

Another incident, this one not related to modern history, also stands out among my early memories. We used to spend the summer holidays at the Rias Bajas in the Galician province of Pontevedra, an enchanting place if ever there was one, embraced by the blue arms of a sea worthy of the Bay of Naples, and favoured with a climate also reminiscent of Italy. It has beautiful beaches of fine, sparkling sand and mother-of-pearl conchs, backed by a line of aloes. There the greyish tone of the Galician skies seems clearer and brighter, and the human race is of lighter blood, dark-haired and pale, more like the people of the south. In such a privileged place we own a vast and picturesque estate, and a very old manor house, the Torre de Miraflores, not at all like the dark, foreboding House of Ulloa. While some repair work was being done to the dilapidated old manor, we rented a house in Sangenjo, a pretty fishing village on the edge of our estate. The owner left us his furniture, among which was a library, and I can still picture now the old books spread out untidily along some worm-eaten, blue-painted shelves. But what a discovery it was for me!

I was one of those children who read whatever falls into their hands, even the cornet wrappings around spices and pastries; one of those children who spend hours sitting quietly in a corner when they are given a book, and who sometimes have black rims round their eyes and a slight squint because of the effort imposed on the still weak optic nerve. Whatever came my way and I happened to like, I would read four, five, or even six times over. I could even keep whole chapters of some books – most notably *Don Quixote* – fresh in my mind, and could recite them with complete accuracy. And so I made that little room full of books my permanent abode. Sometimes the shameless cries of the quarrelling sardine-sellers would rise to its windows, while at other times I could hear the melancholy song of fishermen hauling up their boats. But nothing would pull me away from there. Books, plenty of books! I could pick and choose at random, leaf through them and put them back on the shelf.

* * *

In Madrid, where we spent the winter, I was educated in a French school, highly favoured by the Royal Household and at that time considered the cream of all stylish schools. The headmistress was an old lady who was invariably dressed up to the nines, with little grey ringlets always sticking out beneath one of those typically French lace caps with ribbons. She treated us worse than galley-slaves, and gave us a frugal stew for lunch and rancid peanuts, hazelnuts (most of which were empty) and chestnuts (as hard as fossils – no doubt the worst one could buy in Madrid) for dessert. I think she deliberately kept the nuts in a cupboard until they got so hard no girl could dig her teeth into them. Never in my life have I seen a more miserly Frenchwoman, and heaven knows there are plenty of that sort around. As for our spiritual nourishment, it was *Telemachus* whether we liked it or not, the *Fables* of Lafontaine in great abundance, a lot of mythology, a touch of geography, and once we saw an eclipse of the sun through smoked glass – an experiment that seemed to me at the time the height of astronomic science. But this much I must say: as we were forbidden to speak in Spanish, over the most slow-witted of us came out of that school chattering away in French like little parrots.

Then we settled in La Coruña, in a forbiddingly silent old house, where I was never invited by any child of my own age to play and run about. There I discovered a treasure similar to the one in Sangenjo: next to the iron doors that guarded the archives, rose some no less impressive ones, which one day were left ajar so that I was able to catch a glimpse of a nest of books. I pestered my parents incessantly about these books, until finally they allowed me access to them, for they approved of my eagerness to read. And then what afternoons I spent there, indulging in the pleasure of unexpected discoveries!

* * *

I derived more benefit from this treasure-trove locked behind the iron doors than from any of the lessons given to me at home by my tutors. I secretly rebelled against the piano-teacher: all that grinding of the scales, up and down, and up and down again, seemed to me utterly stupid, especially when it was only to be told that it was all a question of exercising one's fingers! It was good riddance to Liszt as far as I was concerned, and I begged to be allowed to learn Latin instead of the piano: I longed to read the *Aeneid*, the *Georgics* and Ovid's *Tristia*, which were in the iron cabinet. But I was denied the request, which I must admit was rather strange coming from a young lady. I went on hammering the piano-keys and was even told that I was improving. I suppose my permanent dislike for pianos was born then.

* * *

By the age of fourteen I was allowed to read more or less what I liked: history, poetry, science, Cervantes's novels and Quevedo's verses; I was banned only from reading the works of Dumas, Sue, George Sand, Victor Hugo and other leaders of French Romanticism.

* * *

One day I was at the house of one of the few friends I had of my own age. By chance we were left alone in her father's study, and my eyes went straight to the bookshelves. I gave a cry of delight: the first thing I read, on the spine of a thick volume, was: Victor Hugo, *Notre-Dame de Paris*. There was no real struggle within my mind between duty and desire, for the latter won hands down. If I asked my friend's father for the book, it would naturally be denied to me, or at least my parents would have to be consulted first, and then goodbye Victor Hugo. So I took it surreptitiously, hiding it under my coat, and, once I had it home, I hid it in a box in which I kept my rings and ribbons. At night I read it with no regard to time, keeping it half-hidden beneath my pillow until the candle burnt to an end. How I enjoyed the angelic unselfishness of Quasimodo, the wicked plots of Claude Frollo, and all those intrigues between Esmeralda and Captain Phoebus! This really is a novel, I thought with relish. In the world of Victor Hugo nothing seemed to happen in a normal or natural way, as it did in the world of Cervantes, nor was it the everyday world of Fernán: on the contrary, everything seemed extraordinary, exaggerated and fateful. Nor could the ingenuity of the author be compared to that of others either, for it was unique. This conclusion influenced the concept I was to have of the novel for many years to come, considering it something way beyond the field of my aspirations, because it required such a marvellous inventiveness. If anyone were to tell me then that I would eventually write novels myself, I would have thought they were predicting something as unlikely as a royal crown.

Three events of great importance in my life followed one another closely: I made my début, I was married, and the Revolution of September 1868 broke out. My father was elected to the new Cortes of '69, and we began to spend the winters in the capital and the summers in Galicia. My congenital love for letters underwent a long eclipse, darkened by the distractions offered in Madrid to a sixteen-year-old newly-wed, who had emerged from an austere existence, confined to the company of family and serious-minded friends, to the bustle of the court and refined society, which, although at that time dispersed and reduced by the Revolution, did not seem less brilliant to someone who had never known it before. Every morning it was either a lesson at the riding-school or a social call; every afternoon it was a carriage-ride down the Castellana; every evening it was a trip to the theatre or to a soirée; in spring it was Monastery concerts, and after that to the bullfight to see El Tato; in summer we would go to the Retiro park in the evening, and sometimes horse-riding to the Casa de Campo or the Ronda. Once in a blue moon there would be an outing to El Escorial, or to Aranjuez. Very pleasant pastimes indeed, and they helped me correct my tendency to isolation and my distressing shyness – a result of my previous way of life and my childhood interests. However, after I had amused myself in this way over a number of winters, and such a life had become routine, I began to feel a sense of emptiness in my soul, an inexplicable sense of anguish, as one might experience in sleep the night before a duel, oppressed by the fear of not waking up in time to fulfil one's duty.

During the summer I did not have time to pause and collect my thoughts, for the days were filled with entertainments, parties, and excursions to different parts of Galicia by coach, horse or on foot. These excursions were truly delightful, and turned my eyes to the outside world, allowing me to discover the kingdom of Nature, which led me to become the untiring landscape artist I am now, captivated by the grey of the clouds, the smell of chestnut-trees in the damp pastures and country lanes of my homeland, and by the foaming of its rivers through the narrow gullies.

* * *

There was a tendency at the time to disregard the question of literary values in favour of politics. The decadence of taste occasioned by the Revolution was almost proverbial ... But there was little point in wasting one's energy by worrying about the course of literature, when the political situation was so entangled, and particularly when it was further complicated by the terrible religious question, which is the most serious of all, despite what might be said by superficially minded people who cannot distinguish ephemeral politics from the eternal, transcendental forces of society, and who unthinkingly suppose that a civil war occurs simply because a few millions are received from England or France. I am referring to the brutal excesses of the anti-clerical demagogy; the shooting down of holy images; the stupid, vindictive destruction of works of art; the manhandling of nuns, who were treated worse than whores; the greedy confiscation of property. In short, there was a vigorous, systematic, all-embracing war against Catholicism, in which the Cortes itself was turned into the official blasphemer, and this produced an inevitable reaction, which first manifested itself in the form of special three-day masses and other public acts of atonement organized by the Carlists.

In one of those early years of the Revolution I witnessed a spectacle that was to become fixed in my memory. A swarm of urchins were running down the calle de Toledo, their bare little legs in unison, surrounded by a number of prostitutes and other unsavoury-looking characters, and seemingly escorted by a contingent of the Civil Guard. Then, in the middle of this running mob, I caught sight of a priest, with a halo of very white hair round a well-shaven crown, and with his elbows tied together. He was a political criminal, as I later discovered. Indeed, he was not even a criminal, but only a suspect.

This is not the place to recall my many memories of that unforgettable time of the Revolution, and so I shall omit any references to the reactionary atmosphere of the salons, the crusade against Amadeus of Savoy* or the spirit of insurrection among the Carlists, even though these things were not entirely unknown to me. One thing was for sure: in that rough sea there was to be no plain sailing for my beloved literature, about which I thought with growing nostalgia. Nor could I count as an indication of my unsatisfied predilections certain occasional poems which through no fault of my own had a widespread circulation, and which I even saw printed on silk in letters of gold. As literature, God knows they weigh on my conscience, although it is true to say that what is born of political uproar also dies with it.

With the departure of the Italian, the political horizon seemed bleaker than ever. At the same time as the honest Progressive party died (whose dream had been to reconcile religious interests with constitutional freedom), my father decided that his own political life was over, and so we went to France, and from Paris we hoped to watch on in peace as the muddy waters of the Revolution ran their course. By pure chance we passed the frontier without encountering any difficulties, despite the fears of everyone making the journey that we would meet the Carlist forces in Alsasua, they having won a victory the day before in Oñate.

Far from the bustle of Madrid, I led a less active social life, and instead turned my attention to pursuits of a more intellectual nature. After a day spent at a museum or historic monument, I would retire to my hotel and take up my books to practise English grammar, for I had made up my mind to read Byron and Shakespeare in their own language. That same year, on the banks of the River Po and beside the canals of Venice, I relished the poetry of Alfieri and Ugo Foscolo, the prose of Manzoni and Silvio Pellico. In Verona I saw Juliet's balcony, in Trieste the Palace of Miramar and in the Great Exhibition of Vienna all the

* Following the September Revolution of 1868 and the abdication of Isabella II, a constitutional monarchy was established and the Spanish throne offered to Amadeus I of Savoy (1845–90), 'the Italian' (see Historical Note, p. 21).

progress of industry which I considered with Romantic disdain. It was a wonderful journey, time well-spent, in which my sense of vocation was reborn, calling me with a gentle insistence.

* * *

I began to develop an interest in German philosophy, and was honoured with the friendship of a number of those affiliated to the school of Krausism,* which at the time had a splendid following. These gentlemen were distinguished by a certain moral rigidity, which went hand in hand with a number of innovatory and somewhat startling propositions. Unlike the general run of philosophers, who keep their principles tucked away between the leaves of a book in their studies, these insisted on applying theirs in a rather exaggerated and pedantic way to all aspects of daily life. In the opinion of a writer of great talent, they were ungodly penitents, or rather the most aesthetic heretics ever seen on this earth. Such fads do not usually last long, as was to be proved by the speedy collapse and ruin of the school. However, going back to what I was saying, as these 'adepts' considered a knowledge of German to be essential, I set out to learn it. But no sooner had I acquired a simple smattering of the language than I found that I preferred to devote my attentions to the works of Goethe, Schiller, Bürger and Heine, because frankly I believe (though one ought not to admit it) that, unless you are an expert in metaphysics, it is better to read those works in a good French translation, in which the German hyperbole has been given a Latinate construction sufficient for a full and proper understanding of the essentials, if one can get that far.

It is only now I realize how much I owe to this curiosity that led me to peruse the works of the Krausists, for it was that which taught me to read more methodically, with greater concentration and thought, making it a study rather than a pastime. My brain

* Krausism (based on the work of a minor German philosopher) was an extremely popular movement among Spanish intellectuals in the mid-century, who found in it a programme for the moral regeneration of their country. Carr, in *Spain 1808–1939*, describes it as a 'bizarre phenomenon', a 'curious blend of subjective mysticism and vague modernism'.

developed, my intellectual powers awakened and I acquired the intellectual ballast all artists need if they are not to float around without a set course like a cork on the sea. It is true that I ran the risk of becoming a Krause enthusiast: for the very reason that he is not a rigorous thinker and his system abounds in ethics and aesthetics, his books are treacherously attractive. But I resisted this temptation, and Krause and his 'harmonism' served me only as a stepping-stone towards the discovery of the famous 'identity' of Schelling, the eloquence of Fitche and his 'self that makes itself', the pure reason of Kant, the debatable but magnificent aesthetic theories of Hegel, all of which did not altogether convince me, but gave me the same pleasure as one derives from a beautiful poem. Once I had developed this liking, I went back further (chronologically speaking) to St Thomas, Descartes, Plato and Aristotle.

* * *

Men, who from the moment they can walk and talk go to primary schools, and then continue their education without interruption right through to the Academy or the University, have no idea how difficult it is for a woman to acquire culture and fill in the blanks of her education on her own. I am well aware that a lot of what men are taught is very straightforward, and perhaps superfluous or even irksome, but any such intellectual exercise can only help to strengthen the mind and build a foundation for further study. The education of a man starts with the most basic elementary knowledge, but this leads the way to learning of a more superior nature. Thus men become familiar with words and ideas that, generally speaking, are never handled by women, just as women do not handle the fencer's foil or the craftsman's tools. One day they might be attending the lectures of an eminent and famous professor, the next taking a degree, or a public examination, like a boxer flexing and showing off his muscles before entering the ring. In short, for men there are nothing but advantages, while for women there are nothing but obstacles.

* * *

I then nestled in the gentle bosom of mystical philosophy, having exhausted myself on my long excursion into the realms of the German and Greek thinkers, and of the Scholastics. The fatigue of spirit that sometimes sets in following the prolonged reading of serious books obliged me to focus my attention again, and not without pleasure, on the outside world. And I not only allowed myself the luxury of reading poetry, but I also turned, as a relaxing pastime, to consider the novel. Just as in the severity of youth I had scorned the genre, now I was attracted to it and found it delightful, and I soon revised my former strange opinion of it as simply an open field where imagination and invention were allowed to run riot. As I was accustomed to reading more in foreign languages than in my own, I began by reading Manzoni's *The Betrothed* and *The Letters of Jacob Ortis*, followed by the works of Walter Scott, Lytton Bulwer and Charles Dickens. I then went on to discover George Sand and Victor Hugo – and all without even suspecting the existence of contemporary Spanish novels!

To understand my ignorance one has to appreciate what the life of a lady in a provincial capital is like, particularly when she devotes whatever free time allowed to her by her family and social life to studying specialized subjects. At that time I had all the refutations of Draper* off by heart; I was following whatever progress was being made in the field of thermodynamics; I subscribed to the *Revue Philosophique* and the *Revue Scientifique*; I buried myself in books like Father Secchi's *The Sun* and Haeckel's *Natural History of Creation*; the newspapers I read were *The Faith* and *The Future Century*. And all the while my own literary epoch was passing me by, its voice one of those faint, distant rumbles that go unnoticed by our over-occupied minds.

* John William Draper (1811–82), English naturalist and author. His *History of the Conflict between Religion and Science* (1875) was extremely anti-Catholic and when translated into Spanish provoked several refutations by, among others, Cornoldi, Camara and, later, Menendez y Pelayo.

One day I was discussing with a friend, who was less cut off from the world than myself, *Amaya, or the Basques in the Eighteenth Century*, a curious historical novel that was being serialized in *Christian Science*. During our conversation he recommended the novels of Valera and Alarcón, and he also praised some of Galdós's *National Episodes*, though he tempered his praise by saying he found them somewhat over-long and uneventful. And so I set about making my peace with our national *belles-lettres*, beginning with *Pepita Jiménez*,* and then going on to *The Three-Cornered Hat*.† From that point on I needed no further guidance from anyone.

The resemblance I found between my old acquaintances Cervantes, Hurtado and Espinel, and their modern counterparts, was exactly the same as one notices between the figures in an old family portrait, dressed in antique clothes, and one of their descendants in modern-day dress. My new discoveries brought me immense satisfaction and instilled in me the idea of trying to write fiction myself – an idea that would never have occurred to me in the days when I thought that the whole point of a novel was to see its hero being thrown into the sea from a castle-turret, still alive but wrapped in a shroud and with a cannon-ball tied to his feet; or to see him thrown, fresh from the provinces, recklessly into the queen's chamber where he finds out all about her love-affairs and heartaches and performs extraordinary feats to save the honour of the fair lady. If writing a novel amounts to no more than describing the customs and places with which we are familiar, and creating characters by studying the people all around us, then, I thought, I myself might try my hand at it. And so I set to work.

My first attempt was called *Pascual López: The Autobiography of a Medical Student*, and I sent it off to Madrid with a friend who recommended it to the *Spanish Review*.

* By Juan Valera (1824–1905)

† *El sombrero de tres picos* by Pedro Antonio de Alarcón (1833–91)

15

* * *

It was some time before I was able to clarify the doubts that had assailed me after the publication of *Pascual López*. I began to see the importance of the modern novel, to understand the direction it was taking, its singular position in contemporary letters, its incomparable strength and its obligation to re-create and portray nature and society in epic style, but without disregarding truth and substituting it with a fictional beauty of greater or lesser degree. I came to the conclusion that every country has to cultivate its own tradition of the novel – particularly when it boasts such an illustrious one as Spain's – without any prejudice against modern techniques, since they are based on rational principles adapted to the current manner of understanding art, which is certainly not the same as it was in the seventeenth century. And it seemed to me that one should not reject any progress in the novelist's art simply because it originated on the other side of the Pyrenees: a quick glance at literary history is enough to realize that the three Latin nations, Italy, France and the Iberian Peninsula, have since time immemorial enjoyed an exchange of aesthetic ideas and literary influences. The Romans first influenced us, and then we gave to them in return the grand style of our poets and orators. France influenced us through the troubadours, but we paid them back by bestowing upon them our drama. The list of borrowings between nations is interminable – nor should they be called borrowings, but rather cross-fertilizations.

I follow this line of argument in the prologue and text of *The Honeymoon*. The prologue in particular was, if I am not mistaken, one of the first (and perhaps most resounding) echoes of French Naturalism in Spain, against which I set up our own national Realism, which I myself preferred. But I have no wish to make fanciful claims about my work, and, if I am wrong, those who know better are welcome to correct me, and anyway I deserve no great praise for my initiative since I had only just come from Paris.

Before I go any further I will explain how, after returning from the spa,* I stopped in this capital and expressed a wish to meet Victor Hugo, the last of the great Romantics. The author of *Hernani* invited me to one of his literary 'at homes', which was rather like attending his personal court, for he looked like a dethroned monarch in that sumptuous salon, lit by a dazzling chandelier of Venetian glass, and decorated with silks and superb tapestries. On either side, seated silently in a double row, or standing, talking among themselves in low voices as if they did not dare approach the Master, were the last courtiers of fallen majesty, the late neophytes, the stragglers of French Romanticism. Victor Hugo offered me a seat next to him and began to address me. There was an immediate hush as all attention turned to our dialogue that contained all the usual indulgent questions and cautious answers, which are *de rigueur* on these occasions. I tried to hide behind a large bunch of heliotropes I held in my hands in order to cope with the embarrassment of the interview, for I was full of respect for this venerable representative of a bygone age.

However, although Victor Hugo declared he considered Spain as a second homeland, at one point he expressed a sense of regret for its backwardness and added that things could not be otherwise, since the Inquisition had mercilessly burnt at the stake all writers and thinkers. With all the courtesy that good manners require for contradicting someone (especially when it is Victor Hugo), I answered that our greatest literature was written precisely during the time of the Inquisition, and that even the Inquisition had not interfered in the world of letters, nor had it roasted any great writer or thinker, only witches, Jews and the Illuminati heretics. He would not let me convince him, so, driven by my inveterate passion for defending Spain from false accusations, I found myself in the middle of a heated argument with the old gentleman! For my part I conducted myself, I have to say, with the utmost politeness, respectfully choosing my words with the greatest of care, so that when the poet stated that *autos*

* In September 1880 Pardo Bazán went to Vichy to take the waters on medical advice, as she was suffering from 'dark thoughts' attributed to a liver condition.

17

da fé were still being carried out in 1824, I refrained from informing him that he was guilty of an enormous anachronism, but instead begged him simply to consider the facts, for then he would see plainly for himself that although the Inquisition was officially suppressed only in 1812, it had in reality been suppressed long before then.

*   *   *

In the freezing cold of those winter afternoons, between reading Masdeu or Baena's *Songbook* – both of which were most entertaining – I scribbled the articles that were to form *The Burning Question*, and sent one a week to *La Epoca*, in whose literary pages they appeared. My object was to say something in a clear and accessible way about Realism and Naturalism. Both subjects were very much discussed at the time, though not in any great depth, and no one had set out to write specifically about them. I therefore thought it appropriate to go to press and enter the battlefield with no other armour than a thin shield of scholarly anecdotes, which would not frighten the ignorant (on the contrary, it was possible it would act as bait) and would not hinder my own movements.

The success was far greater than my hopes had been. I am continually surprised by the extraordinary dynamism of that little book, which took shape as I wrote; my only plan was that it should be spontaneous and unpremeditated, which was essential if I were to avoid any trace of didacticism.

*   *   *

The originality and independence of *The Burning Question* has been acknowledged by all, including Émile Zola, the highest authority of the French school, and by the numerous foreign critics, who have judged it in the excellent translation just published in Paris by Albert Savine. Its idea of a Catholic Naturalism based on the literary traditions of the homeland is, they say, exactly what might have been expected from a Spanish writer. Heaven knows that when I scribbled away in the cold office of the University rectory of Santiago, nothing was further from my mind than the ambitious and absurd dream of founding a system, a school, or any other foundable thing. But it is equally true – and anyone who reads my book will see this for himself – that I did not simply translate French Naturalism for a Spanish audience, but selected only those aspects of it that seemed to me sensible and commendable, and I opposed the rest repeatedly. I made this same protest, which I repeat now with the encouragement of foreign opinion, in an argument with Luis Alfonso published in *La Epoca*, in 1884: 'I cannot get over my astonishment at people trying to turn me into a female Zola, or, at least, an active disciple of the revolutionary Frenchman,' I wrote. 'I depart from Zola conceptually: as you well know, I have already tracked down all his determinist, fatalist and pessimistic doctrines in *The Burning Question*, published a year and a half ago, and declared that no Catholic could follow him along these paths.' And let it be said that the philosophical concepts are the very heart, the very marrow, of any system.

I have less liking than anyone for the exclusivity of 'schools', and prefer the word 'method', by which I give to understand the greatest sum of critical truths and aesthetic principles on which artists of any one generation can agree. It is obvious to me that these principles change, or are modified, over quite brief periods of time, and only in this sense, accepting the current means of expression, do I sometimes refer to a 'new school' or to a 'restoration'. Well then, I have seen that outside Spain the few people who know our present literature perceive in the works of our best contemporary novelists a common quality, a certain 'something', which characterizes a new phase in the history of our literature; but at the same time they admit that Spanish Naturalism, Realism, Verism, or whatever it is (this is not the time or place to go into all that), is as far from being the same as French Naturalism, as French Naturalism is from being the same as Russian Naturalism. And yet here they will repeat constantly, with the stubbornness of the wilfully deaf, the contention that the Spanish novel is being ruined by obsequiously imitating the French.

* * *

I like the countryside so much that my ambition would be to write a novel in which all the characters are countrymen; but I always come up against the enormous problem of dialogue, which even Zola, the most daring of novelists, cannot defy, according to what I have just read in a newspaper, for the peasants he describes in his latest work, *La Terre*, do not speak in patois, but in French. Genius can achieve anything, and Zola may well be able to get around these difficulties; but I feel that the graphic, timely and witty things said by our country folk are inseparable from the old romanced Latin in which they deliver them, and that a harlequin book, half Galician and half Castilian, would be a monstrosity, as ugly as the Galician poems are lovely when the language of its peasants stands out in them.

* * *

If I could boast of having contributed, in any way and in any measure, to the relative success of the Spanish novel, I would consider those hours well employed when, pen in hand, I confront my blank sheets of paper, in this corner of Las Mariñas, in this cell of the old Granja de Meirás – the place where I feel more continually than anywhere else the light fever that goes with artistic creation.

HISTORICAL NOTE

The *House of Ulloa* takes place against a background of social unrest and political turmoil. A decade of revolts against the monarchy and Government culminated in the Glorious Revolution of 1868, which saw the abdication of Queen Isabella II and the establishment of the Provisional Government of the Revolution. This was made up of a shaky and ill-fated coalition of the Progressive and Unionist parties, and also had the support of the Democrats against opposition from the Carlists and the Republicans. The Cortes of 1869 (to which Don Pedro Moscoso failed to get elected, though Pardo Bazán's own father was more successful) established the new constitution, which included many reforms such as universal male suffrage. General Francisco Serrano was elected regent and Juan Prim, the major statesman of the Revolution, became prime minister. A system of constitutional monarchy was established, with Amadeus I of Savoy being invited to the throne in 1870. Prim, however, was assassinated in December 1870, a month before the new king arrived, and although Serrano went on to become the first prime minister under the new monarchy in the elections of March 1871, he was unable to unite his coalition cabinet and resigned three months later, thus ending the revolutionary coalition of 1868. Although Amadeus was never a popular choice as king, his attempt to establish himself as a constitutional monarch was largely defeated by the political infighting among the parties of the coalition, who were unable to form a stable government. After the resignation of Serrano, Amadeus was left intolerably exposed and abdicated in February 1873, as the radicals took control and declared the short-lived First Republic. Less than two years later Isabella's son, Alfonso XII, was restored to the throne, to more or less general relief.

NOTE ON THE TEXT

This translation of *Los Pazos de Ulloa* is based on the original edition published in two volumes by Daniel Cortezo in Barcelona in 1886.

THE
HOUSE OF ULLOA

Chapter 1

No matter how hard the rider tried to restrain his rough-haired nag – cajoling it with soothing words, tugging at its single rein of thin rope – the villain persisted in going down the hill at something between a stomach-churning trot and a mad, uneven gallop. And that hill on the high road from Santiago to Orense was certainly steep. Travellers would shake their heads and grumble about the gradient far exceeding whatever was permitted by law, while others muttered about the road engineers having known only too well what they were doing, and about some political bigwig in the neighbourhood – someone with real clout at election-time – having had a hand in it somewhere.

The rider's face was bright red – not like a pepper, but with that strawberry flush so typical of lymphatic people. Indeed, at first sight one might have taken him for a boy – he was young, beardless and slightly built – had not his priestly appearance contradicted such an assumption. One could see, despite the yellow dust raised by the hack's trot, that his suit was made of plain black cloth, cut in the loose, graceless fashion that marks the clothes of a priest. And sticking out from under his shapeless frock-coat was about an inch of clerical collar embroidered with beads. His leather gloves, already frayed by the rough rein, were also black as well as new, like his stiff round hat. This he wore pulled down to his eyebrows for fear that with so much bouncing it would fall off, which for him would simply have been the end of the world. His face, meanwhile, showed as much fear of the nag as if it had been a fiery, uncontrollable stallion – for he was hardly a master of horsemanship, and, as he leaned forward, his legs sticking out, he seemed on the brink of tumbling headlong to the ground.

At the bottom of the hill the horse resumed its normal steady pace and the rider was able to straighten up on the pack-saddle – which was so inordinately wide that it jarred his pelvis. He drew in his breath and removed his hat. The sun was now falling at an angle over the brambles and hedgerows, and he welcomed the cool afternoon air on his wet brow. A labourer in shirt-sleeves, his jacket hung over a milestone, was hacking lazily with a mattock at the weeds growing along the edge of the ditch. The rider drew in the rein and his mount stopped at once, for it was tired after the downhill trot. The workman raised his head, and the gilt badge of a municipal roadman glittered for an instant on his hat.

'Would you be kind enough to tell me if it's far to the marquis of Ulloa's house?'

'To the manor house?' replied the labourer, repeating the question.

'Yes.'

'The manor's over there,' he mumbled, indicating a point on the horizon. 'If yer beast's got good legs it won't take yer long. Keep goin' till yer gets to that there pine wood, see? Then turn left, and then down to th' right, that's the short cut to the stone cross. Once there yer can't go wrong, 'cos yer can see it. Great big building it is.'

'But . . . exactly how much further is it?' asked the clergyman anxiously.

The labourer shook his sunburnt head.

'Not more 'an a mite.' And without any further explanation he returned to his weary task, wielding the mattock as if it weighed a ton.

Abandoning any hope of finding out how many miles made a 'mite', the traveller spurred on his horse. The pine wood was not far, and rider and mount disappeared into its dense shadows, along a narrow winding track that proved almost impassable. But the horse was Galician and, true to the special qualities of the breed, it pressed on with its head down, cautiously feeling its way and carefully avoiding the pot-holes made by cart-wheels, rocks, and tree-trunks felled and left where they were least required. The clergyman made steady progress and soon began to leave behind the narrow track and take a clearer path, which gradually emerged into the open, among the young pine-trees and gorse-covered hills. He had not until then perceived any form of cultivation, not even a cabbage-patch, that would point to the presence of human life, but suddenly the horse's hooves fell silent as they sank into a soft carpet. It was the layer of vegetable compost spread out, as was customary in that country, in front of a peasant's hut. At the door of the hut a woman was suckling a baby. The rider stopped.

'Señora, is this the right road for the marquis of Ulloa's house?'

'This is the road, ay.'

'And is there much further to go?'

Her ambiguous reply, in the local dialect, came with a raising of eyebrows and an apathetic yet curious stare.

'It's no more 'n a dog's trot away.'

'Not exactly encouraging,' thought the traveller. Although he was not quite sure how far a dog's trot was, he had a feeling that it was a sizeable distance for a horse. But at least when he arrived at the stone cross he would be able to see the manor. All he had to do was find the short cut, of which, however, there was no sign. The path became wider and the land more mountainous, dotted with a few oaks and chestnut-trees laden with fruit, while dark patches of heather grew here and there on either side of the path. The rider felt ill at ease in a way that was hard to define – but pardonable in someone born and bred in a quiet, sleepy town, who finds himself for the first time face to face with the majestic solitude of Nature, and who remembers tales of travellers robbed, and of people murdered in deserted places.

'What a land of wolves!' he said gloomily, though nevertheless impressed. His spirits rose, however, when he found the short cut – a narrow, steep path just discernible between a double stone wall that marked the boundaries between two hills. He was on his way down, trusting in the horse's skill not to stumble, when he caught sight of something that made him shudder – a wooden crucifix painted black with white stripes, half-fallen and propped against the thick wall, so close he could almost touch it with his hand. The priest knew that these crucifixes marked the spot where a man had met with a violent death. He made the sign of the cross and muttered the Lord's Prayer.

Meanwhile the horse, no doubt scenting a fox, trembled slightly and, raising its ears, broke into a steady trot which soon brought them to a crossroads. There, framed by the branches of a colossal chestnut-tree, stood the stone cross, so crudely carved it looked like a Romanesque relic, though it was in fact only a hundred years old – the work of some quarryman with aspirations to being a sculptor. At that hour of the day, however, and under the natural canopy of the magnificent tree, the rustic monument seemed beautiful and poetic.

The rider, feeling calmer and full of devotion, removed his hat and uttered these words: 'We adore Thee, O Lord Jesus Christ, and we bless Thee, for Thou hast delivered the world through Thy Holy Cross.'

As he prayed, his eyes searched in the distance for the Ulloa manor, which he assumed must be the large, oblong building with towers at the bottom of the valley below. He was unable to watch it for long, however, for suddenly the horse bolted, its ears pricked and mad with fear, and the priest almost found himself kissing the dust. The beast's panic was hardly surprising: two shots had just been fired at very close range.

The clergyman froze with terror, clutching his saddle. He did not even dare look into the bushes to see where his aggressors were hidden. Fortunately, however, his anxiety was brief. Three men were coming down the hill behind the stone cross, preceded by three hunting dogs, the very sight of which reassured him that their masters' guns were a threat only to wild animals.

The hunter who walked in front looked about thirty years old. He was tall, with a full beard and sunburnt neck and face – as his shirt was open, and he carried his hat in his hand, one could see the whiteness of the skin on his forehead and neck where it had not been exposed to the wind and the weather. His broad chest, with its mat of hair, suggested a robust constitution. His legs were covered with thick leather gaiters buckled up to the knees; at his waist hung a full bag of game, and a modern double-barrelled shot-gun rested on his left shoulder.

The second hunter appeared to be middle-aged and of lowly origin. His hair was cropped very close and his face was lean and shaven, with a strong bone-structure and an expression of concealed shrewdness, of savage cunning, more fitting in a Red Indian than a European.

As for the third hunter, the young traveller noted with surprise that he was a fellow clergyman. How could he tell? Certainly not from his clerical collar, for he was not wearing one. Nor from his clothes, for they were similar to those worn by his companions – with the addition of a pair of patent leather riding-boots, peeled and cracked. Nor could the priest be identified by his tonsure, for this was concealed by a jungle of grey bristly hair. Nor by the smoothness of his face, for the bluish stubble on his chin was at least a month old. Nevertheless, he had the unmistakable aura of a clergyman. It was something indefinable about his appearance, his expression, his gait – in fact, about his whole person – that betrayed the formidable mark of ordination that even the flames of hell are unable to efface. There was no doubt about it: he was a priest.

The rider approached the men and asked yet again, 'Is this the way to the marquis of Ulloa's house?'

The tall huntsman turned to the others and said in a casual, but authoritative way:

'What a coincidence . . . It's our visitor! Primitivo, this is your lucky day, for I was going to send you to Cebre tomorrow to look for this gentleman. And you, my dear abbot, at last you have someone here to help you sort out the parish!' Seeing the stranger's hesitation, the hunter added: 'I presume that you are the gentleman recommended to me by my uncle, Señor de la Lage?'

'The very one. The chaplain. At your service,' answered the clergyman, at the same time trying to reach the ground with his foot – an arduous task with which he was helped by the abbot.

'And you, sir, are you the marquis?' he said, turning to the man who had spoken.

'How is my uncle?' the man replied, evasively. 'And you, you've come all the way from Cebre on horseback, eh?'

The chaplain was fascinated by the marquis, who certainly cut a fine figure of a man – unkempt and virile-looking, with beads of sweat on his face, and the shot-gun slung over his shoulder. His arrogance gave him an air of wildness, though the seemingly severe look in his eyes contrasted with his kind, open welcome of the chaplain, who respectfully poured out all the details of his journey.

'Yes, señor. In Cebre I left the coach and was presented with this horse – whose harness, by God, leaves a great deal to be desired. Señor de la Lage is in excellent health and as amusing as ever . . . And still handsome for his age. Indeed, sir, I notice he could not resemble you more even if he were your father . . . The young ladies are also very well – very happy and in the best of health . . . I have news too of the young master who is in Segovia. And, before I forget . . .' He fumbled in the inside pocket of his frock-coat and brought out first a handkerchief, neatly ironed and folded, then a small weekly broadsheet and finally a wallet of black morocco leather, closed with an elastic band. From this he produced a letter which he handed to the marquis.

The sun was setting slowly over the quiet autumn countryside. The hounds lay beside the cross, weary and panting; the abbot of Ulloa busied himself in rolling a cigarette – holding a tip of paper in his lips and tapping his tobacco-pouch – while Primitivo, with the butt of his gun resting on the ground and the barrel against his chin, scrutinized the newcomer with his small, impertinent dark eyes.

Suddenly the marquis laughed out loud. As one might have expected by his appearance, his laugh was arrogant, full-throated and vigorous – despotic rather than communicative.

'My uncle,' he cried, folding the letter, 'is as amusing as ever. He says he has sent a saint to instruct me and convert me. As if

I had any sins on my conscience, eh, abbot? What do you think? Should I have?'

'Certainly not,' mumbled the abbot with a hoarse drawl. 'Here we all preserve our baptismal innocence.' Saying this, he stared at the newcomer through his bristling eyebrows, like a veteran eyeing up an inexperienced recruit. He was deeply scornful of the pretty little priest with his girlish face, whose only signs of priestliness lay in the severity of his brow and his ascetic expression.

'And your name is Julián Alvarez?' asked the marquis.

'At your service, sir.'

'So you couldn't find your way to the house?'

'It was difficult to find. The peasants hereabouts never seem to give a straight answer or have any clear idea of distances. Which meant that – '

'Well, you'll not get lost now. Do you want to ride the rest of the way?'

'Oh no! That is the last thing I should wish.'

'Primitivo, take the horse,' ordered the marquis, and with that he set off, still talking to the chaplain, who followed after him. Primitivo and the abbot, the latter lighting his cigarette with a cardboard match, obediently fell in behind them.

'What do you think of the youngster, then?' Primitivo asked the old priest. 'Nothing to be afraid of, eh?'

'Bah! It's the fashion now to make priests out of scamps like that. Pretty little collars, pretty little gloves . . . All frills and fripperies . . . If I were Archbishop there'd be the devil to pay for those gloves!'

Chapter 2

Night had closed in by the time they reached the coppice behind which lay the massive manor. There was no moon and the darkness made it impossible to distinguish any details of the house, so that one was only aware of its imposing enormity. Not a single light shone from within, and the main door appeared to be firmly locked and bolted. The marquis headed towards a very low side-door, from which a robust young woman emerged to light their way with an oil-lamp.

After passing through several dark corridors they went into what was presumably the wine-cellar, judging from the rows of barrels along the walls. From there they emerged into a large kitchen, lit only by the glow from the chimney, in which a fire blazed like a beacon – a bonfire of thick oak logs regularly stoked up with plenty of kindling. The tall chimney-breast was decorated with strings of red and black sausages and a few cured hams. On either side of the fireplace were benches, which offered a comfortable seat where one could warm oneself and listen to the boiling of the pot hanging on its crook, its black iron bottom licked by the flames.

When they came into the kitchen, an old woman with a mop of white hair, coarse as flax, was crouching beside the pot, her face reddened by the heat. Julián Alvarez caught only a fleeting glimpse of her, however, for the moment she noticed people coming, she straightened up – remarkably for one of her age – and disappeared into the shadows, whining, 'May God grant us a good night.'

The marquis shouted angrily at the servant-girl.

'Haven't I told you before that I won't have any of those old hags around?'

She answered him calmly, hanging the lamp on the chimney-breast. 'She was doing no harm . . . She was just helping me peel the chestnuts.'

The marquis would have flown into a great rage had not Primitivo, with even greater authority and anger than his master, scolded the young woman: 'What are you chattering about? You'd do better to have the food on the table. Hurry up and serve it. Wake yourself up!'

In one corner of the kitchen stood an oak table, blackened with use and covered with a rough cloth that was thick with wine and grease stains. Primitivo dropped his gun and emptied the contents of his gamebag: two young partridges and a hare, its eyes dull and its fur blotched with congealed blood. The young woman pushed these spoils aside and began to set the table with pewter plates and antique, solid-silver cutlery. In the centre she placed an enormous loaf of brown bread and an equally enormous jug of wine. Then she hurriedly uncovered and stirred the contents of some clay pots and took down a great tureen from the shelf.

Once again the marquis rebuked her angrily. 'What about the dogs, then?'

As if the dogs also understood their right to be served before anyone else, they rose from their dark corner and began to sniff, wag their tails and yawn hungrily. At first Julián thought there was one dog more than before, but as they came into the light around the fire he realized that what he had at first taken for another dog was in fact a three- or four-year-old boy whose long brown jacket and white burlap breeches resembled at a distance the patched coats of the dogs – with which the child seemed to live in perfect harmony and fraternity. Primitivo and the girl selected some of the choicest bits from the stew, and served out a feast for the animals in wooden pails. The marquis was supervising the operation and, not content with what he saw, probed the depths of the pot with a metal spoon and brought out three thick chunks of pork, which he put into the pails. The dogs gave short, broken barks, hungry and questioning, not daring to touch the food. Then, at a command from Primitivo, they immediately buried their faces in it, their jaws chomping noisily, their greedy tongues clicking. The little boy crawled between the legs of the dogs, now transformed into wild beasts through unsatisfied hunger. They cast sideways glances at him, growling and snarling. Suddenly he stretched out his hand to take a tempting piece of meat from Chula's bowl. The bitch lifted her head and snapped fiercely. Fortunately she had only caught the boy's sleeve, but it was enough to make him scream and run as fast as he could to take refuge among the maid's skirts, while she was still busy serving the men. Julián, who was removing his gloves, felt sorry for the child. He bent down and took the boy in his arms, to discover that despite the filth and grime, and despite his tears, he was the most beautiful chubby little boy in the world.

'Poor lad!' he murmured lovingly. 'Did the doggie bite you? Is it bleeding? Tell me where it hurts. Don't cry, we'll tell her off. Naughty, bad dog!'

The chaplain noticed that these words had a strange effect on the marquis. His face contracted into a frown and he brusquely snatched the little boy from Julián. Then he held him on his knee to check his hands for any bites or marks. Once he was certain that only the jacket had been harmed, he laughed.

'You humbug!' he shouted. 'Chula didn't even touch you. But why did you bother her? One of these days she'll bite your bottom off and then there'll be tears. Stop crying this instant and let's see you laugh. Now, what do brave boys do?' As he spoke he filled his glass with wine and offered it to the child, who took it without hesitation and drank it down in one gulp. The marquis clapped his hands. 'Well done! Three cheers for brave men!'

'That lad,' mumbled the abbot, 'he really is quite something. No doubt about it.'

'Won't so much wine harm the boy?' objected Julián, who was quite incapable of drinking it himself.

'Harm him? Harm him indeed!' retorted the marquis, adding, with pride in his voice, 'Give him three more and you'll see . . . Shall we put it to the test?'

'He does lap it up,' agreed the abbot.

'No sir, no . . . the child could die . . . I have heard it said that wine is poison for children. What he is, is hungry.'

'Sabel, give the child something to eat,' the marquis ordered harshly, turning to the servant.

Sabel, who had neither moved nor spoken throughout the previous scene, now filled a bowl to the brim with soup and the boy went to sit by the fire, where he could drink it down in peace.

At the table, the company chewed cheerfully at their food. After the thick, floury soup came a meaty stew (on hunting-days the indispensable cooked meal was eaten at night, for there was no way it could be taken to them in the forest). Then a plate of fried eggs and sausages unleashed their thirst, which was already aroused by the saltiness of the pork, and the marquis nudged Primitivo with his elbow: 'Go and fetch a couple of bottles. Bring the '59.' He then turned to Julián and said in an amicable way, 'You're going to taste the best *tostado** in the region. It's from the Melende estate where they claim to have some secret which makes the wine less sweet and syrupy, without losing the flavour of the raisins. It tastes like the finest sherry, and the older it gets, the better it is – not like some wines, which turn to sugar.'

'It has an exquisite taste,' agreed the abbot, soaking up the last of the egg-yolk with a piece of bread.

'I'm afraid I know very little about wines,' said Julián timidly. 'I don't really drink anything except water.' Then, noticing the look of scorn bordering on pity in the abbot's eyes, he added: 'Well . . . on certain feast-days I don't dislike a little anisette with my coffee.'

'Wine cheers the heart,' declared the abbot dogmatically. 'Whoever doesn't drink isn't a real man.'

Primitivo returned from his expedition, clutching a dusty cobwebbed bottle in either hand. For want of a corkscrew they opened the bottles with a knife and then filled the small glasses that had been brought out for the occasion. Primitivo drank hard, and joked freely with the abbot of Ulloa and the master of the house. Sabel, for her part, served with greater familiarity as

* Galician Ribeiro wine.

35

the feast drew on and the wine went to their heads. She leaned across the table and laughed at a joke that made Julián lower his eyes, for he was not accustomed to the after-dinner talk of huntsmen. If the truth be told, however, Julián lowered his eyes not so much because of what he heard but because of what he saw. He wanted to avoid looking at Sabel, whose appearance had disturbed him from the very first moment, despite the fact that she was a good-looking, buxom young woman – or perhaps precisely because of this. Her submissive, moist blue eyes, the bloom in her complexion, and her brown, shell-like curls which hung in tresses down to her waist, made one overlook her imperfections – such as her low, obstinate forehead, her prominent cheekbones and her wide, sensuous, upturned nose. So as not to look at Sabel, Julián fixed his gaze on the little boy, who, encouraged by the kindness in his eyes, slipped on to his knee. Once settled there he lifted his cheeky smiling face, tugged at Julián's waistcoat and said in a low pleading voice:

'Can I have yours?'

Everyone roared with laughter. The chaplain, however, did not understand.

'What does he want?' he asked.

'What do you think he wants?' laughed the marquis, in festive mood. 'He wants the wine, man – your *tostado*!'

'Oh mother!' cried the abbot.

Before Julián had decided what to do about giving him his glass, which was still almost full, the marquis had picked the boy up. Had the brat not been so dirty, he would have been quite beautiful to look at. He resembled Sabel, and indeed even surpassed her in the clearness and merriness of his pale-blue eyes, in the abundance of his curly hair and particularly in the regularity of his features. His small, dark-skinned, dimpled hands reached out towards the amber wine. The marquis put it to the boy's mouth and then teased him for a while by taking it away each time he went to drink. In the end the child managed to snatch the glass, and instantly swallowed the contents and licked his lips.

'This fellow needs no training!' cried the abbot.

36

'Certainly not,' agreed the marquis. 'He's a real veteran. I'll wager you're after downing another glassful, Perucho, eh?'

The little cherub's eyes sparkled, his cheeks glowed and his tiny classical nose quivered with the innocent lustfulness of a young Bacchus. The abbot winked roguishly and poured another glassful, which the child took with both hands and drained to the last drop. He then burst into giggles, but, before his fit of Bacchic laughter had come to an end, he went pale and his head slumped onto the marquis's chest.

'There, gentlemen!' cried Julián, quite beside himself with distress. 'He is far too young to drink in this manner. It will make him ill. These things are not meant for children!'

'Bah!' muttered Primitivo. 'Do you think the lad can't take it? Well he can, and more too, you'll see.' Taking him in his arms, he dipped his fingers in cold water and sprinkled the boy's temples. Perucho opened his eyes and looked around in wonder, his cheeks glowing again.

'How do you feel?' Primitivo asked him. 'Fancy another drop of *tostado*?'

Perucho looked at the bottle and, as if instinctively, shook his thick fleece of curls. Primitivo, however, was not a man to accept defeat so easily. He thrust his hand into his pocket and produced a copper coin.

'That's the way,' grunted the abbot.

'Don't be barbaric, Primitivo,' said the marquis, half serious and half in jest.

'For God and Our Lady's sake!' begged Julián. 'Don't make the boy drunk – you'll kill him. It's a sin – a sin as great as any other. There are certain things one just cannot sit back and watch.' During this remonstration Julián had stood up, flushed with indignation, his natural timidity and meekness momentarily abandoned. Primitivo also stood up. Without letting go of the child he gave the chaplain a cold, sly look full of the scorn that strong-willed people feel for those who lose their heads quickly. He put the copper coin into the boy's hand and raised the uncorked bottle, still a third full, to the boy's lips. Then, tipping it up, he held it there until the entire contents had emptied into the child's stomach. As he took the bottle away, the child's eyes closed and his arms went limp. His face was now more than just pale, it was a deathly white, and he would have fallen flat on the table if Primitivo had not been holding him. The marquis looked worried and began soaking the boy's wrists and forehead with water. Sabel came over and helped him, but to no avail. On this occasion at least, Perucho was blind drunk.

'A real toper,' grunted the abbot.

'Drunk as a lord,' muttered the marquis. 'Off to bed with him this instant. A good night's sleep and tomorrow he'll be as right as rain. It's nothing to worry about.' Sabel carried the boy away, his legs swaying as she walked.

The supper ended less merrily than it had begun. Primitivo said little and Julián was completely silent. Finally it was time to go to bed and Sabel appeared holding an oil-lamp with three wicks. She lit the way up the wide stone staircase, and a further flight of steep spiral stairs.

Julián's room was large and the light from the lamp did little to dispel the gloom. All he could make out was the whiteness of the bed. At the door of the room the marquis wished him goodnight and took his leave, adding:

'Tomorrow you will get your luggage. I'll send someone to Cebre for it.' He sighed deeply. 'Now, get to bed, while I throw out the abbot. He's a little the worse for wear, eh? I shouldn't be surprised if he can't make it home and has to spend the night under a bush!'

Once alone, Julián produced from beneath his waistcoat a picture of Our Lady of Mount Carmel, edged in sequins. He propped it up on the table next to the lamp that Sabel had left, and knelt down to say three decades of the rosary, counting the beads with his fingers. But he felt so exhausted and longed so much for the thick fresh sheets that he omitted the litany and the acts of faith, as well as one or two Our Fathers. He undressed with great propriety, folding every piece of clothing neatly before placing it on a chair. Then he extinguished the lamp and got into bed. All the events of the day began to swim around in his mind. The nag that had almost thrown him flat on his face; the black crucifix that had sent a shiver down his spine; but above all the hubbub over supper and the drunken child. His first impressions of the people here were that Sabel was provocative, Primitivo insolent, the abbot a heavy drinker, over-fond of his hunting, and the dogs far too spoilt. As for the marquis, Julián remembered what Señor de la Lage had said:

'You'll find my nephew rather rough around the edges. When you're brought up in the country and never leave it, you can't help being dull and churlish.'

But as he thought this, the chaplain repented of such severe criticisms. What business was it of his to make such rash judgements? he asked himself, somewhat unhappily. He had come here to say mass and to assist the marquis in the management of his affairs, not to pass judgement on his behaviour and character. With which thought he fell asleep.

Chapter 3

Julián woke as the room filled with soft, golden, autumn sunshine, and while he dressed he examined his new surroundings thoroughly. He was in a vast, high room with bare rafters. The light came in through three windows, in which the missing panes had been patched up with paper and gummed tape. Beneath each window was a wide stone ledge for sitting on, and the rest of the furniture was equally Spartan, and hardly plentiful. Everywhere there remained obvious signs of the habits of the previous tenant, the former chaplain to the marquis and now abbot of Ulloa. Cigar-butts were littered over the floor; in one corner stood two pairs of unserviceable boots; on the table was a packet of gunpowder, and on one of the stone seats were various objects related to the art of hunting: cages for the lairs, collars for the dogs, and a rabbit-skin with a bad tan and a worse smell. Apart from these relics, pale cobwebs dangled between the rafters, and everywhere the dust reposed peacefully, lord and master of the place since time immemorial.

Julián looked at these traces of his predecessor's negligence, and although he was loath to call the abbot a pig, the fact was that so much filth and rusticity filled him with an overwhelming desire for everything to be clean and proper. Julián's aspirations were as much for physical cleanliness as for spiritual purity. He belonged to the vanguard of the excessively prudish, along with those whose sense of virtue is easily shocked, who have the scruples of a nun and the modesty of an untouched maiden. Having never let go of his mother's apron-strings except to attend his classes at the seminary, all Julián knew about life was what could be learned from religious books. The other seminarists had called him St Julián, claiming that all he needed to complete the picture of the saint was a little dove perched on his hand. He could not remember when he had first become aware that he had a vocation. Perhaps his mother, the housekeeper of the de la Lages and a woman with a reputation for piety, had steered him gently towards the Church since his early childhood – and he had simply allowed himself to be steered. As a child he used to play at being a priest, celebrating mass, and when he was older he did not rest until the game had become reality.

For Julián celibacy came easily; he was almost unaware of any restraint and so he remained pure – for, as moralists rightly say, it is easier never to sin at all than to sin only once. Julián's triumph in this matter was thanks not only to the Grace of God, for which he prayed in great earnest, but to the weakness of his nervous-lymphatic system. This meant that he was of a somewhat feminine temperament: tender, gentle, meek and devoid of any aggression or rebelliousness. He also had those sudden, occasional bursts of energy that are so much a part of the female character – for, although women are the weaker sex, in moments of crisis they can draw on vast reserves of hitherto unknown strength, greater than a man's. Thanks to the cleanliness of his habits (learned from his mother, who would perfume all his clothes with lavender and put a pippin apple between each pair of socks), he had gained a reputation as the seminary dandy, especially when it was discovered that he washed his hands and face often. This was indeed his custom, and, had it not been for certain notions of devout modesty, he would have extended these frequent ablutions to the rest of his body, which he tried to keep as clean as possible.

On the first day of his arrival at the manor he was certainly in need of a quick splash in order to wash off the dust from the road. But the abbot of Ulloa had no doubt considered toilet articles an unnecessary luxury, for all Julián could find was a tin basin, with the stone seat as a washstand. No water-jug, no towel, no bucket, no soap. He stood in front of the basin in his shirt-sleeves, at a total loss. Then, convinced of the impossibility of washing, he decided that he could at least bathe in air, and so he opened the window.

The view delighted him. The lush, fertile valley spread out before the house, sloping gently upwards. Vineyards, chestnut groves, fields of maize – some still with cobs, others already harvested – and thick oak copses ascended in terraces up to a small grey hill whose slopes seemed leaden white in the sun. Below, at the foot of the tower, the manor garden lay like a green carpet trimmed with yellow borders, with a huge mirror set in its centre: the shining surface of the pond. Julián filled his lungs with the regenerative air and immediately felt he was beginning to lose some of that initial vague fear he had conceived for the house and what he had seen of its inhabitants. But at the sound of soft, careful footsteps behind him, this fear came surging back. When he turned round, he found Sabel holding a cup and saucer in one hand, and in the other a bowl of fresh water on a pewter dish, with a folded thick napkin on top. The girl's hair was dry and dishevelled, no doubt from having just got out of bed. Her sleeves were rolled up to her elbows and in the daylight the freshness of her skin was even more evident: it was a pure white, diffused with the blue of her veins.

Julián hurriedly put on his coat and muttered, 'Next time please have the courtesy to knock twice before entering . . . As it happens, I am up . . . but I might just as well have been still in bed, or even getting dressed.'

Sabel stared at him fixedly without the slightest hint of embarrassment and cried, 'Forgive me, señor . . . I didn't know . . . and ignorance is like blindness . . .'

'All right, all right . . . I had wanted to say mass before drinking my cup of chocolate.'

'You won't be able to today: the abbot's got the key to the chapel, and the Lord only knows when he'll wake up, or whether there'll be anyone around to go and fetch it.'

Julián suppressed a sigh. Two days now without saying mass! Ever since he had become a priest his religious fervour had intensified. His was the youthful enthusiasm of the newly ordained, in awe of his august investiture. Even now, when he performed the sacrament, he still took great pains, emphasizing every detail of the ceremony, trembling as he elevated the host, feeling overwhelmed when he took the Eucharist, always with indescribable spiritual absorption. Oh well, if there was nothing he could do about it . . .

'Leave the chocolate there,' he told Sabel.

While the young woman did as she was ordered, Julián raised his eyes to the roof, then cast them down on the floor and coughed in an attempt to find the right words with which to express discreetly what he had to say.

'Ahem. Is it . . . long . . . since the abbot slept in this room?'

'No, not long. It must be about two weeks since he went down to the parish.'

'Ah! That's why the place is a little . . . dirty, don't you think? It would be a good idea to sweep up, and run the broom between the beams.'

Sabel shrugged her shoulders. 'The abbot never told me to sweep his room.'

'Well, cleanliness is next to godliness, you know.'

'Yes, señor, of course. Don't worry, I shall tidy it up for you.'

She said these words with such submission that Julián wished in turn to show some charitable interest in her.

'How is the boy?' he asked. 'Did he get ill after last night?'

'No, señor. He slept like a little angel and now he's up running round the garden. See? There he is.'

Looking out of the open window and shading his eyes with his hand, Julián caught sight of Perucho throwing stones into the pond, with the sun on his hatless head.

'What may not happen in a whole year can sometimes happen in a single day, Sabel,' the chaplain warned her gravely. 'You must not let them intoxicate the boy like that. Drunkenness is an ugly vice in a man, and even more so in an innocent child. Why do you allow Primitivo to give him all that drink? It is your duty to stop him.'

Sabel fixed her blue eyes on Julián and it was impossible to distinguish in them the slightest flash of understanding or conviction. At last she said calmly, 'And what can I do about it? I can't go against my own father.'

Astounded, Julián fell silent an instant. So the child had been intoxicated by his own grandfather! He could think of nothing to say, and was incapable even of expressing disapproval. He raised the cup of chocolate to his lips to cover his confusion and Sabel, thinking the conversation had come to an end, was slowly moving away when the chaplain asked her one more question.

'What about the marquis? Is he up yet?'

'Yes, sir. He must be in the garden, or in the outbuildings.'

'Take me to him, please,' said Julián, standing up and hurriedly wiping his mouth on the still folded napkin.

The chaplain and his guide went all round the garden before finding the marquis. It was a vast stretch of land, which at one time had been beautifully cultivated and laid out in the symmetrical and geometrical style of the French. Now, however, there was hardly any evidence left of this. The family coat of arms, once traced along the ground in myrtle, had become a tangled, boxwood bush in which not even the sharpest eye could distinguish any sign of the wolves, pine-trees, towers, roundels and other devices of the illustrious Ulloa escutcheon. Nevertheless, there remained in that tangle the vestiges of an earlier gardener's thoughtfulness and artistry. The stone surround of the pond was half-broken, and the large granite spheres that decorated it had rolled on to the grass and lay scattered and green with moss, like gigantic cannon-balls on some deserted battlefield. The pond was clogged with slime and looked like a pool of mud, adding to the abandoned, derelict impression of the garden. Where once had been arbours and rustic benches were now simply weed-covered crannies. The kitchen garden had been ploughed up and replanted with maize, while, scattered around the edges, a few select rose-bushes – stubborn reminders of the past – had been left to grow wild, their tallest branches touching the tops of the pear- and plum-trees.

Among these vestiges of past grandeur wandered the last of the Ulloas, his hands in his pockets, whistling idly like someone at a loss as to what to do with his time. Julián's arrival on the scene gave him the solution. After exchanging greetings and praising the beauty of the day, the chaplain and his master made a complete tour of the gardens, and even ventured as far as the copse and oak woods that formed the northern boundary of the marquis's vast estate. Julián opened his eyes wide, as if hoping to absorb through them the whole science of agriculture and thus understand all the señorito's comments on the quality of his soil and the state of his forest. But Julián, having come directly from Santiago, had known only life in the city and the seminary cloister, and he found Nature hard to comprehend. Indeed, he was almost frightened by the impetuous vitality he could sense beating within it, in the thickness of the brushwood, in the harsh toughness of the tree-trunks, in the fertility of the fruit-trees, in the sharp purity of the fresh air. With real distress he declared:

'Marquis, I must confess . . . The truth is that I haven't the faintest notion about country life.'

'Well then, let's go back and take a look at the house,' the master of Ulloa replied. 'It's the largest in the entire region,' he added proudly.

They altered direction and headed towards the huge ramshackle house, which they entered through the door by the garden. After crossing the cloister, with its arches of hewn stone, they passed through various rooms in which the furniture was dilapidated, the windows without glass and the paintings faded and ravaged by damp; nor had the woodworm been any more merciful with the floorboards. They came to a halt in a relatively small room, with a grating at the window, but its ceiling was so high that the black rafters in the roof seemed quite remote. Julián was immediately struck by the enormous bookcases made of unvarnished chestnut, with thick iron grille-work on the outside instead of glass. The dismal room also contained a desk on which stood a horn ink-pot, an extremely old leather folder, a number of goose quills and an empty box of gummed paper. Bundles of papers and documents could be glimpsed through the half-open doors of the bookcases, while on the floor, on the two calfskin chairs, on the table and even on the window-sill there were more bundles, all of them creased and torn, yellowed with age, and nibbled by vermin. Such a mass of paper gave off a damp, stale smell that burned the back of one's throat unpleasantly.

The marquis of Ulloa stopped in the doorway and, with a somewhat solemn expression, announced, 'The family archives.'

He immediately cleared the leather chairs and explained with great annoyance that it was all very untidy – an absolutely unnecessary observation – and that all the mess was to be blamed on the negligence of Brother Venancio, his uncle's estate-manager, and of the present abbot of Ulloa in whose sinful hands the archives had reached the state in which Julián now saw them.

'Well, this cannot continue,' declared the chaplain. 'Important papers treated like this! You might even lose one.'

'Exactly! God knows what state things are in, and what damage has already been done. I can't even bear to look. It's a disaster, an absolute ruination. Look! What's that there – at your feet? Under your boot!'

Terrified, Julián lifted his foot and the marquis bent down and picked up a very thin book bound in green leather, from which hung a round lead seal. Julián took it with great deference and opened it to find on the title page a magnificent heraldic miniature in colours that were fresh and bright despite their age.

'Letters patent of nobility,' declared the marquis gravely.

Handling it with care, Julián cleaned away the mould with his folded handkerchief. From his earliest childhood his mother had taught him to respect noble blood, and that parchment written on in red ink and illuminated with gold and vermilion seemed to him venerable indeed, and worthy of pity at having been trodden under his boot. Observing that the young master remained serious, with his elbows on the table and his hands folded under his chin, some other words of Señor de la Lage came to the chaplain's mind. 'Everything to do with my nephew's house must be in complete disarray. You would be performing an act of charity if you cleared things up a bit for him.' The truth was that Julián knew little about official documents and suchlike, but perhaps with patience and good intentions . . .

'Señorito,' he muttered. 'Why don't we put all this into good and proper order? Between the two of us surely we can manage.

46

We could start by separating the old from the new, then copies could be made of what is very damaged. What's torn could be repaired with gummed paper . . .'

The project appealed greatly to the marquis, and they resolved to start work the following morning. However, as luck would have it, that morning Primitivo discovered a whole flock of partridges happily eating the ripe grain in a nearby field, and so the marquis slung his carbine across his back and left his chaplain to struggle alone with the documents – for ever and ever, amen.

Chapter 4

The chaplain struggled with the papers, grappling with them without respite, for three or four hours every morning. First he shook them, then he wiped them clean and pressed them flat with the palm of his hand. The pieces of torn parchment he stuck together with cigarette-papers. He felt as if he were dusting, tidying and glueing back together the House of Ulloa itself, which would shine like a new pin when he had finished with it.

The task, though simple at first sight, was nevertheless irksome for the tidy-minded priest. Sometimes, as he lifted a sheaf of papers that had been left on the floor since heaven knows when, half of the documents would fall to the ground, shredded by the tiny teeth of relentless mice. Moths swarmed like dust, flapping their wings and getting inside his clothes. Cockroaches, pursued to their secret lairs, emerged blind with rage or fear, forcing him to crush them, with great disgust, under his heel, while he covered his ears so as not to hear the dreaded crackle of their exploding bodies. The spiders were usually cleverer and would swiftly take refuge in the dark corners, swinging their dropsical bellies along on their enormous stilts, guided by a mysterious strategic instinct. But of all those disgusting insects, perhaps the one that revolted Julián most was a sort of maggot or mite that thrived on dampness – a cold, black animal he would find curled up motionless among the papers and which, when touched, felt like a sliver of sticky, soft ice.

Finally, through patience and determination, Julián triumphed in his battle against the impertinent pests, and the documents were stacked on the now clear shelves, occupying half as much room as before and fitting where they had never previously fitted

– thanks to the miraculous effect of tidiness. Three or four letters patent of nobility, each with a lead seal, were put aside, wrapped in clean cloth. Everything was now in order, except for one section of the cabinet containing some sombre-looking old books whose dark spines were embossed with gold leaf. It was the library of an Ulloa from the turn of the century. Julián stretched out his hand, took one of the volumes at random and read, '*La Henriade*, a poem by Monsieur Voltaire, translated into Spanish verse . . .' He returned the book to its place, with tight lips and downcast eyes, which was his usual expression when something hurt or shocked him. Not that he was excessively intolerant, but he would gladly have treated Monsieur Voltaire in the same way as he had treated the cockroaches. However, he limited himself to condemning that particular set of books to eternal dustiness, and did not even pass his old rag over their spines, so that moths, maggots and spiders, so ruthlessly pursued in every corner, might find a refuge behind merry Arouet* and his enemy, the sentimental Jean-Jacques, who had also been sleeping there peacefully since 1816.

Cleaning the archives was not child's play, yet the truly arduous task turned out to be the classification of it. 'We've got you now!' the old papers seemed to say every time he tried to disentangle them. A jumble, a puzzled skein without ends, a labyrinth without a guiding thread. There was no lighthouse for him to steer by in this unnavigable sea. There were no record-books, no accounts, nothing, apart from two filthy notebooks, stinking of tobacco. Here his predecessor the abbot had written down the names of the debtors and tenants of the manor, jotting down the state of their account in the margin, with a mark intelligible only to its author, or in words that were even more enigmatic. Some were marked with a cross, others with a squiggle or a cipher, while a very few were distinguished with the phrases

* Voltaire was the pseudonym of François-Marie Arouet (1694–1778), whose books were banned by the Church.

49

'doesn't pay', 'will pay', 'is paying' or 'has paid'. What then did the cross and squiggle mean? An inscrutable mystery. On the same page credit and debit would be mixed together. Here so-and-so would appear as an insolvent debtor, and two lines further on as being owed daily wages. The abbot's book gave Julián a dreadful headache and he blessed the memory of Brother Venancio who, being even more radical, had left no trace of accounts whatever, not even a single receipt to show for his long management.

Julián had set to work with the greatest enthusiasm, certain that it would not prove impossible to find his way through the chaos of papers. He strained his eyes trying to decipher the old-fashioned writing and the complicated flourishes of the signatures. He wanted at least to separate the house's main sources of revenue, and was amazed that to receive such small amounts of money, such miserable quantities of rye and corn, one needed such an array of old bits of paper, so many indigestible documents. He became lost in a labyrinth of leases and sub-leases, apportionments, mortgages, pensions, entails, dowry letters, tithes, tributes, trivial lawsuits about arrears, important lawsuits about partitions . . . And at each step the heap of jumbled papers only created further confusion in his mind. Although he found the work of restoration straightforward enough – such as putting the crumbling old documents into strong white paper folders – he was at a loss when it came to actually understanding the wretched papers, which were unintelligible to someone who did not possess the correct knowledge and experience. Discouraged, he confessed to the marquis:

'Señorito, I just cannot see my way through this muddle . . . What we need is a lawyer, someone who understands these things.'

'That's exactly what I've been thinking for ages. Something really must be done about it. I suppose many of the papers are lost. What sort of state are they in? A pitiful one, I'm sure.'

The marquis spoke these words in the sullen, insistent tone he always employed when speaking about his own affairs, however insignificant they were. And while he spoke, his hands were busy fastening a collar with little bells on Chula, whom he was about to take quail-hunting.

'You are quite right, señor,' Julián muttered. 'They are in a sorry state indeed. However, someone used to dealing with these matters could sort them out in a moment. But whoever it is, he must attend to them soon, for they won't improve on their own.'

The truth was that the archives had given Julián that same sense of unease as the rest of that vast, threatening ruin, which may once have been a symbol of greatness, but which now was rapidly crumbling. Julián had not actually analysed these fears of imminent decay, but, had he known more of the marquis's family history, he would have realized that they were fully justified.

Don Pedro Moscoso de Cabreira y Pardo de la Lage, known as the marquis of Ulloa, had lost his father when he was still only a very young boy. But for that misfortune, he might have gone to university. Ever since the days of the Moscoso grandfather, an encyclopedist, Freemason and francophile who had taken the liberty of reading 'Monsieur Voltaire', the family had kept up certain ancient cultural traditions, already waning but still alive enough to dispatch a Moscoso to attend lectures. On the other hand, his mother's family – Pardo de la Lage – believed in the old proverb that 'a live ass is better than a dead doctor'. In those days the Pardos lived in their manor house, not far from the Ulloa manor. When Don Pedro's mother had become a widow, her brother, the eldest de la Lage and the first in line of succession, had married a lady of distinction in Santiago and settled in the town, while the second-born, Don Gabriel, had come to the Ulloa manor to keep his sister company and look after her, or so he said. Malicious gossips, on the other hand, claimed that he had come to enjoy at his pleasure all his late brother-in-law's revenues. Don Gabriel did indeed take charge of the house in very little time, and it was he who discovered that holy fool Brother Venancio, and had him made estate-manager. Brother Venancio, a secularized monk, had been quite doddery ever since he had left the cloister, as well as being something of a

51

born fool, so that under his cloak Don Gabriel was able to manage his nephew's estate at ease.

Don Gabriel was also an expert at sharing out his sister's money, and thus he skilfully deprived her of most of her rightful legacy – and to this plundering the poor lady gave her consent, being quite incompetent in business matters. Her only talent was for saving money with miserly greed, which she would change, with childish imprudence, into antique doubloons as a reward for her thrift. Few were the profits of the Moscoso property that did not slip through Brother Venancio's shaky fingers into Don Gabriel's robust palms. But if they did manage to reach Doña Micaela, they did not leave her hands again except in the form of gold coins on their way to some mysterious hiding-place, about which a legend soon grew up in the area. While the mother hoarded her gold, Don Gabriel, who had also become his nephew's tutor, brought Don Pedro up in his own image, taking him to fairs, hunts, country fêtes and probably also to less innocent entertainments, and all the while instructing him in the art of hunting the white partridge, as the pursuit of the fairer sex is called in those parts. The boy in turn worshipped his cheerful uncle, who was vigorous and resolute, an expert at outdoor pursuits, and, like all the de la Lages, rudely witty in after-dinner conversation. He was a model of the feudal master, who is treated with such deference in that region, and he taught the Ulloa heir to scorn humanity and abuse his power. One day, while nephew and uncle were hunting five or six leagues from the house, having taken the servant and the stable-boy with them, a band of twenty men, with their faces blackened or disguised by masks, entered the house at four o'clock in the afternoon, when all the doors stood open. They gagged and tied the maid, forced Brother Venancio to lie face down on the floor, and, seizing Doña Micaela, ordered her to show them where she had hidden her famous doubloons. When she refused, they beat her, then they started pricking her with the sharp end of a knife, while a few of them suggested frying her feet in oil. After they had riddled an arm and a breast with cuts, she begged for mercy and revealed the hiding-place: a trapdoor concealed by a huge chest, and cleverly disguised as one of the floorboards, the only difference being that it could be easily lifted. The thieves took the beautiful coins, as well as all the wrought silver they could find, and had left the manor by six o'clock, before it was dark. Some peasant or labourer saw them coming out, but what could he do? There were twenty of them, well-armed with shot-guns, pistols and blunderbusses.

Brother Venancio, who had only been dealt a few scornful kicks and punches, needed no other ticket for making his final journey to the other world – which he did within a week, out of sheer fright. The mistress of the house was not in such a hurry, but, as they say, she never got back on her feet again, and a few months later a serious stroke prevented her from continuing to hide more gold coins in another, even better hiding-place that she had found. People in the neighbourhood talked of the robbery for a long time, and strange rumours circulated. It was said that the robbers were not professional criminals but well-to-do and well-known people, some with official posts. It was even said that one or two of them had been connected since time immemorial with the Ulloa family, and were therefore well informed about their ways – they would have known when the house would be left without men to guard it, and been well aware of Doña Micaela's insatiable obsession with hoarding valuable gold coins.

Whatever the truth may have been, the authorities never discovered the perpetrators of the crime, and Don Pedro was soon left with no other relative but his uncle, Don Gabriel, who found a rough-mannered priest – a dedicated hunter quite incapable of dying of fear at the sight of thieves – to replace Brother Venancio. For a long time they had been assisted in their hunting-expeditions by Primitivo, the best tracker and marksman in the district and father of the most handsome wench to be found in a good many miles. With Doña Micaela's death, father and daughter could move into the house, she as servant, he as – head gamekeeper, we might have said once upon a time, though now there is no adequate name to describe the full weight of his position. Don Gabriel kept them both well within bounds, for he could sense in Primitivo a serious threat to his own influence. Three or four years after his sister's death, however, Don Gabriel had fits of gout that put his life in danger. What had once been whispered about his secret marriage to the daughter of the gaoler in Cebre was now openly revealed, and he went to live, or rather to rant and rave, in the little town. He executed his will, leaving all his goods and chattels to three sons he had, and not even his watch as a token to Don Pedro. When the gout reached his heart, he delivered his soul up to his Maker, very much against his will, and with that the last of the Moscosos was left to be his own master.

Owing to all these vicissitudes, deceits and pilferings, the House of Ulloa was left drained and in a state of utter confusion, though it still retained two or three good sources of revenue. It was, as Julián had imagined, a veritable ruin. Given the complicated Galician system of subdividing property among individuals, a little carelessness or bad management is sufficient to undermine the foundations of even the wealthiest estate. Arrears of tax and the interest accrued on them resulted in the house being burdened with a mortgage. It was not a heavy one, but any mortgage is like a cancer, which starts in one spot and then spreads to attack the whole body. Because of the above-mentioned taxes, the señorito searched assiduously for his mother's second hiding-place, but in vain. Either the lady had not hoarded any more doubloons since the robbery, or else she had hidden them so well that the devil himself would have been unable to find them. The sight of the mortgage saddened Julián, for the kind priest had begun to experience that sense of loyalty chaplains always feel for the houses they serve. But what caused even greater confusion in his mind was the discovery, among the bits of paper, of documents concerning a small land-division claim brought by Don Alberto Moscoso, Don Pedro's father, against . . . the marquis of Ulloa!

For it should now be revealed that the genuine, legal marquis of Ulloa, the one who was listed in the official *Guide to the Peerage*,* was, in that winter of 1866–7 when Julián was

* *Guía de forasteros*, the official calendar of Spanish nobility, an equivalent of the British *Debrett's Peerage*.

exterminating cockroaches in the manor-house archives, in Madrid, calmly riding up and down the Castellana in a calash. The real marquis was quite unaware that the title of nobility, for whose letter of succession he had religiously paid his tribute, was being freely enjoyed by a relative of his in a forgotten corner of Galicia. A grandee of the highest rank – three times a marquis, twice a count as well as duke of somewhere or other – he was never known in Madrid as anything but the duke, for, as they say, a hand full of Aces makes nothing of a Jack – though the title of Ulloa, rooted as it was in the illustrious lineage of Cabreira de Portugal, boasted an antiquity and reputation as great as any. When the estate of the Ulloa manor passed to a collateral branch of the family, the title of marquis went to where it belonged by strict agnation. But the villagers, who knew nothing of agnations, and who were used to the fact that the house lent its name to the title, went on calling the owners of the grand old warren by the name of marquises. The lords of the manor did not complain: they were marquises by common law, and when a peasant, meeting Don Pedro along the lane, would doff his hat respectfully and cry, 'God bless you, marquis!', Don Pedro felt his vanity pleasantly tickled and in reply would boom, 'Good afternoon!'

Chapter 5

All Julián got from his famous reorganization of the archives was an aching head and sore feet. He was anxious to get off to a good start in his new duties as estate-manager, using his intellectual powers and all he had learned about the state of the house to best advantage. But in this he failed, for the job was quite beyond him. His inexperience in rural and legal matters revealed itself at every step he took. He tried to find out what made the manor tick. He took great pains to learn all about the crops grown. He visited the cowsheds and the stables. He inspected the barn, the oven, the granaries, the threshing-floors, the cellars, the tool-sheds, as well as every outhouse and every nook and cranny. He would demand to know what this, that and the other was, as well as how much it cost, and how much it would be sold for. But it was a useless task. He could scent abuses and disorders wherever he went, but he was unable to put a finger on anything and so stop such practices, because of his lack of guile and astuteness.

The señorito did not go with him on these visits: he had quite enough to do, what with fairs, hunting-expeditions and calls on the local gentry in Cebre or in the highlands. Julián's guide therefore was Primitivo – a negative companion if ever there was one. Every improvement Julián wanted to introduce, Primitivo would shrug his shoulders at and deem impossible. Every superfluous thing Julián tried to do away with, the hunter would declare indispensable for the smooth running of the estate. Innumerable small difficulties would rise up at the approach of the earnest Julián, preventing him from making any useful change. And the most alarming thing was to observe Primitivo's disguised but nevertheless real omnipotence. Servants, tenants, labourers, even the cattle in the sheds, seemed to be under his thumb and well-disposed towards him. The flattering respect with which they addressed the master, and the half scornful, half indifferent way in which they greeted the chaplain, turned into utter submission when it came to Primitivo. Submission that was not expressed so much in words, but in the instant observance of Primitivo's every wish, often expressed simply by a fixed cold stare of his small, lashless eyes.

Julián felt humiliated in the presence of a man who ruled over the place like an indubitable autocrat from his uncertain status of servant-cum-majordomo. His spirit was weighed down by Primitivo's penetrating glance as the latter watched over his smallest movements and studied his face, doubtless in order to discover the vulnerable side of that unselfish priest who averted his eyes from the pretty peasant girls. Perhaps it was Primitivo's philosophy that there are no men without vices, and Julián would be no exception.

Meanwhile, winter drew on and the chaplain gradually became accustomed to life in the country. The bracing fresh air gave him a greater appetite. He no longer felt those initial effusions of devotion, and instead was filled with a sort of human charity that made him take an interest in what he saw around him. The young and innocent were the particular objects of his instinctive tenderness, and he felt a growing pity for Perucho, the lad whose own grandfather had intoxicated him. It upset Julián to see him pass his days rolling about in the mud of the yard, or, covered in cow-dung, playing with the young calves and sucking warm milk from the mother cow's teats, or sleeping on the grass meant for the donkey's feed. He decided to devote a few hours of the long winter nights to teaching the child the alphabet and the catechism, as well as how to do his sums. For that task he would settle at the vast table, not far from the fire in the hearth, which Sabel fed with thick logs. He would sit the boy on his lap and patiently, by the light of the three-wick oil-lamp, run his finger through the ABC, repeating the monotonous sing-song with which one begins to learn: 'Ay-ee. Be-ee . . .' Perucho would then be overcome by exaggerated fits of yawning. He would pull funny tearful faces and scowl comically, or he would scream like a trapped starling. He would arm and defend himself against learning in every imaginable way: kicking, grumbling, covering his face, or sneaking off at the teacher's slightest distraction to hide in a corner or go back to the warm shelter of the stables.

In that cold weather the kitchen became an open house, the company consisting almost entirely of women. Some would come barefoot, shuffling in sideways and looking apprehensive, their heads covered by a rough sort of shawl. Many of them groaned with pleasure when they came close to the delectable flames, while others, after warming their hands, would extract a spindle and a tuft of flax from their belts and start spinning, or they would take chestnuts from their pockets and set them on the hot ashes to bake. They all began by talking in whispers and ended up chattering like magpies.

Sabel was the queen of that court: with her face flushed from the heat of the fire, her sleeves rolled up, her eyes bright, she inhaled the incense of their adulation as she buried the iron ladle in the pot to fill a bowl with soup. Then instantly one of the women would leave the circle, take the bowl and huddle in a corner or on a bench, where she could be heard eagerly chewing, blowing on the boiling broth, and slurping her tongue against the spoon. Some evenings the girl did not have a moment's rest from filling cups, as the women kept coming in, eating, and leaving so as to allow room for others. No doubt the whole parish filed through the kitchen as if it were a cheap inn. When they left, they would take Sabel aside, and had the chaplain not been paying so much attention to his unmanageable pupil, he would have seen more than one bit of bacon, bread or pork being quickly hidden in a bodice; or a red sausage, promptly cut from the strings hanging on the chimney, being no less hastily slipped into a bag.

The last of the party to remain, the one whose whispered conversations with Sabel were the longest and most private, was the old woman with the matted hair Julián had caught a glimpse of the night he arrived at the manor. The hag's ugliness was impressive: her eyebrows were white and stood out in profile, as

did the bristles on a birthmark. The fire emphasized the whiteness of her hair, the dark tan of her face and the huge goitre that
so repulsively deformed her neck. While she spoke to the buxom
girl, an artist's fancy might have evoked *The Temptations of St
Anthony*, one of those paintings in which a filthy old witch and a
beautiful, sensuous woman, holding a goat's hoof, are to be seen
side by side.

Without knowing why, Julián began to dislike the chatter and
familiarities of Sabel, who would keep coming over to him, with
the excuse of fetching something from the table-drawer: a knife,
a cup, or some other object she just could not do without. When
the country girl fixed her blue eyes, brimming with moist
warmth, on the chaplain, he felt ill-at-ease and embarrassed, a
sensation comparable only to that caused by Primitivo, whom he
often caught staring at him on the sly. Although he had nothing
certain on which to base his distrust of Primitivo and Sabel,
Julián detected in the way they looked at him the planning of
some trap. Primitivo was a morose character and, except for an
occasional outburst of sudden, wild merriness, his bronze-like
face rarely betrayed any feeling. Despite all this, Julián felt he
was the object of the huntsman's secret hostility. Strictly speaking, it could not even be called hostility; it was more like a kind
of watchful observation, the calm lying in wait for a prey one
does not hate, but wishes to catch as soon as possible. It was an
attitude one could hardly define or express.

However, winter soon passed, and the heat of the fireplace was
no longer so tempting. Julián took shelter in his room where the
boy had to be lugged up to his daily lessons. There the chaplain
was able to observe, better than in the kitchen, the shocking
dirtiness of the chubby little boy. His skin was covered in half an
inch of filth, and, as for his hair, it was a bed of geological layers
– stratifications of earth, tiny stones and all manner of foreign
bodies. Julián managed to drag him to the wash-basin, which
was now well supplied with jugs, towels and soap. He began to
scrub. By the Blessed Virgin Mary, what water came off the first
wash of that fiendish little face! The thickest, greyest ash-water!
For the hair Julián had to use water in plenty, as well as oil,

pomade, and a comb with thick teeth with which to clear the virgin forest. As he advanced in his task, the most beautiful features came to light. They were worthy of an ancient chisel and were coloured by a patina worked by the sun and wind. The ringlets, now cleared of dirt, flowed delicately as if on the head of a Cupid, their golden-brown hue giving the finishing touch to the picture. It was astonishing to see how exquisitely God had created that little doll!

Every day before the lesson Julián washed the boy, whether he screamed or not – but because of the respect he professed for the human flesh he did not dare bathe the child's body, even though it was greatly in need of it. However, the little devil took advantage of Julián's kind nature and the continual washing sessions to leave nothing in the room undamaged. His naughtiness, which grew worse day by day, exasperated the poor priest. Perucho would dip his whole hand in the ink and then press it on to the spelling-book; he would pull the feathers off the quill and break its point by using it to catch flies on the window-pane; he would tear the paper into little shreds or make trumpets with it; he would scatter the sand on the table and build hills and mountains, only to create 'earthquakes' by suddenly burying his finger in it. Moreover, he would rummage through Julián's drawers, mess up the bed by jumping on it, and once he went as far as to set fire to his teacher's boots, by filling them with burning matches.

Julián would have put up with all these pranks if he had entertained any hopes of making something out of that shameless boy. But things became complicated by something far more disagreeable: Sabel's frequent comings and goings to his room. The girl always found some pretext to come up. Either she had forgotten to remove the chocolate-tray, or it had quite gone out of her mind to change the towel. Then she would become absorbed in some task and take a long time to go down, busying herself with tidying up things that were not untidy, or she would lean out of the window, cheerfully boasting a familiarity that Julián, who grew daily more and more reserved, would on no account allow.

One morning, when Sabel brought the priest's jug of water at the usual time, Julián noticed, with a quick glance, that the maid still had her hair down and was wearing only a bodice, a petticoat and a chemise, which was half undone, so that he could not help but see her exposed legs and feet, which were as white as milk. As Sabel always wore shoes and only worked in the kitchen, and as she received considerable help in her work from the peasants and servants, her skin remained quite unblemished, and her figure lost none of its gracefulness. Julián took a step back, and the jug shook in his hand. Some of the water spilt onto the floor.

'Cover yourself up, woman!' he cried, his voice choked with embarrassment. 'Don't ever come in here like this. It's no way to appear in front of people.'

'I was combing my hair and thought you were calling for me,' she answered, not batting an eyelid or even crossing her hands over her bare neck.

'Even if I was calling you, it was not right to come dressed like this. Another time, if you're combing your hair, Cristóbal can bring the water up for me . . . or the milkmaid . . . or anyone . . .'

Saying this he turned his back so as not to look any further at the girl, who slowly left the room. From that moment on, Julián avoided Sabel as one might avoid a harmful, dirty animal. However, it seemed to him rather uncharitable to charge her indecent slovenliness with an evil purpose, and he preferred to blame it instead on ignorance and rusticity. But she was determined to prove the contrary. One afternoon, only a short time after the severe reprimand, Julián was calmly reading the *Guide for Sinners** when he heard Sabel enter. Without raising his head, he noticed that she was tidying up something in the room. Suddenly he heard a bump, like someone falling against a piece of furniture, and saw the girl lying on the bed, moaning pitifully and heaving deep sighs. She complained of being taken ill, of a sudden affliction, and Julián, feeling confused but also concerned, went to soak a towel in water with which to dampen her temples. To do so he drew close to the poor ailing woman. But no sooner

---

* *Guía de Pecadores* by Fray Luis de Granada (1504–88).

61

had he bent over her than he convinced himself – despite his limited experience and complete lack of malice – that the supposed sickness was nothing but a wicked ruse. Julián blushed to the roots. Overcome by the sudden, blind anger that only very rarely inflamed his lymphatic glands, he pointed to the door and shouted:

'Leave the room this instant, before I throw you out! Do you hear? Don't ever cross this door again. Everything, absolutely everything I need will be brought to me in future by Cristóbal. Get out this minute!'

The maid went out with her head down and a sulky look, like someone who has just had a great disappointment. As for Julián he was left trembling, agitated, unhappy with himself, as peaceful people usually are when they give in to a fit of rage: he even felt a pain in his stomach. He was in no doubt that he had gone too far, that he should have delivered some uplifting sermon to the girl, instead of haranguing her contemptuously like that. His duty as a priest was to teach, correct, forgive, not to trample on people as he trampled on insects in the archives. After all, Sabel had a soul, redeemed by the saving blood of Christ, just like any other. But who stops to consider these things when faced by such shamefulness? The chaplain consoled himself with the thought that he had suffered what scholars call a *primo primis* fit, which is beyond one's ability to control. Nevertheless, it was wretched to have to live with that wicked female, who had no more modesty than a cow. How could there exist women like her? Julián remembered his mother, who with her sweet gentle voice was so decorous – her eyes always downcast, her housecoat buttoned up to the top of her throat, and over this, for further modesty, a little black silk shawl, perfectly smooth and creaseless. But oh, what shameful women one finds in the world!

After this unfortunate incident with Sabel, Julián had to sweep his room and bring the water up himself, because neither Cristóbal nor the servant-girls paid any attention to his orders, and he did not want even to set eyes on the maid. But what caused most surprise and fear in Julián was noticing that after the event Primitivo did not hesitate to stare at him most terribly, gauging him with a quick glance that amounted to an open declaration of war. Julián had no doubt that he was unwelcome in the manor. But why? Sometimes the thought distracted him in his reading of Brother Luis de Granada and the six books of St John Chrysostom on the priesthood. But after a while, discouraged by such petty set-backs, and having given up hope of ever being of service in the House of Ulloa, he buried himself once again in the pages of the mystics.

Chapter 6

Of all the parish priests in the district, the one with whom Julián got on best was Don Eugenio, the Naya priest. The abbot of Ulloa, whom he saw most frequently, he did not like, because of his immoderate fondness for the bottle and the gun. The abbot, in turn, was exasperated by Julián, whom he called a sissy. For him, the lowest depravity a man could sink to was to drink water, wash with perfumed soap, and pare his fingernails. And in the case of a priest, the abbot compared these crimes to simony. 'Too damned ladylike,' he would mutter, absolutely convinced that for virtue to be genuine in a clergyman it should have a coarse, rustic appearance. Besides, ordination did not, *ipso facto*, cancel out one's manliness, and a true man, full of vigour, could always be smelt for miles around. Julián did not get along very well with the other priests from the neighbouring parishes, either; thus when he was invited to religious functions he usually left as soon as the ceremony was over, without even accepting the meal, its indispensable complement. But when Don Eugenio asked him with cheerful cordiality to spend the patron saint's feast-day in Naya, he accepted willingly, promising not to fail him.

As arranged, Julián went up to Naya on the eve, refusing the mount Don Pedro offered him. It was only a league and a half away, and on such a beautiful afternoon ... ! Setting off with a walking-stick, he let time slip by and evening fall, stopping every now and then to enjoy the scenery. But it was not long before he reached the small hill that looks down on the hamlet of Naya. It was a timely arrival, right in the middle of the dance that heralded the festivities, with bagpipes, drums and tabors – all lit up by the blaze of the large straw torches that were merrily being waved about. Soon after, the dancers set off down the hill towards the rectory, singing and whooping excitedly, and Julián went down with them.

The priest was waiting for them at the door, his coat-sleeves drawn up; he lifted high a jug of wine, while the maid held out a trayful of glasses. The group came to a halt. The bagpiper, dressed in blue corduroy, looked tired as he let the air out of the wind-bag, with the pipe hanging over the red fringe of the drone, and he wiped his wet forehead with a silk handkerchief. With the gleam of the burning straw and the lights outside the rectory, Julián was able to see his handsome face, with its regular features, enhanced by gallant brown sideburns. When his wine was served, the musical countryman said politely:

'To the health of the abbot and all the company!' And after drinking up he murmured respectfully:

'And may you enjoy your health many years, abbot.'

With this, formalities were set aside and the glasses refilled.

The Naya priest enjoyed a spacious rectory, full of cheer at the time because of the festive preparations, and he witnessed unperturbed the sack and ruin of his larder, cellar, wood-shed and garden. Don Eugenio was young and as happy as a lark. His nature was rather mischievous and roguish for a spiritual adviser, but beneath his boyish exterior lay an exceptional gift for handling people and a knowledge of the practical side of life. He was sociable and tolerant, and had managed to have no enemies among his fellow priests. They thought of him as a harmless youngster.

After a cup of delicious chocolate, Eugenio gave Julián the best bed and room he had. He woke him again at dawn, when the flourish of bagpipes filled the air, and then the two clergymen went together to check the decorations of the altar, which was all set for the solemn mass.

Julián made his inspection with special devotion, for the patron saint of Naya was his very own blessed St Julián – who stood there, on the high altar, with his innocent little face, his ecstatic smile, his frock and short breeches, the white dove on his right hand, and his left hand delicately placed on the frill of his shirt.

The simple effigy, the dilapidated church, whose only ornaments were the plaited candles and some humble wild flowers in modest earthenware pots – everything there aroused a tender sense of devotion in Julián, a sudden feeling of warmth, which did him a great deal of good, softening and reviving his soul. The priests from the neighbourhood were arriving, and, in the porch, carpeted with grass, the bagpiper could be heard painstakingly tuning his instrument. In the church, the fennel spread over the tiles and, stepped on by the people coming in, gave off a lovely fresh country smell.

The procession was ready. St Julián was taken down from the high altar; the cross and the banners swayed above the crowd of people that had already piled into the narrow nave; and the young men in their Sunday clothes, their silken scarves tied like headbands, stepped forward to carry the devotional objects. After going twice round the porch and stopping in front of the stone cross, the saint, still on his stand, was taken back into the church. There he was lifted onto a small table next to the high altar, which was splendidly decked with an antique scarlet damask altar-cloth. The mass began, joyful and rustic, in keeping with the other festivities. Over a dozen priests sang it at the top of their voices, while the rickety censer swung back and forth, with its jingle of old chains, giving off a thick sweet-scented smoke: in that cotton-wool wrapping the introit seemed less harsh and the rasping ecclesiastical throats lost some of their discordance. The bagpiper displayed all his musical skills and accompanied the singers with the pipe, having removed it from the bag to use as a clarinet. When a whole orchestra was called for, he would connect the pipe back in the wind-bag again; that way he could accompany the elevation of the host with a royal march, and the post-communion with one of the latest and merriest *muñeiras*,* which he was to repeat in the vestibule once the mass was over. Then the young men and women took turns to dance to their heart's content and make up for the sobriety they had shown in church during a whole hour. The dance in the sunlit porch; the

* The *muñeira* is a Galician folk dance.

church floor covered with fennel and bulrush, bruised by the trampling feet; the church itself lit up, not so much by the candles as by the light that flooded in through door and window; the priests, out of breath but happy and talkative; the saint, looking so smart, trim and cheerful on his stand, with one leg slightly raised as if to start a minuet, and the innocent dove ready to spread its wings: all contributed to make up a picture of bucolic gaiety, with nothing of the sober melancholy that tends to dominate most religious ceremonies. Julián felt as young and happy as the blessed saint himself, and went out to enjoy the fresh air, with Don Eugenio by his side. Suddenly he saw Sabel, dressed in sumptuous Sunday clothes, in the ring of dancers, twirling round and round with the other girls in step to the bagpipes. The sight somewhat marred his festive mood.

At such a time the Naya rectory was a culinary inferno, if ever there was one. Gathered there were an aunt, and two cousins of Don Eugenio, whom the priest did not like to have around the rectory every day because they were young and shameless. The housekeeper, a weepy and quite useless old woman, continually got in the way, running around in circles like a bewildered old bird. But besides her there was another housekeeper, who worked for the Cebre priest, a resolute woman who in her youth had served the Santiago de Compostela canon and was famed in the district for her skill at churning butter and roasting capons. This stout cook, with her thin moustache, high bosom and jaunty manners, had turned the house upside-down in a few hours – sweeping it the night before with frenzied vigour, putting all the lumber away into the attic – before beginning to prepare for the formidable battle of the banquet. First she put the shoulders of pork and the chick-peas to soak, and then she inspected, with a quick commander-in-chief's glance, the voracious larder, crammed full with parishioners' gifts: chickens, kids, eels, trout, pots of wine, lard and black sausages. Having assessed the state of provisions, she gave the orders to put her strategy into action. The old woman was set to pluck the fowls, the maids to scrub pots and pans till they shone like gold, and a couple of burly young fellows, one of whom was the village idiot, to skin the sheep and prepare the game.

Had a master of the Flemish school been present, one of those painters who poured the poetry of art over the prose of domestic life, with what pleasure he would have observed the spectacle of the big kitchen: the beautiful liveliness of the log-fire, caressing the pan's bright belly; the housekeeper's plump arms, indistinguishable from the round blood-red piece of meat she was preparing for the oven; the pink cheeks of the wenches, who were busy frolicking with the idiot, like nymphs with a helpless satyr, throwing handfuls of rice and peppers down the inside of his shirt. And minutes later, when the bagpiper and musicians came in to demand their breakfast – a stew, known locally as *mataburrillo*, made of goat's tripe, liver and lights – how worthy of his brush would that scene have seemed to him: hearty appetites, expanding stomachs, swollen cheeks and swigs of must quickly snatched among the jokes and laughter!

But what was this compared to the Homeric banquet that was being prepared in the rectory hall? Two spotless damask tablecloths were spread over half a dozen planks, resting on an equal number of baskets, which helped widen the usual table, on top of which stood some large jars full to the brim with vintage red wine. Facing these, in a corner of the room, fat pots, filled with the same liquid, awaited their turn. There was an assortment of crockery, including some real Talavera,* which stood out from the rest and which would have enthralled one of the many collectors who nowadays devote themselves to the arcana of cooking-pots. The priests started taking their seats at the extended table, with a thousand formalities and courtesies, stubbornly insisting on giving up the best places, which finally were allotted to the obese Rural Dean of Loiro – the most respected member of all the neighbouring clergy on account of his age and rank, who had not attended the church ceremony so as not to suffocate among the pressing crowds – and to Julián, in

* Fine glazed ceramic from the town of Talavera de la Reina in the province of Toledo.

whose person Don Eugenio was doing honour to the illustrious House of Ulloa.

Julián sat down feeling rather self-conscious, and his embarrassment grew during the meal. As he was new in the district and had always refused to stay to meals at the country festivities, all eyes were set on him. Around the table, which looked splendid, sat about fifteen priests and about eight laymen, among whom were the doctor, the Cebre judge and notary, the young master of Limioso, the Boán priest's nephew and the famous *cacique*,* known by his nickname Barbacana, 'the Loophole'. With the support of the moderate party, Barbacana ruled the district and almost blotted out the influence of his rival *cacique*, Trampeta, 'the Trickster', who was protected by the Unionists and looked down on by the clergy. To sum up, the most distinguished men in the area were gathered there. Only the marquis of Ulloa was missing, but he would come for the dessert. The monumental bread soup, cooked slowly in fat with red sausage, chick-peas and sliced hard-boiled eggs, was already going round in gigantic pots and being eaten in silence, except for the chomping of busy jaws. Every now and then a priest ventured to let out some words of praise for the cook's abilities; and, having quietly observed which of the guests were chewing slowly, the host would urge them to eat up, assuring them that they must make the most of the soup and stew, for there was hardly anything else. Julián believed him and, not wanting to seem discourteous to Don Eugenio, dug his spoon in. But to his great horror, an endless succession of dishes began to file out, all twenty-six of the traditional recipes for the luncheon of the Naya annual feast – which was not even the most bountiful, for Loiro had many more.

In order to make up the established number, the cook had not had to resort to the contrivances with which French cuisine

---

* The *cacique*, or party boss, was a powerful figure in contemporary politics. The system of *caciquismo* concentrated immense power in the hands of individuals; the local *caciques* of opposing factions were usually bitter enemies and often corrupt.

disguises its dishes, by giving them new names and dressing them up with a whole bag of tricks. Indeed not, for the cooks in these unspoilt regions knew of no Frenchified sauce or condiment, thank the Lord. All was pure, wholesome and classic, like the stew-pot itself. Twenty-six dishes? The list was soon made up. Chickens were baked, fried, or casseroled in an egg-yolk sauce; or stewed with peas, with onions, with potatoes, with eggs . . . The same applied to beef, pork, fish and kid – and thus a wide variety of dishes could be made up without any difficulty.

How the cook would have laughed if a French chef had magically made his appearance and insisted on dictating a new menu, keeping to four or six principles, alternating heavy dishes with light ones, and granting vegetables a place of honour. 'Vegetables indeed!' the Cebre priest's housekeeper would have cried, laughing with all her heart and all her rib-cage too, 'Vegetables on the feast-day of the patron saint! They'll do for the pigs.'

Feeling gorged and sick, Julián was only just able to wave his hand and refuse the dishes that went round endlessly, as the guests passed them from one to another. Now he was not being watched so much, for the conversation had begun to get heated. The Cebre doctor – bad-tempered, thin and argumentative – and the notary – red-faced and bearded – boldly told jokes and stories, while the Boán priest's nephew, a law student who was a regular Don Juan, talked about women, praising the gracefulness of the Molende ladies and the liveliness of a certain bakerwoman in Cebre, who was renowned in the neighbourhood. At first the priests refrained from joining in, while the other guests, observing Julián's downcast gaze, glanced sideways at him and feigned ignorance. But such discretion was short-lived. As the plates and wine-jars were emptied, no one wished to remain silent and the jokes soon began to sparkle.

Máximo Juncal, the young doctor just out of the Santiago lecture halls, dropped a few political innuendoes, as well as some malicious remarks about the serious scandal that then greatly concerned provincial revolutionaries: Sister Patrocinio,* her

* Sister Patrocinio (Maria Rafaela Quiroga) was a nun who enjoyed the protection of Queen Isabella and became notorious for her intrigues at court.

intrigues, and her influence at Court. Two or three of the priests got quite worked up at this, and Barbacana turned his long elegant beard gravely towards Juncal and remarked scornfully, 'We're all well aware that some people prattle on about things without knowing the slightest bit about them.' To this the doctor replied, spite darting from his eyes and mouth, that the day of the big clear-out was at hand, when there'd be the biggest uproar seen this century – and the *neos** could take this news with them back to the house of their father, Judas Iscariot!

Fortunately, as he let fly these terrible threats, most of the priests were busy with a theological dispute – an indispensable complement to any patron-saint's-day luncheon. Involved as they were in their discussion, none of the priests who were capable of answering the doctor paid any attention to what he was saying: neither the gruff abbot of Ulloa, nor the quarrelsome Boán priest, nor the Rural Dean, who, being as deaf as a post, solved all political discussions by shouting and raising his right index finger as if to invoke the anger of heaven. At that moment, while platters of rice-pudding, flavoured with cinnamon and sugar, were being passed round, and the glasses of *tostado* were being emptied, the discussion reached its peak and one could overhear propositions, objections and syllogisms.

'*Nego majorem . . .*'

'*Probo minorem . . .*'

'Ah-hah, Boán, what you are sneakily trying to do is put down the very idea of grace.'

'Careful, my friend. If you go on much further we shall find we've lost our free will.'

'You're on the wrong track, Cebre, you're marching off with Pelagius!'†

'I myself shall stick with St Augustine!'

'Such a proposition could be admitted *simpliciter*; but if it is taken in another sense, one just cannot swallow it.'

---

* Neo-Catholics.

† A British monk whose heresy was to deny the doctrine of Original Sin and the taint of Adam; the Pelagians were attacked by St Augustine ('The Doctor of Grace') and condemned as heretics by Pope Innocent I in 417.

'I can quote as many authorities as you please. But what about you? I'd like to see you come up with even half a dozen.'

'It's the general opinion of the Church, from the earliest synods.'

'That's a debatable point, *ergo*! And don't try to frighten me with synods and synads . . .'

'Do you dare claim to know more than St Thomas?'

'And do you dare go against the Doctor of Grace?'

'No one can refute, gentlemen, that grace – '

'Now we really are in deep water! This is a formal heresy – it's pure Pelagianism!'

'What do you know about these things? I think I could accept as the truth whatever you deny – '

'Let the Dean speak. I'll bet anything you like that the Dean won't go against me.'

The Dean earned his respect more on account of his age than his theological knowledge, and the tremendous din subsided when he sat up with some difficulty, both hands behind his ears and blood flooding into his face, in order to settle the dispute, if he possibly could. But their excitement was interrupted by the entrance of the master of Ulloa, followed by two hounds whose bells accompanied him with a joyful chime. He was coming, as promised, to have a drink at the end of the meal – and he had it standing up, because a flock of partridges awaited him up in the hills.

He was given a warm welcome, and those who were not able to fuss over him fussed over Chula and Turco, who rested their heads on the guests' knees, licked a plate or gulped down a sponge-cake. The master of Limioso stood up, ready to join the marquis on his hunting-expedition. He was already fully equipped, for he rarely left his manor without slinging his gun over his shoulder and tying his gamebag to his belt.

When the two gentlemen had departed, the commotion produced by the discussion on grace had already died down, and the doctor was reciting in a low voice some verses – political satires known as *belenes*, which were very popular at that time. The notary applauded them, particularly when the doctor stressed the more pointed or bawdy lines. The state of the messy, wine-stained table, and of the floor – littered with bones thrown down by the less delicate eaters – was evidence that the banquet was drawing to a close. Julián would have given anything to be able to leave. He felt tired, quite overcome by the loathing that exclusively material things inspired in him. But he did not dare interrupt the talk, and even less now that they were all indulging in the pleasure of lighting a cigarette and exchanging gossip about the most distinguished people in the district. They spoke about the master of Ulloa, of his skill in shooting down partridges, and, without Julián understanding why, they proceeded to talk about Sabel, whom they had all seen that morning in the ring of dancers. They praised her beautiful face and at the same time nodded and winked at Julián, as if the conversation were related to him. The chaplain looked down, as was his habit, and pretended to be folding his napkin. But then all of a sudden, seized by one of those quick, flashing bursts of anger that he was incapable of controlling, he coughed, looked around him and let out a few harsh, severe words which silenced the company.

Realizing that the after-dinner conversation had been spoilt, Don Eugenio stood up and suggested to Julián they go out to the garden for some fresh air. The other clergymen also rose, some announcing that they were going to Compline, while others slipped away with the doctor, the notary, the judge and Barbacana, to play cards till nightfall.

The Naya priest and Julián withdrew to the garden, passing first through the kitchen where the servants, the priest's cousins, the cooks and the musicians were making a tremendous racket, as the wine in the jugs evaporated and their feast threatened to go on till sunset. The garden, on the contrary, maintained its quiet, poetic, spring peacefulness. The last of the pear- and cherry-blossoms swung gently in the fresh breeze, which also rustled the thick foliage of the fig-tree, under the ample shade of which the two priests sat on a bank of soft grass. Don Eugenio took out a chequered pocket handkerchief and covered his head with it, to protect himself from the early, bothersome flies. Julián still felt angry and indignant, though he was sorry he had lost his patience and was resolving to be more tolerant in future. However, on second thoughts . . .

'Would you like to take a siesta?' the Naya priest asked him, seeing him so downcast.

'No. What I do want, Don Eugenio, is to ask you to forgive me for losing my temper at table – I know I am like that at times . . . a bit sharp . . . But then there are conversations which exasperate me. Try to put yourself in my place.'

'I do, I do . . . But they are always making fun of me too, about my cousins . . . One must just put up with it. They don't mean any harm – they only want a bit of a laugh.'

'There are jokes and jokes, and for me those about honesty and purity are embarrassing for a priest. If one puts up with such comments simply out of good manners, people might think one has already lost one's sense of shame. And how do I know whether some, I don't mean priests – I wouldn't like to offend them with such a thought – but some of the laymen don't actually believe that . . .?'

The Naya priest nodded in agreement, as if admiring the strength of the remark. At the same time, however, the smile with which he revealed his uneven teeth was a soft and ironical protest against such strictness.

'One must take the world as it comes,' he said philosophically. 'You can't stop people talking. They'll always say what they think and make whatever jokes they want. What matters is being good. So long as one's own conscience is clear – '

'No sir. No sir! Just a moment,' Julián answered excitedly. 'Not only are we obliged to be good, but to appear good. I am afraid that in the case of a priest, bad example and scandal is worse than the sin itself. You know so yourself, Don Eugenio, better even than me because you have all the souls of your parishioners to care for.'

'You're upsetting yourself over nothing more than a joke, something quite silly, as if everyone was already pointing at you. You need to be very tolerant to live in the world. The way you're taking things, I wouldn't like to be in your place – you'll have nothing but vexations.'

Looking bad-tempered and thoughtful, Julián picked up a twig from the ground and poked the grass with it. Suddenly he raised his head.

'Eugenio, are you my friend?'

'Of course, always,' answered the Naya priest kindly and sincerely.

'Then be frank with me. Speak to me as if we were in the confessional. Do they go around saying . . . *that*?'

'That – what?'

'That I . . . have something to do with that girl. Well? For you can believe me, and I would swear to it, if swearing were permitted, that I even find the woman repulsive – God knows only too well! I can't have looked her in the face more than half a dozen times since I've been at the manor.'

'Well, one can look her in the face all right, for it's as lovely as a rose. Come now, calm yourself down. I'm sure no one entertains any bad thoughts about you and Sabel. The marquis is not over-bright, to be sure, and no doubt she enjoys herself as much as she can with those of her class – just look how she danced to the bagpipes today. But she wouldn't be so shameless as to make a fool of him by going off with the chaplain himself . . . Come on, the marquis isn't *that* stupid . . .'

Julián turned round, half kneeling, half sitting on the grass, his eyes wide open.

'But . . . the marquis . . . what has he got to do with it?'

The Naya priest started, as if he had been stung, and then burst into a roar of youthful laughter. Julián immediately understood and asked:

'So the little boy . . . Perucho?'

Don Eugenio began to laugh again, to the point of having to dry his tears with the chequered handkerchief.

'Don't be offended,' he spluttered between tears and laughter. 'Don't be offended if I laugh like this . . . It's just that, really, I can't stop myself once I start . . . There was one time when I even made myself sick . . . It's like being tickled . . . I just can't help it!'

Once he had managed to bring his fit of laughter under control, Don Eugenio added:

'I know I always took you to be rather naïve – just like our patron saint Julián . . . But this is going too far! To live in the manor and not know what goes on there! Or are you just pretending to be a fool?'

'I promise, I didn't suspect anything, nothing at all. Do you think I would have stayed on there even two days, if I'd found this out earlier? How could I sanction such an illicit union with my presence? But . . . are you quite sure of what you are saying?'

'Come on . . . Do you really not believe it? Are you blind? Haven't you noticed? Well, you'd better take another look.'

'What do I know? I'm not naturally suspicious, and the boy . . . poor child! I feel so sorry for him . . . He is brought up there like a little savage. How can there be such unfeeling parents?'

'Bah! These children born "behind the Church" . . . But then, if you listened to what everyone said . . . People say what they like . . . But the lass is as merry as a pair of castanets. In all the village fiestas everyone seems to owe her something: one invites her to eat pastries, another offers her *resolio**. One asks her to dance, another one grabs hold of her . . . She's the subject of a hundred love stories. Did you notice the bagpiper who played at mass?'

'A good-looking youth with sideburns?'

'That's the one. He's nicknamed The Rooster! Well, they say that he goes for walks in the woods with her . . . Such gossips!'

From the other side of the garden wall came a ripple of laughter and merry voices.

'My cousins,' said Don Eugenio. 'They're off to listen to the bagpipes, down at the stone cross. Would you like to come for a while? You might get over your anger. Back in the house, the choice is prayers or cards. I personally never pray on top of a meal.'

'Let's go,' answered Julián, who had become lost in thought. 'We'll sit at the foot of the cross.'

---

* Cheap brandy to which has been added sweeteners and aromatics.

Chapter 7

It was with a troubled mind that Julián returned to the manor that evening, scolding himself for being so simple-minded. 'I'm as simple as a dove,' he thought, 'when in this crooked world you have to be as wily as a snake.' He could not stay on now at the manor. But how could he go back to being a burden to his mother – with no other remuneration than the church benefice? And how could he suddenly leave Don Pedro, after he had been so friendly? And what about the House of Ulloa, which so desperately needed a keen, devoted restorer? All this was true, but what too of his duty as a Catholic priest?

These thoughts distressed him as he crossed a field of maize, around the edges of which camomile and honeysuckle grew, giving off a delightful scent. The night was warm and mild, and for the first time Julián appreciated the sweet calmness of the countryside – that calmness with which Mother Nature soothes our harassed spirits. He looked up at the dark heavens.

'God knows best,' he murmured with a sigh, reflecting that he would now have to return to the town with its narrow streets, in which one bumped into people at every step.

He was guided on his way by the distant barking of the dogs, and soon he could make out the looming mass of the manor house. The side-door would surely be open, he thought. But when he was only a few steps away, his heart froze as he heard screams – two or three inarticulate yells, like those of a wounded beast, joined by the disconsolate crying of a child.

The chaplain plunged into the shadowy depths of the corridors and the cellar, and quickly reached the kitchen. He stood in the doorway, paralysed by what he saw revealed in the gloomy light of the large hanging oil-lamp. Sabel, lying on the floor, was howling in desperation. Don Pedro, in a frenzy, was hitting her again and again with his rifle-butt. In a corner Perucho was sobbing, with his fists in his eyes. Without knowing what he was doing, Julián dashed towards them, shouting at the top of his voice:

'Señor Don Pedro! . . . Señor Don Pedro!'

The lord of the manor turned round and stood motionless, clutching his rifle by the barrel. He was livid with anger. His lips and hands shook horribly, and, instead of apologizing for his rage or helping the victim, he stammered hoarsely:

'Bitch . . . You miserable bitch! See that you get us some dinner soon, or I'll tear you in pieces! Get up. Or I'll get you up myself, with the gun!'

Sabel got up with the help of the chaplain, groaning with pain. She was still wearing her Sunday dress, which Julián had seen her dancing in a few hours before by the stone cross and in the porch of the church, but the skirt of rich cloth was now covered in dirt. The scarlet shawl had fallen off her shoulders, and one of the long ear-rings, of silver filigree, was dented by a blow of the rifle-butt and had stuck into her nape, which was dripping blood. Five red whip-marks on Sabel's cheek showed quite plainly how the daring dancer had been knocked down.

'The supper, I said!' Don Pedro repeated brutally.

The maid said nothing but went groaning to the corner, where the chubby little lad was still hiccupping and sobbing his heart out. Don Pedro then went up to them, and, with a change of tone, asked:

'What's the matter? Is there something wrong with Perucho?'

He put his hand on the boy's forehead and felt it damp. He lifted his palm and looked at it: blood. Turning his arms away from the child and clenching his fists, he let out a curse which would have horrified Julián even more than it did, had he not known, from what he had learned that afternoon, that the man who stood before him was a father who had just wounded his own son, and whose paternal instincts were now taking a hold on him. Cursing himself again, he drew the boy's curls aside, and tied a wet handkerchief over the head-wound with great care.

'Make sure you look after him properly!' he shouted at Sabel. 'And see that you get the dinner ready immediately. I'll teach you, I'll teach you to spend your whole time dancing and making an exhibition of yourself, you bitch!'

Sabel stopped groaning and stood motionless, staring at the floor and gently rubbing her left shoulder, where she must have had some painful bruise. Speaking in a low, pitiful voice, but with the utmost energy, she said, without looking at the marquis:

'Find someone else to make the dinner . . . and be here . . . I'm leaving, I'm leaving, I'm leaving . . .'

She repeated those words obstinately, with no emphasis, like someone stating something that is natural and inevitable.

'What are you saying, you she-devil?'

'I said I'm leaving . . . I'm going back to my poor little house. Why did they have to bring me here? O Mother of God!'

The maid burst into tears and cried bitterly. The marquis, examining his rifle, snarled in fury and seemed ready to do something really serious, when a new character entered the scene. It was Primitivo, who had come out of some dark corner, where he had probably been hiding for some time. His appearance made Sabel change her attitude immediately, for she trembled, fell silent and held back her tears.

'Can't you hear what the señorito is saying?' the father calmly asked his daughter.

'Yes, s-s-señor, I h-h-heard him,' stuttered the maid, swallowing her tears.

'Well then, get the supper ready right away. I'll go and see whether the other girls are back so they can help you. La Sabia is out there – she can light the fire for you.'

Sabel made no answer. She rolled up her shirt-sleeves and took a frying-pan down from the rack. At that moment, as if conjured up by one of her fellow witches, the old hag with the white matted hair shuffled in sideways, her enormous apron crammed with firewood. Her name was Maria, but she was always called La Sabia, 'the wise one'. Primitivo respectfully took the marquis's gun away from him and put it in its usual place. Julián, who had decided against comforting the boy, thought the moment had come for a diplomatic gesture.

'Marquis, would you like to come outside for some air? It's a pleasant night.' As he said this, he thought, 'In the garden I'll tell him I'm leaving. This house and this life are not for me.'

Outside, the frogs could be heard croaking, but not a single leaf stirred, such was the stillness of the night. The chaplain took heart, for darkness greatly encourages one to say difficult things.

'Señorito, I'm sorry to have to tell you, but – '

The marquis turned round sharply.

'I know! There's no need to waste your breath. You've caught me in one of those moments when a man is not master of himself. They say one should never hit a woman. But quite frankly, Don Julián, that depends on what they're like. Some women are just asking for trouble, hang it all! And some things would make even Job lose his patience, if he were to come back to life. But I'm sorry about the blow that hit the child.'

'That's not what I meant,' Julián mumbled. 'However, if you want me to speak to you from the bottom of my heart, as it is my duty to do, I think it's wrong to ill-treat anyone the way you have done . . . And being late with the supper isn't a good enough reason!'

'Late with the supper!' the marquis spluttered. 'Late with the supper! No Christian man likes to spend all day in the mountains, eating cold food, and then get home and find nothing hot to eat. But if those were the only tricks the wretched woman played! Didn't you see her? Didn't you see her, over in Naya, dancing all day long, without any shame? Didn't you see her on the way back, in good company? Hah! Do you think girls of her kind come home alone? Ha, ha, ha! I've seen her, with these very eyes, and I can assure you that if there's anything I'm sorry about, it's not having broken one of her legs, so that she couldn't dance for a few months.'

The chaplain remained silent, not knowing what to say in the face of this unexpected revelation of fierce jealousy. Finally he felt that the way was open for him to let out what had previously stuck in his throat.

'Marquis,' he murmured, 'forgive me for taking this liberty . . . But a person of your rank really should not stoop to worry about what a servant does or does not do. People can be malicious, and will think you have something to do with the girl – I say "*will* think" but everyone is already thinking that! And the point is that I . . . well . . . I cannot stay on in a house where it is openly said that a Christian is living in sin. It is strictly forbidden for a priest to license a scandal with his presence and so become its accomplice. I am truly sorry, Don Pedro. Believe me when I say that I have not felt so upset for a long time.'

The marquis stopped, and buried his hands in his pockets.

'Nonsense!' he declared. 'You must take youth and vigour into account. Don't preach me a sermon, or ask for the impossible. What the hell! After all, we're all men.'

'I am a sinner,' answered Julián, 'but in this matter I see things clearly, and, because of the favours and hospitality you have bestowed on me, I am duty-bound to repay you with the truth. Don Pedro, tell me frankly: does it not grieve you to be sunk in vice? It is something so inferior to your rank and birth! And with a poor kitchen-maid!'

They continued walking and were nearing the edge of the forest, where the garden came to an end.

'A wanton bitch, which is worse!' cried the marquis, after a moment's silence. 'Listen to me,' he added, leaning on a chest-nut-tree. 'What this woman needs – and Primitivo, and that damned witch, La Sabia, with all her daughters and grand-daughters, and all that gang that turns my house into bedlam – what they need, what the whole village that harbours them needs, is to be picked up like this' – he pulled a branch off the chestnut-tree and snapped it into small twigs – 'and pulled to pieces. They're ruining me. Eating me alive. And when I think that this bitch hates me and prefers to go off with any peasant, of the sort who come barefoot to hire themselves out for grinding rye, I feel like crushing her brains out like a snake!'

Julián listened in astonishment to the wretchedness of a sinful life, and was amazed at how well the devil cast his nets.

'But señorito,' he stammered, 'surely you yourself can see – '

'Of course I see! Do you think I'm so stupid I can't see that the bitch is trying to get away from me, when I have to catch her like a hare every day? She's only happy when she's with the other peasants. Or with the old witch, who fetches and carries her messages to the lads! She hates me. One of these days she'll poison me.'

'Don Pedro, I am astounded,' the chaplain argued skilfully, 'that you should be worried about something which is so easy to solve! All you have to do with a woman like that is to throw her out of the house!'

As both speakers had grown accustomed to the dark, Julián could see that the marquis was not only shaking his head, but screwing up his face.

'It's easy enough to talk,' he said in muffled tones. 'To say it is one thing, but to do it is another. It's when you actually try to do something that the problems start. If I threw her out, I wouldn't find anyone to cook for me or serve me. Don't you believe me? Her father has warned all the other girls that if his daughter goes, whoever takes her place will get her ribs filled with pellets. And they know he's the sort of man who does what he says. One day I grabbed Sabel and put her out of doors. That same night the other maids also left. Primitivo pretended to be ill and I spent a week eating in the rectory and making my own bed . . . And I had to ask Sabel to please come back . . . Believe me, they have the upper hand. The chorus that gathers round them will do anything they say, without question. Do you think I can save a penny here in this desert? Not at all! The whole parish lives off me. They drink my wine. They feed their chickens with my grain. They gather their firewood from my hills and woods. Their bread is made from my flour. They pay their rents late, and then not in full. So I'm hard up. I keep seven or eight cows – and I get no more milk to drink than would fill the palm of your hand. In my stables there's a herd of oxen and bull calves that never get used for ploughing my lands. They are bought with my money, of course, but then they're hired out and I'm never shown any accounts.'

'Why don't you get another majordomo?'

'Hah! That's easily said! It's one or the other: either we would have to find another like Primitivo – and then we wouldn't have got anywhere – or else Primitivo would shoot him through the belly. In fact Primitivo isn't really the majordomo – but in a way it's worse than if he was, because, as it is, he rules over everybody, including me. However, I have never officially given him that position. The majordomo here always used to be the chaplain. But although Primitivo may not be able to read or write very well, he's as bright as they come. Even in my Uncle Gabriel's time they turned to him for everything. The truth is, you see, that if Primitivo decided to sit back and fold his arms, I'd be at a complete loss. Not to mention the hunting, for which there's no one like him. If I lost Primitivo it would be like losing my hands and my feet. And in other matters he's the same. Your predecessor, the abbot of Ulloa, could do nothing without him. And you, who came here as the new manager, be honest, have you been able to do anything alone?'

'I must confess that I haven't,' Julián declared humbly. 'But with time . . . and patience . . .'

'Bah! No peasant will ever take heed of you, because you are a simple soul – you're too good-hearted. They need someone who knows their crafty ways and who can beat them at their own tricks.'

Although this remark wounded the chaplain's self-esteeem, he had to admit its accuracy. But despite being offended, he was determined to win the battle, even though the fight was so uneven, and he applied all his ingenuity to the problem. The result of his thought was the following proposition.

'Don Pedro, why don't you go to town for a while? Wouldn't that be the best way of disentangling yourself? It astounds me that a gentleman like you can bear to stay here all year round, without ever leaving these wild hills. Don't you get bored?'

The marquis was staring at the ground, although there was

nothing worth looking at there. The chaplain's idea did not catch him by surprise.

'Leave this place!' he cried. 'And where the devil would I go? At least here, for better or for worse, I am king. Uncle Gabriel used to tell me this time and time again: in a town you can't tell a decent person from a cobbler. A cobbler who gets rich pushing his awl up and down can rise above any gentleman, such as myself, who is what he is from father to son. I'm used to walking on my own land and seeing trees that I can cut down if I feel like it.'

'But, sir, when all's said and done, it's Primitivo who rules here!'

'Hah! I can kick Primitivo from here to Cebre, if I get really angry, without any magistrate interfering. I don't, but I sleep better knowing I could if I wanted to. Do you think Sabel will take me to court for hitting her today?'

The logic of savagery confused Julián.

'I'm not saying you should leave this place, sir. Only that you should get away for a time, to see how it suits you. If you were to stay away from here for a while, Sabel would no doubt find someone of her own station to marry – and perhaps you too would find someone more . . . suitable, to take as a legitimate wife. Anyone can make a mistake. The flesh is weak, which is why it's not good for a man to live on his own, because he can easily sink into vice. As someone who understood these matters said, it's better to marry than to burn . . . Why don't you marry, señorito?' he cried, joining his hands together. 'There are so many good, honest young ladies in the world!'

If it hadn't been so dark, Julián would have seen the marquis's eyes sparkling.

'And don't you think, you simpleton, that the idea hadn't occurred to me? Don't you think I dream every night of a child who looks like me – not a son of that bitch, but one who can perpetuate the name of the house, who can inherit all this when I die? A boy who can carry on the name of Pedro Moscoso?'

Saying this, the marquis struck his manly chest, as if wanting the coveted heir to spring out of it, strong and adult. Filled with hope, Julián was about to encourage such good resolutions. But suddenly he shuddered as he heard a faint sound behind him, a rustling noise, like the tread of an animal through the undergrowth.

'What's that?' he cried, turning round. 'It sounds like a fox.'

'Primitivo,' the marquis whispered, choking with rage. 'It's Primitivo. He must have been spying on us for the past quarter of an hour, listening to our conversation. Well, you've had it now. We've really made a mess of things. God and all the saints in heaven have mercy on me! I'm getting to the end of my tether. I'd rather go to prison than lead this life!'

Chapter 8

As he shaved the scant fair hairs that grew on his chin, Julián worked out a plan. As soon as he was shaven and clean, he would set off, one foot in front of the other, taking Shanks's mare to Cebre. There he would ask the priest for a cup of chocolate and wait in the rectory until twelve o'clock for the Orense-to-Santiago coach. He would be most unlikely not to find a free seat either inside or with the baggage. His valise was ready, and he would send a boy for it from Cebre. As he worked out these details he looked sadly at the pleasant view: the garden with the sleeping pool; the shady grove; the green of the meadows and the maize fields; the mountain; the clear sky. His heart clung to the charm of that sweet solitude and silence, which delighted him so much that he felt like spending the rest of his life there. But that is the way of the world. God leads us here and there according to His purpose . . .

No! It was not God, but sin, in the shape of Sabel, who was throwing him out of paradise . . . The idea of this disturbed him, so that twice he cut his cheek – and he very nearly cut himself a third time, for a hand suddenly tapped his shoulder.

He turned round. Who would have recognized Don Pedro after such a transformation? He too had shaved, though he had not removed his beard, which now shone, having been smoothed down with perfumed oil. He smelt strongly of soap and clean clothes. He wore a tweed suit, a white piqué waistcoat, a blue bowler hat, and carried a coat over his arm. The marquis of Ulloa looked like a new man – a different man – with twenty times more good manners and education than before. Suddenly Julián understood . . . and his heart surged with joy.

'Marquis!'

'Come on, hurry! It's getting late. You must come with me to Santiago – and we must get to Cebre before midday.'

'Are you really coming, señor? This is a miracle! I was just packing my things! Blessed be the Lord! But perhaps you would rather I stayed on here while you are away . . .'

'Not at all! Going alone would spoil my fun. I want to give Uncle Manolo a surprise – and meet the cousins I haven't seen since they were little girls. If I lose heart now it will take me another ten years to make up my mind again. I've already told Primitivo to saddle the mare and put the pack-saddle on the donkey.'

At that very moment a face peered round the door. It seemed sinister to Julián, and probably to the marquis too, for he asked impatiently:

'Well, well. Now what's the problem?'

'It's the mare,' answered Primitivo, without raising his voice, 'she's not fit.'

'And why not? Am I allowed to know?'

'She hasn't got a single shoe,' the hunter said calmly.

'God damn you!' the marquis shouted, with a furious look in his eyes. 'Now you tell me! Isn't it your job to make sure she is always shoed? Or must *I* take her to the blacksmith myself?'

'As I didn't know that the señorito wanted to go out today – '

'Señorito,' said Julián, joining in, 'I can go on foot. After all, I'd already decided to walk. You can ride the donkey.'

'There's no donkey either,' the hunter objected, without blinking or moving a single muscle of his bronze-like countenance.

'There's . . . no . . . donkey?' Don Pedro muttered, clenching his fists. 'There . . . isn't . . . ? Now, then. Now, then . . . Say that again, to my face.'

Primitivo, statue-like and quite unperturbed, coldly reaffirmed what he had said. 'There's no donkey.'

'Well, God help me, there must be not one, but three. And if there isn't, upon my word I'll put every one of you on all fours and make *you* carry me to Cebre!'

Primitivo did not answer, but remained rooted in the doorway.

'Let's see now. How is it that there's no donkey?'

'Yesterday the boy who looks after it saw that it had a cut as he brought it in from pasture. The señorito can see for himself if he likes.'

Don Pedro let fly a curse and ran downstairs, two steps at a time. Primitivo and Julián followed. In the stables the shepherd – an adolescent with a dumb, scrofulous face – confirmed the hunter's story. There, at the far end of the stable, they caught sight of the poor animal, who was shaking, its ears pressed down, and looking close to death. The blood from its wound formed a black trickle that had coagulated from its croup down to its hooves. In the dark, cobwebbed stable, Julián experienced the same feeling he would have felt at the scene of a crime. As for the marquis, he looked baffled for a moment, and then, all of a sudden, seizing the shepherd by his hair, he pulled and tugged at it with fury, crying:

'This is to remind you not to let animals hurt themselves in future. Take this . . . and this . . . and this too!'

The lad cried out, sounding more like an animal than a person, and looked pitifully at Primitivo, who remained impassive. Don Pedro turned to the latter.

'Fetch my bag and Don Julián's valise right away. Run! We'll walk to Cebre. If we go at a good pace we'll still have time to catch the coach.'

The hunter did as he was told, without losing his icy calm. He brought the bag and the valise down, but, instead of loading both objects on his back, he gave one each to two peasant boys and said laconically:

'Go with the master.'

The marquis was surprised at this and looked at his huntsman suspiciously. Primitivo never missed the chance of going with him, and his sudden reserve was puzzling. A quick flash of suspicion crossed Don Pedro's mind; and Primitivo, as if guessing his thoughts, tried to dispel them:

'I have to see to the thinning of the woods at Rendas. The chestnut-trees are too close together. The woodmen are already down there, but they can't get on without me.'

88

The master shrugged his shoulders. He wondered at first whether Primitivo had perhaps decided to bury the shame of his defeat in the woods, but he knew him too well to believe he was abandoning the game without some attempt at retaliation. He was on the point of ordering Primitivo to come with them, but he foresaw resistance and thought to himself: 'What the devil! It's best to leave him. Even if he tries to, he won't get in my way. And if he thinks he's a match for me . . .' However, he fixed his eyes searchingly on the hunter's lean features, in which he thought he could observe, well-concealed and disguised, a look of evil intent. 'What plot can this fox be hatching now?' the marquis wondered. 'He won't let us get away with this scot-free. But if he gets out of hand, he'll have caught me at the wrong moment!'

Don Pedro went up to his room and came back with his rifle over his shoulder. Julián looked at him, surprised to see he was taking his gun on the journey. Suddenly, the chaplain also remembered something and went off to the kitchen.

'Sabel!' he shouted. 'Sabel! Where's the boy? I wanted to give him a kiss.'

Sabel went out and returned with the child clinging to her skirt. She had found him hidden in the cow-manger, his favourite place, and the little devil's curls had grass and wild flowers woven into them. He looked beautiful, and the bandage over the wound made him look even more like a Cupid. Julián lifted him up in the air and kissed him on both cheeks.

'Sabel, make sure you wash him, at least every now and then . . . In the mornings . . .'

'Come on. Let's be off,' urged the marquis from the door, as if he were wary of going near Sabel and the boy. 'There's no time to spare. We'll miss the coach.'

If Sabel wanted to detain that fugitive Aeneas, she gave not the slightest hint of it, for she turned with great calmness back to her pots and trivets. Don Pedro, however, despite the alleged urgency with which he had hurried Julián, waited at the door for a minute or two, perhaps secretly hoping that the girl would try to stop him. But finally he shrugged his shoulders, went out and set off between the vines, down the path that led to the stone cross.

Although the ground was uneven, it was an open place and the señorito could easily keep an eye on what was happening to right and left. Not even a hare could move without the hunter's sharp eye spotting it. He was conversing with Julián about the surprise he was preparing for the de la Lage family, and about the fact that it looked like rain, but this did not distract him from his vigilance. Suddenly he stopped, thinking he could make out the head of a man in the distance, behind the large thick walls that enclosed the vineyard. But from that distance he could not be sure. He became even more alert.

They approached the Rendas grove, which had to be passed before they reached the stone cross. The trees grew thicker now and vigilance became more difficult. They skirted the grove, reached the foot of the holy symbol and entered the rough, narrow forest track, without seeing anything that might justify any fears. They could hear the repeated sound of an axe in the thicket and the 'Hay! Hay!' of the woodmen thinning the chestnut-trees. Further ahead there was complete silence. The sky filled with clouds that almost blocked out the sun, so that the light filtered through the trees veiled and purplish, portending a storm. Julián remembered the melancholy fact that the black wooden crucifix, which they would soon get to, marked the scene of a crime. He asked:

'Señorito?'

'Eh?' grunted the marquis, hardly opening his mouth.

'A man was killed near here, wasn't he? Where the wooden cross is. What happened exactly – revenge?'

'A quarrel between drunkards, on their way back from the fair,' was the dry answer given by Don Pedro, who was all eyes as he scanned the bushes.

The crucifix loomed above them and Julián began the Lord's Prayer in a very low voice, as was his custom. He walked in front, with the señorito almost at his heels. The lads carrying the baggage had gone on ahead, for they were anxious to get to Cebre as soon as possible and have a drink at the tavern. To hear the almost imperceptible rustle of leaves and undergrowth as someone pushed his way through, one needed all the senses of a hunter. The marquis caught the sound only faintly, but with absolute clarity. Then he saw the barrel of a gun aimed dead on target – not at him, as he might have expected, but at the clergyman's back. The surprise almost paralysed him. But in less than a second he had recovered and, raising his gun to his chin, he took aim at the enemy who lay in ambush. If one of them shot, the other's avenging bullet would have been fired almost simultaneously. For the space of a few seconds, two enemies, worthy of measuring each other's strength, stood face to face, until the more intelligent of the two gave in, realizing he had been discovered. The marquis heard the leaves move as the barrel pointing at Julián was lowered. Primitivo emerged from the trees, brandishing his old, accurate shot-gun, held together with bits of string. Julián finished the *Gloria Patri* in a hurry to say politely:

'Hello . . . Have you decided to come with us to Cebre?'

'Yes, señor,' Primitivo answered, his face resembling more than ever that of a bronze statue. 'I've seen to things in Rendas – and now I'll see if there's anything to be felled between here and Cebre.'

'Give me that shot-gun, Primitivo,' ordered Don Pedro. 'I can hear a quail over there, singing as if it were trying to make fun of me and I've forgotten to load the carbine.'

No sooner said than done, he took the gun, aimed it anywhere and fired. Leaves and bits of branch flew off a nearby oak, but no wounded quail fell.

'Missed,' cried the marquis, pretending great annoyance, while to himself he thought:

'It wasn't a bullet – only buckshot, just enough to fill him up with bits of lead. Of course! A bullet would have been more flagrant, more serious as far as the Law is concerned. He's a sly fox.' Out loud he said: 'Don't load it again. There's no hunting today – the rain will catch us and we must walk faster. Go on ahead, Primitivo, and show us the short cut to Cebre.'

'Doesn't the señorito know the way?'

'Yes, of course I do. But sometimes I get distracted.'

Chapter 9

As the bell had already rung twice and the servants showed no
signs of opening the door, the young de la Lage ladies, imagining
that at that early hour no one would be paying a formal visit, ran
down themselves, all together, despite being still in their dress-
ing-gowns and slippers, and not yet having put their hair up.
They looked perfect sights, and so were quite taken aback when
they opened the door to find an arrogant young man, who
declared in a hearty voice:

'I'll wager nobody here knows who I am!'

They almost fled in panic, but the second youngest, who
seemed to be close on twenty and who was the least pretty of
them all, said softly:

'You must be cousin Perucho Moscoso.'

'Bravo!' cried Don Pedro. 'Here's the cleverest member of the
family!' And he came forward with open arms to embrace her.
She, however, stepped back and instead stretched out a cool little
hand, which had just been washed with eau-de-Cologne.
Immediately they all went back inside, shouting:

'Papa! Papa! Cousin Perucho is here!'

The floor shook under elephantine footsteps as Señor de la
Lage filled the hallway with his bulk. Don Pedro embraced his
uncle, who whisked him off directly to the sitting-room. Julián,
not wishing to spoil the surprise of the cousin's sudden appearance, had meanwhile remained hidden behind the door. But he
now came out of his hiding-place laughing, with the young ladies
teasing him, telling him he looked terribly fat. Then he slinked
off down the hallway in search of his mother.

When seen together, an extraordinary likeness between Señor

de la Lage and his nephew became noticeable: the same lofty stature; the same wide build; the same large bone-structure; the same coarse, thick beard. But what in the nephew was harmonious and titanic, strengthened by an active life in the open air, in the uncle, who was condemned to a sedentary life, was excessive: there just seemed to be too much of him. Without being what is called obese, he somehow overflowed in every part of his body: each foot looked like a barge, each hand like a carpenter's mallet. He suffocated in a suit. He simply did not fit in small rooms. Squeezed into a theatre seat he would gasp, while in church he poked right and left with his elbows to make more room for himself. A magnificent specimen of a race bred to fight wars and live in the mountains, was wasting miserably away in a small town, where he who produces nothing, teaches nothing, and learns nothing, is no use to anyone and spends his days in despicable idleness. What a waste! Had that pure-blooded Pardo de la Lage been born in the fifteenth century, he would have given plenty for archaeologists and historians of the nineteenth century to think about!

He expressed admiration for his nephew's good looks, and, in an attempt to put him at his ease, spoke freely to him.

'Well, my boy! What a size you're getting! If you're not careful, there'll soon be more of you than there is of me! You always were more like Gabriel and me than like your mother, God rest her soul ... As for your father, you're not a bit like him ... No, you're not a Moscoso or a Cabreira, my lad; you're a Pardo through and through. Well, have you had a good look at your cousins, eh? Girls, what have you to say to your cousin?'

'What have they to say? They received me with great formality – as if I were a stranger! I wanted to embrace that one and instead she held out her hand to me, all daintily.'

'What simpletons! Every one a Mrs Grundy! Let's see how you all give your cousin a hug immediately.'

The first one who came forward to fulfil the order was the eldest. As he embraced her, Don Pedro couldn't help noticing the splendid proportions of the human form he was squeezing. Quite a young woman, the eldest cousin!

'You must be Rita, am I right?' he asked merrily. 'I have a terrible memory for names, and I might get you mixed up.'

'Rita, at your service,' answered the cousin with equal kindness. 'And this is Manolita, this is Carmen, and this one is Nucha – '

'Shush! One at a time. Tell me your names as I hug you.'

Two cousins came to pay their tribute, saying good-naturedly:

'I am Manolita, at your service, señorito.'

'I am Carmen, at your orders, señorito.'

And there, hidden between the pleats of a damask curtain, as if hoping to avoid the affectionate ceremony, was the third cousin. But the ploy did not help her. On the contrary, her aloofness made the cousin cry out:

'Doña Hucha,'* or whatever your name is, watch out, I'm owed a hug.'

'My name's Marcelina, silly. But my sisters always call me Marcelinucha, or Nucha.'

She was finding it hard to turn round and face him, so she stayed in the shelter of the red curtain, with her hands crossed over her white, percale peignoir, against which her loose plaits marked two long lines. Without further ado, the father pushed the girl against her cousin, so that not only was she duly embraced, but had her cheek rubbed by the marquis's beard – which made her hide her blushing face in his shirt-front.

After this reconciliation, Señor de la Lage and his nephew began the inevitable conversation concerning the marquis's journey – how it came about, and the adventures he had along the way. The nephew did not explain his unexpected arrival very satisfactorily: Well . . . He was restless . . . and tired of being on his own . . . He needed a bit of a change . . . The uncle did not press the matter, but thought to himself: 'Julián will tell me everything later.' Then he rubbed his enormous hands, smiling at an idea that had been at the bottom of his mind for a long time, but which had never seemed to him as clear and pleasing as it did now. What better husband could his daughters wish for

* 'Miss Moneybox': Hucha is a play on Marcelina's nickname 'Nucha'.

than their Ulloa cousin? Of all the many fathers hoping to marry off their daughters, none were as ardent as Don Manuel Pardo in intentions, yet at the same time so reserved as to ways and means. For that gentleman of ancient stock harboured both a burning desire to marry off the girls and at the same time an intense aristocratic pride, which was sometimes mistaken for arrogance. This prevented him from lowering himself to any of the ruses common among matchmaking fathers, and made him impose the strictest, most scrupulous controls on his daughters' relationships with other people, and on their education. He kept them isolated – shut up, as it were, in their castle – and took them only once in a blue moon to a public entertainment. The de la Lage ladies must marry, Don Manuel would say. It would go against the order of Providence not to find a trunk fit to be grafted with shoots of such noble lineage. But he would rather they were left on the shelf than they married just anyone – the lieutenant of the garrison, for example, or the tradesman who makes it big selling cloth by the yard, or the family doctor. Good God, that would be sacrilege. The de la Lage ladies could only offer their hand to someone whose quality matched theirs. Therefore, Don Manuel, who would not dream of trying to trap a common *nouveau riche*, decided immediately to do whatever was in his means to turn his nephew into his son-in-law, like Sandoval in the operetta.*

Did the young ladies agree with their father's opinions? The fact is that no sooner had the cousin sat down to talk with Don Manuel than each girl slipped out daintily, either to fix her hair, prepare the visitor's room, or fetch the best plates for the table. It was settled that Don Pedro would stay with them, and they sent to the inn for his valise.

The lunch, for which the girls really dolled themselves up, was lighthearted in the extreme. Don Pedro and the de la Lage girls soon established a familiarity that would have been excessive had they not been related. However, it was not the same sort of familiarity that exists between brother and sister, for it was

* *Diamonds in the Crown*, by Francisco Campròdon, first performed in 1854.

95

spiced with a pinch of peppery contrariety, which gave rise to a number of polite but amusing skirmishes. There was a lively crossfire of jokes, puns and witty rejoinders, which between the two sexes are often the prelude to more serious fighting.

'Cousin, I find it very strange that you don't pour out my water, as you're sitting next to me.'

'We country folk don't know anything about good manners. You ought to teach me. With teachers like you . . .'

'You glutton! Who gave you permission to take a second helping?'

'It's so delicious, I can only suppose that you cooked it.'

'Wishful thinking, cousin. It was the cook. I'm not cooking for you – sorry to disappoint you.'

'Cousin, why don't you let me have this little candied egg-yolk. Come on, just one.'

'Don't steal from my plate, you greedy-guts. I'm not letting you have it, so there! There's the serving-dish in front of you!'

'I wager I'll get it from you, when you're not looking.'

'I bet you won't!' And with that the young lady leapt up from her place and ran with the plate in her hands to prevent her cousin, who pursued her round the table, from stealing a meringue or half an apple. The game was played in the midst of deafening laughter, as if it were the funniest thing they had ever seen. Rita and Manolita, the two eldest, presided over these games. Nucha and Carmen, on the other hand, maintained a more distant friendliness, watching, laughing at the fun, but not taking any active part in it. Nucha had an air of natural seriousness, which bordered on placidity, while Carmen's face bore a constant expression of melancholy, as if beset by an overwhelming sense of anxiety.

Don Pedro was blissfully happy. When he had decided to undertake the journey, he had been worried in case his cousins turned out to be very formal, stiff young ladies. That would have put him on the spot, for he was quite unfamiliar with the etiquette required in the company of genteel ladies – a 'white partridge' of a kind he had never before hunted. But the friendly welcome he had received made him recover all his usual self-possession. Once again full of life, and with his warm blood stirred up, he considered the young cousins one by one, trying to work out which he would throw his handkerchief to. There was no doubt that Carmen, the youngest, was very pretty, tall and slender, with white skin and black tresses. But Don Pedro was not a romantic and the girl's passionate spirit, clearly discernible in the purple rings around her eyes, lessened the attraction he felt for her. As for Nucha, the next in age, she looked rather like the youngest, except not so pretty. She was not tall, nor were her features particularly well-formed, apart from her tiny mouth. And her eyes, although magnificently large and black as berries, had a slight squint that gave her a vague, modest look. In all, her physical charms were few, at least for those to whom the subtleties and size of our clay exterior is important.

Manolita was of another type altogether. In her one could admire both extreme gracefulness and vigour, but with one defect, which, although considered by some an enhancement of a woman's beauty, for others – Don Pedro, for example – it inspired repulsion: a certain masculinity blended into the feminine charms. In Manolita it took the form of a down that gradually became a moustache, and an extension of her hair towards her cheeks, which was not just a faint sideburn, but an honest whisker. The one he could find no fault with was Rita, the eldest sister. What really captivated Don Pedro was not so much the beauty of her face, as the perfect proportions of her body – the width and roundness of her hips, the fullness of her bosom. Everything in the bold, harmonious curves of that spirited young girl spoke of a fertile mother and an inexhaustible wetnurse. A superb vase, in truth, for the confinement of a legitimate Moscoso; a magnificent stock on which to graft his heir and namesake! Looking at such a splendid example of the female of the species, the marquis imagined not the pleasures of the flesh, but the numerous and masculine offspring she was capable of producing – rather like the farmer who, surveying a fertile field, does not become enchanted with the little wild flowers that make it beautiful, but calculates instead the crop it will yield at the end of the summer.

They passed the afternoon in the drawing-room, showing Don Pedro numerous knick-knacks, such as stereoscopes and photograph albums, which in those days were very elegant objects and not at all common. Rita and Manolita made sure that their cousin had a good look at the portraits that showed them leaning against chairs or pillars – the classic postures insisted on by photographers at the time – and Nucha opened a tiny album, put it in front of Don Pedro and asked him eagerly:

'Do you know who that is?'

It was a boy of about seventeen, with cropped hair, dressed in the uniform of the Artillery Academy. He bore a remarkable resemblance to Nucha and Carmen, in so much as a boy with a close-cropped head can look like two young ladies with good plaits of hair.

'It's my little boy,' declared Nucha, very seriously.

'Your little boy?'

The other sisters burst into laughter and Don Pedro, catching on, cried:

'Ah-hah! Now I know. It's your brother. The eldest de la Lage, my cousin Gabrieliño.'

'Of course, who else could it be? But Nucha loves him so much she always calls him her little boy.'

As if to corroborate the assertion, Nucha bent over and kissed the photograph with such passionate tenderness, that over in Segovia the poor new student, no doubt the victim of some barbaric initiation ceremony, must have felt something sweet and warm touch his cheek and heart.

When Carmen, the sad-looking one, saw that her sisters were amusing themselves, she slipped out and did not appear again. The other girls, having shown their cousin all there was to see in the drawing-room, gave him a tour of the house from the attic to the wood-shed. It was a large old house, spacious and dilapidated, like many that still stand in the magnificent town of Compostela – the urban brother of the rural and equally dilapidated Ulloa manor. On its stark façade the newfangled glass-covered veranda looked out of place. It had been built by Don

Manuel Pardo de la Lage, who had indulged in the expensive bad habit of building, but it was a continual solace to the girls, who were always to be found perched there, like birds on a favourite branch. It was there they sewed and kept a small garden of potted plants. It was there too that they hung cages with canaries and goldfinches. But that was not all the blessed veranda was useful for, as it was there that they found Carmen, leaning out and gazing down at the street below, so lost in thought that she didn't hear her sisters arrive. Nucha tugged at her dress and the girl turned round – her usually pale cheeks slightly flushed. Then Nucha whispered excitedly in her ear and Carmen moved away from the balcony window as silent and anxious-looking as ever. Rita meanwhile pointed out all the local landmarks to her cousin.

'From here you can see the best streets. That one is Preguntoiro – a lot of people walk along it. That tower is the cathedral ... Don't tell me you haven't been to the cathedral yet? But, have you really never said a *credo* to the Holy Apostle, you Jew?' cried the young girl, her eyes sparkling in a provocative manner. 'Do I have to take you there by the hand and introduce you formally to the saints, so you can shake them by the hand? You haven't been to the Casino either? Or the Alameda? My dear sir, you haven't seen anything!'

'Indeed not, my girl – but remember, I'm just a poor countryman who only arrived last night. And then I went directly to bed.'

'And why didn't you come here straight away – don't you love your family?'

'And cause a commotion late at night? Even if I do come from the wilds, I'm not quite so badly brought up as all that.'

'Well then, today you must see the sights ... And you mustn't miss the promenade ... There are some very beautiful girls here.'

'I've discovered that already, without bothering to go to the Alameda,' answered the cousin, giving Rita a look that she met with blatant boldness and returned without the slightest reserve.

Chapter 10

A number of things the marquis of Ulloa was shown in the town did not, it must be said, impress him very much. Indeed, he liked nothing, and suffered a thousand disappointments, as often happens to people used to living in the country who form an exaggerated idea of town life. He found the streets narrow, crooked and badly paved; the ground was muddy, the walls damp, the buildings blackened – and in all this he was indeed right. The town seemed to him small, its businesses in decline, and its public places almost always deserted. As for the things that in an ancient town can delight a cultivated spirit – the eternity of art kept alive in monuments, ruins and relics – Don Pedro understood these about as well as he understood Latin or Greek. Old mossy stones! He already had plenty of those in the manor! (Notice how a country gentleman, with an antiquated outlook on life, was on the same level as the most loutish, destructive democrat.) Despite knowing Orense, and having been in Santiago as a child, he imagined that a modern city should have wide streets, buildings all looking the same, and everything brand new – as well as a great police force. What less could civilization offer its slaves, after all? It is true that Santiago had two or three spacious buildings: the cathedral, the town hall, Saint Martin's church and convent. But, according to the marquis, these contained a lot of things that were highly over-rated. For example, the Gloria portico in the cathedral. Look how badly made the saints were! The female ones so skinny they didn't even look human! And the pillars – look at how roughly they were carved! It would have been worth seeing one of these learned men who inquire into the *meaning* of a religious monument trying to prove to Don Pedro that the Gloria portico contained great poetry and profound symbolism. Symbolism? Fiddlesticks! The portico was just a piece of shoddy workmanship, with figures that looked all crumbly, which went to show how backward they were in those antediluvian days. In short, of all the sights in Santiago, the marquis paid attention to only one, and that of very recent making: his cousin Rita.

The approach of Corpus Christi gave a little life to the sleepy university town, and every afternoon people strolled elegantly up and down the Alameda. Carmen and Nucha usually went in front, followed by Rita and Manolita with their cousin beside them. The father brought up the rear, talking to some elderly gentleman or other – one of the many who live in Compostela, where, as if by some law of affinity, there seems to be a greater abundance of old people than in other places.

Manolita often talked to a certain young man, very stiff and rigid, with a ridiculously solemn air and an exaggerated pretension to elegance. His name was Don Victor de la Formoseda, and he was a law student at the university. Don Manual Pardo was pleased to see him talking to his daughters, for Master de la Formoseda belonged to a very good family from the highlands, with a far from negligible fortune. Nor was this the only mosquito buzzing round the de la Lage señoritas. From the very start Don Pedro noticed that in the narrow, dark colonnade of the Rua del Villar, and under the leafy trees of the Alameda and the Herradura, a young man with long hair and a strangely cut, old-fashioned grey overcoat, escorted them. He was like a shadow, always behind them. Don Pedro also observed that when the perpetual prowler appeared from behind some pillar or from among the trees, Carmen's sad, haggard face became lively, and her downcast eyes lit up. Don Manuel and Nucha, however, seemed worried and displeased.

Once he was on the track, Don Pedro kept a careful watch, as an expert hunter does. Nucha, he was sure, had no admirer among the crowd of students and good-for-nothings who filled the promenade, or, if she did, she paid no attention to him, for she was always serious and indifferent. Indeed in public she assumed a seriousness beyond her years, while Manolita, on the other hand, did not miss a trick as she flirted with the young de la Formoseda. As for Rita, she was always vivacious and provocative with her cousin – and not only with him. Don Pedro noticed that she responded to the comments and looks of her admirers with lively darting glances. And that gave the marquis of Ulloa a good deal to think about. Perhaps because he was the sort of man who is attracted to lively women, he held a low opinion of them, and expressed this opinion to himself in the crudest of terms.

Julián and the marquis slept in adjoining rooms, for, since his ordination, Julián was given a higher standing in the house. Although his mother was still only the housekeeper, her son ate with the de la Lages, occupied an important room and, in short, was treated, if not as an equal – for there were still some vestiges of patronage left – at least with much kindness and respect. At night, before going to bed, the marquis would go into Julián's room to smoke a cigarette and have a chat. The conversation was rather dull, for it always concerned the same matter. Don Pedro would say that he was amazed by the fact that he had made up his mind both to leave the manor and to take a wife, when previously either course would have seemed to him unthinkable. Like all selfish people, the marquis considered everything he did to be all-important and always newsworthy, and he therefore needed someone of inferior or subordinate rank to talk to – someone, in other words, who also considered what he did to be extraordinarily important.

Julián enjoyed their talks. The prospect of the cousins marrying seemed to him as natural as a vine creeping up an elm-tree. They could not be better suited to each other, and there was no great age difference. Besides, the happy result of such a union would surely be the rescue of the marquis's soul from the clutches of the devil, in the shape of a certain loose woman. The only thing that worried Julián was that Don Pedro should have fixed his attention on Miss Rita, but he said nothing for fear of spoiling the marquis's Christian resolution.

'Rita is a fine-looking girl,' said the marquis, finally taking the chaplain into his confidence. 'She seems as sound as a bell. For sure if she has children, they'll inherit her good constitution. They'll be even stronger than Perucho, Sabel's son.'

What an untimely reminiscence! Julián was quick to answer, without touching on any physiological details:

'The Pardos are a very healthy family, thank heaven.'

One night the confidences took a new turn and entered a very embarrassing field for Julián, who was always afraid that any little slip of his tongue might upset all his master's plans – an awful thing to have on his conscience.

'You know,' Don Pedro began, confidingly, 'my cousin Rita seems to me a bit empty-headed. When we're out walking she's always worried about whether she's being looked at or not, and whether she's being talked to or not. I swear she's fond of being tickled by the picador's lances.'

'The picador's lances?' repeated the chaplain, who was completely unaware of the meaning of that rude phrase.

'Yes, you know. In other words, she enjoys the attention of admirers. And when it comes to marriage, it's no laughing matter if your wife philanders with every Tom, Dick or Harry.'

'Of that there is no doubt, the most essential qualities in a woman are honesty and modesty. But one must not judge by appearances. That's just Miss Rita's nature, to be open and cheerful.'

Julián thought he had safely dodged the issue, but a few nights later Don Pedro squeezed the truth out of him.

'Don Julián, this is no time for mysteries. If I'm to marry I need to know exactly who it is I'm marrying. How people would laugh at me if from the very start I was sold a pig in a poke. It would be out of the frying-pan and into the fire. It's no use saying you don't know anything. You grew up in this house and have known my cousins since the day you were born. Rita . . . She's older than you, isn't she?'

'Yes, señorito,' Julián replied, feeling that to reveal her age was not a moral obligation. 'Miss Rita will soon be twenty-seven or twenty-eight years old, or thereabouts. After her come Miss Manolita and Miss Marcelina, who are close together, and they are twenty-three and twenty-two ... because two boys died in between ... and then comes Miss Carmen, who is twenty. When Master Gabriel, who must be about seventeen or just over, was born, no one had thought the señora would have any more children, because she was very frail, and the birth did her no good at all, for she died a few months later.'

'Then you must know Rita very well. Speak out, come on!'

'To be honest with you, señorito, I was brought up in this house it's true, but without being close to the de la Lage family, because I am not of their class. And my mother, who is very devout, never let me join the young ladies for games or anything. It was a question of decorum – I'm sure you know what I mean! I did spend some time with Master Gabriel, but with the mistresses – it was just a case of good morning and good evening when I met them in the corridors. After that I went off to the seminary.'

'Bah! Don't try to fool me! You must know hundreds of things about the girls. All you need to do is ask your mother. Isn't that right! Look, you're blushing. Aha! We're on the right path. Let me watch your face while you try to deny that your mother has told you a thing or two!'

Julián went purple. Had he been told? Had he indeed! When he arrived, the venerable matron who kept house for the de la Lages had not been alone with her son for more than a minute before giving in to the urge she felt for discussing certain matters, which could of course only be discussed with serious and religious men. Old Mother Rosario, as she was called, would certainly not have talked about such things with the local gossips – after all, she lived under Don Manuel Pardo's roof. But with serious people, capable of good advice – for instance, her confessor, Canon Vicente, or Julián, that precious child of hers who had risen to the highest office on this earth – who could deny her the pleasure of boasting about her discretion, while at the same time saying exactly what she thought about certain things which, if she were a 'lady', she would never have done herself? Or the pleasure of hearing her 'reverend' son praise her good sense and agree with everything she said? Had she told Julián 'a thing or two'? Indeed she had, heaven help him! But it was one thing to be told these things and another to repeat them. How could he reveal Miss Carmen's insanity and disclose that she was set – at all costs and regardless of her father's wishes – on marrying a young medical student, a nobody, the son of a village blacksmith (what a disgrace for the illustrious Pardo line!)? Moreover, the man was raving mad and continually put her in an awkward position by following her everywhere like a lap-dog. And not only that, for it was said that he was a materialist and a member of a secret society. Or how could he tell the marquis that Miss Manolita offered novenas to St Anthony, praying that Don Victor de la Formoseda would make up his mind to ask for her hand, and that she had even gone to the extreme of writing anonymous letters to the gentleman, defaming the other young ladies whose homes he visited? And above all, how could he give even the slightest hint about that business concerning Miss Rita, which, were it interpreted maliciously, could ruin her reputation? He would let them cut his tongue out before he would reveal anything about *that*.

'Señorito,' he stammered, 'I think the young ladies are beyond reproach. But even if I knew anything to the contrary, I would take great care not to divulge it, for after all I . . . my gratefulness towards this family would . . . well . . . as it were . . . tie my tongue.'

He stopped, realizing that he was getting into even deeper water.

'Don't misunderstand me. I beg you not to draw conclusions from my poor ability to express myself.'

'Am I to understand from this,' said the marquis, looking the chaplain up and down, 'that you believe there is absolutely nothing to be said against them? I want you to make it quite clear. Do you consider them all to be absolutely faultless young ladies . . . quite perfect . . . and entirely suitable for me to marry? Eh?'

Julián thought seriously before answering.

'If you insist that I reveal what is hidden in my heart . . . then, to be frank, although all the young ladies are very nice indeed, if I were to have to choose . . . I cannot deny it . . . I would choose Miss Marcelina.'

'Come on! She's cross-eyed . . . and thin . . . All she has is good hair and a good temper.'

'Señorito, she is a perfect treasure.'

'She must be like the others.'

'She's unique. When Master Gabriel was still a baby and left without a mother, she took such care of him it made everyone laugh, because she wasn't much older than him herself. Day and night she always had the baby in her arms. She used to call him "her little boy". They say it was quite a comic sight. But it seems that the child's weight exhausted her, and that is why her health is more delicate than her sisters'. When Don Gabriel went off to school she was ill, which is why she looks so pale. She's an angel, señorito, who spends her time giving good advice to her sisters.'

'A sure sign that they need it,' Don Pedro observed maliciously.

'Lord in heaven! I can't say anything without you – you know well enough that there is such a thing as goodness, but that it can always be bettered. Few people are actually perfect, but Miss Marcelina comes close. She goes to confession and takes Holy Communion so often, and is so religious, that she is an edifying example for others.'

Don Pedro reflected for a while, and then assured Julián that religiousness in a woman pleased him a great deal, and that in his opinion it was an essential condition for being 'good'. 'A pious little thing, eh?' he added. 'Now I know how to annoy her.'

And that, in effect, was the immediate result of that discussion, during which, with more goodwill than tact, Julián had tried to present Nucha as a candidate for matrimony. From then on Don Pedro played a lot of tricks on her, some of which were far from amusing. With the pleasure of a wilful child picking the petals off a flower, he would make Nucha blush, ruffling the purity of her soul with his risqué jokes and indiscreet, over-familiar behaviour, which she rejected vigorously. The marquis's game mortified the chaplain just as much as it did the young girl, while the after-dinner conversation tortured him, for, to Don Manuel's incorrigible habit of telling anecdotes and stories quite lacking in propriety and delicacy, was added Don Pedro's endless teasing of his young cousin. Poor Julián had a terrible time. He kept his eyes fixed firmly on his plate and a slight frown never left his fair brow. He believed that to insult a maiden's modesty, even if only in jest, was an abhorrent sacrilege. From what his mother had told him and from what he could see for himself, Nucha inspired in him a feeling of devout respect, similar to such as he might feel for some holy statue. He never dared address her by her diminutive, for 'Nucha' seemed to him more like a dog's name than a person's. And when Don Pedro let slip some scandalous joke, the chaplain, thinking it would comfort Marcelina, would sit next to her and talk earnestly about some holy or innocent matter – a novena or religious ceremony of the kind Nucha attended so assiduously.

The marquis was still unable to resist the irritating attraction he felt for Rita. Nevertheless, although he was aware of the increasing power his eldest cousin had over him, his own instinctive distrust of her – such as a countryman often feels for town women, whose refined coquetry he tends to confuse with immorality – also became more resolved. He could not but be suspicious of her. For a start, she was so forward! And she led him on shamelessly, and openly. And she got so conceited if a man complimented her!

The villager who arrives in town has heard hundreds of stories about how the unwary are tricked and led unwittingly like lambs to the slaughter. He is therefore suspicious, looking all around him, scared of being cheated by shopkeepers, distrusting everyone, unable even to sleep at night in the inn for fear someone will steal his bag. Allowing for the obvious differences between a simple peasant and the master of Ulloa, this was quite an accurate description of Don Pedro's moral state in Compostela. His self-esteem was not hurt by Primitivo's domination or by Sabel's gross betrayals back in his country lair, but it did indeed hurt him to be led on in town by his artful little cousin. Moreover, the woman who was destined to bear the distinguished name of the Moscosos and carry on the legitimate line would have to be as pure as the driven snow. And Don Pedro was one of those who believe that a woman is no longer pure once she has had an amorous relationship, no matter how innocent and proper, with anyone but her future husband. Even glances exchanged with someone in the street or on the promenade were considered terrible sins. Don Pedro's idea of conjugal honour was a Calderonian* one, a purely Spanish view, indulgent in the highest degree towards the husband, and wholly intolerant when it came to the wife. And it was no use what anyone told him to the contrary, for he was certain that Rita must have had a part in some romantic intrigue or other. As for Carmen and Manolita, there was no need to wonder what was going on, for it was plain for all to see. But Rita . . .

Don Pedro had no close friends in Santiago, but he made a number of acquaintances, mainly on the promenade, at his uncle's house, or in the Casino, where he would go morning and evening, as idle Spaniards do. At the Casino he was often teased about his cousin, and comments were also made about Carmen's mad infatuation with the student, and about how she was continually to be found on the veranda, with her admirer stationed on the opposite side of the street. The marquis, always on the alert, noted carefully the tone of voice with which Rita's name was mentioned. Two or three times he thought he noticed a hint of irony, and perhaps he was not mistaken. In small towns, where nothing is missed or forgotten, and where trivialities are exaggerated and serious matters acquire epic dimensions, a girl can often lose her good name before she actually loses her virtue. And a harmless escapade that gets criticized and condemned for years and years can keep a maiden single to the grave. Besides, because of their ancient lineage, the aristocratic airs of their

* Pedro Calderón de la Barca (1600–1681), Spanish dramatist. In his *El médico de su honra*, a husband kills his wife on the mere suspicion of her infidelity, for the sake of his reputation.

father and the sort of halo he tried to put round them – because of their beauty too – the de la Lage girls were the target of much gossip and back-biting. When they were not branded as stuck-up, they were accused of being coquettish.

Among its dilapidated furniture the Casino boasted an old gutta-percha sofa, the pride of the reading-room. This sofa was the centre of Santiago scandalmongering, for on it gathered the sharpest back-biters in the world – a trio worthy of a more detailed sketch. Its outstanding and most distinguished figure was a master in the art of scandal. Just as scholars pride themselves on knowing even the smallest details of a remote period of history, so this fellow boasted of knowing absolutely everything about the twenty or thirty good families of Santiago: what income they enjoyed, what food they ate, what they talked about and even what they thought. The man would declare with great dignity and the utmost seriousness:

'Yesterday, at the de la Lages, they ate croquettes and stewed meat. And there was cauliflower salad and quince jelly from the nuns for pudding.'

If these details were ever checked, they would invariably turn out to be entirely accurate.

Such a well-informed person managed to kindle even more suspicions in the master of Ulloa's distrustful mind. It was enough for him to say a few words of the sort which, taken literally, appeared entirely without malice, but which on reflection could mean anything . . . After praising Rita's charm and her beauty, and the wonderful shapeliness of her body, he added, nonchalantly:

'She's a first-class girl . . . But she's not likely to find a husband here. Girls like Rita always find their Mr Right in an outsider.'

Chapter 11

For a month now Don Manuel Pardo had been asking himself: 'When will this lad make up his mind and ask me for Rita's hand?' He did not doubt for a moment that he *would* ask for her hand, and the marquis's position in the house was tacitly one of an accepted fiancé. Friends of the de la Lage family allowed themselves direct allusions to the coming wedding, while in the kitchen the servants were already calculating the size of the gratuity they could expect. When the girls retired to bed at night they teased Rita, while during the day they laughed fraternally with their cousin. In all, the ancient house had been transformed into a jabbering aviary by an overflowing of youthful happiness.

One afternoon the marquis was taking a siesta in his room, when someone knocked loudly on his door. He opened it to find Rita, wearing a sack, with a silk handkerchief tied in a stiff bow round her neck, so that it showed off her beautiful bare skin to best advantage. In her right arm she brandished a huge feather duster, and her appearance was that of a good-looking serving-girl. This, far from putting the marquis off, only made his blood boil even more. The girl was out of breath and smiling – her eyes, mouth and cheeks radiant:

'Perucho! Peruchón?'

'Yes, my lovely little Rita?' answered Don Pedro, devouring her with his eyes.

'The girls say you have to come. We're tidying up the attic, where all the old stuff from grandfather's time is kept. There are some wonderful things there.'

'And what use would I be to you? I don't suppose you expect me to do the sweeping.'

'You never know, it *might* occur to us. Come on lazy-bones, you old lie-abed.'

A very steep staircase led up to the attic, which, although not dark, thanks to three large skylights, was rather low. Don Pedro could not stand up straight and the girls bumped their heads against the rafters when they were not careful. Stored in the attic were numerous odds and ends that at one time had been part of the pomp and splendour of the Pardo de la Lage family. Now they lay neglected, their only companions the moths, their only hope a visit from the bustling girls who explored the room every now and then to dig up some priceless old object, which they would renovate according to the current fashion. With the relics that were rotting away up there, one could have written the entire history of the gentry's customs and traditions in Galicia over the past two hundred years. Remains of painted gilt sedan-chairs; small lanterns with which page-boys lit the way for their mistresses on their return from social gatherings, when street-lights were still unknown in Santiago; a uniform from the Ronda riding-club; ladies' gauze coifs and reticules with bead embroidery; doublets embroidered with colourful flowers; old silk stockings with open-work; skirts with fringe trimmings; steel dress-swords gone rusty; a play-advertisement printed on silk, announcing that the *cantatrice* would sing a witty little tune and the comedian perform an amusing *petite pièce*.

All this was jumbled up with other similar bits and pieces that smacked of old-fashioned greatcoats. The most eloquent and symbolic of all these things was a complete set of Masonic paraphernalia: medal, triangle, mallet, square and apron – leftovers from a grandfather who was a francophile and grade 33 in the local lodge. Also a beautiful scarlet jacket with a colonel's insignia embroidered in silver on the cuffs and collar, left by Don Manuel Pardo's grandmother who, as was the custom in her time, used her husband's uniform when she went out riding side-saddle.

'A fine place you've brought me to,' Don Pedro said, suffocating with dust and very annoyed at not being able to move from his seat.

'We brought you up,' Rita and Manolita said, clapping triumphantly, 'because even if you had a mind to, there's no way you can chase us or play any tricks on us here. This is our chance. We're going to dress you up with a sword and doublet. You'll see.'

'I'm not in the mood for fancy-dress.'

'Just for a minute, to see what you look like.'

'I'm not going to dress up like a scarecrow.'

'What do you mean, you're not going to? We've made up our minds.'

'Well, you'll be sorry. Whoever comes near me will wish she hadn't.'

'And what will you do to us, you braggart?'

'I won't say. You'll have to wait and see.'

The mysterious threat seemed to fill the cousins with fear and they confined themselves to innocent pranks, such as occasionally brushing him with the feather duster. The cleaning up of the attic progressed: Manolita, with her sinewy arms, picked out from the pile various bits of rags; Rita sorted them; Nucha shook them carefully and folded them. Carmen took little part in the work and still less in the fun; two or three times she disappeared, doubtless to go and look out of the veranda, judging from the ironic comments of the others.

'What's the weather like, Carmucha? Is it raining or is the sun shining?'

'Are there lots of people going by? Come on, tell us!'

'She's always got her head in the clouds.'

As the clothes were shaken out, the girls tried them on. Because of her masculine build, the colonel's uniform suited Manolita wonderfully. Rita looked charming in her grandmother's bright-green silk dressing-gown. Carmen would only consent to put on an extravagant triple plume, known as 'the three powers' in its day. When it was her turn, Nucha tried on the lace mantillas.

With all this activity the afternoon soon drew to a close and the light grew dim in the cobwebbed attic. The semi-darkness favoured the girls' plans; making the most of a good opportunity, the two eldest went stealthily up behind Don Pedro and, while

Rita clapped a three-cornered hat on him, Manolita threw a dove-coloured doublet, with garlands of blue and yellow flowers, over his shoulders.

A moment of confusion followed this silly prank. As he could not stand up, Don Pedro chased after his cousins virtually on all fours, determined to teach them a lesson they would not forget. The girls ran towards the narrow door to avoid him, screeching like mice and stumbling over the pieces of furniture and odds and ends strewn about the place. While Rita entrenched herself behind the remains of the sedan-chair, two of the girls, the least brave ones, fled. Manolita had the bright idea of blinding her cousin by throwing a shawl over his head, which enabled Rita, the natural leader of the revolt, to escape also. In a single action Don Pedro pulled the shawl off his head, tore it to shreds, and rushed out of the door in pursuit of the fugitive.

He ran quickly down the stairs and into the corridor, groping instinctively in the dark like a hunter who hears before him the quick light trot of a beautiful beast. He caught up with Rita in a bend of the passage. She put up a feeble, half-hearted defence, interrupted by laughter, as Don Pedro wreaked his threatened 'punishment' – noisily and at length – on the neck below her ear. It seemed to him that the victim was not putting up any resistance at all, but this uncharitable thought must have been wrong, for she took advantage of a moment's truce to run away, once more shouting:

'I bet you won't catch me again, you coward!'

Having taken a liking to the game, and forgetting its dangers, the marquis set off after his cousin. She was at an advantage because she was familiar with the territory, and soon disappeared into the winding passage which twisted and turned higgledy-piggledy through the house, narrowing at times like a badly filled sausage. The marquis then heard the hinges of a door squeak, an indication that the girl had taken sanctuary in one of the rooms. Being in no mood to respect sanctuaries, he pushed open the door behind which he reckoned Rita was taking cover. The door resisted, as if it had some obstacle in front of it. But Don Pedro's fists easily knocked down the feeble barricade of two chairs, which crashed to the floor. He pushed his way into a completely dark room, and stretched out his hands instinctively so as not to stumble against the furniture. He noticed something stirring in the darkness, and, groping the air, he touched a woman's breast, which he imprisoned in his arms without uttering a word, intending to repeat the 'punishment'. But what was this? He met with the most tenacious and vigorous resistance – tiny hands with a grip of steel that refused to be held, a nervous body that would not stop wriggling, and loud exclamations of deep, genuine anguish, mixed with truly desperate protests and even two or three real cries for help . . . The devil take it! This was nothing like the last time . . .

Despite his blind excitement, the marquis suddenly realized what had happened . . . He felt confused – a new experience for him – and released the girl.

'Nuchiña, don't cry . . . Come on girl, calm down . . . I've let go, I'm not doing anything . . . Wait a moment.'

He searched hastily in his pockets and struck a match, looked around him, and lit a candle. When Nucha realized that she had been released, she stopped crying, but she was still on the defensive. The marquis apologized once more and comforted her.

'Nucha, don't be a baby . . . I'm very sorry . . . Forgive me, I didn't realize it was you.'

Holding back a sob, Nucha cried:

'It doesn't matter who you thought it was. One should never behave so brutally with young ladies.'

'My dear, your lady sister came looking for me . . . and whoever comes looking for me must not complain if they find me. There now! That's enough, stop upsetting yourself. What will my uncle think of me? Come, come, are you still crying, girl? You really are sensitive, aren't you! Let's see. Let's have a look at you.'

He raised the candlestick to light up Nucha's face, which was flushed and upset, with a tear running slowly down her cheek. But when the light shone in her eyes, Don Pedro could not help smiling gently to himself as he dried her tears with his handkerchief.

'My dear! Who would dare touch you! You're like a little wild animal. By God, you even have a good punch when you get worked up!'

'Go away,' Nucha ordered, regaining her seriousness. 'This is my room, and I don't think it's decent that you should be in here.'

The marquis took a step towards the door, and then turned back.

'Are we friends again? Can we make up?'

'Yes, so long as you don't go back to your old tricks,' answered Nucha, plainly and firmly.

'And what will you do to me if I do?' the country gentleman asked merrily. 'You're quite capable of killing me with one of those punches of yours.'

'No . . . I'm not that strong. I'll do something else.'

'What?'

'I'll tell Papa. I'll spell out to him what so far hasn't even crossed his mind – that it's not right for a man who is not our brother to be living here with four unmarried girls. I know I shouldn't meddle in Papa's affairs – but he just hasn't thought about it. Nor does he think you capable of this sort of behaviour. But as soon as he notices something, I'm sure he'll realize how wrong it is, without me having to say anything. For who am I to give advice to my father?'

'Heavens! You'd think it was a matter of life or death to hear you talk!'

'Well, that's the way I am.'

After this surly reply the marquis left the room and at supper was reticent and reserved, ignoring Rita's attentions. Though still frowning slightly, Nucha behaved as usual, kind, quiet, and observing the proprieties of the table. That night the marquis did not let Julián sleep, but kept him awake until the small hours with his endless talk.

A truce was declared and over the next few days Don Pedro went out frequently, usually to the Casino, where he was to be found by the scandalmongers' corner. He did not waste his time there, but inquired into business of great interest to him, such as, for example, the true state of his uncle's fortune. It was said in Santiago what he himself had already suspected: that Don Manuel Pardo had made an additional bequest to his son Gabriel, which favoured him greatly. And what with this bequest, as well as his birthright and entail, Gabriel would inherit almost all the de la Lage estate. The only hope that remained for the girls was the inheritance from Doña Marcelina, a spinster aunt who, to be more precise, was Nucha's godmother. She lived a miserly existence in Orense, like a rat in its hole.

This news gave Don Pedro a great deal to think about and he kept Julián awake a few more nights. After that he made a final decison.

Don Manuel Pardo trembled with pleasure when he saw his nephew come into his office one morning, with that indefinable expression one notices in the countenance and mien of someone who is about to broach a matter of importance. Don Manuel had heard it said that when there are several daughters to marry off, the problem was to get rid of the eldest. Then the others would slip away gradually, like beads falling one after the other off the end of a string. Once Rita was fixed up, the rest was a piece of cake. The conceited Señorito de la Formoseda would finally be yoked to Manolita. Carmen would have to get rid of certain silly notions, but being so pretty she was sure to make a good match. And as for Nucha . . . Nucha was no burden to him in the house, for she managed it marvellously. Besides, as heir apparent to her godmother, she did not need to seek protection in marriage. If she did not find a husband, she would live with Gabriel, who, after finishing his education, would establish himself as was befitting for the eldest son of the de la Lages. With these pleasant thoughts, Don Manuel opened his ears to listen to the sweet music of his nephew's words. But what he heard resounded in his head like a gunshot.

'Why do you look so alarmed, uncle?' cried Don Pedro, who was enjoying himself immensely with the old gentleman's mortification and surprise. 'Is there any impediment? Is Nucha betrothed to someone else?'

Don Manuel began to make a thousand objections, keeping to

himself a few that were rather far-fetched. He spoke of how young the girl was, of her delicate health, and he even alleged her lack of beauty, throwing in some not very reserved references to Rita's pretty face, and to the marquis's lack of taste in not preferring her. He joked, he clapped his nephew on the back, he gave the young man advice, as if he were a child choosing a toy. Finally he told the marquis that although he would be giving the other girls a dowry, Nucha expected to inherit her aunt's fortune . . . and as times were so difficult . . . Then, looking Don Pedro in the eye, he asked: 'And tell me, what does that two-faced Nucha have to say about all this, eh?'

'You'd better ask her, uncle. I myself haven't mentioned anything to her yet. We're getting too old to go around courting!'

What commotions there were in the de la Lage household during the next two weeks! The girls went to see their father, to talk in private with him; they whispered secretively among themselves; some of them stayed up late into the night, while others rose very early. Tears wept in private were betrayed by swollen eyes. They excused themselves from mealtimes on account of not feeling well. They held long, intimate conversations with the wiser of their friends. Added to this was the insatiable curiosity of a meddlesome matron, who muffled her footsteps so that she could eavesdrop behind the curtains . . .

In other words, the house reverberated with all the drama of a serious domestic crisis. And as in the provinces walls are made of paper, there was incessant and malicious gossiping in Santiago about the girls' *scandalous* behaviour to each other on account of their cousin. Rita was accused of having bitterly insulted her sister because she had stolen her fiancé from her, and Carmen of joining in the attack after Nucha had reprimanded her for her vigils on the veranda. Nucha was also condemned for being a hypocrite. Behind Don Manuel's back, it was said that he had confided to someone, 'My nephew was not to leave my house without one of the girls, and as he fancied Nucha, I had to give her to him.' It was claimed that the sisters no longer spoke to one another at table. This was seemingly confirmed by the fact

that Rita was seen walking ahead with Carmen on the promenade, while the cousin followed behind with Don Manuel and
Nucha who, walking with her head down, looked as if she were
ashamed. The gossip increased when Rita went off to Orense to
keep Aunt Marcelina company, or so she said, and Don Pedro
moved to an inn, because it was not considered proper for the
betrothed to be living under the same roof before the wedding.

The actual ceremony took place after the papal dispensation
had arrived, towards the end of August. There were all the usual
exchanges of mutual courtesies; the gifts from friends and rela-
tives; the little boxes of fancy sweets to hand round; the trousseau
of linen; the wedding-dress sent from Madrid in a huge box. Two
or three days before the ceremony, a little packet had arrived
from Segovia, containing a plain gold ring and, on a piece of
paper instead of a card, the words: 'To my unforgettable little
sister, from her most loving brother, Gabriel.' The bride cried a
good deal over her 'little boy's' present and slipped it on the little
finger of her left hand, where it was joined by the other ring
given to her at the altar by Don Pedro.

They were married in the evening, in a quiet parish church.
The bride wore black* grosgrain, with a lace mantilla and a set
of diamonds. When they returned to the house, refreshments
were served to family and friends. It was all done with great
formality and solemnity in the old Spanish style: syrups, sorbets,
sponge-cakes, and a great variety of sweets, all served on salvers
or trays of solid silver, and washed down with sherry or hot
chocolate. There were no flowers decorating the table, except for
the marzipan and cotton roses on the cakes, and the solemn
atmosphere in the dining-room was increased by two tall candles,
like the ones they have on hearses. The guests, still overcome by
the awe that fills people when they witness the holy sacrament of
matrimony, spoke in low voices, as if at a funeral, even trying to
avoid the gentle tinkle of their dessert-spoons against the plates.
The scene looked like the last meal of criminals sentenced to
death. The man responsible for the happiness of the couple

* It was fashionable then in Spain for the bride to wear black.

whose betrothal he had just blessed, Don Nemesio Angulo* –
an extremely kind and polite clergyman, who was an old friend
of Don Manuel and a frequent guest at his informal gatherings –
tried to liven up the party with a few festive remarks, in a
suitably jovial tone, but his efforts fell flat, given the seriousness
of the other guests. They were all, as is commonly said, 'deeply
moved' – even Señorito de la Formoseda, who perhaps thought
to himself 'it's time I too took the plunge . . .' As for Julián, he
was seeing his greatest wish fulfilled, but, none the less, his heart
was heavy, overwhelmed by a sense of dark foreboding.

The bride was serious and solicitous, attending to everyone.
Two or three times, her unsteady hand spilled the sherry that
she was pouring out for kind Don Nemesio, who was seated in
the place of honour on her right. The bridegroom, in the
meantime, talked to the men, and when he left the table he
handed round a full case of excellent cigars. No one actually
referred to the great event or dared make even the slightest jest
that might make the bride blush. But when the guests took their
leave, some of the men roguishly stresssed their 'have a good
night', while the matrons and maidens alike whispered in
Nucha's ear, as they went to kiss her: 'Goodbye, señora – now
you are a señora: you can't be called señorita any more.'
Delighting in such a trivial observation, they gave a forced laugh
and looked at Nucha as if they wanted to memorize every detail
of her.

When they had all left the room, Don Manuel Pardo went up
to his daughter and, holding her tightly against his gigantic
chest, kissed her affectionately on the forehead. Señor de la Lage
was truly moved. For the first time he was marrying off one of
his daughters and he felt his soul overflowing with paternity. As
he took Nucha's hand to lead her to her wedding-chamber, with
Old Mother Rosario lighting the way with a five-branched
candelabra, he was speechless, though a smile of pride and

---

* Nemesio Angulo also appears as a character in *Pascual López*, Pardo Bazán's
first novel.

pleasure spread across his lips and his eyes filled with tears. When he reached the doorway, at last he said:

'If only your mother, God rest her soul, could see you today!'

On the dressing-table two candles were burning, set in candle-sticks that were just as tall and majestic as the ones in the dining-room. As no other light shone – the classic porcelain lampshade that is *de rigueur* these days in every luxury bridal suite had not even occurred to them – the whole bedroom was filled with an aura of mystery that was more religious than nuptial. The resemblance to a chapel was completed by the bridal bed, for its gold-fringed curtains of red damask looked exactly like the hangings in a church, and the pure-white starched sheets, with their lace borders and trimmings, had the chaste smoothness of altar-cloths. When Don Manuel took his leave, mumbling, 'Good-night, Nuchiña, my dear daughter,' the bride took his right hand and kissed it humbly, her dry lips parched with fever. Then she was left alone.

She trembled nervously like a leaf on a tree, a convulsive shiver running through her. It was not a conscious or reasoned fear, but something indefinable, almost spiritual. The room was filled with such an imposing silence, the candles were so tall and sombre, that she felt she was back in the very temple where, just two hours ago, she had knelt. She went down on her knees again, and in the shadows of the bed caught a glimpse of the old ebony-and-ivory crucifix, for which the curtains formed a severe canopy. She murmured her customary night-time prayer – 'An Our Father for the repose of mama's soul . . .' – as down the passage came the sound of heavy footsteps and the creak of brand new boots. Behind her the door opened.

Chapter 12

Before the bread left over from the wedding was even stale, Don Pedro and Julián had agreed that the chaplain should return to the manor without delay, to make certain essential changes in the household, and to try to some extent to civilize the place before its new mistress took up residence there. But no sooner had Julián accepted the task than the señorito was struck by misgivings and remorse for having asked him.

'Mark my words,' he warned him, 'you'll need a lot of guts. Primitivo is a dangerous man, capable of running rings round you.'

'I'll be all right, with God's help. I don't suppose he'll kill me.'

'Don't be too sure,' said the master of Ulloa, his conscience clearly troubled. 'I've warned you before about Primitivo: he's capable of anything. I don't think he'll harm you just for the sake of it, or on impulse – not even if he's mad for vengeance . . . But . . .' Don Pedro was in fact quite a good judge of character, but this was not enough to make up for his lack of even the most rudimentary sense of morality, culture and tact, of the sort that nowadays is considered essential in those who, either through inherited or created wealth, occupy positions of power in society. He continued: 'Primitivo's not a barbarian . . . But he's a cunning rascal, who'll stop at nothing to get what he wants. The devil! Remember the day we left? If he'd managed to stop us with that shot-gun of his, without any risk to himself, then your life or mine wouldn't have been worth more than two cuartos.'

Julián went pale and shivered. He was not the stuff heroes are made of, and this showed in his face. Don Pedro, on the other hand, was infinitely amused by the chaplain's fear, for there was an undeniably cruel side to his nature, which had been reinforced by his rough way of life.

'I bet you'll be praying when you pass that old black crucifix on the path,' he said, laughing.

'That may well be,' Julián answered, having recovered his calm. 'But it doesn't mean that I refuse to go. It's my duty, so I'm not doing anything extraordinary by performing it. We shall overcome. Sometimes lions aren't as fierce as they're painted.'

'You can be quite sure Primitivo's not thinking about pictures right now.'

Julián was silent. Then after a while he cried:

'Señorito, why don't you make a good resolution? Throw this man out. Throw him out!'

'Come on, Julián, you don't know what you're saying. We'll bring him to heel ... But throw him out? ... What about the dogs? And the hunting? And all the peasants, and the poor who come in for shelter, whom only he can understand? Don't deceive yourself. Without Primitivo I can't manage there. You try, just for the sake of it, to solve some of the things that Primitivo handles in his sleep. Besides, if you throw Primitivo out through the door, he'll come back in through the window. Believe me, it's the gospel truth. As if I didn't know who Primitivo was!'

Julián stammered: 'And ... what about the ... other matter?'

'That ... ? Do whatever you like. I give you full authority.'

That was all very well, but what was he to do with that authority? Now that absolute power had been conferred on him, Julián felt, in the bottom of his heart, a sort of compassion for the shameless concubine and the bastard son. Especially for the latter. How could the poor innocent creature be blamed for his mother's wickedness? It seemed hard to throw him out of a house whose owner, after all, was his own father. Julián would never have undertaken such an unpleasant task had he not considered Don Pedro's salvation to be at stake, as well as the tranquillity of the one whom he continued to call Señorita Marcelina, despite what the other women at the wedding had said.

It was therefore not without apprehension that Julián once again crossed the sad land of wolves that led to the Ulloa valley.

Waiting for him in Cebre was Primitivo. He seemed so submissive and respectful that Julián – who unlike Don Pedro had the gift of making mistakes when it came to judging character, being more at home in the field of abstract reflection – gradually ceased to be suspicious, persuading himself that the old fox no longer wished to bite. As they journeyed together, Primitivo's impassive face revealed no grudge or anger. He spoke, with his usual curtness and lack of humour, about the unpleasant weather – with so much rain it had hardly been possible to reap or grind the maize, or harvest the grapes, or carry out any other of the important agricultural jobs. The path was swamped and full of puddles, and, as it had also rained again that morning, water still dripped off the shining green needles of the pine-branches and fell on the travellers' hats. Julián began to lose his sense of trepidation, and a great surge of joy flooded his spirit as he hailed the stone cross with a truly religious fervour.

'Be blessed, O Lord,' he said to himself, 'for the good work Thou hast allowed me to perform, and which is so pleasing to Thine eyes. A year ago I came to this house to find sin and scandal, wicked passions and depravity. Now I return heralding a Christian matrimony, and the virtues of the home Thou hast sanctified. I have been the instrument of Thy holy will. I thank Thee O Lord.'

His soliloquy was interrupted by the excited barking of the marquis's hounds as they came out to greet the huntsman with wild demonstrations of joy, wagging their tail-stumps and opening wide their red mouths. Primitivo stroked them with his lean hand, for he was extremely affectionate with the dogs. And to his grandson, who was running after them, he gave a sort of good-humoured punch on the nose. Julián wanted to kiss the boy, but he ran off before he could get near him; and once again the chaplain felt compassionate remorse, brought about by the sight of the already rejected child. He found Sabel in the usual place, amongst her pots and pans, but without the usual retinue of old and young peasant women, of La Sabia and her numerous offspring. Perfect order ruled in the simple kitchen, where everything was clean and quiet. Even the most severe critic would have been unable to find fault. The chaplain was confused by the sight of such order brought about in his absence, and feared that his arrival might in some way disturb it – an idea prompted by his natural shyness. At supper his surprise grew as a new, gentle Primitivo told him calmly all that had happened there during the last six months: the cows that had given birth, the jobs that had been undertaken, the rents that had been collected. And while the father thus paid heed to Julián's superior authority, the daughter served him diligently and humbly, with a sticky sweetness, like a pet animal begging for affection. Julián was at a loss to know how to react to such a friendly welcome.

He fully expected them to change their attitude the following day, when, exercising his 'full authority', he ordered the Hagar and the Ishmael of that patriarchy to emigrate to the desert. Miraculously, not even then did Primitivo's tameness alter.

'The señoritos will bring a cook from Santiago with them,' Julián explained, to give some grounds for the expulsion.

'Of course,' answered Primitivo with the greatest naturalness. 'Town people cook differently. It suits me, because I was going to ask you to write to the marquis anyway and ask him to bring someone to do the cooking.'

'You?' asked Julián stupefied.

'Yes, señor . . . You see, my daughter wants to get married.'

'Sabel?'

'That's right . . . She's going to marry the bagpiper from Naya, The Rooster . . . Naturally she insists on going to live with him as soon as they've been blessed.'

Julián blushed, out of pure joy. He couldn't help feeling that in all this business of Sabel, the hand of Providence was visibly intervening. With Sabel married and out of the way, everything would be in order, the danger would have been averted. This was certain salvation! Once again he gave thanks to God who in His goodness removes obstacles that petty humans believe immovable . . . Such was the satisfaction that glowed in his face, that he did not dare show it to Primitivo, and to mask his embarrassment he began talking quickly, congratulating the hunter and predicting a life of happiness for Sabel in her new state. That very night he wrote to the marquis with the good news.

The days went by calmly. Sabel continued to be meek, Primitivo obliging, Perucho invisible, the kitchen deserted. Julián noticed only a certain passive opposition in matters concerned with the management of the estate. In this field he found it impossible to make even the slightest headway. Primitivo maintained his position as the true manager, exercising total power behind the scenes, so that in effect he was absolute dictator. Julián realized that his own 'full authority' was worthless, and it was even clear to him that the influence Primitivo exercised within the boundaries of the manor house was gradually extending to the whole district. Often people from Cebre, Castrodorna, Boán, and even more distant places, came to talk to the majordomo in a respectful and servile manner. Within a radius of four leagues not a leaf moved without Primitivo knowing about it and agreeing to it. Julián did not have the strength to fight against him, nor, indeed, did he try, for to him the harm Primitivo's bad management could do to the House of Ulloa was as nothing compared to the enormous trouble Sabel had been on the point of causing. To get rid of the daughter was the important thing. As for the father . . . he would just have to wait and see . . .

The truth was, however, that the daughter still showed no signs of leaving. But leave she most certainly would, of that there was no doubt! Julián was reassured by a sign that to his mind was infallible: he surprised Sabel and the handsome bagpiper one evening behind the barn, whiling away their time with sweet, rather than edifying, conversation. The discovery made him blush; but he pretended not to notice, considering that what he had seen was, in a way, the ante-chamber of the altar. Feeling sure of victory where this wicked woman was concerned, Julián gave in to the majordomo, especially since the latter did not outrightly reject Julián's suggestions or oppose him in any direct way. If the chaplain condemned some abuse, or had an idea, or insisted in the urgent need for a reform, Primitivo would agree and even suggest ways and means of going about it. Verbally, that is. But when it came to action, that was a horse of a very different colour. Then there began to be unforeseen difficulties and delays. Today it was impossible . . . Maybe tomorrow . . . There is no force comparable to inertia. To comfort him, Primitivo would say to Julian:

'These things are easier said than done.'

The chaplain realized that his only alternative, apart from killing Primitivo, was unconditional surrender. One day he went to unburden his troubles to Don Eugenio, the abbot of Naya, whose prudent advice always gave him great encouragement. He found him in an extremely agitated state because of the important political news just confirmed by the few newspapers received in those out-of-the-way places. The Navy had revolted and deposed the Queen, who was already in France, and a provisional government had been established. There was also talk of a very hard-fought battle on the Alcolea Bridge, and of the army joining the rebels, and the devil and his mother joining the fray . . . Don Eugenio was so agitated he seemed to have gone mad, planning to go to Santiago without delay in order to find out the truth of these events. What would the Dean say? And the abbot of Boán? And what about Barbacana? Barbacana was in a real stew: his eternal enemy Trampeta, who was on the side of the Unionists, would get on top of him now and that would be the end of him, for ever and ever, amen. With all this excitement, the abbot hardly paid any attention to the trials and tribulations of Don Julián.

Chapter 13

After some time of family life with his new in-laws, Don Pedro began to miss his country lair. He could not get used to the cathedral city, which, with its tall, mossy garden walls, narrow porches, gloomy doorways and dark staircases, he likened to a prison. It annoyed him to live in a place where a few drops of rain sent people scuttling indoors, or produced a sad vegetation of gigantic black silk mushrooms. He disliked the perpetual symphony of rain, pouring off the roofs and pattering in pools. He had only two resorts left for fighting boredom: one was to argue with his father-in-law, the other was to gamble in the Casino. Both things soon gave way, however, not to ennui – for true ennui is a moral debility exclusive to highly refined or cultivated minds – but to irritation and anger, which was the product of a secret belief in his own inferiority. Don Manuel seemed superior to his nephew because of the smattering of education and *savoir-faire* he had received during his long years of city life. And also because of the understandable pride he took in his ancestry, which saved him from being 'common', as he called it. He did have a habit of telling after-dinner stories, which, although not offensive to his audience's sense of decency, usually upset their stomachs. But, apart from that, Don Manuel was a courteous, well-mannered person, who could be relied upon, for example, to lead a party of mourners, attend a meeting of the Economic Society for Friends of the Region, carry the standard in a procession, or give his opinion to the civil governor. If he longed to retire to the country, as he claimed, it was not simply because he wanted to give free rein to certain rustic instincts, or because he dreamed of doing away with neckties and all other social formalities, but because he had certain more refined, modern interests, such as gardening, fruit-tree growing, and building – his favourite pursuit, which is, of course, cheaper in the country than in the city.

The traditional coarseness of the de la Lages had been softened in Don Manuel, thanks to the genteel manners of his late wife, and the constant company of his daughters – five refined, amiable women would civilize the most uncouth of men – which is why, despite the fact that he was, strictly speaking, a generation behind his son-in-law, morally speaking he was quite a few years ahead of him.

Don Manuel tried to civilize Don Pedro a bit, but this was not only a waste of time, it was self-defeating, for it exacerbated the arrogant young man and made him want to free himself all the more of any family-tie. Señor de la Lage had hoped that his nephew would settle in Santiago, visiting his country manor only for holidays in the summer, or occasionally to keep an eye on his affairs there. When he suggested this to his son-in-law, he also dropped a few hints to show he knew only too well what went on in the Ulloa household. This meddling in his affairs by Don Manuel was understandable, but it nevertheless annoyed Don Pedro, who, as he himself admitted, didn't take kindly to criticism and hated anyone trying to manipulate him. 'That's why we're clearing out of here as soon as we can,' he said to his wife one day. 'No one has bossed me around since I was a boy. If I don't say anything, it's only because I'm not in my own home.'

The fact that he was in someone else's house exasperated Don Pedro, and, as a result, everything there irritated him, no matter how splendid or decorous: the silver trays and candlesticks; the fine antique furniture; the servants, who, although sometimes careless, would not have dreamed of being insolent or meddlesome. The marquis also despised his uncle's acquaintances, who were among the most respectable people in town, and he poured scorn on the canons and serious people who came to the house of an evening for a game of ombre. For Don Pedro, everything at his uncle's house seemed to mock his own rough, disorderly life at the manor – where the windows had no glass, the dining-table no cloth, and he himself was on such familiar terms with the peasants. But this did not provoke any resolution to mend his ways, only a feeling of envy and bitterness. His one consolation was Carmen's silly love affair. He found it delightfully amusing, and every time there were comments in the Casino about the student's impudence, or the young girl's shamelessness, he rubbed his hands in glee. For all his father-in-law's ranting and raging, his damask-covered chairs and fine carpets didn't make him immune to scandal.

The arguments between Don Pedro and his uncle were becoming sour, particularly when it came to politics, which more than any other subject is a source of rancour among people. This is especially true of those who argue just for the sake of it, with no clear idea – and it must be confessed that the marquis was such a person. Don Manuel was not himself particularly shrewd, but being a habitual newspaper reader, and given his age-old sympathy for the Moderate party, he at least had some notion of what was going on. He was deeply angered by the recent farce of Gonzalez Bravo's failed revolt, and the departure of Queen Isabella II, and would explode almost to choking when his nephew, simply to annoy him, contradicted him and defended the revolutionaries, and even purported to believe as gospel truth the dreadful scandals printed about the deposed monarch in the gutter press. The uncle argued back fiercely, raising his gigantic hands up to heaven.

'You country people will swallow any nonsense. You've got no objectivity, son, that's your trouble. You judge everything by your own standards.' Don Manuel must have got this particular piece of pomposity from some newspaper editorial or other. 'To judge these things you need experience, and common sense.'

'And you think that out in the villages we're all idiots? Well, we may in fact be sharper than you, and able to see things you yourself can't see.' – he was referring to his cousin Carmen, standing on the veranda at that very moment – 'Believe me, uncle, there are dim-wits everywhere!'

In this way, the after-dinner talk became more and more

personal and aggressive. Coffee-cups crashed furiously against saucers, while Don Manuel shook with anger and spilled his anisette. Voices would be raised, and then, after some particularly harsh or rude remark, there would follow a few moments of silent hostility during which the girls would exchange glances, and Nucha, her head down, would roll breadcrumbs into little balls or slowly fold all the napkins, sliding each one into its ring. Then Don Pedro would suddenly jump up, throw back his chair and stomp loudly out; after which he would go off to the Casino, where the card-tables were busy day and night.

Don Pedro did not like the atmosphere there either. As Compostela was a university town, it was only natural that no one wanted to appear stupid, and the señorito realized how people would laugh at him, if they knew he could not spell properly and understood nothing of the numerous 'ologies' bandied about so often there. His pride as lord of the Ulloa manor was aroused when he saw he was thought less of than those chesty, withered professors, or even the hare-brained students with their broken boots who were always worked up about some modern author or other they'd read in the university library or the Casino study. Life in Compostela was thus too active for the señorito's head, and too sedentary for his body. He yearned to be out in the fresh air, his skin beaten by wind and rain, scratched by the harsh hawthorn ... back in the atmosphere he knew – the wildness of Nature.

The social levelling of urban life also annoyed him. He could not get used to thinking of himself as an even number in a town, having always been an odd one in his feudal residence. Who was he in Santiago? Simply Don Pedro Moscoso. Indeed, not even that: he was Señor de la Lage's son-in-law, or Nucha Pardo's husband. His title had dissolved there like salt in water, thanks to the malice of one of the slanderous triumvirate. Because of his great age and prodigious, razor-sharp memory, this little old man had been entrusted with the inquiry into and elucidation of bygone events, in the same manner as the youngest, whom we have already met, was responsible for present-day investigations.

Thus it could be said that one was the historian and the other the chronicler of life in the town.

This 'historian' traced the genealogy of the Cabreira and Moscoso families, and thus proved beyond doubt that the title of Ulloa did not fall to, and could never fall to, anyone but the Duke of such and such, grandee of Spain, etc . . . And as final evidence he produced the appropriate entry in the *Guide to the Peerage*.

A good deal of fun was also made of Señor de la Lage, whom they accused of having the marquisal crown embroidered on a set of sheets given to his daughter – an innocent folly, which was then confirmed by the chronicler, who reported the exact nature of the embroidery, as well as how much the small escutcheon and the silly little crown had cost.

Growing more and more impatient, Don Pedro resolved to leave town even before the severity of the winter was over, and they set off at the end of a very inclement and unpleasant March. The coach for Cebre left early, so that it was bitterly cold and still misty. Nucha curled up in a corner of the uncomfortable vehicle and sat wiping her eyes with a handkerchief. Her husband spoke to her crossly:

'You look as if you're coming with me against your will.'

'What a thing to say!' answered the young girl, uncovering her face and smiling. 'But it's only natural that I should feel sorry to leave poor Papa and . . . the girls.'

'Them!' muttered the señorito. 'I don't think they'll be sending you any written invitations to go back.'

Nucha said nothing. The carriage bounced up and down in the pot-holes as it set off, and the driver urged on the horses in a rasping voice. They came to the road, and the unwieldy coach ran over more even ground. Nucha renewed the dialogue, asking her husband for details concerning the manor. This he did gladly, musing lyrically on the beauty and good condition of the countryside around, exaggerating the antiquity of the mansion and praising the comfortable and independent life one could lead there.

'Don't think,' he said to his wife, raising his voice so it was not drowned by the jingle of the bells and the shaking of the window-panes, 'don't think there aren't any refined people there. We're surrounded by gentry. There's the Molende señoritas, who are very nice. And Ramón Limioso, who's exceedingly polite . . . We'll also have the company of the abbot of Naya . . . And then there's our abbot, the Ulloa abbot, who was put forward by me! He's as much mine as my dogs . . . I don't tell him to bark or fetch things, but I could if I felt like it. You'll see. You'll see! There I'm somebody. People do what I say.'

As they drew nearer to Cebre and came into his estate, Don Pedro's cheerful talkativeness increased. He pointed to the groups of chestnut-trees, to the neat clusters of gorse and cried with delight:

'This is my world . . . My estate! You can't go anywhere here without stepping on my land.'

When they came into the town his excitement was even greater. Primitivo and Julián were waiting for him in front of the inn: the former, with his mysterious, harsh bronze face; the latter with his cheeks broadened in a most affectionate smile. Nucha greeted him with equal affection. The baggage was brought, and Primitivo stepped forward, handing Don Pedro his magnificent chestnut-coloured mare. He was about to get on it, when he noticed the mount that had been prepared for Nucha – a tall, stubborn, bad-tempered mule, with one of those pack-saddles that have a large round bulge in the middle and look as if they were designed expressly to make the rider slip off.

'Why didn't you bring the donkey for the señorita?' asked Don Pedro, stopping with one foot on the stirrup and one hand on the mare's mane. He looked distrustfully at Primitivo, who muttered something about a limp.

'And I suppose there's no other donkey in the neighbourhood? Don't give me that. You had time enough to find ten of them.'

He turned to his wife, and, as if to ease his conscience, asked her:

'Are you scared, girl? I suppose you're not used to riding. Have you ever ridden on one of these pack-saddles? Do you know how to stay on one?'

Nucha stood there undecided, holding her dress up with her right hand, and still clutching her little travelling-bag with the other. After a while she murmured:

'Well, yes ... Last year, when I was at the spa, I rode on a thousand different saddles I'd never seen before. It's just that now ...' Suddenly she let go of her dress, went up to her husband, put an arm round his neck and, hiding her face in his shirt-front, like the first time she had had to embrace him, whispered the rest of the sentence. The look on the marquis's face changed from one of surprise to one of exaltation. Holding his wife close with loving protection, he cried at the top of his voice:

'Even if there isn't a tame donkey in the whole area, and only God in heaven has one and won't lend it to me, Pedro Moscoso gives his word of honour that you'll have it. Wait, child, wait just a minute ... Or better still, go into the inn and sit down ... Now there, a bench, a seat for the señorita ... Wait, Nuchiña, I'll be right back. Primitivo, you come with me. Keep yourself warm, Nucha.'

He came back after half an hour, out of breath and leading a little donkey with a good pack-saddle – a tame and reliable beast that belonged to the Cebre judge's wife. Don Pedro took Nucha in his arms and sat her on the pack-saddle, arranging her clothes with great care.

Chapter 14

As soon as the chaplain and the señorito were able to confer in private, Don Pedro, without looking Julián in the face, asked:

'What about . . . *her*? Is she still around? I didn't see her when we came in.'

Seeing that Julián was frowning, he added:

'She is! I knew it! I could have bet a hundred pesos that you wouldn't be able to get rid of her.'

'Señorito,' Julián mumbled, noticeably upset, 'I don't know what to say . . . It seemed simple at first . . . Primitivo swore again and again that the girl was going to marry the bagpiper from Naya . . .'

'I know who *he* is,' muttered Don Pedro frowning, with his teeth clenched.

'Well I . . . as was only natural . . . believed him. Besides I had the chance of seeing . . . of seeing for myself . . . evidence that the bagpiper and Sabel do indeed . . . have a . . . relationship.'

'And you've managed to work all this out for yourself, have you?' the marquis asked ironically.

'Sir, I . . . Although I admit I'm out of my depth in these matters, I have tried to overcome my ignorance and ascertain exactly what is going on. I've asked around and everyone agrees that they're going to get married. Even Don Eugenio told me the young man has asked him for his papers. But it seems that, with the excuse of some muddle or difficulty concerning these blessed papers, they haven't got round to it yet.'

Don Pedro was silent for a while, and finally he burst out:

'You're a holy innocent. They wouldn't have fooled me with these stories.'

'If their intention was to deceive me, then they must be cunning indeed. And as for Sabel, if she's not dying of grief for her bagpiper, she acts the part wonderfully. Two weeks ago she went to Don Eugenio's house and knelt down crying, begging him in heaven's name to hurry up and arrange for the marriage, for that was going to be the happiest day of her life. Don Eugenio has told me this, and Don Eugenio doesn't make things up.'

'That scoundrel! That total scoundrel!' stammered the señorito, pacing furiously round the room. Then, calming down a little, he continued: 'None of this surprises me. I'm not saying that Don Eugenio is lying, but ... you ... you're a simpleton, you're too gullible. Don't you realize it's not a question of Sabel? It's her father. And he's pulled the wool right over your eyes. I can well understand she's dying to get away. But Primitivo is liable to kill her rather than let such a thing happen.'

'I was beginning to think that myself.'

The señorito shrugged his shoulders disdainfully and cried:

'Well it's a bit late now ... Leave it to me. What about all the other business? How are things, eh?'

'Everyone is being very docile ... like lambs. They haven't objected to anything ... at least, not to my face.'

'But on the side they must have done as they pleased. Sometimes I feel like chopping you up into little pieces and turning you into pigeon-pie.'

Julián answered, greatly distressed:

'You were absolutely right, señorito. There's no way of getting anything done here if Primitivo is against it. People treat him with such respect I'd say they were afraid of him. Even more so since the Revolution, when all these political troubles started – every day brings some other dreadful news. I think Primitivo's mixed up in it all and is recruiting followers in the neighbourhood – so Don Eugenio says. He also says he has lent a lot of people money, charging them interest, and has got a hold over them that way.'

Don Pedro was quiet. Then he raised his head and said:

'Do you remember the donkey we had to find in Cebre for my wife?'

'How could I forget!'

'Well, the judge's wife – this is a real joke – the judge's wife agreed to lend it to me only because Primitivo was with me. If he hadn't been . . .'

The episode had clearly caused Don Pedro great indignation, and Julián made no comment. Finally Don Pedro put his hand on Julián's shoulder, his eyes glowing as they had in Cebre, and cried, 'And why don't you congratulate me? Where are your manners?' Julián looked blank, so the señorito spelled it out to him, drooling with happiness. Yes, sir. In October – the chestnut season – the world would be welcoming a Moscoso. A true, legitimate Moscoso, and a bonny lad he was going to be too.

'But mightn't it be a bonny lass instead?' asked Julián, after he had congratulated the marquis several times.

'Impossible!' shouted the marquis with all his heart. And when the chaplain burst out laughing, he added: 'Don't say such things, not even as a joke, Don Julián . . . not even as a joke. It has to be a little boy. If it isn't I'll wring its neck. I've already told Nucha to make sure she doesn't bring me anything except a boy. And I'm quite capable of beating her black and blue if she does. God wouldn't play a dirty trick like that on me. There's always been a male succession in the family: "Moscoso fathers have Moscoso sons" has almost become a proverb. Didn't you notice this when you were swallowing the dust of the archives? But you wouldn't even have noticed my wife's condition, if I hadn't told you.'

Don Pedro was right. Not only had Julián not noticed the señorita's condition, but such a natural occurrence had not even crossed his mind. The veneration he felt for Nucha, which grew daily, refused to admit the idea that she might be subject to the same natural laws as other women. However, it should be said that Nucha's appearance only encouraged such an innocent fancy: the purity and vagueness in her eyes, as if she were lost in contemplation of an inner world, had not lessened with marriage.

Her cheeks, though a little fuller, still went pink with embarrassment at the slightest thing. Perhaps the only noticeable difference, the only sign that revealed the change from virgin to wife,
was an increase in her modesty, which became more self-aware
and self-assured. In other words, what previously had been an
instinct had now become a virtue. Julián never tired of observing
Nucha's composure when she heard a coarse word or joke, or her
generosity, which meant she was thankful for the smallest
kindness and repaid it with quiet but sincere words. He admired
too her natural dignity, which she wore like a cloak, an impen-
etrable shield that protected her from even her own more daring
thoughts. The serenity of her whole person reminded him of a
tranquil afternoon.

To Julián, Nucha was, in short, the ideal model of the biblical
wife. She was a poetic example of the strong woman, still in her
youth, bearing an aura of innocence but promising future wisdom
and majesty. As time went by, her gracefulness would become
more severe, and her dark tresses would turn to silver, but no sin
would ever stain her pure forehead, no guilt would leave a single
wrinkle. What mellow ripeness was augured by such a gentle
spring!

When he thought about it, Julián congratulated himself on the
part he had played in the señorito's excellent choice of wife. It
was a source of great and selfless satisfaction to him that he had
helped to establish something so pleasing to God, on the one
hand, and so essential to the preservation of stable society on the
other: Christian matrimony – the blessed knot by means of which
the Church takes care, with admirable wisdom, of both man's
material and spiritual needs, sanctifying the first of these with
the second. 'The nature of this sacred institution,' reflected
Julián, 'is far above any shameful passion, any penny-novelette
abandon or breathless billing and cooing . . .'

Thus when Don Pedro addressed his wife in despotic rather
than tender terms, Julián saw it as an affront to the señorita's
simple modesty and virtuous serenity, and feared she was
suffering greatly. It seemed to him that her downcast eyes, and
her blushing silence, were dumb protests against certain unfitting

liberties that her husband took. And if such things happened in front of his eyes – at table, for example – Julián would look the other way, pretending to be lost in thought, or he would drink from his glass, or pat the dogs, who were always sniffing around the place.

At these times Julián suffered certain gentle misgivings. However perfect a wife Nucha might be, her virtuous nature called her to another, even worthier state – one more like the state of angels – in which woman preserves her virginal purity as her most valuable treasure. Julián knew through his mother that Nucha had often expressed an inclination towards monastic life, and that she deeply regretted not having entered a nunnery. Since she made such a good wife for a man, she would undoubtedly make an even better wife for Christ. Moreover, such a spiritual wedding would have preserved the chaste innocence of her body, and protected her against the trials and tribulations of our worldly existence.

Tribulations reminded him once again of Sabel. There was no doubt that her presence in the house was a threat to the true wife's peace of mind. Julián did not foresee any immediate danger, but he had a sense of impending doom – brought about by that loathsome, illegitimate family, who seemed rooted to the ramshackle manor house like the ivy growing up its crumbling walls! The chaplain sometimes felt like seizing a broom, to sweep and sweep with all his might until he had swept away all that wretched breed; but in the end, despite his determination, he always came up against the señorito's selfish calm, and the majordomo's passive, but unyielding, resistance. Moreover, something happened that made such a 'clean sweep' even more problematic. The cook from Santiago soon became bad-tempered and complained about not understanding the stove, about the wood not burning properly, about the smoke, about everything. Sabel very obligingly came to her help, but after a few days the cook, tired of village life, left with ill grace, leaving Sabel in her place. No formalities were necessary: Sabel simply picked up the frying-pan that the other had put down. Julián did not even have time to protest against this return to the old regime. And the truth was that the illegitimate family behaved at this time with extraordinary humility: Primitivo was never around, except when he was needed; Sabel disappeared as soon as she had left the food on the stove, leaving it for the scullery wenches to serve; and as for the little boy, he seemed to have vanished into thin air. Nevertheless, the chaplain was on tenterhooks. What if Nucha found out? And there was no doubt that she would find out – probably when he least expected it.

Unfortunately, the new mistress of the house liked to explore her new domain, inquiring into everything, investigating every nook and cranny – the wine-press, the pigeon-loft, the attics, cellars, granaries, silos, kennels, pigsties, coops, stables, and hay-lofts. Julián was a nervous wreck, fearing that Nucha would make a most regrettable discovery on one of these excursions. Yet how could he oppose this proper exploration of her new responsibilities by such a dedicated mistress – and one whose presence brought cheerfulness, cleanliness and order into every corner of the manor house, making the dust dance and swirl with each sweep of the broom? Wherever she went, the darkness of that old house – protected for years by hundreds of cobwebs – was dispersed by a sudden burst of sunshine.

Julián followed Nucha on these expeditions, to watch over her and, if possible, prevent any unfortunate incident. And indeed, his presence was truly fortunate the day Nucha discovered, in the chicken-house, an unfledged chick. The case deserves telling slowly.

Nucha wondered why the hens there, blessed as they were with food and shelter, never laid eggs (or, if they did, why there was never any trace of them). Don Pedro assured her that they used up more than enough sacks of rye and millet every year, but still the wretched animals produced nothing. They would cackle wildly – a sure sign that they were getting ready to drop an egg. Then the air would fill with the triumphant incantation of fertility, as well as with the soft clucking of broody hens. But when anyone went to inspect the nest, all they would find was a warm, egg-shaped hollow in the straw, with not even a single egg for a tiny omelette. Nucha kept her eyes and ears open until one day, responding to the tell-tale cackle more speedily than usual, she found a small boy hiding at the far end of the chicken-run, crouched down like a little mouse. Only his naked feet were visible, sticking out of the straw in the nesting-box. Nucha pulled. Out came his body, then his hands, which held the omelette the housewife had wanted, for the eggs, which the boy was trying to hide, had broken.

'Aha, you scoundrel!' cried Nucha, seizing him and pulling him out towards the light of the yard. 'I'll skin you alive, you villain! Now we know who the fox is who steals our eggs! I'm going to smack you good and hard!'

The tiny thief wriggled and kicked, until Nucha began to feel sorry for him, thinking he was sobbing disconsolately. But as soon as she managed to pull his arms away from his face, she realized that the insolent boy was really laughing. At the same time she noticed the extraordinary prettiness of the ragged child. Julián, who watched on anxiously, stepped forward and tried to take him away from Nucha.

'Leave him, Don Julián!' she begged. 'Isn't he beautiful? Look at his hair, and his eyes! Who does this child belong to?'

Never had the God-fearing chaplain felt so inclined to tell a lie.

'I think . . .' he stammered, the truth choking him, 'I think he belongs to . . . to Sabel, the girl who does the cooking now.'

'To the maid? But . . . is the girl married?'

Julián's confusion grew. He felt as if he had something stuck in his throat.

'No, señora, she's not married . . . As you know . . . alas . . . the peasant girls hereabouts aren't very modest . . . Human weakness . . .'

Without letting go of the child, Nucha sat down on a stone bench, determined to get a better look at him. He, however, covered his face with his hands and arms, and wriggled like a wild rabbit that has just been caught. All she could see was a sunburnt neck and an unruly mop of chestnut curls, thick with mud and straw.

'Julián, have you got two cuartos on you?'

'Yes, señora.'

'Here you are, little one . . . I don't want you to be afraid of me.'

The magic worked. The child stretched out his hand, and quickly put the coin down his shirt-front. Nucha was then able to see the round, dimpled face, as graceful and well-proportioned as the bronze cupids you find on candlesticks and lamps. Such a pretty work of Nature was made merry by the sound of his half-roguish, half-angelic laughter. Nucha planted a noisy kiss on each cheek.

'You pretty boy! Bless you! What's your name?'

'Perucho,' the young rascal answered in a free and easy manner.

'My husband's name!' cried the señorita, delighted. 'I bet he's his godson! Eh?'

'Yes, his godson, his godson,' Julián declared hurriedly, wishing he could put a stopper on that merry mouth, with its fleshy, Cupid-like lips. Instead, however, he tried to turn the conversation away from such a potentially dangerous subject.

'What did you want the eggs for? Tell me, and I'll give you two more cuartos.'

'I sell them,' said Perucho.

'So you sell them, eh? We have a budding businessman here . . . And who do you sell them to?'

'To women around here, who take them to town.'

'Let's see, how much do they pay you for them?'

'Two cuartos for a dozen.'

'Look here,' said Nucha affectionately, 'from now on, you're going to sell them to me, and I'll pay you the same amount. You're so pretty I don't want to get angry with you. Oh no! You and I are going to be the best of friends. The first thing I'm going to get you is a proper pair of trousers . . . You don't look exactly what we might call decent.'

True enough, the child's healthy, plump flesh burst through the tears and holes of his filthy burlap trousers – its smoothness still visible despite the mud and dirt that served as clothing, for want of anything more seemly.

'Poor little thing!' murmured Nucha. 'How can they let him go around like this? It's a wonder he doesn't kill himself, or die of cold. Julián, we must get some clothes for this little baby Jesus.'

'A fine little baby Jesus *he* is!' Julián grumbled. 'He's the very devil, God forgive me, but you mustn't feel sorry for him, señorita. He's a little demon, naughtier than a monkey. If you knew how hard I tried to teach him to read and write. Or to get him to wash his muzzle and paws! Not even by tying him down, señorita, not even by tying him down! And he's as fit as a fiddle, despite the life he leads. He's already fallen into the pond twice this year, and once he almost drowned.'

'Come now, Julián. What do you expect him to do at his age? He can't behave like a grown-up. Come with me, boy, and I'll fix something to cover your little legs with. Hasn't he got any shoes? Well then, we'll have to order him a pair of really strong wooden clogs ... And I'm going to give his mother a good talking to and see that she washes him with soap every day. You're going to give him lessons again – or we'll send him to school, that would be better.'

There was no way of making Nucha give up her charitable intentions. Julián's heart was hanging on a thread, for he feared that such close contact with the little boy would inevitably end in disaster. However, his natural goodness made him once again take an interest in that pious work, which he had already once attempted without success, but which he now saw as even further proof of Nucha's great moral worth. It seemed to him providential that the señorita should be taking care of that bad chip off a despicable block. And Nucha, in the meantime, found her protégé most entertaining. She was amused by his very shamelessness, by his roguish instincts, his eagerness to swipe eggs, his greed for taking coins, his fondness of wine and good food. She declared an ambition to straighten up that tender tree, civilizing both its body and its soul.

'A Herculean task, señorita,' was the chaplain's only comment.

Chapter 15

During these first few weeks, the Moscoso newly-weds amused themselves by making excursions to the houses of the local gentry – Nucha on the little donkey, her husband on the chestnut-coloured mare, and Julián on the mule. They were accompanied by two servants, footmen whose job it was to hold the saddles when the riders dismounted, and who were dressed in Sunday-best clothes, with highly embroidered sashes and new felt hats, and swung freshly cut switches to and fro as they went. One of the marquis's favourite dogs would invariably also join the party.

Their first visit was to the Cebre judge's wife. The door was opened by a barelegged maid, who, when she saw Nucha dismount and arrange the pleats on her dress with the handle of her parasol, ran horrified into the house, bawling as if there were a fire or a robbery:

'Señora. Oh, señora! It's nobility . . . and they're coming here!'

Nobody answered her frightened screams, but a few minutes later the judge himself appeared in the entrance hall, bursting with excuses for the girl's stupidity. They could not imagine the trouble they had gone to, trying to educate her. 'We tell her the same thing over and over again, but it's no use. She simply refuses to learn how to receive visitors. I mean, what a way . . .' As he muttered on about the maid's shortcomings, he offered Nucha his arm to lean on as they went up the steps. It was too narrow for them to walk side by side, and so it was with enormous difficulty that Señora Moscoso clung to the gentleman's arm with the tips of her fingers, as he preceded her, two steps ahead, his body all twisted and at a slant.

When they reached the door of the sitting-room, the judge

began to feel around for something in his pockets, muttering incoherent monosyllables and confused exclamations under his breath. Suddenly he let out a terrifying bellow:

'Pepa! . . . Pepaaaa!'

The patter of naked feet was heard, and the judge questioned the maid:

'The key. Where is it? What the devil have you done with the key?'

Pepa handed it to him in a flash and the judge, changing the tone of his voice from a furious hoarseness to the most honeyed gentleness, pushed the door open and said to Nucha:

'This way, señora . . . if you would be so kind.'

The sitting-room was completely dark, and Nucha stumbled against a table. 'Please, take a seat, señora . . . do forgive me!'

The judge opened the shutters and revealed a mahogany pedestal table, two matching armchairs and a blue rep sofa, at the foot of which lay a carpet depicting an extremely fierce Bengal tiger, the colour of fine cinnamon. The judge was at pains to make the visitors comfortable, and worried whether the marquis of Ulloa should face the light, or whether it would be better if he had his back to the window. At the same time he kept on looking around anxiously, annoyed because his wife was taking so long to appear. He tried hard to keep the conversation going, but his stiff smile was really more of a grimace, while his stern gaze kept turning back to the door.

Finally the rustle of starched petticoats could be heard in the corridor, and the judge's wife came in. Every little detail of her apparel suggested that she had only just arranged herself, and was still out of breath from the effort. She had hurriedly crammed her respectable flesh into a corset, but had not managed to do up the last buttons of the silk bodice; the false chignon, put into place in a rush, was crooked and twisted towards her left ear; one of her ear-rings was unfastened, and, as she had not had time to put her shoes on, she struggled to hide, under the pompous ruffles of her silk skirt, a pair of selvage slippers.

Nucha did not usually laugh at people, but she could not help being amused by the judge's wife, who was considered the most fashionable woman in Cebre. She gave a secret smile to Julián and pointed out, with an imperceptible wink, the necklaces, lockets and brooches the señora was wearing round her neck. The judge's wife, in turn, studied the newly wedded lady from Santiago with great attention, and made a mental note of the simplicity of her 'accessories'.

The visit was a short one, because the marquis also wanted to pay his respects to the Rural Dean, and Loiro was more than a league from the little town of Cebre. Their leave-taking was as ceremonious and tediously formal as their arrival had been, with the town's legal authority taking the señora by the arm and escorting her to the door, while he assured her that she was always 'most welcome', and that if there was ever anything he could do for her or her husband . . .

The road up the mountain to Loiro ran along cliffs and precipices that only properly became passable as the domain of the Dean was reached – a domain once vast and rich, but now reduced almost to nothing through disentailment. The monastic-looking rectory, however, still boasted signs of past splendour. When they entered and stopped in the doorway, the marquis and marquess of Ulloa felt a certain chill, as if they were in a huge, vaulted crypt, and their voices resounded in a strange, solemn way. Then, laboriously descending the staircase with its wide steps and huge stone banister, came two monstrous, deformed human beings, who seemed even more grotesque because they were together. The Dean and his sister walked with slow, swaying movements like bears on their hind legs, both panting as if after some tremendous exertion. Their triple chins and bulging necks formed a splendid nimbus-like halo round their bloodshot, purplish jaws. And when they turned round, in exactly the same spot as the Dean had his tonsure, his sister displayed a small bun, rather like that of a bullfighter.

Nucha, who had been put into a good mood by the judge's welcome and his wife's attire, smiled again in a furtive manner, especially over the continual misunderstandings that resulted from the extreme deafness of the respectable couple. Not wishing to act contrary to the hospitable country tradition, the hosts made their visitors enter the dining-room, whether they wanted to or not. Even a yokel would have laughed at the table on which the refreshments were served – the same table at which the owners of the house ate their daily meals, and out of which two semi-circles had been cut, one opposite the other, designed to give ample accommodation to the roundness of two gigantic stomachs.

The party's return to the manor house was enlivened by comments and jokes about the visits. Even Julián forgot his usual seriousness and forbearance, laughing at the Dean's table and the store of hardware the judge's wife had displayed on her neck and bosom. They also looked forward to another equally amusing expedition that had been arranged for the following day, when they would make a visit to the Molende señoritas and to the Limiosos.

Next morning, as they had a very full programme, they left the manor nice and early. But despite this, and despite the long summer afternoon, it was only because the Molende sisters were not at home that they had enough time for everything. As it was, a peasant girl, passing by with a bundle of grass, explained with some difficulty that the Molende señoritas had gone to the Vilamorta fair, and heaven only knew when they would be back. Nucha was sorry, because she liked the señoritas, who had previously come to pay her a visit at the manor. They were the only young faces around, the only people who reminded her of the merry prattle and bold tongues of her sisters, whom she could not forget. They left a courtesy message with the peasant girl, and turned up the hill, on the road to the Limioso manor.

The path was difficult, twisting in an upward spiral around the mountain, and almost obliterated by leafy vines leaning over from either side. As they neared the summit, they caught sight of a building that shone golden in the setting sun, with a tower on its left side, and on its right a tumbled-down dovecote with no roof. It was the Limioso country mansion, which had once been a castle. Perched on an outcrop of rock, it was like a goshawk nest suspended on the craggy slope of the lonely hillside, behind which, in the distance, towered the majestic peak of the inaccessible Leiro. In the whole district – perhaps even in the whole province – there was not a more illustrious or ancient stately home, nor another referred to by the local people with such respect as a 'mansion'.

From close up, the Limioso manor looked as though it was uninhabited, and that increased the melancholy impression given by the dilapidated dovecote. There were signs of abandonment and ruin all around. The small patio was overgrown with nettles, and though in truth it could be said that there were no panes missing from the window-frames, this was only because there *were* no frames in the first place, only wooden shutters, and even some of these were wrenched off their hinges and dangled crookedly, like a tear in an old suit. The weeds grew right up to the gratings of the ground-floor windows, which were devoured by rust, and garlands of dry, stunted grass ran along the spaces left between the disjointed stones.

The main door stood wide open, as if the inhabitants had nothing to fear from thieves. But the dull sound of the horses' hooves on the grassy floor of the patio was answered by the feeble barks of a mastiff and two setters, which pounced on the visitors, snarling with what little vigour they still possessed – for all three animals were little more than bags of bones covered with bristly coats that seemed likely to fall apart at any moment. The setters calmed down when they heard the marquis of Ulloa's voice, for they had been out hunting with him hundreds of times. But the mastiff, which could only just manage a bark, the effort making his legs tremble and his tongue hang down through his carious, yellow teeth, seemed none the less resolved to die in the enterprise, and was only silenced by the appearance of his master, Señorito de Limioso.

Who, in these mountains, has not known one of these gentlemen, direct descendants of the Galician paladins and grandees? An indefatigable hunter and a staunch Carlist, Ramonciño Limioso must have been about twenty-six years old at the time, but already his moustache, his eyebrows, his hair and all his features bore a serious, melancholy and dignified expression, which seemed a little comical to those who set eyes upon him for the first time. The sad arching of his brows gave him a vague resemblance to portraits of Quevedo. His lean neck seemed to cry out for a ruff, and in place of the stick he held in his hand, one's imagination supplied him with an old-fashioned sword. Despite his lanky body, his threadbare overcoat, patched-up trousers, and general poor appearance, there was no doubt that Ramón Limioso was a true 'gentleman born' – as the villagers said – and had not 'fought his way up' as others had. This was apparent even in the way he helped Nucha dismount from the donkey – in the naturally courteous fashion with which he offered her not his arm to lean on but, as in bygone days, the two fingers of his left hand. Then, with the elegance of a minuet, the couple climbed the exterior staircase that led up to the cloister (not without some risk of falling back down again, such was the state of the venerable, but worm-eaten, steps), and entered the Limioso manor house.

The roof of the cloister was like a piece of open-work: through the tiles and beams one could see strips of sky-blue velvet. Swallows sang sweetly in their nests, well-sheltered behind the Limioso coat of arms – three fish haurient in a lake and a lion holding a cross – which was coarsely engraved on the capital of every column.

Even worse awaited them in the entrance hall. It had been years since woodworm and time had destroyed the floor-boards, and, doubtless because the Limiosos' means were not sufficient to meet the expense of new flooring, they had contented themselves with throwing down a few loose planks over the logs and beams. The señorito walked calmly along this dangerous path, never ceasing to offer his fingers to Nucha, and with the latter not daring to request a steadier support. Each plank she stepped on would rise and tremble, revealing the black depths of the wine-cellar underneath, with its barrels clothed in cobwebs. Dauntlessly, they crossed the abyss and went into the sitting-room, which at least had a nailed-down floor, even though it was broken in many places and everywhere almost reduced to powder by the insects' resolute drilling.

Nucha was so surprised by what she saw that she stood there motionless. In one corner of the room a magnificent piece of furniture, a credenza inlaid with tortoise-shell and ivory, was half-hidden under a huge heap of wheat. On the walls hung old, blackened pictures, in which one could just make out the shrivelled leg of a martyred saint, or a horse's croup, or the chubby-cheeked face of an angel. On the side opposite the heap of wheat there was a dais carpeted with Cordoba leather that still retained its rich colours and deep golds. In front of this, set in a semicircle, were some magnificent carved ceremonial chairs, also with leather seats; and between the wheat and the dais, sitting on rustic oak stumps, such as are used as stools by the poorest peasants, two thin, pale, upright old women, dressed in the habit of the Carmelite Order, were actually spinning.

Señora de Moscoso had never imagined she would see anyone spin – except perhaps some village women – other than in novels or stories. She was thus greatly impressed by the sight of these two Byzantine statues – for that is what they looked like, since they had both simultaneously stopped working the spindle and distaff when she came in, and had remained perfectly still ever since. They were the paternal aunts of Señorito de Limioso, and in their name the latter had previously paid a visit to Nucha. The father, who was paralysed and confined to his bed, also lived in the house, but no one had ever actually seen him, and his existence was like a myth, a mountain legend. The two old ladies stood up and in the same instant stretched out their arms to Nucha, so that she did not know which of the two to turn to first. At once, on either cheek, she felt an icy kiss, a kiss given without lips, just the rub of inert skin. She also felt her hands being grabbed by other, bony hands, and realized they were guiding her towards the dais and offering her one of the ceremonial chairs. But no sooner had she sat in it than she felt to her horror the seat coming apart and sinking. Without even a creak of resistance the chair began to collapse in all directions. Nucha stood up, following the instinct of a woman with child, and let one of the last vestiges of the Limiosos' splendour collapse on to the floor for ever.

They left the leaking manor house when it was already growing dark, and were silent during the whole journey home. Although they made no comment on it, perhaps even being unaware of it, they had been touched by that inexplicable sadness evoked when one witnesses something coming to its inevitable end.

Chapter 16

The Moscoso heir was clearly soon to enter the world, for Nucha sat endlessly sewing at clothes so tiny they seemed made for a doll. The strain of carrying the child, however, had done nothing to impair her health: on the contrary, one would have thought that every little step the child took towards daylight was taken for its mother's benefit.

Nucha had not grown fat, exactly, but she had 'filled out', sharp angles and flat surfaces turning into soft, round curves. Her usually pale cheeks were now rosy, though her forehead and temples were shadowed with that blotchiness common in women with child. Her black hair seemed shinier and thicker; her eyes less vague and more moist; her mouth, fresher and redder. Even her voice had changed, becoming deeper. As for the natural enlargement of her body, this was only slight and not at all unseemly, like the gentle heaviness of the Holy Mother in pictures of the Visitation. The way she stretched her hands over her belly, as if to protect her tiny charge, completed the likeness to paintings of such a tender subject.

It must be admitted that Don Pedro treated his wife very well during this time of waiting. Setting aside his usual excursions to the woods and hills, he would take her out every day, without fail, for constitutional walks which gradually grew longer. Nucha, leaning on his arm, walked through the valley in which the manor house lay hidden, pausing to rest on walls and banks whenever she felt tired. Don Pedro endeavoured to satisfy her smallest wishes: on occasions he was even gallant, fetching for her the wild flowers that drew her attention, or branches of arbutus trees, or blackberry bushes heavy with fruit. As gunshots always made Nucha jump, the señorito never carried a gun with him, and he had expressly forbidden Primitivo to hunt around there. It seemed as though the marquis was slowly coming out of his rough shell, and his heart, so indomitable and selfish, was changing, letting the tender feelings proper to a husband and father show through, like little weeds peeping out of the cracks in a wall. If this was not exactly the Christian matrimony envisaged by the excellent chaplain, then it was certainly very close to it.

Julián thanked the Lord every single day. His devotion had not been reborn, for it had never died, but it had been revived and rekindled. As the hour of Nucha's confinement drew near, Julián remained even longer on his knees at the end of mass, giving thanks to God. He extended the litanies and the rosaries. He put more feeling and fervour into his daily prayers, which now always included a very devout novena: either to Our Lady of August, or to Our Lady of September. He believed this Marian cult to be extremely appropriate in the circumstances, for he was convinced, and every day more firmly so, that Nucha was the living image of the Virgin Mary, inasmuch as any mortal woman, conceived in sin, could be.

One October afternoon, as it was getting dark, Julián was sitting on the stone bench under his window, engrossed in the writings of Father Nieremberg, when he heard hurried footsteps on the stairs. He recognized Don Pedro's tread, and, when he saw the señorito's face, it was beaming with satisfaction.

'Is there any news?' asked Julián, dropping the book.

'You bet there is. We've had to hurry back from the walk.'

'Have you sent to Cebre for the doctor?'

'Primitivo is on his way.'

Julián pulled a face.

'Don't worry . . . I've just sent two other messengers to follow him there . . . I wanted to go myself, but Nucha says she doesn't want to be left without me now.'

'The best thing would be for me to go too, just in case,' cried Julián. 'Even if I have to go on foot and by night.'

Don Pedro let out one of his terrible, mocking guffaws.

'You!' he cried, without restraining his laughter. 'What an idea, Don Julián!'

The chaplain looked down and wrinkled his fair eyebrows. He felt ashamed of his cassock, for it disqualified him from rendering even the smallest service in such a difficult situation. And because a priest is also a man, he was not allowed to enter the chamber where the mystery was being fulfilled, either. Only two males possessed that right: the husband and the representative of human knowledge, whom Primitivo had been sent to fetch. It distressed Julián to think that Nucha's modesty would be profaned, and that her pure body would perhaps be treated with no more respect than an anatomist treats a corpse – as inert matter that no longer lodges a soul. He felt humiliated and upset.

'Call me if you need me for anything, señor,' he mumbled faintly.

'A thousand thanks, man. I only came to give you the good news.'

Don Pedro hurried down the stairs again, whistling a *riveirana*,* and the chaplain stood motionless for a moment, wiping some beads of sweat from his brow and contemplating the little illustrations that hung on the wall, framed with spangles and sequins. From these he selected two: Raymond the Unborn, and Our Lady of Anguish, holding her dead son on her lap. He would have preferred Our Lady of Milk and Good Childbirth, but he had no picture of her, for the idea had only just occurred to him. He cleared all the bits and pieces that cluttered the top of the bureau and stood the prints on it. Then he opened the drawer where he kept a few candles for use in the chapel and, taking two, placed them in tin candlesticks, and set up his little altar. As soon as the yellow light of the candles was reflected on the ornaments and glass of the pictures, Julián's soul felt an indescribable comfort. Uplifted and full of hope, the chaplain scolded himself for having thought he was useless at such a time. Useless indeed! For precisely what pertained to him was the most

* A Galician folk dance.

important task of all: to ask for heaven's protection. Full of faith, he knelt down and began his prayers.

Time went by with no interruption, no news from below. At about ten o'clock the pins and needles in Julián's knees became intolerable. A painful weariness took hold of his limbs, and he felt dizzy. With a great effort he stood up and tottered unsteadily. Someone came in. It was Sabel, and the chaplain looked at her in surprise, for she had not been up to his room for a long time.

'The señorito says you are to come down to supper.'

'Has your father come back? Has the doctor arrived?' Julián asked anxiously, not daring to inquire any further.

'No sir . . . It's quite a way to Cebre.'

In the dining-room, Julián found the marquis eating with a voracious appetite, like someone whose meal has been delayed two or more hours. Julián tried to assume a similar calmness by sitting down and unfolding his napkin.

'How is the señorita?' he asked, eagerly.

'Bah! . . . Not feeling very well, as you can imagine.'

'Will she need anything while you're here?'

'No. She has her maid Filomena with her. Sabel is also helping with whatever's needed.'

Julián did not answer, his thoughts on this matter being best kept to himself. It was outrageous that Sabel should be assisting the lawful wife at such a moment; but if the husband did not see it like that, who was bold enough to tell him? On the other hand, Sabel had plenty of experience in domestic matters, and would certainly be useful. Julián noticed that the marquis, unlike a few hours before, now seemed ill-humoured and impatient. Therefore, it was with some trepidation that he asked, 'And . . . will the doctor get here in time?'

'In time, did you say?' answered the señorito, cramming the food into his mouth and chewing bad-temperedly. 'With time to spare, probably! These refined ladies are too delicate for a job like this. They make such heavy weather of it . . . If only she were like her sister Rita . . .' He banged his glass violently on the table and added sententiously: 'Town women are a calamity . . . There's nothing to them, you'd think they were made of icing sugar . . . She's so weak, and has such a tendency to get convulsions and fainting spells that . . . Nothing but fuss, the deuce! Fuss and nonsense they grow used to when they're children!'

He banged the table again with his fist and got up, leaving Julián alone in the dining-room and once more at a loss as to what to do with himself. Then, having decided to renew his conversation with the saints, he went upstairs, where the candles were still burning, and went down on his knees again. The hours went by and the only sounds to be heard were the night wind as it groaned through the chestnut-trees, and the low sobbing of water in the sluice of the nearby mill. Julián felt the muscles in his legs prickle and stiffen. His bones grew cold, and his head became heavy. Two or three times he looked longingly at the bed, but each time the thought of the poor girl suffering in the room downstairs made him ashamed of such temptation. His eyes closed none the less, and his head, drunk with sleep, fell on his chest. He lay down with his clothes on, promising himself that he would sleep for just a few minutes.

Dawn had already broken when he awoke. Finding himself dressed, he remembered what had happened during the night, and cursed himself for being such a sleepyhead, as he wondered whether the new Moscoso had arrived in this world. He hurried downstairs, still half-dazed and rubbing his eyes. In the room next to the kitchen he bumped into Máximo Juncal, the Cebre doctor, who was wearing a grey woollen scarf wound round his neck, a brown flannel overcoat, boots and spurs.

'Have you just arrived?' The chaplain asked in amazement.

'Yes, sir. Primitivo says he and two others were knocking on my door last night, but nobody answered. The truth is that my maid is rather deaf. But even so . . . if they had called properly . . . Anyhow, the message didn't reach me until dawn. Still, it seems I've got here in plenty of time. After all, this is her first child. These battles tend to drag on and on. I'm going up now, to see what's happening.'

Preceded by Don Pedro, he set off, whip in hand, his spurs rattling, so that the warlike image he had just used seemed to fit exactly, and anyone could have taken him to be the general who arrives on the battlefield at the last minute, to ensure victory with his presence and his orders. He reappeared shortly after and asked for a hot cup of coffee, for in the rush of coming over he had not had time for breakfast. The marquis was given chocolate. The doctor, whose resolute countenance inspired confidence, warned that in his professional opinion the business promised to be a long one, and so they should arm themselves with patience. Don Pedro, whose face was swollen from lack of sleep and who was in a gruff mood, asked if there was any danger.

'No sir, no sir,' answered Máximo, stirring the sugar with his spoon and adding rum to the coffee. 'If any complications should arise, here we are. You, Sabel, bring me a small glass.' He poured some more rum into the little glass, which he tasted while the coffee was cooling down. The marquis offered him a cigar.

'Thank you very much,' said the doctor, lighting one. 'For the moment we must wait and see. This is the señora's first delivery, and she's not very strong ... Townswomen receive a most insanitary education. They're taught to wear corsets and so make narrow what should be wide. Being always indoors, they grow anaemic, and, all in all, the life they lead is far too sedentary, they eat too much, and their lymph glands get out of control ... Country women are a thousand times better prepared for the great battle of gestation and childbirth – which, after all, is the true function of women.'

He continued to expatiate on this theory, keen to show he was not ignorant of the latest and most daring scientific hypotheses. He boasted the results of improved sanitation, and praised the enormous healing power of Mother Nature, when left to her own devices. He was clearly a clever young man, well-read and determined to fight the illnesses of others. However, the champion of hygiene and clean living did not set an example to his patients, and with his bilious yellow face and his dry, thin pale lips he was not exactly a picture of health. It was said that this was to be blamed on rum and a certain baker-girl from Cebre, robust enough to be able to sell or give her health to at least four hygienist doctors, and still have more to spare.

Don Pedro puffed bad-temperedly at his cigar, and pondered on the doctor's words. Strangely enough, considering the difference between the two men – one with a mind overflowing with science and the other an intellectual virgin, so to speak – they were in complete agreement on the subject. The gentleman of ancient lineage also believed that the purpose of women was first and foremost the reproduction of the species. Any suggestion to the contrary would have seemed to him criminal. He thought a great deal – with strange, almost incestuous regret – about his robust, buxom sister-in-law, Rita. He also recalled Perucho's birth. Sabel had been kneading the dough to make corn bread, which did not even have time to bake before the child was already crying, declaring in his own way that he too was a creature of God, the same as everyone else, and needed sustenance. These memories provoked a very important thought in the marquis's mind.

'Tell me, Máximo . . . do you think my wife'll be able to suckle the child?'

Máximo burst out laughing, as he sipped his rum.

'Don't ask for too much, Don Pedro . . . Suckle the child! That august function requires an extremely vigorous constitution and a sanguine temperament . . . Your wife is not up to it.'

'She's the one who insists on it,' said the marquis spitefully. 'I could see it was an absurd idea, even though I didn't realize then that my wife was quite so feeble. Oh well, we must at least make sure the child isn't going to starve when he's born. Will I have time to go to Castrodorna? The daughter of Felipe, one of the tenants – a big strapping young girl . . . Do you know who I mean?'

'Yes, of course I know! A big cow of a woman! You have a doctor's eye all right . . . And she had her child just two months ago. What I don't know is whether her parents will let her come. I believe they're honest people for their class, and don't want others to know about their daughter's shame.'

'Gibberish! If he doesn't like it I'll drag her here by the plaits of her hair . . . No tenant of mine says no to me. Is there or isn't there time to fetch her?'

'Oh yes, there's time enough. I wish we could be finished before then, but it doesn't look likely.'

When the señorito went out, Máximo helped himself to another glass of rum and spoke confidingly to the chaplain:

'If I were in Felipe's skin, I'd have a message for Don Pedro. When will these señoritos understand that their tenants aren't their slaves? That's the way things are going here in Spain – a lot of revolution, and talk of freedom, and rights for the individual . . . But in fact there's still tyranny, privilege and feudalism, everywhere you look! It's no different from the bad old days of tithes and serfdom. I need your daughter, so bam! I'll take her, even if you don't like it. I need some milk, a human cow, so, bam! if you don't want to suckle my baby, you'll do it all the same. But I'm shocking you, Don Julián. You don't share my ideas on social matters, to be sure.'

'No sir, I'm not shocked,' answered Julián calmly. 'On the contrary, I'm amused to see you getting so worked up. You can be sure Felipe's daughter will jump at the chance to be a wetnurse here, where she'll be well-fed, well looked after, and not have to work. Just think about it.'

'And what about free will? Don't you want people to have any rights and to do what they want? Imagine that the girl prefers to stay at home in honest poverty rather than come here, despite all the benefits and advantages you talk about. Don't you think it's wrong to drag her here by the hair just because she's the daughter of a tenant? But naturally you don't think so. That's clear. Wearing a cassock, you can't be expected to think any other way: you must be in favour of feudalism and theocracy. Am I right? You can't deny it.'

'I have no political ideas,' Julián declared quietly. Then, as if suddenly remembering, he added: 'Wouldn't it be a good thing to go and see how the señorita is feeling?'

'Pooh! I'm not needed there at the moment, but I'll go and see. Don't let them take the bottle of rum away, eh? I'll be back in a moment.'

He returned shortly afterwards and, after settling down by his glass, showed signs of wishing to resume the political debate he was so fond of. He secretly preferred to be contradicted, for this spurred his mind into finding unexpected arguments. Moreover, he argued for the sake of his health: it was, he considered, excellent exercise for both the larynx and the brain, and these in turn cleared his liver – while really violent arguments that ended in shouts and insults made his stagnant bile flow and activated his digestive and respiratory systems, giving him great comfort.

'So you have no political ideas? Give that bone to another dog, Father Julián . . . All birds with black plumage fly backwards – in other words, I don't believe you. Let's see, let's put you to the test: what do you think of the Revolution? Do you agree with religious freedom? That's a hard one for you! Do you think Suñer's right?'*

'The things you say, Don Máximo! How could I agree with Suñer? Isn't he the one who said those dreadfully blasphemous things in the Cortes? May God enlighten him!'

'Make yourself clear, man. Do you hold the same opinions as the abbot of Boán? He says that Suñer and the revolutionaries will never be won over by reason, but only by a well-aimed shot from a blunderbuss, and no nonsense. What do you think?'

'That's the sort of thing one says in the heat of the moment. A priest is a man, like any other, and is liable to lose his temper in an argument and say things he doesn't mean.'

'You bet he does. And exactly because he is a man like any other, he's quite capable of selfish interest, quite capable of living a life of idleness and luxury by exploiting his neighbours' gullibility, and helping himself to roast kid and roast capon – kindly supplied by his parishioners . . . You can't deny that.'

'We are all sinners, Don Máximo.'

'And he can do even worse things than that . . . you know what I mean, eh? Don't blush.'

* Francisco Suñer was a Republican politician and celebrated doctor, who as a Deputy at the Congress in 1869 declared war against 'God, the monarchy and tuberculosis'.

'Yes, sir, a priest can indeed commit every sin in the book. If we were incapable of sin, that would really be a great privilege, for it would mean we gained salvation at the very moment of our ordination, which wouldn't be a bad deal at all. In fact ordination imposes harder duties on us than on other Christians, which makes it twice as difficult for one of us to be good. Our efforts can never be enough, if we are to follow the path of perfection we should enter upon when we are ordained priests. We must always rely on the help of God's grace, and that's saying something.'

He said these words with such sincerity and unaffectedness, that the doctor calmed down for a few moments.

'If they were all like you, Don Julián . . .'

'I'm the last in the row, the worst of all. You mustn't judge by appearances.'

'Nonsense! The rest are a lot of rogues – and even with the Revolution we haven't been able to undermine their position. You wouldn't believe what they got up to, just to please that villain Barbacana.'

Not knowing what the story was, Julián remained silent as the doctor continued.

'There's a scoundrel from Castrodorna, known as El Tuerto, who works for Barbacana – does everything he says. But because one night he stabbed his wife and her lover, he's always on the run, always having to slip over the border into Portugal. However, it seems that not long ago the police finally managed to lay their hands on him, but Barbacana was resolved to set him free. Well, both he and the priests worked so hard at it that finally the man was let out on bail, and now walks around freely . . . So you see, despite everything, here we are as usual, under the rule of that vile Barbacana.'

'But I've heard,' objected Julián, 'that when Barbacana isn't ruling over the district, his place is taken by another *cacique* who is even worse – the one they call Trampeta, who swindles the poor peasants and sucks every drop of their blood . . . So there's not much to choose between them.'

'Sure enough. There's some truth in what you say. But look here, at least Trampeta doesn't try to set up a party. We must put an end to Barbacana's doings, for he's in league with the provincial Carlist committees to put the country to the sword. Are you a supporter of the Young Pretender?'*

'I've already told you I hold no opinions.'

'You're just not in the mood for arguing.'

'Quite frankly, Don Máximo, you've guessed right. I'm worried about the poor señorita ... thinking of what might happen to her. And I don't understand politics. Don't laugh, I really don't understand. All I know is how to say mass, and the fact is I haven't said mass yet today, and, until I have, I can't have my breakfast, and my stomach is getting weak ... I·shall devote today's service to present needs,' he added in a melancholy voice, 'for I can't give her any other help.'

He left, leaving the doctor surprised to have found a priest who shrank from political discussions, which in those days took the place of theological arguments in every rectory in the country. Julián celebrated mass with great concentration, and, as the chime of the acolyte's bell sounded clear and silvery in the old empty chapel, so outside could be heard the calming sounds of the countryside – bird-song in the trees, the distant creak of carts going out to work. Julián had chosen to dedicate the mass to St Raymond the Unborn, and, when he said the words, '*ejus nobis intercessione concede, ut a peccatorum vinculis absoluti . . .*', it seemed to him that the chains of pain that still bound the poor little virgin – for in his mind he still saw her as such – suddenly broke, leaving her free, triumphant and radiant with the joy of motherhood.

However, when he got back to the house the said chains still showed no signs of breaking. Instead of the hurried comings and goings of servants that always indicate some important event, he noticed an ill-omened calm. The señorito had not yet returned, although it was true that it was quite a journey to Castrodorna, and so they had to sit down to dinner without him. The doctor no longer wished to argue, for he too was getting worried about

* Carlos VII of the Carlist dynasty, known as the Duke of Madrid (1848–1909); he reconstructed the Carlist party in the 1860s.

the late arrival of the Moscoso heir. It must be said, in all fairness to the argumentative hygienist, that he took his profession seriously and respected it as much as Julián respected his. Proof of this was his very obsession with the cult of hygiene and health, a cult instilled by numerous weighty modern books that strove to replace the God of Sinai with the goddess Hygeia. To Máximo Juncal, immorality was synonymous with scrofula, and duty was very similar to a 'perfect oxidation of assimilable elements'. Meanwhile he was able to pardon certain misdemeanours on his own part, blaming them on the obstruction of his liver passages.

At that moment, the danger that threatened the señora aroused his instinct to fight all the positive evils of the world, such as pain, illness, and death. He ate absent-mindedly, and drank only two glasses of rum. Julián, meanwhile, barely tasted his food and asked the doctor several times what he thought was happening with regard to the birth at that particular moment. He only stopped asking when the doctor had given him, in a half-whisper, a rather explicit medical description of all the details.

Night began to fall and Máximo now hardly left the patient's room. Julián felt so sad and lonely that he was already on the point of going upstairs to his little altar, in order at least to enjoy the company of the candles and little prints, when Don Pedro burst in impetuously, like a hurricane, clutching the hand of a sturdy-looking girl, the colour of earth, who was built like a castle: a perfect specimen of the human cow.

Chapter 17

To the amazement of all who saw, the marquis had brought the wetnurse to the manor on the front of his saddle, for there had been no other means of transport available in Castrodorna, and he had been too impatient to let her come on foot. The poor mare will shudder for ever after remembering the day she had to bear the weight of both the present Moscoso and the wetnurse of his future heir; for the girl was as strong and large as an ox, with a veritable fountain of milk – as Máximo Juncal, who was, after all, the expert, readily agreed.

Don Pedro lost heart, however, when he found that the child had still not arrived. Indeed, it seemed to him that now the expected birth would never happen. He was ferociously hungry and hurried Sabel with his supper. She served it to him personally, for Filomena, the maid who usually served in the dining-room, was busy elsewhere. The lass looked fresher and more appetizing than ever; the flesh on her bare arm, the copper-coloured shine of her curls, the soft tenderness and sensuality of her blue eyes, all seemed in contrast with the woman who lay prostrated in agony only a short distance away. It was a long time since the marquis had seen Sabel closely. Rather than merely look at her, it would be more exact to say that he examined her carefully for several minutes. He noticed the girl was not wearing ear-rings and that one of her ears was disfigured: then he remembered that he himself had torn it, when he crushed the filigree ear-drop with the butt of his rifle in a brutal fit of jealousy. The wound had healed, but the ear now appeared to have two lobes instead of one.

'Doesn't the señora sleep at all?' Julián was asking the doctor.

'At times, between contractions . . . But to tell the truth, I don't like this drowsiness she falls into at all. We're not getting anywhere, and the worst thing is she's losing strength. She gets weaker and weaker, and hasn't tasted food for forty-eight hours – she confessed to me that before telling her husband, long before that, she was already feeling ill and couldn't eat. All this falling asleep looks wrong to me. I would say that rather than drowsiness, what we have here are real fainting-spells.'

Dismayed, Don Pedro rested his head on his clenched fist.

'I'm convinced,' he said emphatically, 'that these things only happen to señoritas brought up in the towns. Only one of them would get so worked up over such a trifle . . . I'd like to see the girls around here faint . . . they'd give themselves half a jugful of wine and finish off the job singing.'

'No, sir, there are all sorts everywhere. The lymphatic-nervous ones lose their vigour quickly. I've had some cases . . .' and he went on to explain in detail the various battles he had fought – which in truth were not many, for he had only just entered the fray, so to speak. He was in favour of waiting: the best obstetrician is the one who knows how to wait the longest. However, there comes a point at which to lose a second is to lose everything. As he asserted this, he sipped his rum with relish.

'Sabel!' he suddenly called out.

'What do you want, Señorito Máximo?' answered the girl solicitously.

'Where did you put that box I brought with me?'

'In your room, on the bed.'

'That's all right then.'

Don Pedro looked at the doctor, realizing what it was all about. But not Julián, who, frightened by the deep silence that followed the dialogue between Máximo and Sabel, asked indirect questions to discover what the mysterious box contained.

'Instruments,' answered the doctor drily.

'Instruments? . . . What for?' asked the chaplain, feeling the sweat break out on his scalp.

'For operating on her, damn it all! If we were able to hold a medical conference here, then perhaps I would let things take

164

their natural course. But the full responsibility of what will happen falls on me. I cannot sit back and do nothing, or let myself in for a surprise like an ignoramus. If by dawn the prostration has increased and I see no clear symptoms to indicate that this will sort itself out . . . I will have to take a decision. You'd better start praying to the blessed St Raymond, chaplain.'

'If it were just a question of praying!' cried the unworldly Julián, 'I've been praying to him since yesterday!'

The doctor used that simple admission as a pretext to tell a hundred amusing stories, in which devotion and obstetrics were closely mixed and St Raymond played a central role. He told of how his teacher, in the Santiago hospital, would go into the room where the women in labour stayed, and, when he saw the picture of the saint, with all its little candles, would cry furiously: 'Sirs, either I'm in the way here, or that saint is. For if I am unsuccessful they will blame me, and if things go well they'll say it was his miracle.' He also made some rather outrageous remarks concerning the roses of Jericho, the ribbons of Our Lady of Tortosa, and other devout charms used in critical moments. Finally overcome by a rum-induced sleepiness, he stopped his prattle. But so as not to become too lethargic in the comfort of his bed, he lay down on the dining-room bench, using a basket as a pillow. The señorito crossed his arms on the table and rested his head on them, as a muffled whistle, prelude to snoring, announced that the need to sleep was getting the better of him too.

The tall grandfather clock struck midnight wearily. Julián, the only one left awake, felt a chill in his marrow and the burning of a fever in his cheeks. He went up to his room and, after wetting a towel with cold water, pressed it against his temples. The altar-candles had burnt away; he replaced them, put a pillow on the floor on which to kneel, for the most tiresome thing was always the wretched pins and needles, and began to climb the hill of prayer in high spirits. Sometimes he felt weak, and his young body, wrapped in the grey mists of sleep, longed for the clean bed. Then he would cross his hands, digging the nails of one into the back of the other to wake himself up. He wanted to pray with real devotion, and be fully aware of what he was asking God to grant, rather than pray by rote. But, despite himself, he slowly began to lose strength. Then he remembered the passage from the Bible in which Moses prayed with his arms raised high, for to have lowered them would have meant the defeat of Israel, and it occurred to him to do something that had been floating round in his imagination: he removed the pillow, so that his knees rested on the bare floor; then he raised his eyes, searching for God up above the holy pictures and the roof rafters; and, opening his arms like Moses, he began to pray even more fervently.

A faint light, more ashen and opaque than the light of the moon, slowly appeared from behind the mountain, and an icy chill filled the air. Two or three birds began to chirp in the garden and the murmur of water in the mill-sluice became less deep and sobbing. Dawn placed first one of her rosy fingers over that little corner of the world, and then slowly stretched out her whole hand, spreading a cheerful, pure radiance over the slate rocks, making them shine like polished plates of steel, and, entering the chaplain's room, engulfed the yellow light of the candles. But Julián did not see the dawn, nor anything else apart from the spots in his mind's eye caused by the movement of blood – those little violet, green, scarlet or sulphur-coloured stars that quiver without shedding light, which we confuse with the ringing of our ears or the sound of the giant pendulum of the arteries, near to bursting. He felt as if he were about to lose consciousness and die. His lips no longer spoke in sentences, but only produced a mutter that still had the singsong of prayer. In the midst of his painful giddiness he heard a voice that seemed to him as resonant as a bugle call. The voice was saying something. Julián only understood two words:

'A girl.'

He tried to get up, heaving a deep sigh, and managed to do so, helped by the person who had come in and who was none other than Primitivo. But no sooner had he got to his feet than a dreadful pain in his joints, a feeling that he had been hit on the head with a hammer, made him fall to the ground again. He fainted.

Downstairs, Máximo Juncal was washing his hands in the pewter basin Sabel held out for him. His face bore the joyful expression of triumph mixed with the sweat of the fight, which ran down in drops, half-frozen already by the cold dawn air. The marquis, strained and bad-tempered, paced round the room scowling, with that grim and at the same time stupid expression that lack of sleep gives people who are very vigorous and subject to the laws of Nature.

'Now you must be happy, Don Pedro,' said the doctor. 'The worst is over. What you desired so much has been achieved. Didn't you want the child to come out alive and unharmed? Well then, there she is, safe and sound. It's been a hard job, but in the end . . .'

The marquis shrugged his shoulders contemptuously, as if he were diminishing the doctor's merits, and mumbled something inaudible. He continued pacing up and down, down and up, his hands thrust in his pockets, his trousers stretched tight, like his own nerves.

'It's a little angel, as the old women say,' added Juncal mischievously, seemingly enjoying the nobleman's anger. 'Only it's a female angel. One must resign oneself to these things. Writing off to heaven with an order, specifying what sex one wants, is something that hasn't been invented yet.'

Don Pedro's lips foamed once more with rage and rudeness. Juncal burst out laughing, while he dried himself with the towel.

'You must be at least half to blame, marquis,' he cried. 'Will you be so kind as to hand me a little cigar?'

As he offered him the open case, Don Pedro asked him a question. Máximo recovered his seriousness before answering.

'I didn't say as much as that . . . I don't think so. It's true that when battles are very persistent and bitter, the combatant may as a result become disabled. But nature is very wise, and, while she subjects women to such harsh tests, she also offers them the most unforeseen amends. However, now is not the moment to think about that, but about your wife getting better and the little one gaining weight. I fear some more immediate calamity, as the señora is still in a poor state . . .'

Primitivo came in, and, without showing any signs of disturbance or fright, said: 'Don Máximo must come upstairs, something's wrong with the chaplain. He looks like a corpse.'

'Let's go and see, man, let's go and see. This was not on the programme,' mumbled Juncal. 'This priest is just like a woman! What a useless fellow! One thing is certain: he'll never take up the blunderbuss, even if those gangs that the lion of Boán dreams of were to revolt.'

Chapter 18

For many a day Nucha lay hovering before that gloomy portal known as death's door, with one foot on the threshold, as if to say: 'Shall I go in, or not?' Propelling her forward were the dreadful physical tortures that had shaken her nerves; the all-consuming fever that disturbed her mind when the wave of useless milk flowed in her chest; the distress at not being able to offer her little girl the liquid that was choking her; and the exhaustion of her body, from which life drained hopelessly drop by drop. But holding her back from the door was her youth; the desire to exist that drives every living being; the knowledge of that great hygienist, Juncal; and, more than anything else, a soft, tiny pink hand – a little closed fist that peeped through the laces of a matinée coat and the tight folds of a shawl.

The first day Julián was able to see the patient, she had only just been allowed out of bed – and then only to lie down, wrapped in blankets and coats, on the old, wide couch. She was not yet permitted to sit up, and her head rested on pillows folded in half. Her thin bloodless face, yellow like the face of an ivory image, was framed by her black shiny hair, and her squint was more pronounced than previously, for the ordeal had weakened the nerve. She smiled sweetly at the chaplain, and pointed to a chair. Julián fixed his eyes on her with the look of overflowing compassion that betrays us in the presence of a seriously ill person, when in vain we wish to hide or suppress it.

'You're looking very well, señorita,' said the chaplain, lying like a rascal.

'Well, looking at you,' she answered languidly, 'I'd say you don't appear to be in very good health.'

He confessed that, in effect, he was not feeling too well since . . . since he had caught a bit of a cold. He felt ashamed to speak about the sleepless night, the fainting fit, the great physical and moral suffering he had endured on her behalf. Nucha began to talk to him about some trivial matters, and then, without a pause, asked him:

'Have you seen the little one?'

'Yes, señora . . . on the day of the christening. The little angel! How she cried when they put the salt on her and when she felt the cold water . . .'

'Ah! Well, since then she's grown at least a quarter of a foot and has become a real beauty!' And raising her voice with an effort, she added: 'Nurse, nurse! Bring the baby.'

Footsteps were heard, like those of a gigantic walking statue, and in came the young earth-coloured peasant girl. She seemed very self-satisfied in her new blue woollen dress trimmed with black velvet ribbon, that made her look like *La Coca*, the famous giantess of Santiago Cathedral. The innocent infant lay on the great bosom that nourished her, like a little bird perched on a thick tree-trunk. She was asleep, breathing in that calm, sweet and imperceptible way that makes a child's sleep so sacred. Julián did not tire of looking at her.

'God's little saint!' he murmured, pressing his lips very softly against her cap, not daring to do so on the forehead.

'Hold her, Julián . . . Feel how heavy she is. Nurse, give him the baby.'

She weighed no more than a bunch of flowers, but the chaplain swore time and time again that she seemed to be made of lead. The nurse stood and waited, while he sat with the little girl in his arms.

'Leave her with me for a while,' he begged. 'Now that she's sleeping. I'm sure she won't wake up for a long time.'

'I'll call you when I need you, nurse. You may go.'

The conversation revolved round a very well-stocked subject, and one that pleased Nucha immensely: the baby's charms. She most certainly had plenty of those, and whoever doubted it would be an utter fool. She opened her eyes with incomparable mischievousness. She sneezed so funnily, and held your finger so tightly with her little hand, you needed the strength of a Hercules to disengage yourself. And she performed even more little tricks, best omitted from the annals of history. When she talked about them, Nucha's bloodless face livened up, her eyes shone, and laughter spread across her lips once or twice. But all of a sudden her face clouded over, and tears flickered between her eyelashes, though she withheld them.

'They haven't let me feed her, Julián – one of Señor Juncal's silly ideas. He applies "hygiene" to everything. It's always hygiene this, hygiene that . . . I don't think it would have killed me to try for a couple of months. Just two months . . . I might even have felt better than I do now, and might not have had to spend such ages glued to this sofa, with my body tied down and my imagination roaming wild. Because, as it is, I don't get any rest. I'm always imagining that the nurse is suffocating the baby, or that she's going to drop her. But now I feel happy, having her so close to me.'

She smiled at the sleeping child and added:

'Don't you see the resemblance?'

'To you?'

'To her father! The shape of her forehead is exactly like his.'

The chaplain did not give his opinion. He changed the subject and continued that day and the following days to perform the act of charity of visiting the sick. During her slow convalescence and complete solitude, Nucha badly needed someone to devote himself to such a pious occupation. Máximo Juncal came on alternate days, but always in a hurry because his practice was expanding rapidly. He was even called for from Vilamorta. The doctor spoke about politics with a breath that smelt of rum, trying to provoke and anger Julián; and, in fact, had Julián been capable of getting irritated, he would have found good reason in the news Don Máximo brought. Nothing but accounts of antireligious outrages, churches being demolished, Protestant chapels being founded here and there, freedom of education, of religion, of this, that and the other . . . Julián limited himself to deploring such enormous excesses and wishing that things would mend, which did not give Máximo grounds enough to start one of his beloved arguments – so beneficial for the flow of his bile, and so rich in drama when he came up against bragging Carlist priests, like the abbot of Boán or the Rural Dean.

While the belligerent doctor was away, all was peace and calm in the sick-room. Only the child's crying disturbed it, and this was soon hushed. The chaplain read the *Christian Yearbook* aloud, and the air was filled with stories that had a novelesque and poetic flavour: 'Cecilia, a most beautiful young woman and a distinguished Roman lady, dedicated her body to Jesus Christ. Her parents betrothed her to a gentleman named Valerian and the wedding took place with many banquets, celebrations and dances. Only Cecilia's heart was sad . . .' There followed the account of the mystical wedding night, of the angel who guarded Cecilia in order to preserve her purity, of Valerian's conversion, and the ending of the glorious epic in martyrdom. At other times it would be the martyrdom of a soldier, like St Menna, or a bishop, like St Severus. The story would describe in dramatic detail the judge's cross-examination, the spirited and free answers given by the martyrs, and then the tortures – scourging with ox's sinews, the rack, the iron nail, the red-hot axes applied to the skin . . . 'And the heart of this knight of Christ was brave and calm, his face serene, his mouth filled with laughter, as though it were not he, but another who was suffering – laughing at his own tortures and asking for them to be increased . . .'

Such readings produced an air of unreality in the room, particularly when the austere winter afternoons drew to their close, the dry leaves swirled and danced about, and the thick cotton-wool clouds passed slowly across the panes of the deep window. In the distance one could hear the endless sob of the sluice, and the creak of the carts as they went along carrying maize stalks or pine-branches. Nucha listened attentively, her chin resting on her hand. From time to time her bosom rose as she heaved a sigh.

Not for the first time since the birth, Julián noticed a great sadness in the señorita. He had recently received a letter from his mother which he thought might hold the clue to Nucha's sorrows, for it seemed that Señorita Rita had inveigled the old aunt from Orense to name her the sole heiress, thus disinheriting her godchild. To add to this, it appeared that Señorita Carmen was getting more and more foolishly fond of her student, and it was believed in town that if Don Manuel Pardo did not give her his consent, the girl would ask for court protection. Terrible things were also happening to Señorita Manolita: Don Victor de la Formoseda had left her high and dry for a working girl, an artisan who was the niece of some canon. To end the letter, Old Mother Rosario asked God for patience to bear such tribulations – for any affliction that fell upon the Pardo household she considered as her own. If all this had reached Nucha's ears either through her husband or her father, it was not surprising that she sighed the way she did. On the other hand, her physical weakness was more than clear! The only figure of Our Lady that Nucha resembled now was the emaciated image of Our Lady of Solitude. Juncal took her pulse attentively, ordered her to eat the most nourishing food, and looked at her with grave concern.

The one thing that would cheer Nucha up was taking care of the baby, which she did with a feverish activity, wanting to do everything herself, only allowing the wetnurse the actual job of feeding the child. The nurse, said Nucha, was a barrel full of milk that was there so she could open its tap whenever necessary and let it gush out: no more than that. The comparison with a barrel was absolutely exact: the nurse had the shape, the colour and intelligence of a barrel. And like a barrel, she had a great belly. It was quite a spectacle to watch her eat, or, rather, gulp down her food: in the kitchen Sabel busied herself filling up her plate or cup to the very brim, putting half a loaf of bread in front of her, and stuffing her like a turkey. Next to such a fat, dull person, Sabel assumed the airs of a princess, and was like a model of delicate refinement. As everything in this world is relative, for the people below stairs in the manor house the wetnurse was like an amusing and ridiculous savage, and they laughed heartily at her blunders, when in fact they themselves were prone to make even worse ones.

The nurse was indeed a curiosity, not only for the country folk, but also – for different reasons – for an anthropologist. Máximo Juncal gave Julián some interesting details. In the valley where the nurse's parish lay – a valley on the Galician border with Portugal – the women are distinguished by their physical characteristics and their way of life: they are descendants of the Galician warrior-women that Latin geographers talk about. And though today they can wage war only with their husbands, they go around half-naked, displaying their strong, robust flesh, and breaking up clods of earth with the same fury with which they once fought. They plough, dig, reap, load up carts with branches and crops, bear enormous weights on their shoulders like caryatids, and live without the aid of man, for the men of the valley usually emigrate to Lisbon to look for jobs from the age of fourteen, and return to the country for only a couple of months, to get married and propagate their race, taking to their heels as soon as they have performed their duty as beehive males. Sometimes in Portugal they hear news of conjugal infidelities, and then, crossing over the border at night, they stab the sleeping lovers. This was the crime committed by El Tuerto, the 'wall-eyed', Barbacana's protégé, whose story Juncal had also told. However, the women of Castrodorna are usually as chaste as they are wild.

The wetnurse was true to her race in the inordinate width of her hips and the chubbiness of her coarse limbs. It was a great struggle for Nucha to dress her sensibly, and make her change the short green baize skirt that did not cover her calves for a longer, more dignified one. She allowed her to keep only her bodice – which is traditionally worn by wetnurses, for it lets the full udders overflow – and the typical huge ear-rings, the Roman *torquis* preserved in the valley from time immemorial; but she had to fight to make her wear shoes every day, because all her friends kept them for important feast-days. To teach her the name and use of each object, even the most simple and common ones, was quite a penance, and it was utterly useless to try to convince her that the girl she was suckling was a delicate, fragile being, and that, unlike the new-born of Castrodorna valley, she could not be carelessly wrapped in bits of red baize cloth or put in a wicker

Moses-basket with a bedding of fern and then be left under an oak-tree at the mercy of wind, sun and rain. Although a great believer in hygiene, Dr Juncal was also a defender of the miraculous virtues of Nature, and he found some difficulty in reconciling both extremes. He got himself out of the fix, however, by referring to the latest book he had read, Darwin's *The Origin of Species*, and applying certain laws of adaptation to environment, descent, and so forth, which allowed him to assert that the wetnurse's method, unless it made the child explode like a firecracker, would strengthen her admirably.

Nucha, however, had no such faith in the theory, and thus devoted herself to looking after her treasure personally, leading the busy, meticulous life of a mother, in which it is quite an event if the soup is burnt, and a catastrophe if the brazier goes out. She washed her little daughter, dressed her, swaddled her, watched her while she slept and amused her while she was awake. Life was busy, and at the same time monotonous. Kind Julián, a witness to all these chores, learned little by little what for him were the mysterious secrets of the cleaning and dressing of infants, and in the end became familiar with all the objects that form the complicated trousseau of the new-born: caps, navel bandages, napkins, swaddling-clothes, tiny crocheted shoes, bonnets and bibs. These garments were pure white, decorated with lace and embroidery, scented with lavender and warmed by the healthy heat of the brazier – a homely heat if ever there was one. They often lay on Julián's lap, while the mother, holding the baby face-down on her oilcloth apron, ran the sponge time and time again over the silky flesh, which was so excessively delicate it looked sore and almost broken. Then she would sprinkle refreshing starch powder on the skin, and squeeze the buttocks with her fingers to make dimples appear. She would show these to Julián and cry joyfully:

'Look, isn't she lovely? Isn't she getting nice and plump?'

Julián was not an expert on the nakedness of infants, apart from the cherubs on the altar-pieces. But he thought to himself that although original sin had corrupted all flesh, what he now beheld was the purest, most saintly thing in the world – as innocent as a madonna lily. The soft little head, covered by a fair, gentle down over the milk-crust, and with that special smell one notices in pigeon's nests where there are still unfledged chicks; the tiny hands, their skin already filling out with soft fat and their fingers curved like those of the Christ-child when he blesses; the face that looked like a pink wax sculpture; the toothless moist mouth, like a piece of coral just out of the sea; the little feet, their heels red with endless and amusing kicking: these were just some of the little delights that inspire such mixed feelings in even the hardest hearts – feelings both complex and humorous, combining compassion, selflessness, a little respect and a lot of gentle, unsatirical mockery.

For Nucha, now both nervous and frail, it was like a maternal honeymoon, something in which she could absorb herself fully. The soft bundle of what still seemed little more than a mass of gelatinous protoplasm had as yet no self-awareness and lived only for sensations. But its mother breathed her own soul into the child with wild kisses, and believed that the baby was so clever and intuitive that she understood everything and was deliberately being amusing in a thousand different ways – even discreetly mocking at what the wetnurse said and did.

'This is a form of delirium imposed on the señora by Nature with a very wise purpose,' explained Dr Juncal. And oh the day when for the first time a smile erased the seriousness, both grave and comical, of the tiny little face, and half opened, with a heavenly expression, the thin line of her lips! It was impossible not to think of the hackneyed simile of the light of dawn dispelling the darkness.

'Again, again!' cried Nucha. 'My darling, my little angel, my pretty little girl! Smile for Mama!' For the time being, however, the smile refused to appear again, and the stupid nurse denied the fact, which infuriated the mother. But the following day Julián had the honour of lighting the tiny, ephemeral light of the new-born intelligence, by waving some shiny trinkets before her eyes. He was slowly losing his fear of the baby girl, whom at first he had thought might easily dissolve like a meringue between his fingers; and while the mother wound up the swaddling bandages or warmed the napkin, he usually held her on his lap.

'I trust you more than I trust the nurse,' Nucha would say to him confidentially, relieving herself of her secret maternal jealousy. 'She's not even fit to take the sacraments . . . Imagine, to part her hair she places the comb on her chin and then runs it up over her mouth and nose until she finds the middle of her forehead. There's no other way she can do it. I have insisted that she doesn't eat with her fingers, so what happens? Now she eats roast meat with a spoon. She's a farce, Julián. One of these days she'll drop my baby.'

The chaplain perfected the art of holding a baby without it crying or getting angry. One day, there was a little incident which ought perhaps to be silently overlooked, but which strengthened Julián's friendship with the little one: holding the baby on his lap, he suddenly felt a certain damp warmth making its way through his trousers . . . What an event! Nucha and he celebrated it with roaring laughter, as if it were the most amusing and roguish thing. Julián jumped for joy, his hands on his waist, which hurt from so much laughter. The mother offered him her oilcloth apron, but he refused it: he was already wearing an old pair of trousers, destined to perish in the enterprise, and for nothing in the world would he deny himself the pleasure of feeling that warm flood . . . Its contact melted the strange snow of austerity that had set on his effeminate virgin heart back in the days of the seminary, when he had made up his mind to renounce having a family and home on earth by entering the priesthood. At the same time it lit a mysterious fire in him, a human tenderness that was both effusive and sweet. The priest began to love the child blindly, and to imagine that, if he were to see her die, he would die with her, and many other similar absurdities, which he glossed over with the idea that, after all, the baby was truly a little angel. He never tired of admiring her, of devouring her with his eyes, of examining her pupils, which were watery and nebulous, as if they were flooded with milk, and seemed to contain in their depths serenity itself.

A painful thought crossed his mind every now and then. He

recalled his dream of establishing Christian matrimony in that house, based on the model of the Holy Family. But this holy family had already broken up: St Joseph was missing, or, what was even worse, he had been replaced by a clergyman. The marquis was almost never to be seen. Instead of being more home-loving and sociable since the child had been born, he had gone back to his old tricks. He would go off to the homes of abbots and gentlemen who owned good dogs and enjoyed the woodland, and to far-off hunting-grounds. Sometimes he would spend a whole week away from the manor house. He spoke in harsher tones, his temper was more selfish and impatient than ever, and his wishes and orders were expressed more severely. And Julián noticed other signs that were even more alarming. It worried him to see that once again Sabel held court like a favoured sultana, and that La Sabia and her offspring, together with all the gossiping peasant women and ragged beggars of the parish, were there in swarms, fleeing quick as lightning when he approached, carrying with them, in their bosoms or under their aprons, suspicious-looking lumps. Perucho no longer hid. On the contrary, one found him everywhere, always getting tangled in one's feet. In short, things were returning to their previous state.

In his goodness, the chaplain tried to pull the wool over his own eyes and tell himself that none of this meant anything. But as luck would have it, he was forced to open his eyes when he least wanted to. One morning, when he rose earlier than usual to say mass, he decided to go and tell Sabel to have his chocolate ready in half an hour. He knocked in vain on the door of her room, which was near the tower where he slept. Then he went downstairs in the hope of finding her in the kitchen and, as he went by the door of the large office next to the archives, where Don Pedro had moved to since the birth of his daughter, he saw the girl coming out, carelessly dressed and looking drowsy. The psychological laws that apply to guilty consciences demanded that Sabel should have been the one to feel embarrassed, but in fact it was Julián who blushed. Not only that, but he went back upstairs with a strange feeling, as if someone had given him a strong blow on his legs and broken them. As he entered the room he said something to himself like, 'Let's see – which bright spark is going to say mass today?'

Chapter 19

Well, Julián was no such 'bright spark'. A fine mass he would have said, with his head swimming like that! Until he was able to bring his thoughts under some sort of control, and make a calm, objective decision about what he should do, he did not even dare think about the Holy Sacrament.

Quite clearly, things were back to the way they were the year before last, and it was equally clear that it was wrong for him to remain in that house another moment. He would have to leave, driven away by vice and vile wickedness. The Christian marriage, which, in a way, was his doing, had fallen apart and there was no trace left of a home, only a den of corruption and sin. It was therefore time to strike camp.

Only ... well ... some things are easier said than done. Everything seemed impossibly difficult: having to think of an excuse, take his leave, pack all his things up ... The first time he had thought of leaving the place, it had already seemed a hardship, but now it was worse: it felt as if a rag, dripping with cold water, had been thrown over his soul. Yet, why did the idea of leaving the manor upset him so much? After all, he was a stranger in that house. Well, not exactly a stranger ... because he lived spiritually united with the family, through respect, through loyalty, through habit. And then there was the baby. The very thought of her left him spellbound. He could not explain why he felt so miserable at the prospect of never being able to hold her in his arms again. It was just that he loved the dear little doll so very much! His eyes filled with tears.

'They were right in the seminary,' he mumbled unhappily, 'I'm spineless, I'm just like ... just like a woman, getting worked up over everything. A fine priest I make! If I'm so fond of children, I should never have embraced the vocational life. No, no ... What I'm saying now is even more foolish. If I like children and I feel it's my vocation to take care of them, who's to say I shouldn't look after the ones that go barefoot in the streets, begging for alms? They are just as much God's children as this poor little mite ... I know I was wrong, very wrong to grow so fond of her ... But the fact is that only a dog – no, not even dog – only a wild beast could kiss such a little cherub and not wish it well.'

Summing up his thoughts, he said to himself: 'I'm an idiot, a fool. I don't know why I ever came back here. I should never have returned. It was obvious that the señorito would end up doing this. I have only my own weakness to blame, for even if it was at the risk of my life I should have seen that rogue Primitivo off, if not by fair means, then with a whip. But I'm not a brave man, as the señorito rightly says, and, however coarse they might be, they are stronger and cleverer than me. They've tricked me, they've led me right up the garden path. I've failed to throw out that shameless hussy ... and they've laughed at me. Evil has triumphed.

As he kept up this monologue he took some articles of linen from a drawer and started packing, for like all irresolute people he tended to act impulsively at first, only then to adopt certain measures designed to deceive no other person but himself. Thus at the same time as putting his things into the valise, he began to follow a different line of reason.

'Lord, Lord, why does there have to be so much wickedness and stupidity in this world? Why must man let the Devil fish him with such a rough hook and such a mean bait' – as he said this he put a neat row of socks in the valise – 'and here we have a man who possesses the pearl of all women, the very image of female strength, the chastest of wives' – this superlative occurred to him while he was carefully folding a cassock – 'and then he has to go and mix himself up with such a trollop – a servant, a dishwasher, a shameless wench who'll tumble in the hay with the first farmhand she meets!'

As he reached this point in the soliloquy, he tried unsuccessfully to fit his shovel hat into the valise without squashing it. The soft, musical groan of the leather lid as it was being closed seemed to him like an ironical voice answering:

'That's the very reason!'

'But how is it possible?' mumbled the good chaplain. 'How can someone actually be attracted to sinful filth and abjectness, which like a hot pepper seems to stimulate the corrupt palates of the slaves of vice and increase their appetite for more! And here we're not just talking about any old people, but about people of noble birth, people of rank . . . Gentlemen, who . . .'

He paused, and thoughtfully counted out a pile of handkerchieves that lay on the top of the chest of drawers.

'Four, six, seven . . . I had a dozen, all marked with my name . . . A lot of clothes seem to get lost here.'

He counted again.

'Six, seven . . . And one in my pocket makes eight . . . There might be another one in the wash.'

Suddenly he let them drop. He had just remembered that he had tied one of those handkerchieves under the little girl's chin, to stop her dribbles wetting her neck. He heaved a deep sigh, and opening the valise once more, noticed that the lid had crumpled the silk on the shovel hat. 'It won't fit,' he thought, and the fact of not being able to find a place for it seemed to him an insurmountable obstacle to his journey. At ten, or just a little after, the little one would be eating her soup, and it was the funniest thing in the world to see her with her face smeared with mush, determined to grab the spoon but without ever managing to do so. She would look so sweet! He decided to go downstairs. Tomorrow he would find it easier to fit his hat in and make up his mind to go. Twenty-four hours more or less were not going to make much difference.

Delay, a soothing medicine, is usually an infallible remedy, and one should not condemn its use, considering the comfort it gives. After all, life is but a series of postponements, with only one definite conclusion, the last. Once Julián had had the brilliant idea of waiting a little, he felt calmer. In fact, better still, he felt happy. His character was not exactly jovial, for he was inclined to a sort of dreamy, morbid apathy, like an anaemic young girl. But at that moment he breathed with such relief after having found a solution, that his hands trembled, as with cheerful haste they unpacked the sausage of socks and undergarments and kindly gave freedom to the shovel hat and the long cloak. Then he rushed downstairs, heading for Nucha's room.

Nothing happened in the nursery that day to make it any different from the rest, for there the only change was in the greater or smaller number of times the baby was fed, or the amount of napkins put out to dry. And yet, in that calm interior, the chaplain could now see the development of a mute and terrible tragedy, and understood only too well Nucha's melancholy moods, her suppressed sighs. Looking into her face and seeing how emaciated it was – her skin the colour of earth, her eyes larger and more vague than before, her beautiful mouth always tightened, except when she was smiling at her daughter – he reckoned that she must perforce *know everything*, and a profound pity filled his soul. He scolded himself for even having thought of leaving. If the señorita needed a friend, a defender, in whom would she find one if not in him? And need one she most certainly did.

That same night, before going to bed, the chaplain witnessed a strange scene that confused him even further. As there was no oil left in his three-wick lamp, he could neither pray nor read, and therefore he went down to the kitchen to ask for fuel. He found Sabel's soirée very well attended. There was no room left for anyone on the benches surrounding the hearth: girls spinning, others peeling potatoes, and all listening to the ribald jokes of Uncle Pepe of Naya. This was an old rogue who, having come to grind a sack of wheat at the Ulloa mill, where he also planned to spend the night, saw no harm in enjoying himself in the manor house, eating the bowl of pork broth offered him by the hospitable Sabel, and paying for it by telling spicy stories. On the large kitchen table, which since Don Pedro's marriage had not been used by the masters of the house, the cloudy light of the lamp showed the remains of a more sumptuous feast – left-over meat on greasy plates, an opened bottle of wine, and half a cheese. Everything was piled up in a corner, as if it had been disdainfully shoved aside by those who had eaten to their full, and in the empty space about twelve cards were set out, which, although not oval from excessive use like the ones Rinconete and Cortadillo* played with, were certainly just as greasy and filthy. Standing in front of the cards, Señora Maria La Sabia stretched out her black knotted finger, which was like the dry branch of a tree, and consulted them thoughtfully. The horrendous, stooping sibyl, lit by the lively flames of the hearth and the light of the lamp, cut a fearful figure with her thick, tow-like hair: she looked like a witch at a sabbath, and was made even more monstrous by the now enormous goitre that deformed her neck and mimicked a second face, a face out of an infernal vision, with no eyes or lips, smooth and shiny like a cooked apple. Julián stopped at the top of the stairs, watching the superstitious practices, which would no doubt be interrupted if his slippers made a noise and betrayed his presence.

Had he properly understood that sinister and yet still undiscredited art of cartomancy, how much more interesting the spectacle would have been to him! He would then have been able to see gathered there, like the dramatis personae in a play, all those characters who played a part in his life and who occupied his imagination. That King of Clubs, with his blue smock edged in red, his feet symmetrically apart, the big green mace over his shoulder, would have seemed quite frightening to him had he known that he represented a dark married man – Don Pedro. The Knave of the same suit he would have considered less ugly if he understood that it symbolized a young lady, also dark – Nucha. The Knave of Goblets he would have kicked away as an insolent person and a drunk, for it represented Sabel, a fair unmarried girl. But the worst thing would have been seeing himself – a fair young man – represented by the Horse of Goblets, which was blue, to be precise, though all the colours had disappeared under the grime.

* *Rinconete and Cortadillo*, a novel by Cervantes (1547–1616).

And what would have happened, if then, after the hag had shuffled the cards and set them out in four piles in order to decipher their prophetic meaning, he had been able to hear distinctly all the words that came out of her appalling, cavernous mouth! An association between the Knave of Clubs and the Eight of Goblets signified no less than a long-term secret romance. The Eight of Clubs foretold quarrels between husband and wife. The Knave of Spades, coming with the Knave of Goblets upside-down, was a sombre omen of widowhood, through the death of the wife, even though later the Five prophesied a happy union. All this, uttered by the sibyl in a low, hollow voice, was listened to only by Sabel, the beautiful scullery maid, who, with her arms crossed behind her back and her cheeks flushed, bent over the oracle that seemed to provoke in her more curiosity than joy. The revelry with which Señor Pepe's jokes were received prevented anyone from hearing the old woman's halting voice.

Thanks to the position of the stairs, Julián was able to get a good view of the table – the tripod and altar of the fearful rite – and, without being seen himself, he could see and even hear a little. But as he leant on the banister to try to catch the words that he could hear only indistinctly, it creaked slightly, and the witch raised her horrible mask. In a flash she gathered the cards, and the chaplain came down, confused by his involuntary spying, but so worried about what he thought he had come upon that it did not even occur to him to censure the practice of witchcraft. The witch, using her customary humble and servile tone of voice, hastened to explain to him that it was just a way of passing the time, 'just a bit of fun'.

Julián returned to his room in a terrible state of mind. Even he did not know what was running through his imagination. He had always been aware that Nucha and her daughter were exposed to certain dangers by living in the manor house. But now . . . now he saw these dangers as imminent, and with utmost clarity. What a dreadful situation! The chaplain turned it over and over in his agitated mind: the baby girl would be stolen and starved to death; Nucha would probably be poisoned . . . He tried to calm himself down. Come now! Not that many crimes abound in the world, thank God. There are judges, magistrates, executioners. That gang of rogues would content itself with exploiting the señorito and the house, taking it over for their own camp, robbing him of his dignity and usurping his power. But . . . what if that was not enough for them?

He turned the wick up in his lamp, and with his elbows resting on the table, he tried to read the works of Balmes, lent him by the Naya priest, in which he found a gratifying spiritual relief. He preferred that pleasant, persuasive intelligence to the scholastic depths of Priscus and St Severinus. But that night he could not understand a single line of the philosopher's writings and only heard the sad sounds coming from outdoors, the constant groan of the sluice, the moan of the wind in the trees. His overheated imagination made him hear an even more sorrowful sound among those plaintive murmurs – a human cry. What an absurd idea! He paid no attention and went on reading. But once again he thought he heard the miserable cry. Could it be the dogs? He looked out of the window: the moon sailed in a misty sky, and in the distance the howling of a dog could be heard, that mournful howling of an animal supposedly on the scent of death, according to country folk, who are sure it predicts an imminent death in the neighbourhood. Julián shuddered and closed the window. He was not noted for his bravery, and his instinctive fears grew in the manor house, which once again produced the same sense of anguish it had given him on his first days there. His lymphatic temperament did not possess the secret of certain healthy reactions with which one can dispel any imaginary fear, every phantom of the imagination. He was capable, and had proved it, of facing up to any serious risk, if he felt that his duty required him to; but not of doing it with a calm spirit, with a fine disdain for danger, with the phlegmatic heroism that only people with rich red blood and strong muscles are capable of. Julián's courage was a shaky courage, one might say: the short-lived, nervous impulsiveness of a woman.

He was returning to his discourse with Balmes, when . . . The Lord help us! There it was again, and this time there was no doubt about it! A high-pitched scream of terror had come up the dark spiral staircase and entered through the half-open door. What a scream! Julián's oil-lamp trembled in his hands, as he ran quickly down the stairs without feeling he was even moving, like in those horrific falls one has in dreams. He flew through the rooms and passageways and finally arrived at the family archives, where it seemed to him the horrible cry had originated. The oil-lamp, flickering more and more in his trembling right hand, cast bizarre patches of shadow on the whitewashed walls. He was about to round the corner of the passage that divided the record-room from Don Pedro's, when he saw – Holy God! Yes, the very scene, exactly as he had imagined it – Nucha against the wall, her face distorted with fear, her eyes no longer vague but filled with a lost look of death. Before her stood her husband, brandishing a huge weapon. Julián flung himself between them and Nucha screamed again.

'Oh, oh! What are you doing! It's getting away, it's getting away!'

The misguided chaplain then realized what was happening, much to his embarrassment and confusion. Scuttling up the wall, trying to flee from the light, was an inordinately large spider, a monstrous belly swinging on eight hairy stilts. It ran so fast that the señorito's attempts to catch it with his boot were unsuccessful. Suddenly Nucha stepped forward, and in a voice that was both grave and frightened, artlessly repeated what she had said a thousand times in her childhood:

'St George – stop the spider!'

The ugly creature stopped when it reached the shadows, and the boot fell on it. Julián, in a natural reaction to dispel fear that has turned to unimaginable joy, was about to laugh at the incident, but he noticed that Nucha, closing her eyes and leaning against the wall, was covering up her face with a handkerchief.

'It's nothing,' she sobbed, 'a few nervous tears ... It will pass ... I'm still a bit weak ...'

'What a lot of fuss about nothing!' cried the marquis, shrugging his shoulders. 'You're so spoilt! I've never seen anything like it. Don Julián, you must have thought the house was falling down! There, can we go back to bed now? Good night.'

The chaplain took a long time to fall asleep. He reflected upon his fears and admitted they had been ridiculous. He promised himself to try to overcome his feebleness, but a sense of unease remained lodged in the most inaccessible parts of his brain and no sooner had sleep granted him its favours than a legion of nightmares appeared, each one blacker and more oppressive than the last. He began by dreaming about the manor, about the large ramshackle house. But as is usual in this state, in which reality has been jumbled up, confused and disarranged by the anarchic influence of the imagination, he did not see the old warren as he usually saw it: a vast oblong mass with enormous halls and a wide, harmless-looking doorway – a dull, almost monastic eighteenth-century building. Now, although still recognizably the same place, it had changed its shape: the garden with boxwood trees and ponds was now a wide, deep moat; the thick walls were filled with arrow-slits and crowned with battlements; the doorway had become a drawbridge, with creaking chains – in other words, a real medieval castle with even the romantic detail of the Moscoso standard floating above the keep. No doubt Julián had seen some painting or read some fearful description of these ancient horrors, which our century restores with such loving care. The only thing that the castle had in common with the manor itself was the majestic coat of arms. But even this was different, for Julián could clearly see that the stone emblems had been animated so that the pine was a green tree, with the wind moaning in its topmost branches, and two rampant wolves moved their heads and let out doleful howls. Julián was looking up in fascination to the top of the castle, when he saw an alarming figure: a knight in full armour, his visor down. Although not even one of his fingers was visible, Julián, with that gift for divination that one acquires in dreams, could see Don Pedro's face through the helmet. With a furious, menacing look, Don Pedro raised a strange weapon, a steel boot, which he was going to let drop on the chaplain's head. The latter made no movement to avoid it, nor did the boot ever stop falling. It was an intolerable anguish, an endless agony. Suddenly he felt that a horrible-looking owl, with matted feathers, was perching on his shoulder. He wanted to shout, but in a dream shouts remain stuck in the throat. The owl laughed silently. To get away from it, Julián jumped into the moat. But it was no longer the moat, for it had turned into the mill-sluice. The feudal castle also changed shape inexplicably: now it looked more like the classical tower that in pictures St Barbara holds in her hands, a painted cardboard construction, made of neat little squares. The pale, distorted face of a woman was looking out of the window. The woman brought out a foot, then another. She started to climb out of the window and let herself down. How amazing! It was the Knave of Clubs, the same filthy, greasy Knave of Clubs! At the foot of the castle the Horse of Spades was waiting for her, a strange blue animal, with black stripes on its tail. But soon Julián realized his mistake, for it was no Horse of Spades! It was really St George in person, the valiant knight-errant of the heavenly forces, with his dragon underneath, a dragon that looked like a spider, and in whose claw-like mouth the knight boldly dug his spear. The shining sharp spear came down, thrust itself in, deeper and deeper. The surprising thing was that Julián could feel the thrust of the spear in his own side. He wept very softly, wanting to cry out for mercy. But no one came to his help and the spear had run right through his body . . . He woke up with a start, feeling a painful stab in his right hand on which the full weight of his body had rested as he lay on his left side – the position most favourable for nightmares.

Chapter 20

Nightmares often seem ludicrous when the new day dawns, but, as Julián jumped out of bed next morning, he was unable to shake off the thought of his, and his over-excited imagination still ran wild. Looking out of the window, the view seemed to him sombre and sinister: large, lead-like clouds with their pale reflections formed an awning over the sky's vault, and the wind whistled intermittently, bending the trees with sudden gusts. The chaplain went down the spiral staircase intending to say mass, which, because of the bad state of the manor-house chapel, he was in the habit of celebrating in the parish church. On his return, when he approached the entrance of the house, a whirl of dead leaves surrounded his feet, a cold wind made him shudder and the big stone mansion seemed an imposing, frowning and even terrifying sight: it reminded him of a prison, or the castle he had seen in his dreams. Under the canopy of black clouds, and with the fearful sound of the cold north wind whistling through it, the house looked grim and menacing.

Julián entered with his heart full of fear. He hurriedly crossed the freezing cold hall, the cavern-like kitchen, and a few empty rooms, until he was able to take refuge in Nucha's room, where he was usually served chocolate at the señorita's orders.

He found her looking more worried than usual. To her normal look of dejection was added a tautness and a bewilderment that indicated great nervous strain. She was holding her daughter in her arms, and, when she saw Julián, she quickly signalled to him not to say a word or move about, for the little angel was growing drowsy with the heat of her mother's bosom. Leaning over the baby, Nucha breathed on her to help her fall asleep, and with feverish movements arranged the knitted shawl that was wrapped round the new-born baby, like a cocoon around a caterpillar. The baby blinked two or three times, and then closed her little eyes, while the mother rocked her to sleep with a lullaby she had learned from the wetnurse – a sort of wail based on the sad *lai, lai!*, the long, slow moan of all Galician folk songs. The singing became softer and softer until it ended with the melancholy and loving pronunciation of a single note, a long, drawn-out 'ee'. Then, standing on tiptoe, Nucha placed her daughter in the cradle with great delicacy and care, for the little girl was so bright – in her mother's opinion – that she could immediately distinguish the cradle from the arm, and would wake up from the deepest of sleeps if she was aware of the substitution.

For that reason Julián and Nucha spoke very quietly, while the señorita crocheted a pair of boots that looked like little bags. Julián began by asking whether she had got over the fright of the night before.

'Yes, but I'm still feeling a bit shaky.'

'I'm not very fond of those disgusting creatures, either,' said Julián, 'I hadn't seen such fat ones until I came here. In town there are hardly any.'

'Well, before,' answered Nucha, 'I used to be very brave, but since ... since the baby was born, I don't know what's the matter with me. It's as if I'd become stupid, I'm frightened of everything.'

She interrupted her work to look up. Her large eyes were dilated, her lips trembled slightly.

'It's an illness, a sort of phobia ... I'm aware of it, but I can't help it, no matter how hard I try. My mind's weak. I think only of frightening, horrifying things. Just look how I screamed last night because of the wretched spider! Well, at night, when I'm left alone with the baby – when the nurse is asleep she may as well be dead, she wouldn't wake up even if you fired a huge cannon-ball in her ear – I would be making scenes like that one every moment, if I didn't control myself. I don't tell Dr Juncal because I'm ashamed. But things look so strange to me. The clothes I hang up seem like corpses hanging on the gallows, or dead men that have come out of their coffins wearing their shrouds. It makes no difference even if I rearrange the things before I go to sleep, when the lamp is still alight. As soon as I've turned out the lamp and lit the candle, these strange creatures always appear. Sometimes I see people with no heads. Other times, I can see their faces with every feature, their mouths gaping and grinning. Then the silly figures painted on the screen start moving; and when the windows creak with the wind, like last night, I start wondering whether they are souls from the other world, groaning – '

'Señorita!' cried Julián painfully, 'that goes against the faith! We must not believe in apparitions and witchcraft.'

'But I *don't* believe in them!' answered the señorita laughing nervously. 'Do you think I'm like the nurse who says she has really seen the *Compaña,** with its procession of lights, in the middle of the night? Never in my life have I believed in such nonsense. That's why I say I must be ill, when I'm persecuted by such visions and horrible monsters. Señor Juncal is always insisting on getting one's strength up and producing new blood. What a pity one can't buy blood in shops, don't you think?'

'And what a pity those of us who are healthy can't give it to ... the ones who ... need it.' The priest said this hesitatingly, blushing down to the nape of his neck, because his first impulse had been to cry out: 'Señorita Marcelina, here's my blood at your service!'

The silence created by such a strong outburst lasted a few seconds, during which both speakers, their minds absent and thoughtful, fixed their gaze upon the view that could be seen from the deep, wide window facing them. At first they did not notice it, but then, even against their wishes, the sombre vision began to make its way through their eyes into their souls: the mountains, black, hard and massive under the dark roof of the stormy sky; the valley, lit up by the pale rays of an anguished sun; the chestnut-trees, some still, others violently shaken by

* The *Compaña* was, in Galician rural superstition, a procession of souls that emerged from the village graveyard at night.

sudden gusts of furious wild wind . . . A sight that made both the chaplain and the Señorita cry aloud at the same time, 'What a miserable day!'

Julián reflected on the curious coincidence of Nucha's terrors and his own, and, thinking aloud, he burst out:

'Señorita, the truth is that this house – well, it's not that I wish to speak badly of it, but . . . it's a bit eerie, don't you think?'

Nucha's eyes livened up, as if the chaplain had guessed a feeling she had not dared to reveal.

'Since winter has set in,' she murmured, almost talking to herself, 'there's something about the house, about the way it looks . . . It just doesn't seem the same to me. Even the walls have become thicker and the stones darker. It's foolish, I know, but I hardly dare come out of my room, whereas before I used to explore every corner and wander about everywhere. The only answer is to take a walk around. I need to see if downstairs, in the basement, there are trunks for the linen. Please come with me, Julián, now the baby is asleep. I want to drive these fears and silly ideas out of my mind.'

The chaplain tried to dissuade her: he was afraid she would tire herself, that she would catch cold going through all those halls on the way down to the cloister. The señorita's answer was to leave her work, wrap herself up in her shawl and start walking. They crossed the row of large, unfurnished, almost empty rooms at a good pace, their footsteps echoing dully. Every now and then Nucha betrayed her anxiety by turning her head to make sure her escort was following her, and by swinging a bunch of keys with her right hand. They came out into the upper cloister, and then, descending a very steep staircase, they headed for the lower one, which had stone arches.

When they reached the small courtyard enclosed by the solemn cloister, Nucha pointed at a pillar with an iron ring buried in it, from which still hung a rust-eaten link.

'Do you know what that was?' she mumbled in a low voice.

'No, I don't,' answered Julián.

'Pedro says it's where his grandparents used to chain up a

black slave. Doesn't it seem incredible that such cruelties were committed? What terrible times those were, Julián!'

'Don Máximo Juncal, who can only think about politics, is always talking about that. But mark my words, all times have their stretch of bad road. People are pretty barbaric these days too, and religion is in a bad way since all this uproar.'

'But here,' Nucha observed, putting in simple words a historic and philosophical observation of great significance, 'one sees only the past atrocities of the old aristocracy. So they seem to be the only ones that count. Oh, how can people be such bad Christians?' she added, with her mouth half open in innocent wonder.

As Nucha spoke, the sky grew darker. Then a flash of lightning suddenly lit up the depths of the cloister's arcade, and in the greenish light the señorita's face took on a tragic look as in a holy picture.

'St Barbara protect us!' the chaplain pronounced devoutly, with a shudder. 'Let's go back upstairs, señorita. I hear thunder. We didn't have bad weather for St Francis's feast this year, so now the equinox is demanding this. Shall we go up?'

'No,' said Nucha, determined to fight her own fears. 'This is the door to the basement. I wonder which is the right key?'

She took some time to find it in the bunch, and, when she put it into the keyhole and pushed the door open, there was another flash of lightning and the basement was lit by a ghostly clarity. The thunder rolled, slowly at first, then harsh and formidable, like a voice that was swollen with anger, and Nucha stepped back in terror.

'What's the matter, señorita? What's the matter?' shouted the chaplain.

'Nothing . . . nothing at all!' she stammered in reply. 'When I opened the door, I thought I saw a great big dog there, sitting down, and that he was getting up to attack me . . . How silly I am! I could have sworn I saw it.'

'In the sweet name of Jesus! No, señorita, it's just that it's cold here. There's more thunder. It's mad to go and rummage around the basement now. You go back, I'll look for whatever you need.'

'No,' replied Nucha energetically. 'I'm really fed up with being such a simpleton. I want to go in ahead so you can see I am perfectly aware that this is all nonsense . . . Have you got the match?' she cried from inside.

The chaplain lit the match, and in this less than certain light they saw the basement. That is to say, they could just make out the walls, which oozed dampness, and a jumble of useless objects left down there to rot away in a corner – shapeless things, whose shapelessness made them even more sinister and mysterious. In the subterranean darkness, in the pile of old mementos now pensioned off as obsolete and left to the rats, the foot of a table looked like a mummified arm, the face of a clock was the white face of a dead man, and the worm-eaten riding-boots, sticking out from under a pile of papers and rags, made one imagine that the corpse of a murdered man lay hidden there. Nevertheless, Nucha went boldly towards the damp, macabre muddle and, with the choked and shaky voice of someone who has just achieved a great personal triumph, she shouted:

'Here's the trunk! Have them bring it up to me later.'

She emerged in a lively mood, pleased with her persistence, having won the hand-to-hand fight with the large ramshackle house that frightened her so much. As she went back up the narrow staircase, she was startled once again by the roar of an even stronger clap of thunder, nearer and louder than the previous ones. They decided to light the pentecostal candle and say the Trisagion at once. The candle was placed on Nucha's chest of drawers: a long candle of orange-coloured wax, with lots of drips and a wick that spat out sparks and never quite burnt properly. Before they knelt they closed the wooden shutters to stop the lightning flashes continually dazzling them. The wind roared with growing anger, and the thunderstorm settled over the manor house, so that it sounded like a herd of wild horses galloping over the roof, or a giant rolling a huge boulder over the tiles. The chaplain said the mysterious Trisagion with such urgency! With his spirit overwhelmed by the divine anger whose violence shook the building and made it tremble like a hut, he prayed:

From death unforeseen,
From thunder and lightning
deliver us, and bless us
with this Trisagion . . .

Suddenly Nucha stood up, screamed, and ran to the sofa, where she lay down and let out broken hysterical laughs that sounded like sobs. Her trembling hands tore off the hooks on her dress, pressed against her temples, grabbed the sofa cushions and tore at them furiously. Despite his lack of experience, Julián realized what was happening: the inevitable fit, the outburst of suppressed fear, the price to pay for poor Nucha's boasts of courage.

'Filomena, Filomena! Come here, woman, here! Water, vinegar . . . That little bottle . . . Where's the bottle from the Cebre chemist's? Undo her dress . . . Of course I'm already turning my back, woman, there's no need to tell me . . . Put some cold cloths on her temples . . . Never mind the thunder! Don't worry about that . . . Look after the señorita . . . Fan her with this piece of paper, it's better than nothing . . . Are her clothes loose – and is she covered? I'll give it to her, a little bit at a time . . . She must take deep breaths of the vinegar.'

Chapter 21

Some days later a general improvement was noticed in the señora's health, and with that the chaplain also began to look more cheerful. The marquis, meanwhile, was totally absorbed in the preparations for a hunting-expedition to the distant mountains of Castrodorna, beyond the river. The weather was settling: the nights were frosty, clear and icy-cold; the moon was almost full, and everything indicated a happy outcome to the expedition. The night before setting off, the hunters all came to sleep at the manor: the notary from Cebre, Señorito de Limioso, the priests from Boán and Naya, and a poacher, who was an infallible sharpshooter known as Mouse-face – a most appropriate nickname given his dark skin and his small, lively, darting eyes. The house was filled with the scratch of the dogs' claws on the wooden floors, the tinkle of their tiny collar bells, and the deep-voiced orders of the men to have all the hunting-gear ready at dawn. At dinner everyone was lively and boisterous: they joked, counted in advance the number of partridges they would catch, savoured in their minds the provisions they were taking to the woodlands, and in anticipation wet their whistles with jugs of a glorious vintage red wine. Nucha was worried about the baby and retired early, before the dessert and coffee were served. At that point Primitivo and Mouse-face came up from the kitchen to fraternize with their future comrades in glory and woe, who began smoking and drinking in competition with one another. It was the moment they all relished, the real instant of spiritual happiness for a true hunter: the time for telling hunting-stories, especially tall hunting-stories.

Each patiently waited his turn, for no one would give up the chance to tell his own tall tale – which became taller and taller as the night went on. The hunters formed a circle, and the dogs, all with one eye closed and the other quivering and half-open, curled up at their feet. Sometimes, when the laughter and jokes abated, the dogs could be heard 'strumming the guitar' – getting rid of their fleas like a full orchestra playing – or barking in their sleep, shaking their ears and sighing in resignation. No one paid any attention to them.

It was Mouse-face's turn to have the floor:

'You may not believe me, but it's as true as we're all going to die and the earth will swallow us up! To be precise it happened on one St Sylvester's Day – '

'The witches must have been loose,' interrupted the Boán priest.

'I don't know whether they were witches or hobgoblins. But as true as we'll have to account for our deeds before the Lord, what I tell you is what happened to me. I was after this partridge, all stealthy like' – Mouse-face had a habit of acting out everything he said and so crouched down low – 'for I had neither dog nor devil with me and I was, if the honest company will excuse the expression, on the point of getting my leg over a fence like it were a horse, when I hear pit-a-pat, pit-a-pat, pit-a-pat! A hare, which was as quick as lightning! Well, sirs, it turns its head just like this . . . and, if the gentlemen will excuse my words, I grabs me gun tighter than a papal bull . . . and suddenly, bam! Something from another world flies over my head, and I fall off the fence.'

A general outburst of laughter, protests and questions ensued.

'Something from another world?'

'A soul from purgatory?'

'But was it a person, or an animal, or what the devil was it?'

'Open the door! There's not enough room for that lie in here!'

'It's true, may God help me!' cried Mouse-face, looking extremely hurt. 'It was, if you'll forgive the expression, that damned hare, who jumped over me and knocked me down with my feet in the air!'

The explanation caused general hysteria. Don Eugenio, the abbot of Naya, was almost bursting with laughter, and tried helplessly to protest as he held his sides with both hands, tears rolling down his cheeks. The marquis gave a loud guffaw. Even Primitivo smiled dully. Good old Mouse-face could not open his lips without making everyone laugh again.

Hunters love practical jokes and whenever they get together you will always find a clown, an entertainer, an unfailing comedian and this was, by right, the role of the poacher, who here willingly offered to play it. Being used to spending days and nights in the open, waiting for a hare, rabbit or partridge; accustomed to tightening his waist with a rope, the way savages do, on the many occasions when he did not have a crust of bread to take to his mouth, poor old Mouse-face was happy when he could go hunting with worthy people, of the sort who take wineskins swollen with mellow wine, cooked shoulders of pork and cigars on their hunting-expeditions. He felt proud when they laughed at his preposterous stories. Every day he told them with greater seriousness, conviction and ingenuousness, and defended himself from their ragging by calling upon God and the saints in heaven above to support his outlandish claims.

Standing up, his hands in the pockets of a pair of trousers so full of patches they looked like a map of the world, he comically twitched his nose and mouth, which was the colour of rancid pork fat, while he waited for someone to ask for a new story as credible as the one about the hare. But now it was Don Eugenio's turn.

'Do you know,' he said, still tearful and choking with laughter, 'the story of what happened between the canon of Castrelo and a very amusing gentleman called Don Ramírez de Orense?'

'The Castrelo canon!' cried the Boán priest and the marquis together. 'Now there's a real rascal! His lies are as big as the cathedral tower.'

'Wait and see, then, wait and see how he found his perfect match where he least expected to. It happened one night, in the Casino, when they were playing ombre. Castrelo, as usual, started telling hunting-stories . . . Real whoppers! When he had had enough, he wanted to make them swallow the biggest lie of all, and so he said, with a straight face: "You know, one morning

I went out to the woods, and there, in some bushes, I heard something . . . well . . . something suspicious. I went closer, very slowly. The noise persisted. I went a bit nearer, until I was sure that here was a piece of game waiting for me. I loaded the gun, took aim, and fired. Bang! And what do you think I killed, gentlemen?" Everyone started to name different animals: a wolf, a fox, a boar, and one even suggested a bear. But Castrelo shook his head, until finally he came out with: "It wasn't a fox, or a wolf, or a boar . . . What I killed was a Bengal tiger!"'

'Come on, Don Eugenio! You can't mean it!' the hunters all cried in chorus. 'Even Castrelo wouldn't go as far as that. Didn't they break his jaw then and there?'

Unable to make them hear, Don Eugenio made signals with his hands to show that the best part of the story was still to come.

'Patience!' he cried at last. 'I haven't finished. Well, gentlemen, you can imagine the uproar that ensued in the Casino. They started to insult Castrelo, calling him a liar to his face. Only Señor Ramírez kept his composure and he tried to calm the noisy ones down. "Don't look so surprised. I'll tell you something that happened to me when I was out hunting that's even stranger than what happened to Señor Castrelo." The canon looked at him suspiciously, but everyone listened carefully. "Well, gentlemen, one day I went out to the woods and I heard, in the bushes, something . . . something suspicious. I went closer, very slowly, until I was sure that here was a piece of game waiting for me. I loaded the gun, took aim, and fired. Bang! And what do you think I killed, canon?"

'"How the devil am I to know?" answered Castrelo. '"I suppose it was a lion."

'"Bah!"

'"All right, then, it was . . . an elephant!"

'"Rubbish!"

'"It was . . . whatever you like, damn it!"

'"It was the Jack of Clubs, canon!" cried Ramírez, "It was the Jack of Clubs!"'

This provoked an uproar. Mouse-face laughed with a sort of sharp hiccup, Señorito de Limioso in a deep, grating voice, and the Boán priest, not knowing how to vent his mirth, stamped his feet on the floor and banged on the table.

'Hey, Mouse-face!' shouted Don Eugenio. 'Have you never come across a tiger? Have another drink and tell us, man.'

Mouse-face emptied the pint-tankard, his small eyes sparkling. Then he wiped his lips on the cuff of his filthy jacket and declared in a sincere and naïve tone of voice:

'Tiggers? No . . . There can't be any round these hills, or I'd have killed 'un. But I'll tell you what happened to me once, on Our Lady of August's Day – '

'At ten past three in the afternoon?' asked Don Eugenio.

'No . . . It must have been about eleven o'clock in the morning, and maybe not even that late. But believe it, for it's as true as there's daylight! I was on my way back from going after some pigeons in a field, and I met Pepe of Naya's little girl, who was leading a cow like this.' He mimicked tying a piece of rope round his wrist.

' "Good morning."

' "Good morning to you," I says.

' "Will you let me have the pigeons?" she asks.

' "And what will you give me for them, girl, eh?"

' "I haven't got a miserable ochavo," she says.

' "Then let me suck from your cow, for I'm dying of thirst," I tells her.

' "Suck then, but don't take it all," she says. So I kneels down like this' – Mouse-face half knelt in front of the abbot of Naya – 'and squeezed the udder, if you'll forgive the expression, and swallowed up the milk. It was lovely and fresh.

' "Well, girl," I says, "may St Anthony look after your cow!" I walk on, and about half a mile further I come over all drowsy like. And my head goes all dopey. So I think, have a sleep! I go up into the woods, and I get to where there are some gorse bushes as big as men. I lie down like this – with your permission – and take off my hat, and leave it on the grass like this – that's how I left it. Did I sleep? I didn't come back to life for over an hour and a half. Then I'm about to pick up my hat and go on and as true as we all here must die and rise from the dead on

Judgement Day, I find, underneath it, a snake as fat as my right arm – if you'll excuse the expression!'

'But not as fat as your left arm?' interrupted Don Eugenio mischievously.

'Much, much fatter!' continued Mouse-face unperturbed. 'And all curled up in a cirle, so it fitted underneath . . . and fast asleep, like a little saint!'

'But it wasn't actually snoring, was it?'

'The rascal had come there because it smelt the milk. And then it had the idea of hiding under the hat. But I knew what it was up to. It wanted to get down my throat, forgive me, gentlemen!'

Although this produced a great uproar, it was slightly subdued by the Boán priest, who recalled various occasions in which similar cases had been described: snakes found in stables sucking from the cows' teats, others sliding into babies' cradles to drink the milk in their stomachs.

Julián took part in the gathering, amused and happy, because the merriness and good mood of the hunters drove away the distressing ideas he had had a few days back – his fear of La Sabia, of Primitivo, of the manor house, and of the dark premonitions increased by Nucha's nervous terrors. Seeing that he was in such high spirits, Don Eugenio pressed him to come and pay them a visit at the hunting-grounds. Julián refused, with the excuse that he needed to say his office and celebrate mass, but the truth was that he did not wish to leave the señorita completely alone. In the end, Don Eugenio insisted so much that he had to promise, putting it off until the last day.

'Nothing of the sort!' cried the boisterous priest. 'Tomorrow morning we take you with us. And you can come back early the day after tomorrow.'

All resistance would have been useless, and more so at that particular moment, when the revelries increased as the level of the wine in the jugs went down. Moreover, Julián knew that such roguishly playful people were likely to take him by force if he refused to go with them willingly.

Chapter 22

Julián was thus obliged to leave at dawn on his gentle donkey, his teeth chattering. He became the butt of the hunters' jokes, as he was dressed most inappropriately for the occasion, with neither sheepskin jacket, leather gaiters, hunting-hat, nor any kind of offensive weapon. The new day was clear and magnificent: crystal dew-drops shone on the grass, the earth shuddered with the cold and steamed slightly with the first caresses of the sun. The lively energetic steps of the hunters echoed on the hard, frosty earth as if it were a parade ground.

They reached the hunting-ground at about nine o'clock and then dispersed into the woodland. Not knowing what to do with himself, Julián stayed by Don Eugenio's side, and watched him as he shot down two partridge fledgelings and put them into his gamebag, still warm from the life that had just been snatched from them. It must be said that Don Eugenio was not famous for his shooting skills, which is why, when the hunters gathered at midday for lunch in a secluded oak-grove, the Naya priest called upon Julián as a witness to prove he had shot them on the wing. 'And what does "on the wing" mean, exactly, Don Julián?' they all asked him. Seeing that the chaplain fell silent when such an insidious question was put to him, it occurred to the hunters that it would be amusing to give Julián a rifle and a dog and let him try to shoot something himself. Whether he liked it or not, he had to accept. They chose for him an infallible setter called Chonito, a brave hound with a cleft muzzle, the pluckiest, most trustworthy of all the dogs there.

'As soon as you see the dog stop,' Don Eugenio explained to the inexperienced hunter, who hardly knew how to hold the deadly weapon, 'you get ready and encourage him to go in. And when the partridges fly out, you aim at them and fire. It's the easiest thing in the world.'

Chonito walked with his nose to the ground, his muscles quivering with excitement. Every now and then he would turn round to make sure the hunter was following him. Suddenly he trotted off to a heather bush, and came to a dead stop, standing like a statue, tense and motionless, as if he had been cast in bronze to be placed on a plinth.

'Now!' cried the Naya priest. 'Julián! Tell him to go in.'

'Go in, Chonito, go in,' the chaplain muttered half-heartedly. The dog, being surprised at the gentle tone of the order, hesitated, but at last he threw himself into the heather, and at the same moment a fluttering was heard, and the flock flew out in all directions.

'Now, you fool, now! Shoot!' shouted Don Eugenio.

Julián pulled the trigger . . . The birds flew swiftly away and disappeared in a second. Chonito looked in bewilderment at the person who had fired the shot, then at the rifle, then at the ground. The noble animal seemed to be asking with his eyes where the wounded partridge was, so he could retrieve it.

Half an hour later the same scene was repeated, as was Chonito's disappointment. Nor was that the last one, for further on, in a ploughed field, the hound raised such a large number of them, so near and so much within range, that it was almost impossible not to knock down two or three partridges by just shooting straight into the flock. Once again Julián fired. The setter barked with joy and enthusiasm. But no partridge fell. Then Chonito, giving the chaplain an almost human look full of spite, turned his back on him and ran off at full speed, without deigning to listen to the imperious shouts with which he was being called back.

There is no way of exaggerating how this trace of canine intelligence was applauded at the dinner-table. Julián was made fun of, and in penance for his clumsiness was condemned to go immediately, tired as he was, to join the hunters who lay in wait for hares.

That December night the moon looked like a polished silver disc hanging from a dark-blue glass dome. In that almost boreal clear stillness, the sky seemed to have become wider and higher. The air began to freeze, with thousands of tiny pin-pricks tightening the skin and thickening the blood. For the hare, however, dressed in its soft, thick fur, it was a night for feasting – on the tender shoots of the pine-trees, the fresh dewy grass and the sweet-smelling plants of the forest – and a night for love. A night for chasing the shy young maiden with the long ears and short tail, startling her, catching her and dragging her to the dark depths of the pine wood . . .

On nights such as these the hunters wait in ambush sometimes for hours behind the pine-trees and the bushes. Lying face down, the barrel of the rifle covered with a piece of paper so that the smell of the gunpowder does not alert the keen-scented hare, they put their ears to the ground. And when the fitful patter of the prey echoes clearly in the ice-hardened ground, the hunter shudders slightly and then, half-kneeling, he puts his rifle to his right shoulder, lowers his sight and twitches nervously at the trigger. Then, in the clear moonlight, he sees a grotesque monster leaping prodigiously in the air, appearing and disappearing like a vision. In the alternating darkness of the trees and the spectral moonlight, the harmless hare looks enormous, its ears gigantic, its leaps acrobatic and fearful, its movements astonishingly quick. But the hunter, his finger on the trigger, restrains himself and does not fire. He knows that the phantom that has just crossed his path within range is the female, the pursued Dulcinea desired by countless lovers in their ardour: modesty compels her to hide during the day in her warren, and she comes out at night, tired and hungry, to eat the tips of pine-shoots, followed by at least three or four anxious males who are melting with love and yearning for romantic adventure. And if the hunters allow Dulcinea to pass, her nocturnal suitors will without fail continue their mad pursuit – even if a shot rings out and cuts a rival down, even if they trip over the blood-stained corpse, even if a whiff of gunpowder warns them: 'At the end of this idyll, death awaits you.' No, nothing will stop them. The hares might, in a moment of instinctive cowardice for which they are known, crouch down for a second behind a bush or rock. But at the first scent of love on the breeze, at the first hint of female breath among the pines, the hot-blooded lover will set off again with renewed vigour, mad with love, convulsed with desire. Then the hunter, who lies in wait, will pick them off one by one, and they will finally come to lie at his feet, on the very grass that they had dreamed of for their bridal bed.

Chapter 23

For some time now the chaplain had had a joyful and victorious rival for the tender heart of the Ulloa heiress: Perucho, whose mere presence in the nursery was enough to ensure his triumph ever since the day he had first crept in on tiptoe and gone right up to the cradle without being heard. Nucha often gave him sweets and money, and the boy, as often happens with domesticated animals, became overfamiliar, outstaying his welcome until finally he would have to be banished from the room. He seemed to get everywhere, especially when he was least expected, and behaved like a kitten that has been spoilt by too much pampering and attention.

Perucho was wholly captivated by the little one, who fascinated him even more than Linda's puppies, the cow's suckling calf or the new-born chicks breaking out of their shells. He would ponder for hours on how such a novelty had appeared, and on where it had come from. He hovered continually around the cradle, despite the risk of being cuffed on the ear by the wetnurse. He would stand for ages – until he had to be thrown out – totally entranced, sucking his thumb like one of those garden cupids who seem to be saying 'hush'. He had never been seen to stay still for so long at a time. As for the baby, when she became aware of the world around her, she made it clear that if Perucho was interested in her, she was no less interested in him. They took each other's stock immediately, and acknowledged the fact with clear signs of mutual satisfaction. As soon as the baby caught sight of Perucho, her eyes would light up and she would begin to gurgle lovingly – dribbling at the same time, for she was now teething. Then she would stretch out her hands, and

Perucho, understanding instinctively what she wanted, would put his head close to her, his eyes shut tight, and let her tug at his curly hair or poke him in the mouth and nose to her heart's content, gurgling happily, or occasionally shrieking for joy if, for example, she discovered an ear.

As babies get older and they start teething they often become more irritable and, when this happened to Nucha's baby, Perucho was often used as a lucky charm to calm her down. On one occasion the baby screamed so much that Nucha was driven to the desperate remedy of sitting Perucho on a low chair and placing the baby in his arms. He sat wide-eyed and motionless, a picture of innocence, and the baby soon forgot her tears and laughed, her mouth wide-open, her eyes sparkling and her little legs kicking frantically. The boy was so enchanted he did not dare even blink.

As the baby began to take more notice of things, Perucho brought her little toys of his own devising, which amused her enormously. He never failed to find something – a flower, a bow made of cane, even a little bird, which of course was what the baby loved best. Living toys were his speciality and he brought in all manner of horrid little things. Once he turned up with a frog held by a piece of string tied to its leg, which wriggled grotesquely; another time he produced a pathetic, terrified new-born mouse. In his moth-eaten cap he kept salamanders, butterflies and ladybirds; down his shirt-front, as well as the odd piece of fruit, he kept worms and birds' nests. The señorita would pull his ears kindly and say, 'I'm warning you . . . If you bring any of these disgusting things in here again I'll . . . I'll hang you over the chimney like a string of sausages and smoke you!'

Julián turned a blind eye to these little intimacies until he discovered the existence of other, far less innocent ones. Ever since he had caught Sabel emerging early one morning from her master's room, Julián's heart had missed a beat every time he found the boy in the nursery and noticed how affectionate Nucha was with him. Then one day he went in to find a totally unexpected scene. In the centre of the room stood a huge tub full of steaming hot water, in which both Perucho and the baby sat naked, hugging each other tightly. Nucha, squatting beside the tub, watched them closely. 'It was the only way I could get her to have a bath!' she cried, noticing Julián's astonishment. 'And as Dr Juncal says bathing is good for her . . .'

'I'm not surprised at seeing her in the bath – it's him . . . He's more frightened of water than he is of fire.'

'If it meant he was allowed to be with the baby he'd sit in boiling tar. Look at them, they're so happy. They're just like brother and sister, aren't they?' As she said this, the look on Julián's face changed profoundly. Nucha, noticing this, got up and stood before him. Her face was pale and emaciated by the long illness, but her big, dreamy eyes, surrounded by thick dark rings and black eyelashes, flashed a sudden certainty, mixed with amazement and fear. She did not speak, either because she was unable to, or because she wanted to conceal her evident agitation.

The little girl smiled happily in the water as Perucho rocked her back and forth, talking tender nonsense and running the water over her legs as he had seen Nucha do. They were in one of the smallest rooms in the house, divided in two by a large, dilapidated eighteenth-century screen. A fantastic landscape was painted on it, with trees like rows of lettuces, mountains like cream cheese and clouds like bread rolls; there were also little two-dimensional houses, each with a red roof, two windows and a door. Behind the screen was Nucha's bed, with its gilt headboard and Salomonic pillars, and the baby's cradle. Nucha stood motionless for a few moments, and then suddenly bent down and seized the baby from Perucho's arms.

Surprised by this sudden rough interruption of her fun, the baby broke into sobs as her mother, paying no attention to her protestations, took her behind the screen and quickly put her in the cradle and covered her with a blanket. She came back and grabbed Perucho, who was so shocked that he had remained in the water, dragged him roughly out of the bath and chased him, still naked, out of the room. 'Get out!' she screamed, her eyes blazing and her face paler than ever. 'And don't dare come back! If you do, I'll whip you, d'you understand? I'll whip you!'

She went back behind the screen, followed by a dazed, bewildered Julián. Señora Moscoso, her head bowed, arranged the baby's nappies, not attempting to conceal the shaking of her hands. 'Call the nurse,' she ordered curtly, her lips trembling.

Julián ran to do as he was told, but was obstructed by something lying on the floor outside the door. He looked down and saw Perucho, still naked and curled up in a ball, large tears glistening on his face, and his chest sighing with silent sobs. Feeling sorry for the child, the chaplain picked him up. His skin, still wet, was blue with cold.

'Come and get your clothes on,' he said. 'Take them to your mother and she'll dress you. Don't cry.'

Perucho had a Spartan's resistance to pain, and thought only of the injustice he had suffered. 'I wasn't doing anything wrong,' he stammered, choking. 'I wa-wasn't doin' anything wrong . . .'

Julián fetched the nurse, who fed the baby, but she took a long time to calm down: she would put her mouth to the breast, and then turn away, whining. Nucha, walking like an automaton, emerged from behind the screen and went towards the window, signalling to the chaplain to follow her. Both distraught, they exchanged looks for some moments – Nucha with a persistent, questioning gaze, Julián in return trying to be evasive, even deceitful. What can seem an insurmountable problem, when looked at in the cold light of reason, can often be solved instinctively in a moment of crisis. Thus it was that Julián resolved on the spur of the moment to lie unscrupulously.

Finally Nucha spoke, her voice trembling. 'This isn't the first time that I've thought he might be my husband's son. But I didn't believe it . . . Until, that is . . . I only had to see the look on your face.'

'Lord above, Señorita Marcelina! What's my face got to do with it? Please don't get worked up, I beg you! This is the devil's doing . . . Lord above!'

'I'm not getting worked up!' she cried, breathing heavily and running her hand through her hair.

'In heaven's name, señorita, you don't look well. You're a strange colour . . . Take some medicine, I'm afraid you might have one of your turns.'

'It's nothing. I often feel like this . . . as if I've got a lump stuck in my throat . . . and as if someone's boring a hole in my temples. But don't try to get out of it, tell me what you know. Tell me everything.'

'Señorita . . . I can't be responsible for my face' – Julián now resorting to what is known as Jesuitic subterfuge, the natural recourse of those who hate lies but who nevertheless fear the truth – 'What an idea! I wasn't thinking anything of the sort. Indeed not, señora, indeed not . . .'

She looked the chaplain in the eyes, questioning him closely as he resorted more and more to Jesuitic caution – picking up the sharp knife of truth by the blunt end, so to speak.

'Believe me . . . Why would I lie to you? I don't know who the child's father is. No one knows for certain. It's presumably the girl's lover . . .'

'So she has a lover? Are you sure?'

'As sure as daylight.'

'And this lover . . . Is he one of the young men in the village?'

'Yes, señora. A handsome youth he is too – the one who plays the bagpipes at the fiestas. I've seen him here hundreds of times, and I've seen them . . . together. In fact I know for sure they were trying to get the papers ready to get married. So you see . . .'

Nucha breathed normally again, and put her hand to her throat as if to touch the lump she felt there. She had calmed down somewhat, though she had still not regained her composure or her usual air of gentleness. She frowned, with a vague look in her eyes.

'And to think my little girl was hugging him,' she mumbled. 'No matter what you say, Julián, or how hard you swear, this must stop. How can I go on like this? You should have told me sooner. If that woman and the boy don't leave, I think I'll go mad! I'm not well, and these things hurt . . . they really hurt.' She smiled bitterly, and added, 'I don't have much luck, do I? I've never done anyone any harm, I only married to please Papa . . . and look how things have turned out.'

'Señorita – '

'Don't you deceive me as well, Julián' – she stressed the 'as well' – 'You were brought up in my house, and for me you're one of the family. I've no other friend here . . . Please advise me.'

'Señorita,' declared the chaplain, in earnest. 'I wish I could wash away all your cares. If I could, I would gladly shed my own blood.'

'Either that woman gets married and leaves,' said Nucha, 'or . . .' She did not continue. Sometimes the mind can figure a solution of such extreme violence that the tongue, being more cowardly, dare not speak.

'But Señorita Marcelina, stop worrying yourself to death like this. It's all in your imagination.'

Her hand, which was burning, reached out and touched his. 'Tell my husband to throw her out, Julián. By the Lord Jesus Christ and His Holy Mother . . .'

The contact of her feverish hands, and the imploring tone of her voice moved the chaplain deeply and, without thinking, he blurted out:

'I've told him that several times!'

'You see!' she cried, shaking her head and wringing her hands.

A silence fell between them. They could hear the hoarse squawking of the crows outside in the fields, while behind the screen the baby whimpered inconsolably. Nucha shivered and then struck the window-pane with her fist, saying, 'In that case I'll tell him!'

The chaplain mumbled, as if saying office. 'Señorita, please. Put an end to these thoughts . . . Let it be . . .'

Nucha closed her eyes and leaned against the window, trying to control herself, trying to save her energies and her peace of mind in the face of that terrible storm. But the shudder that ran down her back betrayed the tyranny of her nervous system, taking control of her weakened metabolism. Finally she stopped shivering and turned round, her eyes dry, her nerves under control once again.

Chapter 24

It was not long after this that the quiet, sleepy life of Los Pazos was transformed by the arrival of a certain witch with far greater powers than Maria La Sabia: politics – if indeed the tangle of squalid intrigue that passes as such in the villages deserves that name. Everywhere, it is true, politics is a cloak for self-interest, hypocrisy and lack of principle. But in the city there can at least be an element of greatness in the outward show, and sometimes in the tenacity of the fight. And the very scale of the urban battlefield lends the squabble some dignity, as greed becomes ambition and material profits are at times sacrificed for the idealized profit of victory for victory's sake. In the country, on the other hand, not even the hypocrites and demagogues pretend to be interested in the loftier, universal issues. Ideas have no part in the game, only people, and the issues at stake are the meanest imaginable: petty grudges, personal enmities, miserly gains and primordial vanities. In short, a full-scale naval battle staged on the village pond.

However, it must be said that, during the Revolution, political extremism (when belief in one system or another reaches the point of fanaticism) spread to even the furthest corner of the land, like a gale blowing away the fetid stench of everyday intrigue. The fate of Spain hung at the time on a debate that was carried on not only in the Cortes, but across the entire land, whether in munitions factories or in mountain wildernesses. Every two or three weeks a new issue arose, which had to be debated, demonstrated over and decided once and for all – complicated issues, which legislators, sociologists and statisticians would take years to ponder over, but which the revolutionary mob could now resolve in a matter of hours, with a heated debate in the Cortes or a noisy demonstration in the streets. Between breakfast and lunch, society would be radically reformed, and later, over the cigars, new theories would be hatched. But at the centre of the whirlpool, the battle raged between the two great historical systems of the Spanish people, long nurtured and matured into strength: absolute monarchy versus constitutional monarchy, which in those days appeared under the guise of 'democratic monarchy'.

The commotion caused by this confrontation was felt throughout the land. Even in the wild mountains around Ulloa, people were talking about politics. Religious freedom; human rights; the abolition of conscription; federation; 'plebiscites' (pronounced in all sorts of ways) – these were the subjects that filled the Cebre taverns at fair-time. The priests would linger in the church porches after mass, and exchange excitedly all the latest snippets of information about the troubles, such as the first campaign of those famous 'four sextons'. Señorito de Limioso, who, like his father and grandfather before him was an inveterate traditionalist, had made two or three mysterious trips to Miño, across the border with Portugal, and it was rumoured that he had met up with certain big shots in Tuy. It was also said that the señoritas of Molende were frantically busy making cartridge-cases and goodness knows what other weapons, and that they were regularly being tipped off that their house was going to be searched.

However, those who knew what they were talking about realized that any attempt at an armed uprising in Galicia would be a washout, and that despite all the rumours about the mustering of troops and the appointment of officers in Portugal, the real battle would be fought not in the fields but in the ballot-boxes. Though that, of course, did not mean that it would be any the less bloody.

Control of the region was at the time in the hands of two local *caciques* – one a lawyer, the other the town secretary of Cebre. The town and surrounding district trembled under their power. They were perpetual enemies, and their struggle could only end, like those of the Romans, in the defeat and death of one or other of the combatants. The full chronicle of their exploits, with all their intrigues and acts of revenge, would be endless. But, lest anyone should fail to take them seriously, certain crosses met by travellers on the wayside, certain charred remains of houses, certain men condemned to life imprisonment, were testaments of their savagery.

It should be pointed out that neither entertained any political conviction or gave a hoot about the burning issues of the day in Spain. But for reasons of expediency each one represented and upheld a party and a particular creed. Barbacana, who, before the Revolution, had been a moderate, now declared himself a Carlist. Trampeta, who had been a Unionist in O'Donnell's day,* had now progressed to the extremes of victorious liberalism.

Barbacana was the more serious, authoritarian and obstinate, the more ruthless when it came to revenge; he was also more avaricious and hypocritical, and better at covering up the ways in which he stole the bread from the mouths of the local tenant farmers. Added to this, he was a man who preferred to make use of the law in his battles, declaring that there was no surer way of dealing with an enemy than wrapping him up in red tape; and although Barbacana may not have decorated the roadsides with many crosses, the stinking rural prisons in the past, and the town walls of Ceuta and Melilla in the present, held a great deal of evidence to prove the extent of his power.

Trampeta too, as one would imagine from his nickname (the Trickster), was fond of lawsuits. But on the whole he was more impetuous and violent than Barbacana, and was not quite so adept at covering his tracks, so that he had at times been caught out by his adversaries and almost defeated. On the other hand, he was extremely bold and had a fertile imagination, which enabled him to extricate himself from the most awkward situations. Barbacana's strength lay in planning an attack from behind his desk, and later staying on the sidelines; Trampeta, however, would carry it out in person – and would win. Both

---

* Leopoldo O'Donnell y Jorris (1809–67), Spanish soldier and politician of Irish descent; founder and leader of the Liberal Union party.

men were hated in the district, but it was Barbacana who inspired the greater fear because of his fierce temper.

In the present circumstances, since he represented the party currently in power, Trampeta felt certain of impunity, even if he were to burn down half the town and beat up, sue or imprison the other half. Barbacana, however, with his superior intelligence and education, was aware of two things: he had his back to a wall that would not fall down – friends who would not betray him; secondly, that, should he decide to defect to the opposing camp, he could always overthrow Trampeta and assume the leadership himself. He had already planned his strategy in the forthcoming election for parliamentary representatives.

Trampeta worked with boundless energy to pave the way for the victory of the government's candidate, and often went to the provincial capital to consult with the governor there. On such occasions the Cebre town secretary, preferring to be safe than sorry, made sure he carried a brace of pistols and went accompanied by one of his toughest men, for he was well aware that Barbacana employed some extremely ruthless characters – in particular a wall-eyed man from Castrodorna. Each visit Trampeta made to the capital was a resounding success, both for himself and his party, as, one by one, Barbacana's followers fell by the wayside. Soon Trampeta held in his pocket not only the police, the prison-guards, the government storekeepers and the municipal roadworkers, but all the officialdom of Cebre. The only one he was unable to unseat was the judge, who was protected by his wife's influential relations. Thanks to the extent of Trampeta's machinations, many of the things he did were winked at, or a blind eye was turned to them. Given this, as well as his own innate abilities, he was able to put his hand on his heart and declare himself 'fully responsible' for the outcome of the Cebre election.

Meanwhile, Barbacana was keeping a low profile. His support for the candidate proposed by the Carlist Assembly in Orense (who was also backed by the rural Dean of Loiro and others of the more active clergy, such as the priests of Boán, Naya and Ulloa) was only lukewarm, done out of a sense of duty, as it were. He made it clear that he did not expect the party to win the election. The candidate was a good man from Orense; he was well-educated and thoroughly traditionalist, but he had no connection with the district and, besides, his lack of political guile was self-evident. Even his supporters were unhappy with him as a candidate, seeing that he was more at home behind a desk than in the rough-and-tumble of political intrigue.

This is how matters stood when it was suddenly remarked that Primitivo had begun to make frequent visits to Cebre. And, as one can do nothing there without being seen, it was also noticed that, as well as his usual stint at the tavern, Primitivo passed many hours with Barbacana. The lawyer virtually never ventured out of the house now, except occasionally and then only with Primitivo, for Trampeta had begun to go around swearing – power having completely gone to his head – that Barbacana could expect to get his due in some dark alleyway. A number of influential clerics and local bigwigs were seen coming and going from Barbacana's house – many of whom were also visitors at the manor. And as it is impossible to keep a secret between three – let alone three dozen – the government and the people soon heard the great news: the Assembly's candidate was withdrawing of his own free will, and instead Barbacana was supporting an independent candidate, Don Pedro Moscoso, known as the marquis of Ulloa.

As soon as he discovered this, Trampeta seemed struck with an attack of St Vitus's dance. He made numerous trips to the capital, where his comments to the governor, and the excuses he made to him, were well worth listening to.

'It's all a plot – set up by that prize pig, the Dean, and the trouble-maker priest from Boán. They set to work on the majordomo at the manor, an out-and-out usurer who can get his uncouth master to do whatever he likes since he got tangled up with his daughter. I ask you, what kind of a candidate have the neo-Catholics got themselves this time? At least the other one was a gentleman!' He raised his voice to a shout on the word gentleman.

The governor, observing that the town secretary was completely losing his sang-froid, realized that things must really be going badly, and demanded angrily:

'I thought you took full responsibility for the outcome of the election – no matter who stood against us?'

'Indeed, indeed,' Trampeta answered hurriedly. 'But you must take into account that no one could have imagined such an extraordinary turn of events . . .'

He blurted out in incoherent fury that no one could have expected the marquis of Ulloa, a señorito who thought about nothing except hunting, to start meddling in politics; and that although his family had great influence and he himself was respected by the local gentry and clergy, as well as by the peasants, he would have been doomed to failure if Barbacana hadn't taken him up – and if Barbacana had not been in league with a certain person of influence who had hitherto vacillated between the two opposing factions. This was none other than the aforementioned majordomo, who was as sly and resolute as a fox, and who could count on a good many votes from all the people who owed him money. He had made himself rich by underhandedly sucking dry the House of Ulloa and, now that he had joined forces with that master of the writ, Barbacana, the villain would snatch the whole district from them if they didn't deal with him once and for all.

Anyone who knows anything about the conduct of elections will not be surprised to hear that the governor soon had the telegraph humming and promptly arranged for the removal of the Cebre judge – despite his influence – and the few of Barbacana's protégés who still held on to their posts. The governor had hoped to win Cebre without resorting to foul play, for although he knew that it was unlikely any party would actively take up arms there, on the other hand he was well aware that all too often blood was spilled over a ballot-box. But the situation now ruled out any half-measures, and demanded that he grant Trampeta an absolutely free hand.

While the town secretary was laying his plans, the lawyer did not exactly stay in bed. The señorito's acceptance of the candidature had made Barbacana wildly happy. Don Pedro was without any political beliefs, though he was inclined towards despotism, innocently believing that it would bring the restoration of entails and other such things that appealed to his aristocratic pride. Apart from this, he shared the peasants' indifference and scepticism and was incapable of dreaming, like the chivalrous hidalgo from Limioso, of anything as quixotic as leading 200 men across the Miño border. It was not conviction that had led Don Pedro to accept the candidature, but vanity. He was the noblest person in the district, and the most important. His family, since time immemorial, had been the foremost among the local aristocracy. These were the facts used by the Rural Dean of Loiro to convince him that the representation of the district was really his by right. Primitivo, for his part, did not rely on eloquence in his support of the Dean's proposal, but simply clenched his fist and declared: 'We've got the whole place – like that!' His use of the plural was not insignificant.

From the moment the news spread, Don Pedro was flattered by the attentions of countless people – all the local gentry, most of the clergy and most of Barbacana's faction, led by the man himself. It all went to Don Pedro's head. He was well aware of Primitivo's machinations behind the scenes, but when all was said and done it was him they were paying homage to. He was in an excellent mood these days, and very affectionate with his daughter, for whom he ordered a new embroidered dress so that the Molende señoritas could admire her (for they had promised at least a hundred votes towards the victory of the mountain aristocracy's representative). And, as candidates court the Deputy's post in the same way as they might court a young lady, taking great care of their appearance and showing off their good looks to best effect, so Don Pedro too smartened himself up (having more or less neglected his appearance since his return from Santiago). Indeed, as he was then in his prime and extremely manly-looking, the ladies of the party could relish the fact that they were sending such a handsome representative to the Cortes – these being the days when a man's political career depended on every detail, including his figure, hair and age.

There was now open house at the manor. Filomena and Sabel were continually running backwards and forwards with trays of sherry, *tostado* and biscuits. The tinkle of coffee-spoons and the chink of glasses filled the air above stairs, while below, in the kitchen, Primitivo received his guests with rough Borde wine and huge plates of fish, meat and cabbage. Often the two groups, from upstairs and down, would join up, and then they would argue, laugh, and tell risqué stories, continually interrupting each other. They skinned, metaphorically speaking, Trampeta and his cohorts alive with a hatchet (to say with a scalpel would give too fine an impression). Puffing on their cigars and chuckling, they ransacked the whole rag-bag of dirty tricks on which the town secretary's fortune was based.

'This time we'll really get them *quoniam*!' said the priest from Boán, an old braggart with blazing eyes, who enjoyed the reputation of being the best shot around, after Primitivo.

Nucha did not attend these 'committee meetings'. She saw to the arrangements of the never-ending banquet, but did not partake herself. In fact she was never to be seen, unless the occasion absolutely demanded it. Julián was also absent from the company, except on rare occasions, and even then never said a word – confirming the abbot of Ulloa's opinion that these daintified priests were useless. However, as soon as the committee discovered that Julián not only had elegant handwriting but also could spell, he was put to work drawing up the more important electoral communications.

He was also given another duty. The Rural Dean of Loiro had known Don Pedro's mother, Doña Micaela, well, and now wished to revisit the house where she had lived and the chapel where he had occasionally celebrated mass when the señora – God rest her soul – was still alive. Don Pedro grudgingly showed him round, and the Dean was scandalized at the state of the chapel. It was virtually without a roof, and the rain fell directly on to the altar; the clothes of the statues hung in tatters and everything was in a state of total neglect, exuding the air of stark melancholy peculiar to abandoned churches. Julián himself had long tired of dropping hints to the marquis about the need for repairs, but the Dean's astonishment and criticism touched Don Pedro's pride, and he decided that now was a particularly opportune moment to make a good impression by having the place smartened up a bit.

The building was swiftly retiled, and a painter, brought in from Orense, transformed the interior by painting and gilding the main and side altars. Don Pedro proudly showed off the restoration work to various priests, señoritos and friends of Barbacana. The only task that remained was to repair the vestments and altar-cloths, and dress the statues. This Nucha set herself to do, guided by Julián, and thus, tucked away in the lonely chapel, they were both spared the incessant noise made by the electoral committee. Between them, they undressed Saint Peter, combed out the Virgin Mother's curls, sewed trimmings onto St Anthony's coarse woollen robe and scrubbed clean the infant Jesus' halo. Even the alms box, dedicated to the souls in purgatory, was carefully cleaned and varnished, revealing the tortured naked souls, surrounded by red flames, in all their disturbing grotesqueness. Julián enjoyed this work immensely. The hours flew by in their silent retreat which smelled of fresh paint and bulrush – brought by Nucha to decorate the altars with. As he busied himself by attaching a silver leaf to a wire stalk, or wiping down a glass case with a damp cloth, a great sense of peace filled his soul and he felt no need to talk. Sometimes Nucha did no more than sit on a low chair with the baby in her arms (she would not be parted from her for a single moment) and give out orders. Julián then worked as hard as two people, climbing his step-ladder to reach the highest part of the altar-piece.

In their conversations together he did not dare broach any confidential matter, such as whether or not the señorita had yet managed to resolve the matter of Sabel with her husband, but he noticed her air of dejection, the black rings around her eyes, her frequent sighs . . . and he drew the obvious conclusion. There were other symptoms also, which set his imagination running and gave him great cause for concern. For some time now

Nucha's maternal affection had been over-intense, and, if she lost sight of the child, she would immediately set off to look for her, in a state of great anxiety. Once, when the child was not where she thought she would be, she started screaming hysterically:

'They've taken her away from me! They've taken her away from me!'

Fortunately, on that occasion the nurse had appeared at once, carrying the baby in her arms. At other times Nucha would kiss the child with such frenzy that she made her cry, or else she would gaze at the little girl with such a sweet, ineffable smile that Julián could not help but think of the Virgin Mary and wonder at the miracle of motherhood. But the moments of peace were rare compared to those of fear and anxious affection, which were almost continuous. As for Perucho, she could not bear to have him anywhere near her, and her expression changed whenever she caught sight of him. He, for his part, would forget his usual devilish pranks and his fondness for the stables, in order to lie in wait at the chapel door and thus see the baby. Then he would babble away to her and she would shriek with angelic joy, wriggling in her nurse's arms in an attempt to go to him.

One day Julián noticed a turn for the worse in Nucha: not only did she look sad, but she was beginning to show signs of a deep physical and emotional decline. Her eyes were red and swollen, as if she had been crying for hours on end. Her voice was strained and weak, her lips dry from fever and lack of sleep. He saw in this not the thorn of pain working its way slowly under the skin, but the dagger thrust in to the very hilt. It was enough to make him forget his usual reticence.

'Señorita, you are not well. Something is wrong with you today.'

Nucha shook her head and forced a smile.

'There's nothing wrong with me.'

'For heaven's sake, señorita, don't deny it. I can see something's wrong. Señorita Marcelina . . . St Julián give me strength! Can't I help you in any way? Let me comfort you. I'm useless, I know, but my intentions are as great as any mountain. I beg you from the bottom of my heart, tell me how I can help you!' As he spoke he rubbed a cloth dabbed in chalk over the metal frame of a prayer-card, but without looking at it.

Nucha raised her eyes, and for a moment they flashed with an impulse to cry out and ask for help . . . But she only shrugged her shoulders and said again, 'There's nothing wrong with me, Julián.'

On the floor was a basket of hydrangeas and ferns, ready to put in the vases. Nucha began to arrange them with the graceful skill with which she carried out all her domestic tasks. Julián, entranced yet at the same time heart-broken, watched the delicate hands place the blue flowers into the earthenware jars. A large, clear drop of water, which was not dew, fell onto the leaves, and at the same time Julián noticed with horror a dark, round purplish mark on her wrist . . . With sudden clarity his mind flashed back to events of two years ago and he heard once again the groans of a woman being hit with a rifle-butt. He remembered the kitchen, the fury of the marquis . . . Totally beside himself he dropped the prayer-card and seized Nucha's hands to check that what he had seen was really there. At that very moment the chapel door was flung open and in walked the señoritas from Molende, the Cebre judge, and the abbot of Ulloa – all led by Don Pedro, who had brought them to admire the restoration work. Nucha turned hurriedly. Julián, confused, could only stammer when the young ladies greeted him. Primitivo, who brought up the rear of the party, fixed him with a penetrating stare.

Chapter 25

An election – with all its acrimonious suspicions, promises, recriminations, relentless toing and froing, letters flying here and there – makes life intolerable. Indeed, if it was not for the fact that it is soon over, it would surely kill those involved, through stress and total exhaustion. As for the poor inhabitants of the manor stables – the donkey, the mare and the fine young stallion recently acquired by the majordomo for his own use – all agreed on the inconvenience of the parliamentary system and, as they panted and sweated from so much exertion, their minds were full of unkind thoughts on the subject of elections.

And as for the little mule on which Trampeta made his visits to Santiago, it had grown so thin its ribs were sticking through! The *cacique* was to be found making the same journey night and morn, as every day brought further complications and the outcome of the election seemed ever more doubtful. In despair Trampeta shouted at the governor that it was time to make a show of force. They had to intimidate and cajole the voters, and had to replace certain people in key positions with others. And, above all, the Government's candidate had to untie his purse-strings, for they were losing their hold on the entire region.

'But, did you not say,' shouted the governor one day, wishing the town secretary in hell, 'that this election was not going to cost us money? Did you not say that the opposition had nothing to spend? That the Carlist Assembly wouldn't give them a centimo, and that the manor, despite all the rents it collects, was always stony-broke?'

'Indeed, indeed,' Trampeta replied, 'all this is true enough. But there are times when a leopard does, so to speak, change his spots, as you yourself would say' – this last was one of Trampeta's favourite phrases – 'Now, the marquis of Ulloa – '

'He's no more a marquis than I am!' the governor interrupted, impatiently.

'Well, it's customary to call him that . . . And believe me, I've spent the last month telling everyone that he's no marquis, that the Government stripped him of the title to give it to a liberal . . . And that the one who'll give him the title back is Carlos VII at the same time as he brings back the Inquisition and the tithes. As you yourself would say – '

'Get on with it!' The governor was in a state of nervous tension on this particular occasion. 'You were saying that the marquis or whatever he is . . . in the present circumstances – '

'Thinks nothing of spending a couple of thousand duros, more or less, señor.'

'As he has not got the money, I presume he has borrowed it?'

'Exactly. He asked his father-in-law in Santiago to lend it to him, but as you yourself would say, he's not got a peseta either . . . So it follows that he must have asked his father-in-law in Ulloa.'

'Does this Carlist have two fathers-in-law then?' asked the governor, who despite everything enjoyed listening to the town secretary's gossip.

'Well, if he has, he won't be the first, as you yourself would say,' said Trampeta, laughing. 'You know who I'm talking about, of course . . . ?'

'You mean the girl who lived at the house before Moscoso married, and who he had a son by . . .? See how I remember these things!'

'The son – only God knows for sure who he belongs to, señor, for I think the girl herself might be in some doubt – '

'But all this has damn all to do with the elections. Let's get to the point, which is the money Moscoso has at his disposal.'

'It's provided by his "natural" father-in-law, the majordomo, Primitivo. And now, you might ask, how is it that a simple majordomo can possess thousands of duros? Well, I'll tell you: by lending at eight-per-cent interest a month – more when the harvests fail – and by intimidating everyone into paying him back on time, and not a single peseta short. But, I hear you say, where does Primitivo, or this thief rather, get the money to lend in the first place? The answer: from his own master's coffers – stealing from him when he sells his produce. Not all the money he makes at market reaches the marquis. And so he cheats the estate, one way and another. Now, I hear you say – ' This was one of Trampeta's favourite rhetorical devices, designed to convince his audience. But the governor interrupted him.

'And I *will* say it myself, if you don't mind. What exactly does this scoundrel stand to gain by lending his master the thousands of duros he has taken such pains to rob him of?'

'Hell's bells! Primitivo wasn't born yesterday, you know. Money isn't lent without mortgages, securities. This way his capital is safe and his master's tied hand and foot.'

'I see, I see,' the governor exclaimed. And just to prove his understanding of the situation, he added: 'And of course he wants the señorito in the Cortes so that he himself can have more influence, and then do what he likes.'

Trampeta regarded the governor with that mixture of irony and amazement with which the lower classes always react to stupidity in their superiors.

'As you yourself would say, governor,' he declared, 'he wants nothing of the sort. Don Pedro, whether he's in the opposition or an independent, or whatever, will be a dead loss for his supporters. If Primitivo had come to you, or to that Jew – begging your pardon – Barbacana, he would have got whatever he wanted well enough, without having to get his boss made a Deputy. And Primitivo was always on my side, until he took to this game. There's no fox more cunning than him in the whole province. Mark my words, he'll get the better of Barbacana and me yet.'

'So why has Barbacana come out in support of the señorito?'

'Because Barbacana will always side with the priests, no matter what. He knows what he's doing. You, for instance, are here today and gone tomorrow, but the priests are here for good, like the aristocrats – the Limiosos and the Méndezes.' Then, giving vent to his rage, the *cacique* swore. 'God's blood! Until we deal with Barbacana we'll get nowhere in Cebre!'

'Exactly. But tell me how we are supposed to deal with him. I'm only too willing.'

Trampeta looked thoughtful, scratching his beard with a stubby, tobacco-stained thumb. 'What I can't understand is this: exactly what does that scoundrel stand to gain by getting his master elected? Certainly, he stands to gain on two counts: he'll fleece him with the mortgage and, as you yourself would say, he'll present a pretty hefty bill for his campaign expenses. But if they win and his honour Don Pedro sets off to Madrid and then starts borrowing money from someone else there – and of that you can be sure – then the marquis will start to realize what a crook his steward is. And he'll forget too all about the girl and her child. So . . .'

He scratched his beard again, like a man trying to unravel the most complicated of problems. But despite his keen mind, he was defeated by it.

'Let's get back to the point,' insisted the governor. 'What matters now is not to suffer a humiliating defeat. Our candidate is the minister's cousin, and we've promised to get him elected.'

'Against the committee of Orense's candidate.'

'Do you think they are going to listen to excuses like that? We should be able to defeat anyone. Let's not beat about the bush. Are we going to end up with egg on our chin over this?'

Trampeta looked doubtful. Then he lifted his head with the pride of a great strategist, always ready with a plan to trap the enemy.

'Listen. Up to now Barbacana has never got the better of me, despite his dirty tricks. When it comes to tricks of any sort neither he nor the devil can beat me. The trouble is, my best ideas only come when the shooting starts. Then Lucifer himself couldn't match me. I can feel things starting to stir up here' – he tapped his dark forehead – 'but try as I might nothing's coming out yet. However, it will, when the time comes.' He flung his fist in the air, as if it held a sword, and declared in a hoarse voice: 'That's enough of worrying – we're going to win!'

While the town secretary was thus engaged in intrigue with the highest civil authority in the province, Barbacana was receiving the Rural Dean of Loiro, who had decided to go to Cebre in person to find out how matters were progressing.

The Dean, who was known in Santiago by the nickname *Monsieur Sachet pour la poste*, after an innocent attempt at refinement when buying stationery in a shop, made himself comfortable in the lawyer's office, sniffing at a silver snuff-bottle full of ground macouba – a kind of snuff that no one but he used in the whole of Galicia, obtained for him by smugglers at vast expense. There had been a time, while he was still the abbot of Anles, when he was a leading force in elections. It was said that once, when he was told his candidate was losing, he had shouted: 'The abbot of Anles lose an election? Never!' And with that he had kicked the ballot-box – a clay cooking-pot – which instantly broke into a thousand pieces, scattering ballot-papers everywhere. This simple action not only won him the election, but also the Great Cross of Isabella the Catholic. Now, however, obesity, old age and deafness prevented him from taking any active part in affairs, though he still liked to keep up with all the goings on, and was never more at home than in an electoral rough-house.

Whenever the Dean came to Cebre he always paid a visit to the tobacconist's, which was also the post office. Politics were discussed there incessantly, the Madrid newspapers were read, and all politicians, past, present and future, attacked for their failings, while many there thought they could do better. 'If I were the prime minister, I'd solve it with a stroke of the pen!' was frequently heard, as were other comments such as, 'If I were Prim, I wouldn't be put off by such a trifle!' Even a clergyman was heard to declare, 'Make me Pope and you'd soon see me sort the lot out, with no messing!'

It was here that, after leaving Barbacana's house, the Dean met the judge and the town secretary. Also, on the way in, he spotted Don Eugenio untying his horse and about to mount it.

'Wait a minute, Naya,' he said, addressing him familiarly by the name of his parish, as priests have a habit of doing amongst themselves. 'I'm just going to see what's in the newspapers, and then we can leave together.'

'I'm going to the manor.'

'So am I. Go to the inn and tell them to bring my mule around here.'

Don Eugenio obeyed immediately and soon the two clergymen were riding slowly down the steep hill, both wrapped in wide capes, with their hats held on against the wind by a handkerchief tied under the chin. They talked, naturally, about the parliamentary candidate and his coming battle. The Dean saw everything through rose-coloured spectacles, and was so certain of victory that he was already thinking of engaging musicians to come to the manor house and serenade the victor. Don Eugenio was also cheerful, although not so optimistic. The Government was powerful, heaven knows! And when it saw an election not going its way, it brought in the Civil Guard to make sure it did. According to the abbot of Boán, the Cortes was nothing but a solemn farce, from beginning to end.

'Well this time,' puffed the Dean as he struggled to clear the cape from his face, 'they're going to have to choke on this. At last Cebre will send someone decent to the Cortes – the head of an old and respected family. And someone who belongs here and who knows what's what better than the scoundrels they send in from outside.'

'That's right enough,' said Don Eugenio, who rarely contradicted people to their face. 'I'm as much in favour as anyone else that the House of Ulloa should represent Cebre. And if it weren't for certain things we all know about . . .'

The Dean's face darkened and he sniffed at his snuff-bottle. He loved Don Eugenio dearly – he had seen him grow up, as they say, and what's more he professed to respect the aristocracy. 'Indeed,' muttered the Dean. 'But let's not spread rumours. We all have our faults and none of us are innocent. We all have to answer to the Lord. One shouldn't interfere in other people's lives.'

Don Eugenio, however, persisted, pretending not to have understood. Raising his voice almost to a shout, so that the

Dean's deafness, made worse by the wind, should not prevent him from hearing, Don Eugenio repeated all he had heard at the Cebre post office, where the news brought by Trampeta to the governor had been elaborated with even more scandalous comments. The mischievous priest took delight in seeing the Dean, out of breath and red in the face, put his hand to his ear like a funnel, or furiously take another pinch of snuff. According to Don Eugenio, Cebre was surging with indignation at the behaviour of Don Pedro Moscoso. The village people wished him well enough, but in the town, which was dominated by Trampeta's people, it was said that terrible things went on at the manor house. Ever since the marquis had declared himself a candidate, the people of Cebre had developed a devout hatred of sin and a sense of righteousness that were extraordinary. To have a mistress and an illegitimate son now became totally reprehensible, though it must be said that this sudden moral fervour was really conspicuous only among the town secretary's followers – most of whom were a thoroughly bad lot and whose own behaviour left much to be desired.

'Pharisees! Scribes!' snorted the Dean. 'And then they have the nerve to call us hypocrites. How right and proper the uncircumcised of Cebre have suddenly become!' – for the Dean, 'uncircumcised' was a tremendous insult – 'As if the whole lot of them didn't deserve prison – or hanging, indeed. Yes, hanging!'

Don Eugenio could not help but laugh.

'It's been seven years . . . seven years,' the Dean stammered, calming down a little but still breathing hard because of the high wind, 'since all that happened . . . And now it's suddenly a scandal, when no one has ever mentioned it before. But with the elections – What a dreadful wind . . . It'll blow us away my boy!'

'Well, even worse things are being said than that,' shouted the Naya priest.

'Eh? I can't hear a thing in this wind.'

'I said that even worse things are being said!' shouted Don Eugenio, bringing his restless little mare alongside the Dean's more dignified mule.

'I suppose they're saying they're going to shoot the lot of us.

Speaking for myself, the town secretary has already threatened to issue me with seven lawsuits and put me under lock and key.'

'That's nothing . . . Lean your head a bit closer, I don't want to shout it out, even if we are alone.'

Don Eugenio explained, holding onto the Dean's cloak as his words were carried off in the gale with a strident, scornful whistle.

'Glory be!' gasped the Dean, and then was speechless. It was another two minutes before he recovered and was able to blurt out into the raging wind, which grew wilder every moment, a string of insults against the scandalmongers of Trampeta's party. The mischievous Don Eugenio allowed him to finish before adding, triumphantly:

'There's worse to come.'

'What could be worse? Do they claim the marquis is a highwayman? An uncircumcised bunch of scoundrels! With no other God than the hunger in their bellies!'

'They claim to have heard it from someone living in the house itself.'

'What? The devil take this wind . . .'

'I said that someone in the house told them about it. Now do you understand?' and with that Don Eugenio winked at the Dean.

'Yes, yes, I understand. The chicken-hearted, mealy-mouthed . . . And this of a lady who is the very soul of virtue, from such a good family, and who has a good word for everyone. To say such slanderous things about her . . . and with a man of the cloth, what's worse. These damned liberals around here would sell their souls for a cuarto. What's the world coming to, Naya, I don't know.'

'Well, that's not all.'

'Glory be! Aren't you ever going to stop? Holy Mary, there's a real storm brewing! What a wind . . .'

'This is what Barbacana says, not the others. That the person who told them – Primitivo – is out to trick the lot of us in the elections.'

'Eh? Are you mad? Whoa, mule, stop so I can hear properly! Are you telling me that it was Primitivo . . .?'

'There's nothing certain, nothing certain!' shouted the priest, who was enjoying himself as much as if he were at the theatre.

'Upon my soul, this is too much for me! Be so kind as not to drive me out of my senses. This wind is bad enough . . . I don't want to hear another word.' As he spoke, his cloak was lifted up by the wind and blown inside-out over his head, making him look like Venus in her shell. Pulling it back as quickly as he could he set off at a trot, and not a sound was heard except for the majestic symphony of the great north-east wind howling through the oaks and chestnuts.

Chapter 26

Having recovered from the initial shock, Julián still did not dare question Nucha about what he had seen. He was even afraid to visit her in her room, though in this he was not without reason. It was his nature to trust other people, but now he felt sure that he was being spied upon. By whom? By everyone: Primitivo, Sabel, the old witch, and by the servants. Just as sometimes at night we feel the mist come down and surround us, penetrating us, although we cannot see it, so Julián was aware of the suspicion, hatred and malevolence that had begun to engulf him. There was nothing tangible, but he was sure it was there. At several religious services he attended, he felt that the Dean was frowning at him and that the other priests treated him with hostility. Only Don Eugenio remained friendly. And yet perhaps he was only imagining these things, such as the way Don Pedro seemed to watch his every movement at table, and follow the direction of his gaze. This was particularly exhausting because of his frequent and irrepressible urge to look at Nucha, to see if she ate with an appetite or whether she had become thinner, and to check whether she had any new marks on her wrists. The bruise that had been so dark at first later turned green and then disappeared altogether.

Finally, however, his need to see the baby girl was greater than his sense of caution. Now that the restoration of the chapel was complete, he could only see her in her mother's room, and there he went one day, not content with the kiss he had stolen in the passageway as the nurse had carried her by. The baby had passed the stage of being a mere wrapped-up bundle, and now, although she maintained that charm peculiar to defenceless creatures, she was even more appealing because of a growing personality and a greater freedom of movement and self-awareness. She put all sorts of things in her warm mouth because she was teething; she stretched out her whole body with absolute abandon to be picked up by someone she liked; she adopted poses reminiscent of the angels painted by Murillo. Her sudden, melodious, bird-like laughter was now to be heard twice as often as before, and, although she could not yet talk, she managed to express beautifully all her feelings and wants, with the onomatopoeic sounds that some philologists believe to be the basis of primitive language. The soft spot on her head still pulsated, but her hair, smooth as moleskin, grew thicker and darker day by day. As for her feet, these were beginning to straighten, and the toes that had previously been twisted – the big ones turned up, the little pink ones bent down – had set in the horizontal position necessary for walking.

Each one of these great steps forward in growing up came as a delightful surprise to Julián, and intensified the fatherly affection he felt for the little creature, who did him the enormous favour of tugging at his watch-chain, playing with his waistcoat buttons, and dribbling milk all over him. What he would not have done to be of service to this adorable child! Sometimes his love for her inspired the wildest ideas in him: he planned to take a stick and thrash Primitivo, and Sabel too. But, alas, no one can replace the head of the house, the head of the family . . . Though in this particular case, what sort of head . . . The founding of this house through Christian matrimony was a source of deep regret for the chaplain. The intention had been perfectly honourable, but it had produced a bitter fruit, and now he would have given his heart's blood to see Nucha in a convent!

But what was he to do now? Julián foresaw the enormous disadvantages that would result if he interfered directly. He was sure of his ground, sure of what was right, but he lacked initiative, the mainspring of human action. That a number of things in that household were not as they should be, the chaplain was in no doubt, as the drama unfolded before his eyes and he feared a tragic end – the more so since he had seen the famous

234

marks on Nucha's wrists, which he could not get out of his mind. He now said little; his fresh complexion grew pale and waxen; he prayed even more than usual; he fasted; he said mass with the same sense of exaltation as is described in the lives of the martyrs; he wanted to be able to offer his own life in return for the señorita's well-being. But apart from his sudden, unexpected nervous impulses, he was quite incapable of any action, even something as easy and straightforward as a letter informing Don Manuel Pardo de la Lage of what was happening to his daughter. Instead he would say to himself, 'Let's wait until the election is over or some equally convenient opportunity.'

His hope was that if the señorito was elected to the Cortes and left his country lair – and with it all the people who spun their webs around him – then God might touch his heart, and he would change his ways.

One thing greatly troubled the gentle chaplain: would the marquis go to Madrid alone, or would he take his wife and child with him? Julián swore before God that he hoped the latter would be the case, but he also feared that the separation would make him ill to the point of death. The thought of not seeing the 'baba' for some months or perhaps even years, of no longer being able to play 'horsy' with her, bouncing her up and down on his knee, and of remaining behind alone with Sabel, as if down a dark well infested with vermin, was intolerable to Julián. The idea that the señorita might be going away was hard enough to bear, but that the baby too . . .

'I could look after her myself perfectly well,' he thought. 'If only they would let me.'

The day of the decisive battle approached. The manor house bustled with the coming and going of messengers and gossips; orders were dispatched and received, as if it were a general's headquarters. The stables were never without an extra horse or mule to feed, while the drawing-rooms resounded continually with the tramp of heavy shoes, the clatter of clogs and the creak of high leather boots. Julián would run into priests, breathless with their warlike ardour, who talked of their fight for the cause, and who were astonished to see him take no part in it. At such a critical moment the chaplain of the house should not even have stopped to eat or sleep!

He noticed that some of the priests resented his behaviour, particularly the Dean, who was very attached to the family. For while the priests of Boán and Naya thought only of political triumph, the Dean was concerned above all with upholding the name of Moscoso and increasing the splendour of the ancestral line.

Everything pointed towards a victory for the marquis, despite the enormous electoral machine deployed by the Government. The register was drawn up, supporters on each side were counted, and such was the marquis's majority that it seemed not even Trampeta's dirtiest tricks could affect the outcome. The Government's influence was confined to what might be called the bureaucratic element, and, although in rural Galicia this is often inordinately powerful because of the submissiveness of the peasants, it was no match for the combined forces of the priests and aristocrats of Cebre, led by the formidable *cacique*, Barbacana. The Dean snorted with pleasure, but Barbacana, oddly enough, was the only one not sure of the outcome. He was worried, his mood grew steadily worse, and he would scowl every time a priest entered his office rubbing his hands in satisfaction as he told the lawyer about the capture of some new vote.

And, Lord Almighty, what an election it was! What a fight, each side struggling to gain ground inch by inch, using every trick in the book. Trampeta seemed to have been multiplied into half a dozen men, laying his traps everywhere at the same time. Ballot-papers were tampered with, and voting-times were altered without notification. Forgery, intimidation and violence are not unusual during an election, but in this one they were combined with certain strokes of ingenuity that were entirely unprecedented. In one of the polling-stations, the cloaks of those voting for the marquis were secretly splashed with turpentine and set on fire with a match, so that the unfortunate men ran out shouting, never to return. In another, the ballot-box table was placed up a flight of stairs, on a landing, so that only one voter at a time could approach it, while twelve of Trampeta's henchmen stood in line all morning, gleefully kicking and punching any who dared make an attempt.

In Cebre itself a particularly subtle trick was played. There the priests escorted the voters to the ballot, so as to hurry them along and avoid a last-minute panic. To prevent themselves from being swindled, Don Eugenio availed himself of his right of intervention and sat one of his most dependable parishioners, a labourer, next to the table, with the strict instruction not to take his eyes off the ballot-box for a moment. 'Do you understand, Roque? Watch that box, even if there's an earthquake!' The peasant sat, his elbows on the table and his head resting in his hands, staring intently at the mysterious box as if he were part of some experiment in hypnosis. He hardly dared to breathe and sat motionless like a statue. Finally even Trampeta himself, who was making his rounds, grew impatient with the unmoving witness, for a second box, already filled with ballots marked to the satisfaction of the mayor and the returning officer, was hidden beneath the table, waiting for an opportune moment to replace the real one. He ordered one of his most trusted followers to distract the man, to invite him to have a drink and something to eat, and to use all sorts of flattery. A waste of time. Don Eugenio's sentry did not even look to see who was talking to him: his round, shaggy head and his prominent cheekbones were the very image of obstinacy. But move him they must, for it would soon be four o'clock – the solemn hour when the ballot-box would be whisked away for counting. Trampeta grew anxious and ordered his men to find out all they could about the peasant. It turned out that he was involved in a lawsuit as a result of which all his oxen and fruit had been impounded by the High Court. So Trampeta went quietly up to the table, clapped his hand on the man's shoulder and cried: 'Hey, whatever your name is, you've won your case!' The peasant sprang up as if he had received an electric shock.

'What's that you say?'

'The judge decided yesterday.'

'You're joking . . .'

'No, it's as I say.'

During this interval the returning officer switched boxes in a flash, without being seen or heard. Then the mayor rose solemnly.

'Gentl'min, we'll now proceed with the countin' out o' the ballits . . .'

People crowded into the room and the ballots were read out. The priests looked at one another in astonishment, as no one seemed to have voted for their candidate. 'Did you move from here?' the Naya priest asked his sentry. 'No, señor,' he replied, with such honesty in his voice that no one could doubt him. 'Someone's betrayed us,' declared the abbot of Ulloa in a hoarse voice, looking suspiciously at Don Eugenio. Trampeta, meanwhile, stood with his hands in his pockets and laughed quietly to himself.

Rigging the results in this way robbed the marquis of many of his votes, and in the end it was all to be decided on a tiny margin. At this critical moment, when the Ulloaists already thought themselves victorious, the scales were tipped in favour of the Government by the completely unforeseen desertion, not to say betrayal, of certain people whose loyalty Primitivo himself had answered for. So sudden and treacherous a calamity could have been neither foreseen nor averted, but Primitivo, abandoning his normal air of impassivity, gave free rein to his fury with absurdly wild threats about what he would do to the turncoats.

The only one to be stoical in the face of defeat was Barbacana. On the evening after the results became known, he was in his office with three or four people gathered round him, when in came the Dean, purple with rage and puffing like a whale left high and dry, as he collapsed into a leather armchair. He tore off his dog-collar, ripped open his shirt and vest. Then, still trembling and with his spectacles crooked and the snuff-bottle gripped tightly in his left hand, he wiped the sweat from his brow with a scented handkerchief. The *cacique*'s calmness only served to irritate him further.

'It amazes me, in God's name it amazes me to see you take things so calmly. Don't you know what's happened?'

'I don't get worked up about something that was a foregone conclusion. Where elections are concerned, I'm never taken by surprise.'

'You were expecting this to happen?'

'I saw it coming quite clearly. The Naya priest here will tell you so himself. I don't call on the dead for witness.'

'It's true,' said Don Eugenio, tired and full of remorse.

'In that case, in God's name why did you make such fools of us all?'

'We weren't going to let him have the district without even putting up a fight. How would you have liked that? Anyway, legally we won.'

'The devil take it – legally! Of course we won legally – but who cares about legalities? And as for those Judases who betrayed us when everything depended on them – may they be damned for eternity. The blacksmith from Gondas, the Ponlles brothers, the vet . . . !'

'They aren't Judases. Don't be so innocent, Dean. They are just people who obey orders, who do what they are told. The real Judas is another.'

'What? Ah, now I see . . . It's hard to believe in such wickedness, but if it's true, then such a traitor deserves worse than Judas himself got for his sins. But my dear fellow, why didn't you do something to stop him? Why didn't you warn us? Why didn't you unmask the villain? If the marquis had known there was a traitor in his own house he would have tied him to a bedpost and horsewhipped him. His own majordomo! I can't understand how you've stood by and calmly watched it happen.'

'It's easy enough to say that now. But when an election depends on one man alone, and you can't be sure if he's acting in good or bad faith, it's no use showing you're suspicious. Your hands and feet are tied, and all you can do is wait for the blow to fall. You have to just stand back and see how things turn out, and if they go against you, well you just have to keep your mouth shut. But that doesn't mean you forget!'

As he said this, Barbacana struck his breast with a hollow thud, just as St Jerome's breast must have resounded when he

239

struck it with that famous rock. Indeed, Barbacana was of the same mould as those Jeromes painted by the Spanish school – lean and bony, with a long, unkempt beard and dark, flaming eyes.

'They won't escape,' he added in a grim tone, 'and we won't waste any time. No one has yet played a dirty trick on Barbacana and got away with it. And as for the Judas . . . How do you think we could have unmasked him if, just as in Our Lord's day, he held the purse? Now tell me, Dean, who provided the munitions for this battle?'

'Who provided . . . ? Well, I suppose, in actual fact it was the House of Ulloa.'

'And was the House in a position to supply them, would you say? That's the point. As these noble houses are nothing but vanity and more vanity, and as the marquis didn't want to admit he was broke and ask someone honest, like myself, to lend him the money, he goes and asks this scoundrel, this leech who's sucking him dry.'

'I can just imagine what those good-for-nothings of the Orense Assembly will be saying about us. They'll say we're a load of Aunt Sallys! Lose an election! It's never happened to me before, in all my life.'

'Frankly, what they'll say is that we chose a simpleton as a candidate.'

'Steady on,' cried the Dean, always ready to defend his beloved señorito. 'I don't agree there . . .'

Here the conversation came to a halt, with everyone, including the priests of Boán and Naya and señorito de Limioso, falling silent out of humiliation and defeat. But then suddenly a terrific noise filled the room, the most discordant, threatening din, which deafened their ear-drums: frying-pans beaten with metal forks and spoons; cooking-pots knocked together like cymbals; sauce-pans scraped furiously with egg-whisks; copper kettles struck with pestles till they rang out; tins tied to a string and dragged along the ground; iron trivets banged with pokers . . . And above all this, the hoarse, mournful drone of horns and the hollow cries of those who have drunk too much wine. In fact, the 'musicians' had just polished off a full skin of wine generously provided by the town secretary (the country voters still had not refined their taste to demand 'the wine that bubbles and froths', as they did some years later, but were content with the simple, honest Borde red). The tavern-like smell of wine that emanated from the mob, which was drunk with more than just the excitement of victory, wafted through Barbacana's window, together with the terrible racket of their instruments. The Dean, his flushed face full of anxiety, straightened his spectacles. The Boán priest frowned, while Limioso went calmly over to the window and lifted the lace curtain.

The frantic serenade continued unabated, the frenzied noise of the mob sounding like tom-cats fighting on a tin roof. Then suddenly amid the din rose a cry that in Spain has such tragic reverberations: *muera* . . ., 'death to . . .'

'Death to the King!'

This sparked off a whole train of *mueras* and their opposites, *vivas*:

'Death to the priests!'

'Death to tyranny!'

'Long live Cebre and our Deputy!'

'Long live national sovereignty!'

'Death to the marquis of Ulloa!'

And then came a shout that was clearer and more deliberately stated than the rest:

'Death to that factious thief Barbacana!'

This was taken up with one voice by the crowd, who chanted in unison:

'Death! Death! Death!'

At that moment a sinister figure, who until then had remained in the shadows in one corner of the room, approached the lawyer's desk. He was not dressed as a peasant, but as a lower-class townsman, in a black jacket, red belt and grey bowler hat. His mutton-chop whiskers emphasized the hardness of his face, with its prominent cheekbones and broad forehead. One of his eyes shone green like a cat's; the other was set in a fixed stare, veiled with a thick white cloud, and looked as if it were made of glass.

Barbacana opened a drawer in his desk and produced two enormous, seemingly prehistoric, saddle pistols, which he examined to make sure they were loaded. He looked intently at the newcomer and appeared to offer the pistols to him with a slight raising of his eyebrows. El Tuerto, 'the wall-eyed one from Castrodorna', as he was known, replied by simply lifting his jacket to expose the yellow handle of a dagger protruding from the top of his belt, and then quickly concealing it again. The Dean, who had lost whatever courage he once had through obesity and old age, grew agitated.

'Don't do anything foolish, my friend. But just in case, it strikes me we ought to slip out the back door, eh? We don't want to sit here and wait for those uncircumcised rascals to come and poison us.'

But the Boán priest and Limioso had already joined El Tuerto, and were clearly determined to make a stand. The blue-blooded Limioso waited calmly, neither aggressive nor afraid; the priest, whose true vocation lay with the army rather than the Church, handled one of the guns with obvious pleasure: he scented danger and would have neighed with delight, had he been a horse; El Tuerto crouched behind the door, ready to spring like a tiger and tear out the guts of the first man to enter.

'Don't be scared, Dean,' murmured Barbacana gravely, 'their bark is worse than their bite. They're all talk, and wouldn't even dare to break one of my windows. But we should be prepared to show our teeth to them if need be.'

Indeed, although the chanting grew even louder and wilder, not a single stone was thrown at the window. Limioso again lifted the curtain and looked out. Then he beckoned to Don Eugenio.

'Naya, look . . . They've got no thought of coming up here, nor of throwing stones . . . They're dancing!'

Don Eugenio went to the window and burst out laughing. In among the drunken mob stood two of Trampeta's supporters, one a gaoler, the other a bailiff, trying to incite those who were shouting the hardest to attack the lawyer's house. They pointed towards the door, and demonstrated with their hands how easy it would be to knock it down. But although drunk, the revellers had not lost their caution nor forgotten the fear *caciques* inspire in peasants, and so they pretended not to understand as they continued to beat their pots and pans with ever greater gusto. In the middle of the mob those who were most inebriated, the real topers, danced like madmen to the rhythm.

'Gentlemen,' said Ramón Limioso in a grave, hoarse voice, 'it's shameful that those scoundrels should try and besiege us like this. I myself would like to go out and see them off, and give them such a fright they won't stop running till they reach the town hall.'

'Well said,' muttered the Boán priest. 'You don't talk much, Limioso, but I like what you say. Let's give them a fright, *quoniam*! I could scare off half a dozen of those drunkards just by sneezing.'

El Tuerto said nothing, but his green eye shone and he looked to Barbacana as if asking for permission to join in the enterprise. Barbacana nodded, but at the same time indicated that he should not make use of his knife.

'You're right,' exclaimed the nobleman, lifting his chin and altering his usually sad, listless expression to one of haughty arrogance. 'People of this sort you take a whip to, rather than dirty a weapon you use for partridges and hares, which are far worthier creatures – apart from their souls of course.' As he said this, the señorito made the sign of the cross.

'Be careful, gentlemen, be careful,' gasped the Dean breathlessly, stretching out his arms as if to quell the general anger. Gone were the days when an election was decided just by kicking a few backsides!

Barbacana did nothing to oppose the venture, and even went to another room and fetched back a bundle of walking-sticks and canes. The Boán priest wanted no other stick but his own, which was a stout one. Ramón Limioso took a riding-crop, which expressed his contempt for the common people. El Tuerto seized a horsewhip, which in his hands was a fearsome sight.

They crept down the stairs, trying not to make a sound – a completely unnecessary precaution given the tremendous din made by the revellers. The door was fitted with a bolt and an iron crossbar, which the lawyer's cook had secured as soon as she had heard the commotion outside. The Boán priest released the bolt impatiently, while El Tuerto removed the crossbar and turned the key in the lock. Then, without a word, they threw themselves forward and set about the mob, wielding their sticks and whips.

Less than five minutes later Barbacana, who followed the engagement from his window, smiled to himself (or, to be strictly accurate, bared his yellow teeth) and gripped the window-rail with such force that his knuckles whitened.

The terrified drunkards were fleeing in all directions, screaming as if they were under attack from a full regiment of cavalry. Some tripped and fell flat on their faces, only to cry out with pain as El Tuerto's whip caught them on the back. Limioso was less violent, swiping at the crowd with utter disdain, as if it were a herd of swine. The Boán priest lashed out tirelessly, while Don Eugenio exceeded his role of meting out justice, as he simultaneously cursed, flogged and laughed at the drunkards.

'Take that, you wine-bibbers! And that and that, drunkards! This'll teach you! Get back to the tavern where you belong! Off to the gaol with you, where you can lie in your own vomit!'

The street was now clear, completely clear, and total silence replaced the death-cries and the fearful cacophony. The ground was strewn with battle-spoils: saucepans, pestles, cowhorns. On the staircase, the returning victors revelled noisily in their easy triumph. Don Eugenio entered the lawyer's office first and threw himself into a chair, clapping his hands and rolling with laughter. He was followed by the Boán priest, who wiped the sweat from his brow. Then came Ramón Limioso, grave and melancholy as ever, handing the crop back to Barbacana without a word.

'My, my, they are in a sorry state,' laughed Don Eugenio.

'I thrashed them as if I were thrashing corn!' cried the other clergyman joyfully.

'Upon my soul,' said Limioso, 'if I had known they were such cowards and were going to turn tail and run like that, I wouldn't have bothered to go out.'

'Don't be too confident,' warned the Dean. 'Right now in the town hall Trampeta will be making them feel ashamed of themselves – and he's quite capable of coming back here in person, with that uncircumcised rabble, to make trouble for our learned friend' (as Barbacana was called by those who knew him). 'To be on the safe side, it would be wise for you gentlemen to spend the night here. I would myself, but I must say mass in Loiro tomorrow morning, and my sister would be worried sick.'

'I won't hear of it,' declared Barbacana. 'These gentlemen must return to their homes. There's nothing to worry about. I'll be quite all right with this chap here – ' He nodded towards El Tuerto, who had returned to his station in the shadows.

It was impossible to make the lawyer see reason and accept the guard of honour offered him. On the other hand, there was no sign of any further trouble stirring. Cebre had sunk back into its usual sleepy silence, and not even the occasional cheer of a triumphant voter was to be heard. The Dean and three of the heroes of the recent battle set off together towards the mountains. None were crestfallen, as might have been expected given the outcome of the election, but they were cheerful and talkative, congratulating themselves on the thrashing they had given the drunken mob. Don Eugenio in particular was quite inspired, and extremely amusing as he imitated the screams of the revellers and the face of the Boán priest pounding them with his stick, and joked about how they had fallen flat on their faces in the mud.

Barbacana was left alone with El Tuerto. Had one of the beaten 'musicians' dared show his head around a corner and looked up at the lawyer's window, he would have observed that, out of either carelessness or arrogance, the shutters had been left open; and he would have observed further, through the lace curtains, the heads of the lawyer and his faithful henchman silhouetted against the back wall. Their conversation was no doubt serious, for it lasted a great while. More than an hour elapsed between the lighting of the lamp and the closing of the shutters, and then the house stood silent and sombre, like someone with a dark secret to hide.

245

Chapter 27

The person who was seemingly most affected by the loss of the election was Nucha. Her already poor health declined even further and she became utterly exhausted, both physically and morally. She lived a slave to her daughter, bound to her day and night, and hardly ever emerged from her room. During meals she ate with little or no appetite and was completely silent, though on several occasions Julián, who never took his eyes off her, noticed she talked to herself quietly as obsessed people sometimes do. Don Pedro was more ill-tempered than ever. He ate moodily, drank heavily and stared at his plate or at the ceiling, but never at his fellow diners, not bothering to maintain even the semblance of a conversation.

So frail and wasted did the señorita look that one day Julián summoned all his courage and approached the marquis, asking him in a shaking voice if he did not think it a good idea to send for Dr Juncal . . .

'Are you mad?' exclaimed Don Pedro, contemptuously. 'Send for Juncal? After the way he worked against me during the election? He'll never set foot inside this house again!'

The chaplain said nothing, but a few days later, as he returned from a visit to Naya, he encountered the doctor by chance. Juncal reined in his horse and answered the chaplain's questions without dismounting.

'It may well be something serious,' he said. 'She was extremely weak after the birth and needed very special care. Nervous women only regain their health if they're kept happy, and have their mind taken off their troubles . . . Listen, Julián, we'd be here for hours if I told you all I thought about that poor girl and

246

what goes on at the manor, but I'll keep it to myself. A fine Deputy you wanted to send to the Cortes! He'd be better off going to school first!'

It may well be something serious . . . These words stuck in Julián's mind. It could indeed be serious, but what powers did he have in the face of sickness and death? None at all, which made him envy doctors. He could care only for the soul, and in this case even that was useless as he was not even Nucha's confessor. He had often envisaged the possibility of her being overwhelmed with the need for spiritual comfort, and throwing herself at his feet in the house of penance, asking for advice and strength, for the power of resignation, but the very idea of her confessing, the idea of seeing her beautiful soul naked, left him confused and disturbed. 'Who am I,' Julián asked himself, 'to guide someone like Señorita Marcelina? I am neither old enough, nor experienced nor wise enough. And even worse, I am without virtue, for if I were truly virtuous I'd accept joyfully all the señorita's sufferings as having been sent by God to test her, make her a better person, and give her even more glory in heaven. But I'm wicked, worldly, blind, wretched . . . spending my life doubting God's goodness just because I see this poor woman suffering ephemeral trials and tribulations . . . It's time I woke up,' he said finally, with great determination. 'After all, I have the light of faith to guide me. The light denied to unbelievers, to the godless, to those in mortal sin. And if the señorita asks me to help her carry her cross, then I must teach her how to embrace it lovingly. It's most important for her, and me, to understand what this cross means. With it she will achieve the only true happiness. For even if she were happier in this world, how long would it last? Even if her husband loved her as she deserves to be loved and set her above all else in his eyes, would that save her from sickness, worry, old age, death? And when the final hour comes, what does it matter whether one has been more or less content in this transitory, worthless life?'

Julián always had a copy of Father Nieremberg's admirable translation of *The Imitation of Christ* near at hand; it was a modest edition published by the Religious Library, with a picture on the front cover which, although of no value as a work of art, was a source of great comfort to the chaplain. It depicted the hill of Golgotha, with Jesus walking slowly up the narrow path to the place of execution, carrying the Cross on his back and with his head turned towards a monk in the distance, who carried another cross. Although the technique was poor, the picture expressed a feeling of melancholy resignation that fitted in exactly with the chaplain's own state of mind. And after contemplating it for a while the chaplain would imagine he could feel a weight on his own shoulders, both crushing and sweet, that filled him with a deep calmness, as if (or so he said to himself) he was lying on the bottom of the sea, immersed in the water but not drowned by it. Then he would read a passage from the book that went through him like a red-hot iron, touching his soul:

Why therefore fearest thou to take up the Cross which leadeth thee to a kingdom?

In the Cross is salvation, in the Cross is life, in the Cross is protection against our enemies, in the Cross is infusion of heavenly sweetness, in the Cross is strength of mind, in the Cross joy of spirit, in the Cross the height of virtue, in the Cross the perfection of sanctity. Take up therefore thy Cross and follow Jesus.

Behold! in the Cross all doth consist, and all lieth in our dying thereon; for there is no other way unto life, and unto true inward peace, but the way of the Holy Cross, and of daily mortification . . . Dispose and order all things according to thy will and judgement; yet thou shalt ever find that of necessity thou must suffer somewhat, either willingly or against thy will, and so thou shalt ever find the Cross. For either thou shalt feel pain in thy body, or in thy soul thou shalt feel tribulation of spirit.

When thou shalt come to this estate, that tribulation shall seem sweet, and thou shalt relish it for Christ's sake; then think it to be well with thee, for thou hast found a paradise upon earth.

'O Lord, when will I reach this blissful state?' murmured the chaplain, putting a mark at the page. He had sometimes heard that God granted whatever a priest prayed for inwardly at the moment of consecrating the host, and he prayed fervently that his cross – no, Kempis was right, the señorita's cross too would become sweet and she would relish it . . .

Nucha always attended mass in the restored chapel, listening on her knees and leaving as Julián said the Thanksgiving. Without turning round or being distracted from his prayer, he always knew when she stood up, and always followed the almost imperceptible sound of her light footsteps across the new floorboards. One morning, however, he did not hear her, and it was enough to prevent him concentrating on his prayers. When he rose to his feet he saw Nucha, also standing and with her finger pressed to her lips. Perucho, who served at mass with great naturalness, was busy snuffing out the candles with the help of a long cane. The señorita's look clearly said: 'Send the boy away,' and the chaplain told Perucho to go off and play. The boy hesitated, slowly folding up the towel the priest used when he washed his hands. Then he left reluctantly. The chapel was filled with the smell of flowers and fresh varnish, while the warm light filtering through the crimson silk curtains gave life to the altar saints and an artificial rosiness to Nucha's normally pale complexion.

'Julián,' she said, in an uncharacteristically firm voice.

'Señorita?' he replied softly, respecting the holiness of the place. His lips trembled as he spoke, and his hands went cold, as he thought that the awesome moment of confession had arrived.

'Julián, we must speak. Here, for they spy on us everywhere else.'

'That is true enough.'

'If I ask you something, will you do it?'

'You know I will.'

'Whatever it is?'

'I . . .' His confusion grew and his heart thudded dully. He leaned on the altar.

'You must help me get away from here,' declared Nucha,

249

fixing him with her eyes, which now were more than vague, they were distracted. 'Help me get away from this house.'

'Help you ... get ... away ...' stammered Julián, beside himself.

'I must leave, and take my daughter with me ... back to my father. But we must keep it a secret. If they find out they'll lock me up. They'll take the baby from me. Then they'll kill her. I know they'll kill her.' Her voice, her expression and everything about her indicated that she was not in full possession of her mental faculties, but was in a state of nervous hysteria bordering on madness.

'Señorita,' said the chaplain, equally disturbed. 'Don't stand up. Sit on this bench. Let's talk calmly. I know you have more than enough to be upset about, but one must be patient, prudent. Try to stay calm ...'

Nucha sank onto the bench, breathing with difficulty but trying to regain her composure. The light shone through her pale, slightly prominent ears.

'Patience? Prudence? I have as much as any woman could! This is no time for beating about the bush. Julián, you know when I started to feel all this misery – it was the day I decided to find out the truth, not that it was hard to discover. No, that's not true ... it was ... a battle ... for me. But that doesn't matter now. I'm not thinking of leaving for my own sake. I'm ill, and feel I don't have much longer. But what about the baby?'

'The baby –'

'These people will kill her, Julián. Don't you see she's in their way? Don't you see it?'

'For the Lord's sake, let's keep calm, señorita. Let's be reasonable ...'

'I'm tired of being calm!' cried Nucha angrily, as if he had said something incredibly stupid. 'I've prayed and prayed. I've done everything I can. I can't wait any longer. I waited for the elections to be over, because I thought then we might leave this place and I'd stop being afraid. I'm scared in this house, Julián, terribly scared. Especially at night.'

By the light filtering through the crimson curtains Julián saw a look of terror on Nucha's face, her eyes wide, her mouth open, her brow furrowed.

'Terribly scared,' she repeated, shuddering.

Julián cursed his own stupidity. How he wished he knew the right words to say! But he could think of nothing, nothing at all. The mystic comforts he had prepared for her, his theory of embracing the cross she bore – all were swept aside by this boundless, vibrant sorrow.

'From the moment I arrived,' Nucha continued, 'this huge old house has sent shivers down my spine. And it's not that I'm just a spoiled child, not now . . . They'll kill my baby. You'll see. Every time I leave her with the nurse I'm on tenterhooks. But enough is enough, we're going to resolve things right now. I've come to you, because I can't confide in anyone else . . . You love my daughter.'

'Indeed I do,' stammered Julián, almost hoarse with emotion.

'I'm alone, alone,' said Nucha, putting her hand to her face. Her voice faltered because of the tears she held back. 'I thought of confessing to you, but . . . a fine confession I'd have made! I would not have obeyed you if you'd ordered me to stay on here. I know it's my duty, a wife should not leave her husband. My intention when I married was – ' Suddenly she stopped and, facing Julián, asked him, 'Don't you agree, that from the start this marriage was bound to end badly? My sister Rita was almost engaged to our cousin when he asked for my hand. Through no fault of mine, Rita hasn't spoken to me since. I don't know how it happened. God knows I did nothing to make Pedro notice me. And Papa advised me that, all the same, I ought to marry him. So I followed his advice. I resolved to be good, to love him, obey him, look after his children . . . Tell me, Julián, have I failed in anything?'

Julián crossed his hands. His knees trembled so much he could hardly stand. He said with great feeling: 'Señorita Marcelina, you are an angel.'

'No,' she answered, 'I'm no angel, but I think I can say I have never hurt anyone. I took great care of my little brother Gabriel, who was a sickly child, and had no mother . . .' As she said this, she finally lost control and burst into tears. Then her breathing calmed, as if these memories of her childhood brought her some relief. 'In fact I grew so fond of him I thought, "If ever I have children, I couldn't possibly love them more than I love my brother." Now I realize what a foolish thought that was, for one loves one's own children far more than that.'

The sky clouded over and the chapel grew dark. The señorita spoke with melancholy calmness. 'When my brother went to the Artillery School, my only thought was to make Papa happy, and to make him miss Mama as little as possible. My sisters preferred their walks, and since they were so pretty they loved to amuse themselves. They used to say I was ugly and cross-eyed, and told me I'd never find a husband.'

'I wish they'd been right!' cried Julián, unable to restrain himself.

'I used to laugh. What did I want to get married for? I had Papa and Gabriel, and could live with them for ever. If they died, then I would enter a nunnery. I like the Carmelite convent where my aunt Dolores is very much. In short, I'm in no way to blame for Rita's anger. When Papa told me about my cousin's intentions, I said I didn't want to take my sister's fiancé away from her. Then he kissed me many times on the cheeks, like he used to when I was a little girl, and I can still hear him say "Rita is a silly girl, don't say another word." However, no matter what Papa says, our cousin still preferred Rita!'

After a few moments' silence she continued.

'As you can see, my sister has not had much cause to envy me. What a lot of sorrows I've had to endure, Julián. When I think about it, I get a knot in my stomach.'

The chaplain at last managed to express something of what he felt.

'That doesn't surprise me in the least. I feel a knot in my stomach too. I think about your troubles day and night, señorita. When I saw that mark, the bruise on your wrist . . .'

For the first time during their conversation, Nucha's pale face lit up. Her eyes were concealed beneath the long lashes, and when she spoke it was indirectly.

'It's strange how misfortunes happen to me through no fault of my own,' she said, with the faint trace of a bitter smile. 'Pedro insisted that I should claim my share of Mama's estate from Papa, because he had refused to give him the money he needed to fight the election. He also got angry because Aunt Marcelina, who was going to make me her heiress, will now probably leave everything to Rita. I've got nothing at all to do with such things. Why are they trying to kill me? I know I'm poor, they don't have to keep reminding me of that. But that's the least of it. What really hurt was when my husband blamed me for leaving the House of Ulloa without an heir! Without an heir, indeed! What about my little girl – my beautiful little angel?'

The wretched woman cried in silence, the red rims of her eyes making her look like an image of Our Lady of Sorrows.

'I don't care about myself,' she added. 'I could put up with it till I die. If they . . . treat me in one way . . . or another, if the maid . . . takes my place . . . well, it's just a question of being patient, and suffering quietly till the end. But what about my little girl? There's that other child, the boy . . . my husband's bastard . . . She's in his way . . . They'll kill her!' Then after a pause she repeated slowly and deliberately, 'They'll kill her. Don't look at me like that, I'm not mad – just excited. I've made up my mind to leave, to go back and live with my father. I don't think it's a sin to do that, nor to take the little one with me either. And if it is a sin, please don't tell me, dear Julián! I've made up my mind. And you must come with me, because I can't carry out my plan without your help. Will you come with me?'

Julián wanted to make an objection, but he could think of none. The way she had spoken with such feverish determination, the way she had called him 'dear', waved aside all his possible objections. How could he refuse to help the poor woman? It was unthinkable. The difficulties of carrying out the plan, or its irregularity, did not even occur to him. In his innocence such an absurd flight seemed even easy. How could he oppose her going away? He too had felt – and still did feel at every moment – a terrible fear, not only for the baby's safety, but for the mother's too. Had he not thought a thousand times that both their lives were in imminent danger? Besides, what wouldn't he do in order to dry her beautiful, pure eyes, calm her anxious breast, and to see her again safe, honoured, respected and looked after, back in her paternal home?

The chaplain tried to envisage the escape. They would leave at dawn. Nucha would be wrapped up in layers of coats. He would carry the baby, swaddled and fast asleep. He would take a bottle of warm milk in his pocket in case she woke. At a good pace they could reach Cebre in three hours. There they would be able to have some soup. The baby would not go hungry. In the coach they could sit in the front closed compartment, the most comfortable place. Every turn of the wheels would take them further away from that evil house . . .

They began to discuss these details in a whisper, as if he were hearing her confession. The sun burst through the clouds and lit up the faces of the saints in their niches, so that they appeared to be smiling down on the young couple seated on the bench. Neither the Virgin Mother, in her blue and white robe and with her loose ringlets, nor St Anthony, patting a chubby Christ-child, nor St Michael, with his shining sword always ready for the assault on Satan, showed the slightest sign of annoyance at a chaplain who was busy working out a way of taking a wife from her legal master and snatching a child from her proper father.

Chapter 28

To give a full picture of that morning at Ulloa, we must recall certain other events witnessed by the young Perucho – events that he was unable to forget for the rest of his life. It was the last morning he ever served mass for kind Don Julián – who, by the way, usually gave him two cuartos once the Divine Office was over.

Perucho's first recollection of what happened that morning was that when he left the chapel, he leaned against the door outside, feeling sad because the chaplain had not given him anything at all that day. For a few moments he just stood there, lost in thought and sucking his thumb; but worrying about the loss of his two cuartos suddenly made him remember that his grandfather had once offered him another two if he let him know whenever the señora lingered on in the chapel after mass. With surprising mathematical astuteness, he realized that since he was two cuartos short in one way, it was important to make them up in another. No sooner had this thought occurred to him than he ran off as fast as his legs would carry him in search of his grandfather.

He slipped through the kitchen and went to the room where his grandfather did all his business. He pushed open the door and saw the old man sitting at a large table on which lay a tumultuous sea of papers covered with notes and figures in a clumsy handwriting. The table, and in fact the whole room, intrigued and enchanted Perucho, who, like all children, loved such chaos for the hidden treasures it promised. However, Perucho hardly ever entered the room and when he did his grandfather usually chased him out again, for he did not want any witness to certain of his financial practices. Seated at that table, Primitivo's hard, metallic face could have been confused with the piles of copper coins heaped in rows before him. Perucho was dazzled by such fabulous wealth. There were his two cuartos! A tiny nugget in a huge mass of precious metal. Filled with hope, and raising his voice to speak as loud as he could, he informed his grandfather that the señora was in the chapel with the chaplain, who had sent him away.

He was about to add that he was owed two cuartos for this information, or words to that effect, but his grandfather gave him no chance as he leaped nimbly from the chair, with the animal swiftness that characterized all his movements, and knocked down the great towers of coins, scattering them across the table. The boy was left alone, facing the two greatest temptations he had ever met. Firstly there was a tin of inviting red and white wafer biscuits. Although it would have been to the greater glory of our hero if we could report that he controlled this greedy impulse, honesty compels us to divulge that, licking his finger and reaching for the tin, he first removed and ate one, then two, then three wafers, and then the whole tinful. Having given in to this first temptation, he was then confronted by a second dilemma: whether or not he should help himself to the two cuartos he had been promised, and which lay there before him for the taking. Not only did he want his due, but he was seduced further by the sight of some grimy ochavos, known as 'lucky coins' in those parts, and which in his childish innocence seemed preferable to the larger coins. An ochavo was usually sufficient to satisfy Perucho's needs. With an ochavo the woman of the cake-stand at the country fair would give him a number of sweets and cakes; with an ochavo he could buy enough string for his spinning-top, or enough gunpowder from the firework-maker to lay down a little train; with an ochavo he could buy cardboard matches, holy pictures on bright yellow paper, clay cocks with whistles in immodest places . . . And all this was spread out before him, waiting for his touch, like the wafers, with no one to see him or tell on him! The little angel then stood on tiptoe to reach the table more easily, and plunged both hands into the sea of copper coins. For a while he simply let them run through his outspread fingers, which he did not dare to close. But finally he seized a handful of ochavos and held them as tight as he could, with that intensity of children who fear happiness can slip away easily through their fingers.

He stood motionless, not daring to withdraw his hand which held its sinful bounty, or move it to the safety of his shirt-front, where he always stored his little thefts – for, although it must be admitted that Perucho was a hardened thief, who did not think twice about helping himself to eggs, fruit or anything else he fancied, he had never yet touched a single coin – out of the superstitious regard for money typical of countrymen, who consider it to be the only property that can really belong to someone. A conflict went on in Perucho's soul between duty and passion, between the good angel and the bad angel who were pulling him in opposite directions. It was a tremendous battle, but finally, to the joy of heaven and honest men, the spirit of light triumphed! Was this the first awakening in him of the sense of honour that inspires men to heroic sacrifices? Was it the trace of Moscoso blood that coursed through his veins and, with the mysterious force of heredity, guided his will? Was it the fruit of Julián and Nucha's earlier lessons? Whatever, the fact is that the boy opened his hands and let the coveted ochavos tumble onto the table, where they landed with a clatter amid the rest of the pile.

That is not to say, however, that Perucho renounced his claim to the two cuartos, gained honestly by the swiftness of his legs. Certainly not! That same seed of conscience in his heart (where we all have engraved from birth the major part of the Decalogue), which had cried out to him 'Thou shalt not steal!' said, with no less energy, 'Thou hast a right to demand what is rightly thine!' And so, obeying this impulse, he ran off after his grandfather.

He discovered him by chance in the kitchen, where he was questioning Sabel in a low voice. Perucho went up to him and tugged his sleeve, crying, 'What about my two cuartos?'

Primitivo ignored him. He was busy talking to his daughter, who, from what Perucho could understand, was explaining to him that the señorito had left at dawn to shoot partridges down by the Cebre road. The grandfather let out a vulgar oath that he used often (and which Perucho would sometimes copy just to show off), and then, having no more to say, he stormed out.

Perucho later declared, on reflection, that he had been surprised to see his grandfather go out without his gun or his hat, neither of which he ever left behind. But at the time Perucho only had one thought: to catch up with his grandfather, and this he did at the top of the path that leads down to the manor. Although the hunter was exceptionally fleet of foot, the boy too had strong legs.

'What the devil do you want?' muttered Primitivo when he saw his grandson.

'My two cuartos!'

'I'll give you four when we get back to the house, if you help me find the señorito and tell him exactly what you told me – that the chaplain is in the chapel with the señora, and that they sent you away so that they could be alone. Do you understand?'

The cherub-faced boy fixed his clear eyes on the fascinating, snake-like eyes of his grandfather. Then, without waiting for any further instructions, he raced off to where he instinctively judged the señorito to be. He ran with his mouth open, his fists clenched, and scattering stones as his little feet pounded the earth. He dashed through the gorse without noticing the thorns, flattened the flowering heather, leaped over bushes almost as tall as himself, and scared off a hare hiding behind a strawberry-tree and a magpie perching amid the branches of a pine. Suddenly he heard steps, and then saw the señorito emerge from a cluster of oaks. Mad with delight, he ran to give him the message, for which he expected some reward. But all he received for his pains was the same vulgar oath his grandfather had used in the kitchen, and with that the señorito set off like a tornado towards the manor.

For some moments Perucho remained there, confused. Then, as he can still recall to this day, his desire for the cuartos – which now had reached the respectable sum of four – once again overwhelmed him. To obtain them, he first had to find his grandfather and tell him he had delivered the message to the señorito; he did not expect this to be hard, as he knew more or less where he had left Primitivo. Taking a short cut, accessible only to rabbits and himself, the boy ran off again. He was in the process of climbing a thick, half-ruined stone wall – the boundary of a vineyard that hung, so to speak, on that steep slope – when he detected on the other side the sound of footsteps. He did not recognize them as those of his grandfather and, with the cautious instinct of a child who has grown up wild and who is used to taking care of himself, he crouched down behind the wall, with only the top of his head visible. He was in no doubt that they were human footsteps – totally distinct from the noise made by a hare rustling through the leaves, or the short, steady tramping of a dog. They were human footsteps, but they were suspiciously slow and stealthy, as if the person to whom they belonged was trying to conceal his presence.

Sure enough, the boy soon caught sight of a man crawling through the bushes, a man whom he recognized from a hundred fearful descriptions he had heard at the night-time gatherings in the kitchen. The grey bowler hat, the red belt, the close-cut whiskers and, above all, the white, sightless eye – cold as a piece of quartz embedded in the ground. In short, the boy had been astounded to find himself in the presence of the dreaded El Tuerto from Castrodorna. The man carried a short, wide blunderbuss against his chest; he looked all around him with the only good eye in his ugly face, pricked up his ears, sniffed the air thoughtfully and then squatted down behind a blackberry bush, close in to the wall.

Perucho seemed to become a part of the same wall, his feet resting in its cracks; he did not dare get down, and was even afraid of breathing, for the ugly stranger filled him with an irrational panic that children sometimes feel when in the presence of a danger they do not fully comprehend. However much he longed to get his cuartos, he did not jump down for fear of making a noise and becoming the target of that terrifying gun, whose muzzle no doubt spat out fire and death. Several seconds passed, with the boy in a state of terror. But before he could think what to do, something happened. He heard more footsteps, this time not the stealthy tread of someone who doesn't want to be seen, but the hurried steps of someone who wants to get somewhere fast. Then he saw his grandfather on the path parallel to the wall, heading for the manor. No doubt his eagle's eye had already spotted the señorito, and he was following his steps in the hope of catching up with him. Primitivo walked along without the least caution, thinking only of Don Pedro, looking only straight ahead.

He passed in front of the wall. The boy then witnessed something that was to remain fixed in his memory for the rest of his life. The man in hiding stood up and put the enormous gun to his shoulder, his single eye blazing like fire. He heard a terrible bang, as the black mouth roared; then there was a small puff of smoke, which dispersed immediately, but through its grey haze Perucho saw his grandfather reel like a spinning-top and fall forwards, biting the grass and mud in his last convulsion.

Perucho is unsure now whether he made a conscious decision, or simply reacted in fear when he climbed off the wall and bounded down the short cut. He tore his clothes as he ran and knocked himself against obstacles, but without the least regard. He jumped over the knotted vines, leapt over stone walls, raced through maize-fields like an arrow; he waded through streams, with water up to his waist, so as not to lose time following the stepping-stones. He scrambled over fences three times his own height, pushed through the hedgerows and sprang over ditches. Not knowing which way he went, nor how he had arrived, the boy found himself back at the manor, scratched, bleeding, panting and perspiring. He automatically returned to his starting-point, the chapel, having completely forgotten about the four cuartos, the original source of all his adventures.

That morning was destined to be full of extraordinary surprises. Perucho was used to hearing people speak and walk softly in the chapel – indeed, if you didn't you were severely scolded by Don Julián. Thus, out of habit, he managed to control his agitation and enter the chapel in a respectful manner, only to find something happening there that amazed him almost more than the catastrophe that had overcome his grandfather. Leaning against the altar was Señora de Moscoso, her face deathly pale, her eyes closed, her whole body sobbing. The señorito stood before her menacingly, shouting something the boy did not understand. The chaplain, meanwhile, had his hands clasped together and his face bore a look of terrific fear, such as Perucho had never seen in a human being; he was imploring the señorito, the señora, the saints, the angels . . . Suddenly abandoning his entreaties, the chaplain then stood before the marquis, as if challenging him, his eyes sparkling. Although unaware of the cause of all the commotion, Perucho deduced that the señorito was ferociously angry, that he was going to hit the señora – perhaps kill her – as well as tear the chaplain apart limb from limb, overturn the altar-table and, who knows, perhaps even burn down the chapel . . .

The boy then recalled similar scenes in the manor kitchen, when the victims were his mother and himself. On those occasions the señorito had said the same things and had the same look on his face. In the midst of the confusion, a brilliant idea shone through Perucho's muddled, terrified brain. There was no doubt in his mind that the señorito was about to deal a mortal blow both to his wife and his chaplain: his grandfather had just been murdered in the woods; as far as he could understand, it was a day of general massacre. And what, if after killing Don Julián and the señora, the señorito took it into his head to put an end to the little baby too? The very idea of this brought back all the usual energy and power with which Perucho applied himself to his adventures in the stables and the farmyard.

He slipped cautiously out of the chapel, determined at all costs to save the life of the little Moscoso heiress. How would he manage it? He had no time to devise a plan – the important thing was to be quick and not lose heart if he met with any obstacles. He passed unseen through the kitchen and hurried up the stairs. When he reached the upper floors where the señores lived, he tiptoed so quietly that even the sharpest ear would have mistaken the sound for the wind rustling a curtain. What he feared most was finding Nucha's bedroom door locked, so when he discovered it ajar his heart leapt for joy.

He pushed it open with the gentleness of a cat who has drawn in its claws. The wretched door usually squeaked, but he pushed it so carefully that it only gave out a dull groan. Perucho stole into the room and hid behind the screen, peeping through one of its many holes at the cradle. He saw the baby asleep, and the nurse lying face down on Nucha's bed, snoring softly. There was no danger of waking *this* sleeping beauty, so Perucho could go ahead with his plan in safety.

However, it was important not to wake the baby either, for she would alert the whole household if she began to cry. Perucho lifted her from the cradle, handling her as if she were a precious and very fragile glass doll. His rough hands, accustomed to throwing well-aimed stones and smacking the bulls on their heads, suddenly assumed a great gentleness, and the baby, wrapped in a knitted shawl, did not utter a sound as she was moved from her bed to the arms of her young kidnapper. The boy held his breath and stole cautiously out, like a cat carrying her young in her teeth. He decided to go out by the cloister and thus avoid the kitchen, where he might be surprised.

Once in the cloister he paused for a few seconds. Where should he hide his treasure? In the hay-loft, in the granary or in the stables? He opted for the granary – the darkest and least frequented place. He decided to descend the staircase, slip through the stables, across the threshing-floor and into his hide-out.

This was no sooner said than done, and shortly afterwards Perucho climbed the ladder leading up to the granary. But it was difficult, particularly with the little girl in his arms, for the ladder was steep and narrow, and one had to hold on with both hands and feet to get up. Perucho had his hands full, but the strength of his will-power made his toes almost prehensile, as they clung to the smooth wooden bars. Half-way up he thought he was about to fall, and grasped the baby tightly to his chest. This woke her up and she began to cry. Let her cry, no one will hear her now, he thought, for there was not a living soul around, apart from a few chickens and sparrows arguing over a cabbage-leaf on the threshing-floor. Then, reaching the top, Perucho went triumphantly through the door to the granary.

There was just enough space for two tiny people, like Perucho and his protégée, to make themselves comfortable and have room to play among the enormous pile of maize-cobs. The boy sat down, still holding the little girl, quietening her with a stream of witty and affectionate rustic babble.

'Oh my little queenie, my sweetie, my tootsie-wootsie, don't cry, don't cry . . . I'm going to give you some pretty, pretty things . . . but if you don't hush, the bogeyman will eat you . . . Sssh, here he comes! Ssssh my little darling, little doveykins, my pretty little flower . . .'

It was not what he said, but the fact that the baby recognized her favourite friend that stopped her crying. She smiled happily, put out her hands to touch his face, gurgled, dribbled and looked all around her with a curious gaze. She found the place strange. Above her, beneath her, all around her, all she could see was an ocean of golden grain, which at Perucho's slightest movement cascaded down, and which the bright sun, streaming through the lattice window, lit up in stripes. Perucho realized that the cobs offered him a way of entertaining the baby. He gave her one to hold, and built a pyramid with a number of others. Then the baby would amuse herself by knocking these pyramids down, or rather imagining she knocked them down, for it was Perucho who performed this apparent miracle by kicking them. She laughed out loud and signalled impatiently for him to start all over again.

Though she soon tired of the game, she remained in a good mood thanks to Perucho's company. Her gentle, radiant eyes were fixed on her companion and seemed to say: 'What better game than this, to be together? Let's enjoy it while we can, for they grudge us it so much.' As she was so affectionate in return, Perucho fussed over her to his heart's content. He tickled her on the cheek to make her laugh; he used his fingers to imitate a lizard, wriggling up her body; he pretended to be angry, with his eyes glaring, his cheeks puffed out, his fists clenched, and with great raging snorts . . . He held her up and pretended to let her fall down on to the grain. Finally, fearing he might exhaust her, he sat down with his legs crossed and began rocking her softly with as much tenderness as her own mother might have shown.

He was overcome with a powerful emotion. The times he had been allowed into the intimacy of Nucha's room and permitted to go up to the baby and thus be a part in her life, he had not dared . . . Perhaps it was the fear of being scolded or dismissed, perhaps it was a vague religious awe imposed on his roguish little soul, or perhaps just embarrassment, for his lips had never kissed anyone . . . All this together had prevented him from satisfying a desire he considered almost sacrilegious . . . But now he owned the treasure. 'Nené' belonged to him. He had won her fair and square, she was one of the spoils of war, a right even savages understand! He pursed his lips, as if he were about to eat a sweet, and, lowering his head, he touched the baby's eyes and forehead. Then he slowly unwrapped the shawl from her legs, which were as warm as toast and started to kick with delight as soon as they felt free. Perucho kissed first one foot, then the other, and spent some time doing this. His kisses tickled her so that she laughed, and then she would look suddenly serious again. Soon she started to feel cold, reacting quickly to a drop in temperature as small babies do. Perucho noticed that her feet were freezing; he blew on them several times (as he had seen the cows do with their calves), wrapped them in the shawl and, holding the baby tight, began rocking her again.

The greatest of conquering heroes could not have felt more proud of himself than did Perucho, for he was certain he had saved the baby from death and had brought her to safety where no one could find her. He did not think for a moment of his hard, sunburnt grandfather lying by the wall . . . Just as a child weeping at the body of his dead mother can comfort himself with a toy or a bag of sweets, pushing sadness and memory momentarily aside and forgetting his first impression of grief, so it was with Perucho. The happiness of having his adored Nené to himself, the glory of having saved her life, distracted him from the recent tragic events. He gave no thought at all to his grandfather or to the shot that had knocked him down like a partridge.

Nevertheless, his imagination must have been affected, for the tale he now told the baby (as if she could understand everything he said) contained a streak of fear and gloom. Where did this story of an ogre originate? Had he heard it one evening by the kitchen fire, listening as the old women sat spinning and the young ones peeled chestnuts? Was it a product of his imagination, excited by the terror he had witnessed earlier that day? 'Once upon a time,' the story began, 'there was a bad, bad king, who ate up people alive. He had a pretty, pretty Nené, like a little flower. She was teeny-weeny, like a maize-cob. And the 'orrible king wanted to eat her all up too, 'cos he was the bogeyman. He was ugly as a devil.' Perucho pulled a terrible face to make the point. 'Then one night he says this. "Tomorrow morning really early I'm gonna eat up the Nené . . . just like this!"' Perucho opened his mouth wide, like a gargoyle. 'A teeny birdie on the tree heard the king and he said, "Don't eat the Nené, you ugly bogeyman." And then guess what the bird did? It flew through the window when the king was sleepin' in his bed' – Perucho laid his head on the maize and pretended to snore loudly – 'and with his beak pecks out the king's eye.' He put one hand over an eye, to show how the king would have looked. 'The king woke up and cried a lot' – pretend sobs – ''cos of his eye, and the little bird laffed up in a tree. Then he says to the king, "If you don't eat Nené up and you give her to me, you can have your eye back." And so the king says all right, and the little bird married the Nené and they were always singing lovely songs and playing the bagpipes' – solo of this instrument – 'And they lived happily ever after.'

The baby did not hear the end of the story, which of course had not meant anything to her. The singsong of Perucho's voice, the fact that she was warm again, and the joy of being with her favourite, lulled her imperceptibly back to sleep. Perucho was about to give out the loud cheer with which you always end a bogeyman story, but saw that she had closed her eyes. He arranged her bed of cobs as best he could, drawing the shawl up to her face, the way Nucha did, so that she didn't get cold. Then, determined to stay on guard, he went bravely to the door of the granary and leaned against a heap of maize in the corner. But out of sheer physical and emotional exhaustion, he too began to feel a heaviness in his head. He yawned, and tried to fight off the overwhelming drowsiness . . . Before long the two angelic little refugees in the granary were fast asleep.

Among the fearful images that filled Perucho's dreams, there was a ferocious wild animal that roared out and wanted to scratch him with its huge claws, and then eat him. His hair stood on end, he shivered, a cold sweat broke out on his temples. What a terrifying monster! It came closer . . . It grabbed hold of Perucho, and dug its claws deep into the boy's flesh, its body descended on him like a huge boulder . . . The little boy opened his eyes. There, breathless with rage, was the nurse, seemingly bigger and more brutal than ever, hitting and scratching him, pulling his hair and kicking him with all her might. To the end, Perucho conducted himself like a hero. He lowered his head and barred the entrance to the granary with his whole body, defending his charge. But the massive bulk of the nurse pushing against him was finally too much and he collapsed, unable to move. When the poor lad, who almost suffocated, felt the great weight lift from on top of him, he looked back . . . to see that the baby had vanished. Perucho will never forget the tears he shed for over half an hour, writhing in despair among the maize-cobs.

Chapter 29

Julián also will always remember that extraordinary day, the most dramatic day of his life. He had never imagined such things could happen to him, to find himself accused by a husband of having an illicit relationship with his wife! To be accused of such an outrage! And then threatened by the offended husband and thrown ignominiously out of his house for ever! And then on top of this, to see the unfortunate wife, who could truly complain of having been outraged, powerless to disprove the ridiculous, horrible calumny. And what would have happened if they had indeed carried out their plan of escape the following day? Then they would certainly have had to hang their heads in shame! And to think that five minutes earlier the very thought of Don Pedro, or anyone else, seeing their exodus in such a light had not even entered their minds!

No, Julián will never forget that day. He will never forget that sudden moment of distress, or the unexpected courage, which surprised even himself, as he had thrown in the marquis's face all that had been raging in his breast, all the indignation that was usually restrained by his shyness, and his defiance in the face of such a barbarous insult. He had used words he had never imagined himself using, not being used to speak in anger – not to mention the 'man to man' challenge he had thrown at the marquis as he left the chapel. No, he will never forget that dreadful scene, no matter how long he lives, nor will he forget how quickly he had to leave the manor without time even to pack his things. He had saddled the mare himself, with his own inexperienced hands, and, displaying a determination born of the moment, had mounted and ridden off at a gallop. All this he did mechanically, as if it were a dream, without allowing his boiling blood time to cool. He did not even pause to have a last look at the baby, or to give her a farewell kiss, for he knew that to have done so would have reduced him to throwing himself at the señorito's feet and begging him to let him stay, even if only as a cowherd or a labourer.

Nor will he forget that ascent up the path from the manor, which had seemed to him so sad and oppressive the day he had arrived. As he climbed, thick clouds gathered about the sun and the sky grew dark. The swaying tree-tops seemed to whisper secrets to each other. The air was full of the sweet fragrance of sap and honey from the copses full of broom. And soon the stone cross, covered with golden lichen, loomed before him. The horse began to tremble and then started suddenly, rearing up. Julián instinctively dropped the reins and clung to the horse's mane. There, on the ground, was the body of a dead man. The grass beside it was thick with already blackening blood. Julián froze. All strength left his body. He was overwhelmed by a mixture of astonishment and thankfulness, for although the body was lying face down he realized that it was none other than Primitivo. Without pausing even to wonder who had done the deed – for he was sure that whoever it was was the instrument of God – he steered the horse round the body, made the sign of the cross and continued defiantly on his journey, turning back every now and then to look at the black hump that stood out starkly against the green grass and white wall.

No, Julián does not forget. When he reached Santiago, the story of the elections, the chaplain's departure and the major-domo's murder, was soon embellished, and entertained the town for over a month. People would stop him in the street and ask him how things were 'back there'; ask him if it was true that Nucha Pardo was ill-treated by her husband, if it was true that she was ill and that the elections were a tremendous scandal. Nor can he forget how the Archbishop had summoned him to his presence. Julián had knelt before him, and told him the whole story without omitting a single detail, finding immense relief in the confession. Afterwards he had kissed the Archbishop's ring, his heart feeling considerably lighter. Then he had been sent to a distant parish, to endure a form of banishment, totally removed from the world.

It is a mountain parish in the heart of Galicia – with higher, rougher mountains than those of Ulloa. There is not a single manor house within four leagues, only a ruined stone castle standing alone on its crag, inhabited by bats and lizards. The peasants in that part speak in a very thick accent that is hard to understand; they wear rough clothes and have their long, unkempt hair cut straight across the forehead, like ancient serfs. On feast-days and at times of offerings they present Julián with goat's milk, sheep's cheese and lard in earthenware pots. In the winter, snow covers the parish and wolves howl near the rectory. When Julián has to go out in the middle of the night to offer extreme unction to someone in their final hour, he has to stuff his clothes with a layer of straw and wear wooden clogs; at these times the sexton lights the path for him with a lantern, through the dark woods where the oak-trees seem like ghosts.

Six months after his arrival, he received a letter edged in black. At first he did not fully understand, but when he did he showed no sign of grief. On the contrary, he experienced a sense of comfort and elation, in the sure knowledge that in heaven Señorita Nucha would be rewarded for all her suffering on this miserable earth, where a soul as pure as hers could only know martyrdom. Julián's own spirit bowed once more to the strict rule of Kempis's *Imitation*. Even the shock occasioned by receiving the news of her death soon wore off, while a peaceful passivity cauterized, as it were, his spirit.

Now Julián concentrates only on his immediate surroundings, applying himself to the restoration of the dilapidated church and to the elementary education of the half-savage mountain children. He has founded a Guild of the Daughters of Mary to prevent the young girls going out dancing on Sundays. Thus for him time passes with neither joy nor sorrow, and the peace of Nature enters his soul. He is growing used to living with the peasants, worrying about their crops, seeing rain or fine weather as the greatest gifts God can give to man. He says mass very early, and later sits by the open fire, retiring to bed before even lighting the lamp. He is now able to predict the weather simply by looking at the stars and, as he helps to harvest the chestnuts or the potatoes, resigns himself to following the monotonous, sleepy, endlessly recurring agricultural cycle, as regular as the return of the swallows in springtime, and the eternal revolutions of our globe on its axis, wheeling for ever in its permanent ellipse through the universe.

And yet, he still does not forget. And now, in this humble backwater, promotion has suddenly come to him. He is to be transferred to the parish of Ulloa. The Archbishop shares the privilege of appointing the abbot with the marquis, and they take it in turns to do so. The Archbishop has now decided to show the humble priest, buried in the wildest mountain district of his diocese for the past ten years, that although slander may cloud a man's honour, it never destroys it.

Epilogue

A decade is a stage not only in the life of an individual, but in the life of a nation. A decade is long enough for both change and renewal, and, looking back, one is often surprised at the distance one has travelled in such a short space of time. But there are people on whom ten years leave no trace, and indeed the same applies to places. The House of Ulloa, for example. That great warren stands just as gloomy, just as austere and sinister as ever. There have been no changes, either practical or decorative, in its furniture, in its garden or even in its farmlands. On the coat of arms, the wolves have not been tamed, nor has the pine-tree developed new shoots, and still the same parallel stone waves wash the pillars of the bridge.

The little town of Cebre, however, has paid homage to the cult of progress and applied itself to both moral and material improvements, according to one illustrious inhabitant who is the correspondent there for the newspapers in Orense and Pontevedra. The post office is no longer the only place where politics are debated, for a literary and scientific society has been established for study and leisure (or so it says in the rules). Several small shops, which the correspondent calls bazaars, have also been opened.

The two *caciques* still, it is true, vie for control of the local legal system, but it already seems certain that Barbacana, who represents reaction and tradition, is giving in to Trampeta, who personifies the advanced ideas of the new age. Certain malicious people claim that the liberal's triumph is due mainly to the fact that Barbacana, who has become a follower of Cánovas, is now extremely old and frail, having lost most of his vigour and temper. Whatever the reasons, there is no doubt that Barbacana's influence has been greatly reduced.

Another person who has aged a great deal, this time prematurely, is the former chaplain of the manor. His hair is streaked with silver; the line of his mouth has drooped; his eyes are hazy and his back is bent. He walks slowly down the narrow path that winds through the vineyards and the heath to the church of Ulloa. What a sad and humble church it is too. It looks more like a peasant's hut, with only a simple cross over the porch to denote its holy purpose. It is extremely damp, the grassy courtyard in front sodden with dew at all times of day, even at noon. The courtyard is now higher than the pillars of the church entrance, for the building is sinking as the earth around it slowly crumbles down the hillside. In a corner of the courtyard a small tower houses the cracked bell, while in the middle a small cross on a short pillar of stone gives a pensive, almost poetic touch to the scene. There, in that quiet corner of the world, lives the Lord Jesus Christ – but how alone, and how forgotten!

Julián stopped before the cross. He did indeed look old, but also more manly. His rather delicate features had hardened, while his pale, tight lips were those of a man who controls his emotions and all his earthly impulses. Maturity had taught him the true merit and reward of the pure priest: to be extremely tolerant of others while at the same time very severe with oneself.

A curious impression struck him as he walked across the courtyard. It seemed to him that someone very dear to him was close by; he sensed a presence beside him, and felt warmed as if by its breath. Who could it be? Good Lord, he had almost for a moment believed that Señora de Moscoso was still alive, despite the fact that he had read her obituary notice! This hallucination was caused no doubt by his sudden return to Ulloa after a long absence. Señora de Moscoso dead? To see the truth with his own eyes he had only to push open the little door in the ivy-clad wall and go into the graveyard.

It was a sombre enough place, even without the willows and cypresses that so theatrically adorn the solemnity of Spanish cemeteries. On one side it was bounded by the church, on the others by three low, ivy-clad walls. The outer door, next to the one that joined with the courtyard, was made of wooden lattice-work, and through this, in the clear distance, one could see the mountain, which at that early hour had a violet hue as the sun began its climb and Nature awoke fresh and chill. Above the gate leaned an old olive-tree, in which nested hundreds of noisy sparrows, who shook the leaves and branches with their busy toing and froing. In front of the gate was an enormous hydrangea, shrunken and bowed by the force of wind and rain, but retaining its gracefulness, with its spiky blue and yellow flowers.

This was the cemetery's only ornament, but it was not its only vegetation. The rank, luxuriant undergrowth there inspired one with superstitious fear, and into one's imagination strayed fantasies that those massive nettles, half the height of a man, that dense grass and those hardy, wax-like thistles were perhaps the mysterious metamorphoses of the souls that lay for eternity beneath them. Souls that in their own way were like the plants, for they had never really lived or loved, their hearts had never yearned after some great ideal, or their minds worried over the spiritual or intellectual matters that occupy more serious thinkers and artists. The substance that nourished the lugubrious, lush flora was human – a coarse, primitive, inferior substance, steeped in ignorance and materialism. Unlike the smooth courtyard, the ground here was covered with little mounds. Underfoot in some places the hard surface of a badly covered coffin could be felt, while in others there was a repulsive softness, as if one were treading on a bloated, flabby corpse.

A distinct smell of mould and putrefaction, a sudden chill . . . A real sense of the grave rose from that bumpy ground, crammed with corpses, one on top of the other. Black wooden crucifixes stood awry amid the damp foliage, criss-crossed by the slimy spoors of snails and slugs. On them were painted thin white stripes and curious inscriptions, full of spelling-mistakes and absurd oddities. Julián shuddered, as if he had trodden on something soft and alive – or something that at least had once been imbued with sensibility and life. Suddenly, what until then had been a sense of unease in him was replaced by a feeling of alarm and deep confusion. He went over to a cross that was taller than the rest, with the name written in large letters, and read the inscription, ignoring the mistakes:

HER LY THE REMAYNS OF PRIMITIBO SUAREZ
HIS FAMLY AND FRENDS PRAY TO GOD FOR HIS SOL

Below the cross the earth was swollen into a mound. Julián mumbled a prayer and then quickly stepped back, imagining he felt underfoot the bronzed body of his formidable enemy.

At that same moment a small white butterfly flew off the cross. It was one of those last butterflies of the year, which fly so slowly they seem shrivelled by the cold, and settle on the first suitable spot they find. The new abbot of Ulloa followed it and saw it alight on a small, shabby mausoleum, tucked away in a recess between the corner of the church and the mud wall of the cemetery. Where the insect stopped, so Julián stopped too. His heart beat fast, his vision blurred. For the first time in many years his spirit was shaken to its depths. Even he was unable to explain how such a turbulent emotion could have overtaken him, could have overwhelmed him, the way it did, crashing through barriers and dams, trampling over everything else with the superhuman force of feelings long suppressed but which finally fill the spirit to overflowing and so inundate it. He did not even notice how ridiculous the mausoleum was, built of stone and lime and embellished with skulls, bones and other *mementos mori* by the unskilled hand of some village dauber. He had no need to read the inscription here, knowing for certain that where the butterfly had landed, Nucha lay. Here Señorita Marcelina, the saint, the eternally innocent and holy virgin, the victim, lay at rest. Here she was alone, abandoned, sold, abused, slandered, her wrists bruised by brutal hands, her face withered by illness, pain and terror . . . Julián's prayer froze on his lips as these thoughts came to his mind, and he went back in time ten years. Then in one of his rare but sudden and irrepressible fits of rapture, he fell to his knees, opened his arms wide, kissed the wall of the niche with

274

passion and sobbed like a child or woman, his face rubbing against the cold, hard surface, his nails scratching at the lime.

He heard whispering and laughter, then merry shrieks of fun inappropriate to either the time or place. He stood up and turned round, confused. Before him, in the bright midday sunlight, stood the most beautiful young man imaginable; if in childhood he had looked like a tiny Cupid, the change from infancy to puberty had lent his features a resemblance to the travelling angels and archangels of biblical engravings, in which graceful locks and feminine prettiness are combined with a charming virile severity. With him was a girl, a tall, slender eleven-year-old. Julián's heart ached when he saw how closely she resembled her poor mother at the same age: the identical long black tresses; the same pale face, though slightly darker and more oval, and with brighter eyes and a firmer gaze. Did Julián not know this young couple? He had held them on his lap a hundred times!

There was only one point which gave him cause to doubt that these two charming youngsters were indeed the bastard son and legitimate heiress of the House of Ulloa. For while the clothes worn by Sabel's son were of a good quality and well-cut, so that one might have placed him as something between a well-to-do peasant and a señorito, Nucha's daughter wore an old percale dress and shoes that were so broken one could almost say she was barefoot.

Paris, March 1886

FOR THE BEST IN PAPERBACKS, LOOK FOR THE 🐧

In every corner of the world, on every subject under the sun, Penguin represents quality and variety – the very best in publishing today.

For complete information about books available from Penguin – including Puffins, Penguin Classics and Arkana – and how to order them, write to us at the appropriate address below. Please note that for copyright reasons the selection of books varies from country to country.

In the United Kingdom: Please write to *Dept E.P., Penguin Books Ltd, Harmondsworth, Middlesex, UB7 0DA.*

If you have any difficulty in obtaining a title, please send your order with the correct money, plus ten per cent for postage and packaging, to *PO Box No 11, West Drayton, Middlesex*

In the United States: Please write to *Dept BA, Penguin, 299 Murray Hill Parkway, East Rutherford, New Jersey 07073*

In Canada: Please write to *Penguin Books Canada Ltd, 2801 John Street, Markham, Ontario L3R 1B4*

In Australia: Please write to the *Marketing Department, Penguin Books Australia Ltd, P.O. Box 257, Ringwood, Victoria 3134*

In New Zealand: Please write to the *Marketing Department, Penguin Books (NZ) Ltd, Private Bag, Takapuna, Auckland 9*

In India: Please write to *Penguin Overseas Ltd, 706 Eros Apartments, 56 Nehru Place, New Delhi, 110019*

In the Netherlands: Please write to *Penguin Books Netherlands B.V., Postbus 195, NL–1380AD Weesp*

In West Germany: Please write to *Penguin Books Ltd, Friedrichstrasse 10–12, D–6000 Frankfurt Main 1*

In Spain: Please write to *Longman Penguin España, Calle San Nicolas 15, E–28013 Madrid*

In Italy: Please write to *Penguin Italia s.r.l., Via Como 4, I-20096 Pioltello (Milano)*

In France: Please write to *Penguin Books Ltd, 39 Rue de Montmorency, F-75003 Paris*

In Japan: Please write to *Longman Penguin Japan Co Ltd, Yamaguchi Building, 2–12–9 Kanda Jimbocho, Chiyoda-Ku, Tokyo 101*

FOR THE BEST IN PAPERBACKS, LOOK FOR THE 🐧

PENGUIN CLASSICS

A Passage to India   E. M. Forster

Centred on the unresolved mystery in the Marabar Caves, Forster's great work provides the definitive evocation of the British Raj.

The Republic   Plato

The best-known of Plato's dialogues, *The Republic* is also one of the supreme masterpieces of Western philosophy whose influence cannot be overestimated.

The Life of Johnson   James Boswell

Perhaps the finest 'life' ever written, Boswell's *Johnson* captures for all time one of the most colourful and talented figures in English literary history.

Metamorphoses   Ovid

A golden treasury of myths and legends which has proved a major influence on Western literature.

A Nietzsche Reader   Friedrich Nietzsche

A superb selection from all the major works of one of the greatest thinkers and writers in world literature, translated into clear, modern English.

Madame Bovary   Gustave Flaubert

With *Madame Bovary* Flaubert established the realistic novel in France; while his central character of Emma Bovary, the bored wife of a provincial doctor, remains one of the great creations of modern literature.